WICKED IS THE HOLLOW

WICKED IS THE HOLLOW

TALES FROM THE HOLLOW

BOOK ONE

K.E. GANSHERT

For my mom

I have no doubt that if it were within your power, the whole world would be reading my books. Thank you for your unending support, generosity, and encouragement.

"There are more things in Heaven and Earth, Horatio, than are dreamt of in your philosophy."

~ William Shakespeare, Hamlet

PROLOGUE
THE DREAM

When I was eight, I watched my mother disappear in fading pixels. I remember it clear as day. My frantic hands trying to plug up those tiny square holes as she begged me to hurry.

Hurry, Selah. Hurry!

But there was nothing I could do. How do you put a person back together when the pieces are gone? Then the monster came. It descended like a windstorm—spidery tendrils of swirling darkness that swept her off her feet and dragged her away. I grabbed onto what was left of her arm as she screamed for me to save her.

Save me, Selah. Save me!

But I wasn't strong enough to save her. Those spidery tendrils gathered into a black mouth that sucked her up. Then she was gone. The black hole vanished and I bolted upright in bed, my pajama top sticking to my back.

"A monster ate Mommy! A monster ate Mommy! A monster ate Mommy!"

I screamed the words over and over, macabre images flashing through my mind like vignettes on a broken film reel.

My mother, disappearing in bits.

My mother, swept off her feet.

My mother, gobbled up by a terrifying, bodiless mouth.

I screamed until Dad crashed into my room, and not until his calloused hands clamped over my small shoulders did that scream finally die in my throat.

"Selah, sweetheart," my father cried, his eyes wide, his grip firm. "It was a dream. You were just having a bad dream."

But I couldn't stop seeing it.

I would never be able to unsee it.

That broken film reel played on and on as I whimpered in the dark.

Dad sat beside me, the mattress springs squeaking as he wrapped me in a hug and rubbed soothing circles onto my back. "It's okay, peanut. Mommy's fine. It was just a dream."

His words were a lie.

Mommy wasn't fine.

I knew this at eight. Heck, I'd known it at five.

My mother had been anything and everything other than fine. And that nightmare? I couldn't let it go. It became a fixation. I was so convinced in the truth of it, so stalwartly adamant that a monster had, in fact, eaten my mother, Dad took me to a therapist named Dr. Penny—a soft-spoken woman with skin like papier-mâché. She said things like, "That must've been very scary, watching your mom disappear like that."

I thought she believed me.

Then I overheard her talking to Dad after one of our appointments. She called my nightmare a *trauma dream*—a vivid, disturbing dream related to a past traumatic event. Or, in my case, multiple traumatic events. She said it was my subconscious way of processing my mother's unreliable presence, which was true enough. My mother's presence was unequivocally unreliable. The thing is, she always came back eventually.

Until that nightmare.

At first, nobody was surprised. She'd left before. So often, in fact, it had become a predictable, normal thing—my mother leaving. Usually for days. Sometimes weeks. Once, when I was five, she stayed gone for three whole months. So when one month turned into two, no one panicked. When two turned into three, nobody sounded an alarm. By the time eleven months slipped into twelve, Dad had grown silently resigned. A year had passed without a glance or a peep. There were no staticky phone calls filled with apology. No tear-stained postcards promising to see me soon. From the moment I woke up screaming like a banshee, we never saw her or heard from her again.

She vanished into thin air.

Dad decided I didn't need a therapist anymore. Or maybe he just couldn't afford the copays. What I needed—what *we* needed—was a fresh start. A place where I wasn't the drug addict's daughter and he wasn't that "poor man." He found himself a landscaping job two states away in the town of Foggy Hollow, West Virginia, where, unbeknownst to him, an entire family had vanished just like my mother.

It should surprise nobody that such a disappearance would capture my imagination so thoroughly. Dr. Penny would probably blame it on trauma. Maybe she'd call it a *trauma obsession.* Maybe she would've been right. Whatever the case, whether from trauma or some invisible force drawing me in, I took it upon myself to learn everything I could about the Vandenberg family cold case, having no idea that several years later, my life would intertwine with theirs in the most astonishing of ways.

THE FOGGY
HOLLOW TRIBUNE

NO BODIES, NO CLUES, JUST QUESTIONS
By Walt Jensen, Staff Writer
April 17, 1995 | Foggy Hollow, WV

In a case that has authorities baffled, the prestigious and enigmatic Vandenberg family—John, Maureen, and their children, Simon (16) and Lily (15)—have disappeared without a trace from their historic estate on the outskirts of town.

The family's longtime butler, Mr. Denis Tulane, left the estate shortly after 7:00 p.m. Thursday evening to run errands just as the family was sitting down to dinner. Not long after, a 911 call was placed from the residence. Though patchy and brief, the caller—believed to be Maureen Vandenberg—sounded distressed.

"It cut out before we could get a clear read," said Sheriff Doyle Whitmore. "By the time deputies arrived, the house was empty. Dinner still on their plates."

There were no signs of forced entry. No indication of struggle. The only unusual detail noted at the scene was a fallen candelabra near the dining room table.

"Smells like a cover up, if you ask me," said longtime resident Opal Farnsworth. "People don't just vanish into thin air. Something horrible happened to that family. And whatever it is, the people of this town deserve to know."

The estate, a prominent fixture in Foggy Hollow history, has stood for over two centuries and has long been the subject of local legend and lore. Now, it's the center of a real-life mystery.

The investigation is ongoing. Authorities urge anyone with information to contact the sheriff's office.

1

THE STAKEOUT

"Today is Saturday, August ninth. I'm positioned one hundred yards southwest of our trail cam. The time is ten-oh-six p.m. So far, no signs of paranormal activity."

And no sign of Twig, either.

Which could be considered paranormal, as Twig is nothing if not punctual.

I push pause on the small recording device and swat at a mosquito buzzing by my ear. A lock of auburn hair falls in front of my eye. I blow it out of the way and peer through my binoculars. They don't have night-vision, so all I really see is the dark outline of trees, and if I squint really hard, the vague impression of headstones poking through fog.

The scent of damp moss and decaying leaves hangs in the air. Thin shafts of moonlight poke through the canopy above. They trickle through what's left of the windows, empty eye sockets of shattered stained glass, and stretch down charred beams and crumbled stone. Crickets chirp uneasily, occasionally interrupted by the haunting hoot of an owl.

This is where we do our stakeouts—inside the ruins of St. Fortuna's church, a once-sacred space that's being slowly consumed by time and the Monongahela National Forest. Foggy Hollow is nestled in a valley of the Allegheny Mountains. The ruins sit on the outskirts of town and offer an elevated view.

I lay on my stomach, elbows propped on the tarp spread beneath me, peering at the cemetery in search of my target, the Woman of the Woods. A ghostly figure with long, raven hair and a white flowing gown who has been rumored to wander the cemetery on nights when the moon is full. Over the past two years, Twig and I have made it our mission to capture her on camera.

A bat flits through St. Fortuna's skeletal frame. I'm not afraid. I welcome the bats. I would prefer more, honestly. Anything to get rid of these mosquitos.

I swat at another.

I'm wearing a long-sleeve dry-fit top, black leggings, and black combat boots. Everything is covered, except for my hands and my neck and my face, which would maybe be sufficient at any other time. But this is August, peak mosquito season, and they're especially bad in these particular ruins, where puddles of water sit stagnant.

I could use some bug spray.

At the moment, I could also use a Xanax.

"There has to be a solution," I mutter to the night.

One that doesn't involve moving.

Away from Twig.

Away from this town.

The knots in my stomach tie tighter.

Foggy Hollow has been my home for seven years. And while I didn't move here willingly—my nine-year-old self convinced that leaving Ohio would mean losing my mother forever—it took no time at all to fall head over heels in love with the town and the boy who introduced me to it. It felt like destiny, coming here. Like Twig and I were meant to be best friends, and Foggy Hollow was meant to be my home. But now, I might have to leave. Right on the cusp of my favorite season, too.

Fall in Foggy Hollow is a magical time any year. But this year, we're celebrating our bicentennial. Not its birth, but its rebirth, when the town rose from the literal ashes of a devastating fire. Which means all the festivities will be bigger and better. The reenactment, the lantern ceremony, the Phoenix parade, the fire festival, the masquerade ball. Not to mention Halloween, which will occur under the blaze of Dante's comet —an astronomical event that only comes once every two hundred sixty-eight years. There's a distinct possibility I won't be here for any of it, which makes me want to stand up and scream into the void.

My rage toward Evergreen Landscaping Solutions swells.

Due to the company's mismanagement and mounting debt, they went under. And my dad's paying the price. *I'm* paying the price. Seven years as a faithful employee, and not even a severance package to show for it. Bills are piling up on our kitchen counter and our landlord keeps lurking like a vulture. Yesterday, I offered Dad my car money. I've been working extra hours at Evermore Books to save up. It's not much, but it could buy us some time. Pay some of the bills.

I should have kept my mouth shut. The offer only seemed to make Dad more desperate, because tonight, after dinner, I overheard him conversing with his cousin on the phone.

He needs a job.

His cousin offered him one.

In Illinois.

I bite my lip and scan the tops of the tombstones.

"Think, Selah. Think."

But my brain boycotts. It's done nothing but frantically think for the past few weeks, ever since Dad came home with the awful news. Now it's exhausted and desperate and filled with panicked static. A hard lump settles in my throat as a red-eyed glow bounces through the fog.

Not the Woman of the Woods, but Twig with a headlamp on his forehead. The red light bobs up and down in rhythm with his tall, gangly frame as he weaves his way toward our hiding spot in the ruins. His face materializes beneath the headlamp's glow, which turns his brown skin into molten copper.

The lump in my throat tightens.

I can't bear the thought of leaving him. Twig Calloway has been my best friend since my first day at Riverbend Elementary.

A book brought us together. *Scary Stories to Tell in the Dark* by Alvin Schwartz. Not the tattered copy I had at home, with my mother's name scrawled inside the cover. But a newer version from the school library. All the fourth graders were selecting books for silent reading after recess, and we were the caboose in a very long checkout line. Me, the new girl in Ms. Lyman's class. Him, the Black kid in Mr. Brunson's.

He kept casting furtive glances from my hair, which had been cut painfully short two days earlier, to the book I clutched in my hands. Perhaps, if a group of girls hadn't taken cruel turns making fun of my hand-me-down clothes at recess, I would have introduced myself. Instead, I was trying very hard to keep the tears at bay. To this day, I can still remember how lonely I felt, how very out of place. Perhaps this was why I'd opted for a book I already had—the familiarity of it brought a sense of comfort.

Sometimes I wonder how things would have panned out if I'd chosen a different book, one that wouldn't have caught his eye so determinedly. As shy as he'd been back then and could still be to this day, would he have struck up a conversation if I'd been holding a copy of *Nate the Great*?

Whatever it was, whether the book or destiny, the next

time our eyes met, he pushed his glasses up his nose and blurted out, "My name's Spencer. But everyone calls me Twig."

The nickname was unusual enough to distract me from the mean girls at recess. When I asked why everyone called him Twig, my chin only wobbled a little.

"Because I look like one," he said, looking down at himself. And it was true. Twig was as stick-thin then as he is now, with knobby elbows and ashy knees.

"Do you like to be called Twig?" I asked. "Because if you don't like it, I can call you Spencer."

He seemed to seriously consider the question, as though nobody had ever asked him before. After a moment, he gave his head a singular, decisive nod. "I like the way it sounds."

I introduced myself then, officially with a handshake. His was a bit noodle-like, but I didn't hold it against him.

As we shuffled forward, he peeked at my book. "Do you like scary stories?"

"I love them."

That's when he told me all about the Woman of the Woods, and when he finished, he told me he liked my hair, too.

Normally, I didn't mind my hair. But something about the haircut made it look extra red. I looked around at my new class-mates—the ones in front of us still waiting in line, and the rest quietly scrambling for the limited selection of bean bag chairs. "I think I'm the only ginger in our whole grade."

"I'm the only one with brown skin," he said with a shrug. "I don't match anyone. Not even my family." At my puzzled expression, he told me he was adopted. And as we made our way to a table—by then, all the bean bag chairs had been taken —he invited me to ride bikes with him after school.

He brought me to the Vandenberg Estate.

I remember peering through the wrought iron bars of the black gate, beholding a home that might as well have been a castle while he told me about the family that went missing. When he finished, I told him about my mother.

A sting pinches my temple.

I smack the spot. My hand comes away with a smear of blood and a smushed mosquito, injecting me with a momentary surge of vindictive glee. I'm not normally a murderer of living things. If I find a spider and don't like where it is, I'll catch it in a cup and move it elsewhere. If I'm put in charge of a plant, I'll go through extra pains to ensure it doesn't suffer under my watch. Once, I accidentally ran over a squirrel and assigned it an entire human life, complete with a squirrel husband and squirrel daughter waiting for its squirrel mother to come home. I spent the rest of the day in mourning. But I draw the line with sanguinivores.

I wipe its guts on the tarp.

Twig ducks under a crumbling archway and slides the proton pack off his shoulders. It's not really a proton pack. It doesn't suck up ghosts like the one from *Ghostbusters*. But it does house our most important supernatural gear—a full-spectrum camera, a night-vision camcorder, an EMF meter, and a temperature gun, along with glow sticks and flashlights and an air horn in case of emergency. This was Carl Calloway's idea—Twig's dad—who isn't nearly as concerned with ghosts and cryptids as he is about a potential run in with a territorial bear or a mean coyote.

I unzip the front pouch, where Twig keeps our non-paranormal essentials. He apologizes about being late and takes a seat beside me. The tarp rustles beneath him. I dig past spare batteries, a power pack, a Swiss army knife, a first aid kit, some granola bars, and grab the can of bug spray. Squeezing my eyes shut and holding my breath, I spray my face, my hands, and the air around us with no sympathy at all.

Die, bloodsuckers. Die.

When I'm finished, I wave my hands through the toxic cloud.

"Any sign of her?" Twig asks with a cough.

"Not yet," I reply.

He removes the night-vision camcorder from his bag, along with a folded up tripod.

I tear open a granola bar. "So, why the late arrival?"

"Mom needed help cleaning up after the parade committee meeting, and I got cornered by Mrs. Tibbs, who went on a full tirade about her workload." He lifts a finger and launches into the perfect Mrs. Tibbs impression. "*There's only so many pioneer frocks one retired teacher can sew!* By the time we got her out the door, Dad was just getting home from his bowling league. And get this." He pushes his glasses up his nose, a habit leftover from elementary school. "He told me that Denis Tulane is looking for a groundskeeper."

I nearly choke on a bite of granola bar. "*What*?"

"He heard it from Red. Apparently, he did some repairs on the estate a couple days ago, and Mr. Tulane asked if he knew of anyone who might be interested in a groundskeeping position. Red mentioned Benny, but of course, Benny already has a job working for the city. So Benny told Red to tell Mr. Tulane about your dad."

My mind has gone spastic—a swirl of chaotic energy.

Mr. Denis Tulane is the recluse I've been pestering with emails and handwritten letters ever since Twig and I started our podcast, *Accounts of the Uncanny*. He's the former butler for the Vandenbergs, the last known person to see the family of four alive before they vanished without a trace thirty years ago. For five years after, the estate sat abandoned. Then reports of trespassing and vandalism had Denis moving back in. And there he has lived ever since. All by himself for the past two and a half decades.

"Why would he be looking for a groundskeeper now?" I ask.

"Because," Twig says, his eyes twinkling in the dark. "A new Vandenberg family is moving to town."

2

MOVING DAY
ONE MONTH LATER

I step out of Dad's Ford Bronco beneath a moody sky, feeling like a princess in a dream. Up until now, I've only ever seen the Vandenberg Estate through the gaps of its black iron fence. This evening, I'm standing *inside* that fence, unable to take a proper breath. Judging by the look on Twig's face, he can't either.

Dad lets out a low whistle.

It isn't directed at the gothic manor looming before us—a sprawling mansion with stone gargoyles, lancet windows, and towering turrets. It's directed at the grounds. Two thousand, five hundred acres of them, most of which have gone wild and overgrown. Caring for them will be a massive undertaking. So massive, in fact, Mr. Tulane requires his new groundskeeper to live on site. Which means we said *arrivederci* to our dingy doublewide and *buongiorno* to our very own carriage house, with walls of gray stone covered in creeping ivy, and a set of old-fashioned carriage doors that are no longer functional but offer plenty of charm.

My new home.

Dad walks around his Bronco to the small trailer hitched to

the back, gravel crunching beneath his work boots. He slides open the hatch, revealing the sparse interior.

The carriage house comes fully furnished, which means we didn't have to bring any of our derelict furniture. Twig and I sold it all in a yard sale last week. Unpacking should be a breeze.

We each grab a box.

Inside, the main level is wide open—one giant room with a kitchen, a dining area, a living area, and a ceiling two stories high. My attention travels up the staircase, where the bedrooms are.

Dad gives the first stair a test with his boot, like he's checking its sturdiness, then turns to me with a fond tip of his chin, his brown eyes soft with amusement. "You know I don't care where I sleep."

The invitation is clear.

With matching grins, Twig and I clamber up the stairs.

Of the two options, I know which one I want immediately. The floorboards creak as I set the box on my new daybed and tiptoe past the antique furniture, to the mullioned window on the far wall. I unlatch the brass fastener and push it open, letting in a soft breeze that stirs lace-trimmed curtains. I imagine sitting here in the window seat, staring out at the misty grounds with a stunning view of the manor—my own private stakeout every single night.

With a happy sigh, Twig and I rejoin my dad.

In short order, the boxes are unloaded and we're back in my room. I close the door behind me with a soft click. Twig catches my eye, and we start laughing. Actually laughing. Because how is this real life? A month ago, I would have given anything to stay in our trailer home. Today, I'm standing in the guest house on the Vandenberg estate. *Inside* my new bedroom. Our fourth-grade selves would never believe it.

"Imagine if we could tour the manor," Twig says, gazing out my window.

"You're getting greedy," I reply, opening the wardrobe. Warped mirrors line the inside of the doors, and a row of hangers dangle from a bar. It smells like cedar and dust.

Twig opens one of the boxes. "It's not farfetched."

He's right. It isn't.

The new Vandenberg family has a son our age. And instead of getting private tutors, like the Vandenberg teenagers before him, he's officially enrolled at Foggy Hollow High, information Twig gleaned from his mother, the high school secretary. We searched for a picture of him online. It shouldn't have been difficult. Surely he'd be on social media. But no. Jude Vandenberg remains a complete enigma. We only know that he and his stepmother have spent the past several years overseas—she in France, and he in England at an elite all-boys boarding school. He's also the great nephew of John Vandenberg, the patriarch of the Vandenberg four who vanished thirty years ago.

On Monday, we'll get to meet him.

One more unbelievable fact in a long line of them.

I start unpacking my clothes.

Twig takes out a stack of books from the box. The one on top is my journal. I've been using it to record my dreams, which have been wild and vivid ever since I found out I was moving here.

"Did I tell you about the dream I had last night?" I ask, hanging up a jean jacket that once belonged to my mother. It's one of the few items of clothing I own that doesn't come from The Lucky Penny, a consignment shop downtown.

"Not yet," Twig says, opening the top drawer of my new writing desk.

"There was fire everywhere. I was trapped inside The Silver Lantern. Some man outside kept screaming for a woman named Florence. And then I realized it was me. *I* was Florence."

I hang my cream-colored turtleneck and move on to my collection of grunge band tees. "It makes a person wonder. What if these dreams are me in past lives?"

"Or rehearsals are getting to your head."

He's referring to the reenactment. *The Burning of Foggy Hollow, a Living History,* performed every September in town square. An ode to our tragic past, when fire consumed the town in 1822. Dozens died. Those who survived lost nearly everything. But the town would not be broken. Led by Amos Vandenberg, Kit Bogaard, and Alexander Doorn, the people rallied, and three years later, Foggy Hollow rose again like a phoenix from the ashes.

"I'm not playing a woman named Florence, though. And what about the dream I had a few nights ago?" Bombs raining from the sky. Alarms blaring. "I was hunkered in a basement wearing a ruby necklace and a utility dress with a CC41 label, clutching a little boy to my chest. How do you explain that?"

"What's Langley teaching in U.S. History?"

"Not World War II."

Twig's phone vibrates.

His mom is here.

Outside, Dad is conversing with an old man dressed in a black suit with a waistcoat. I take in his hollow cheeks and neatly combed snow-white hair—a jarring contrast to the unruly state of his eyebrows—and I have to intentionally avoid eye contact with Twig lest the two of us geek out.

Mr. Denis Tulane, in the flesh.

Dad calls us over.

"This is my daughter, Selah," he says, "and her friend, Spencer. This is Mr. Tulane, the estate's caretaker."

Oh, we know.

We've only been pestering him for an interview the past two years, which is probably why he's looking at me so strangely now, like I'm the paparazzi ready to bulrush him with a microphone and an onslaught of questions.

Mr. Tulane bows in our direction, then continues his conversation with Dad like Twig and I never interrupted. "As I was saying, everything should be in order. The cleaning crew attended to the carriage house earlier today. The beds have been made. There are fresh linens in the closet. The bathrooms have toiletries, and you will find your refrigerator stocked with the basics."

"That was very generous of you," Dad says.

"Yes, well. I expect you will be busy clearing out the overgrowth along the front drive so it's presentable when the family arrives on Sunday."

Dad flattens his palm over the crown of his head, his cheeks puffing with air. Today is Friday, and the front drive is massive, with *a lot* of overgrowth.

I nod toward the front gate, where Mrs. Calloway idles in her Honda Accord.

Dad's cheeks deflate with an exhale. "You're not joining us for dinner?" he asks Twig.

"Kate's singing the National Anthem at the football game. My parents want to grab dinner downtown before we go."

"Tomorrow, then," Dad says.

Twig nods enthusiastically before casting one last longing glance at the manor. He obviously doesn't want to leave. I'm thrilled I don't have to.

As I walk him out, Mrs. Calloway rolls down the passenger side window and waves cheerfully. She's a tiny white woman with a big smile, an older version of Twig's sister, Kate. Twig looks nothing like either of them, just like he told me the day we first met. He doesn't match his family because he's adopted, a story he would elaborate upon later in our friendship—how as an infant, he was left on a doorstep in a basket without any information at all, leading us both to wonder, where exactly did

Twig come from? We've brainstormed origin stories ranging from wizarding worlds to fae kingdoms to alien planets.

"This must be so exciting for you two," Mrs. Calloway says, her narrow shoulders lifting toward her ears.

Dad might not fully appreciate how big of a deal living here is to me, but Mrs. Calloway does. She also knows how close we were to moving. Given the fact that I'm Twig's best and oldest friend, she really didn't want that to happen. Mrs. Calloway dotes on her son. And by proxy, Mrs. Calloway dotes on me.

Almost like a mother.

Twig opens the door and folds himself into the car. After a bit of small talk, I watch them drive away, then turn back to the gate. Not closed, but open. Because this is where I live now. I trace my finger along the Vandenberg Family crest, branded into the black iron—a shield with two crisscrossing keys at the bottom. In the center, a sun with thorny rays is cradled by what could be mistaken as a crescent moon, but is actually a claw.

A breeze swirls around my ankles and flutters through my hair. With it comes a vague whisper, like breath on the back of my neck. My skin prickles as I turn toward the house. And there, framed inside a window on the second floor, is a shadowed silhouette. Not a profile, but someone facing the grounds.

As though watching.

Staring.

At me.

My prickling skin turns into a full battalion of goosebumps as my attention darts to Mr. Tulane, still conversing with my dad. Then the circular drive, which is empty. No cleaning vans. No work trucks. By the time I look back at the second floor window, the shadowed figure is gone.

3
KEEPSAKES

Our new home smells like pizza, even upstairs in my bedroom. Dad ordered out from The Ember Oven. We split his favorite, the Phoenix Special—a spicy pepperoni with roasted red peppers and a drizzle of hot honey. Now he's downstairs, hunting for the antacids. Unfortunately for him, his tastebuds and his digestion don't see eye-to-eye.

I curl up in my window seat, listening to the night sounds outside. A chorus of cicadas and crickets. The soft chirping of tree frogs. The rustle of leaves. The creaking of branches. Somewhere in the distance, a coyote howls at the moon.

Fog rolls over the unkempt grounds. Ground lights shine through the mist, casting eerie shadows up the manor's front. I stare at the window that caught my attention earlier this evening, now dark and empty. The Vandenbergs aren't arriving until Sunday. So who was that, watching us move in?

The question sends a tickle up my spine.

I'm itching to explore.

But first, I must sleep.

I pull the window closed. As much as I'd love to leave it open, there isn't a screen. Bugs will get in. So I secure the latch and face my room with a smile. I'm all finished unpacking. Every box has been broken down and neatly stacked. Except for the one on my writing desk, set atop a tattered copy of *Where the Wild Things Are* by Maurice Sendak and an equally tattered copy of the book that brought Twig and I together, *Scary Stories to Tell in the Dark.*

I sit down at the desk and open the box. Years ago, it held a brand new pair of light-up Sketchers, a Christmas gift from Dad. Now, it houses an assortment of odds and ends, carefully curated over the years. A few faded postcards. The front page of a tabloid folded into a small square. A pair of movie ticket stubs. A meager stack of photographs. An antique necklace my mother never took off, more relic than adornment. A tiny hospital bracelet that once fit my wrist. A beaded rosary. A half-used tube of lipstick. A Chinese finger trap. And an old sour cream container.

Once upon a time, containers like these lined our windowsills. Mom would rinse them out and fill them with soil and seed, then set them in the sun and wait. She didn't have a green thumb. Not like Dad. But she didn't let her lack of natural aptitude stop her from trying. My mother loved to plant. She loved the miracle of something sprouting up from the soil when nothing had been there before. She loved waiting for new life—the anticipation, the possibility.

Of fresh vegetables.

Flowers.

Me.

I touch the tiny wristband.

Selah Mae Whitlock.

A name from the Bible. Found in the Psalms, mostly— breaking apart songs and poems, denoting a peaceful pause. A moment of reflection. According to Dad, my mother battled demons all her life. Most times, the demons won. But for awhile, when Mom found herself pregnant, the demons let go.

Her life entered an extended moment of peace and reflection. For the first time since she could remember, she was clear-headed enough to think about the life she had lived and the life she wanted to live, and she felt hopeful that it was all possible. So, when she gave birth to a healthy baby girl, she named her Selah.

Her own peaceful pause.

The problem is, hope of a thing is different than the thing itself. She intended to take care of the plants in those sour cream containers, to nurture them and watch them grow, just as she intended to be everything a little girl might need a mother to be. But keeping life alive proved a task too arduous for my mother.

I pick up the ticket stubs, from a theater in Ohio that played old films on the big screen. Mom took me to one on my seventh birthday—*Little Monsters*, a favorite from her childhood—and I was only a little bit scared. But it was the fun kind of fear, like riding a roller coaster at an amusement park. A jolt of adrenaline. An exciting thrill. It left such an impression, I made Twig watch it in fifth grade. From there, we discovered *Labyrinth*, *Gremlins*, and every other supernatural cult classic from the 1980s.

I unfold the tabloid, the front page of an old *National Enquirer*. The headline is in bold caps, *Vampire Baby Born in Idaho, Doctors Baffled*. It still smells of cigarettes. I picture her at Save-A-Lot, snagging a copy to read while waiting in the checkout line. Every now and then, she'd splurge and buy one and read it cover to cover, then set it on our coffee table next to her ashtray while reruns of *Unsolved Mysteries* played on our television. Perhaps this is where my obsession with the strange and mysterious comes from—she was always drawn to it, too. And then I had that dream ...

I shuffle through the meager stack of photographs, pausing on a glossy 4x6—a picture of my parents when they first started dating. Unlike Twig, I bear a strong resemblance to my mom. I have her auburn hair, thick with a slight wave. I wear mine long, halfway down my back or up in a messy bun. In this picture, hers is cut just above her shoulders with the kind of layers popular in the nineties. We share the same eyes—wide set and deep blue. The same straight nose with a spray of freckles across the bridge. The same petal pink lips and pointy chins.

I'm so locked in, so utterly focused on the photograph in front of me, the loud thwack against glass sends a strangled scream up my throat. Staticky adrenaline zips through my veins as I send the photographs flying and duck for cover, arms covering my head like they might protect me from whatever just hurled itself at my window.

What was that?

Slowly, I lower my arms and come out of my chair. With one hand set over my chest, I unlock the latch, push open the window, and look down at the grounds.

A crow struggles in the grass, its right wing bent at an unnatural angle.

My thudding heart twists.

That poor bird!

Unwilling to let it suffer alone, I hurry downstairs and out into the night where the grass is damp beneath my bare feet. But the bird isn't there.

A shadow slips across the yard, fast and wrong. A branch snaps behind me. Somewhere in the distance, a coyote howls. The sound lifts the hair on my arms, and I bolt back inside, heart hammering.

4

DG + DB

The next morning, the bird remains a mystery, only not such a frightening one in the light of day. I search around the spot where it fell. There's not even a vague imprint. It's as gone as Dad's Bronco, but at least he left a note.

Went to Home Depot. Will bring home biscuits from Tudor's.

I swipe at the dewy grass with my tennis shoe, wondering if it somehow hobbled away. Surely it didn't fly away, not with how bent its poor wing was. I imagine it slowly dying somewhere under a bush, then shake the image away with a shudder. I refuse to let the fate of a bird dampen my first morning as an official resident of the Vandenberg Estate.

I pull my hair into a ponytail and slip my phone into the side pocket of my leggings. The summer heat is finally relenting, Hollowed Grounds Cafe has rolled out its pumpkin spice latte, some leaves are just beginning to change, and pale fog stretches across the landscape. Soon, the sun will rise over the manor and chase it away. For now, mist floats over the grass like a blanket spun from gossamer, wrapping the property in sleep.

And it's mine to explore.

With an excited inhale, I roll my shoulders and jog up the

service road, around the west end of the manor until my heart is pumping. Typically, I record voice memos when I jog—verbal notes almost always related to *Accounts of the Uncanny.* An idea for an episode, edits for an episode, cuts to an episode, additions to an episode, my favorite cult classics to mention in an episode.

Today, however?

I jog in silence, soaking it all in.

The orchard on the northwest lawn boasts row upon row of gnarled apple and twisted pear trees, their branches tangled like skeletal fingers, the ground thick with rotting fruit. The black iron fence gives way to low stone walls and iron posts with missing chains. The gravel road narrows and turns to dirt. I follow its winding path to a large paddock choked with weeds. Beyond it, a long wooden barn sits weathered and still.

With my breath coming in quick puffs, I stop in front of the barn's massive double doors. They're marked with the faded insignia of the Vandenberg crest, just like the front gate. I give them a push. They don't budge. Panting, I lean my whole weight against them. The hinges groan. I give another shove, and with a shuddering creak, one door gives way just enough for me to slip through.

Inside, the air is stagnant. Nameplates mark empty stalls where prized horses once lived. A splintered ladder ascends to a hayloft. In the back, something hides beneath a tarp. I pull it away with a flourish and a cloud of dust to find a carriage underneath. In the wooden panel of the door, someone has carved a heart around a pair of initials.

"DG + DB," I whisper.

I snap a picture with my phone and send it to Twig, imagining a stablehand enamored with a chambermaid. Star-crossed lovers who died tragically and now haunt this very stable. We could make it into a Valentine's Day special on *Accounts of the Uncanny.*

Stretching out my muscles, my attention wanders to the hayloft, where dust motes float in the sunlight. And perhaps, a lovelorn specter or two? *DG + DB*. Maybe I could dig up their identities on the second floor of Evermore Books, where my boss, Maggie Henshaw, runs the town's historical society.

I resume my jog, following the dirt path to the back of the estate, where a service gate opens to a road I didn't know existed. By now, my legs are fatigued, and I'm so removed from everything, it feels like I'm the only person in the world. Two paths stretch before me. The dirt road that goes all the way around the estate, which would equate to the longest run of my life. And a trail that cuts through the woods toward the back of the manor.

The path is dark.

The trees, dense.

The fog, stubborn.

A chill races down my spine.

I can't help but think of Episode 8, *Cryptid Craze*, the only one that has ever kept me up at night. If I had to choose between a ghost and cryptid, I'd take the ghost every time. My thoughts drift to the *Nachtdier*, otherwise known as the Night Beast, rumored to have slaughtered two girls in these very woods back in 1832. The story gave me nightmares for days.

For a moment, I consider option three—turning around and going back the way I came. But then, how can I call myself an expert on all things supernatural if I can't handle jogging through the woods in the morning?

I set my hands on my hips.

Muted light glistens off dew drops, which have gathered on leaves and spiderwebs. It's a beautiful scene, not a scary one.

"C'mon, Selah," I say to the trees. "Do it for the pod."

With that, I take off, hopping over fallen branches and jutting tree roots. Not until I'm properly winded, do I reach something worth stopping for. A murky pond with statues of nymphs half-submerged in the mossy waters, and a rotting rowboat tied to a wooden post. I imagine DG + DB taking a moonlit boat ride, kissing under the stars. I take some more pictures, then continue around a bend.

An old well comes into view—cracked stone creeping with ivy, the rope and bucket long gone. Maybe DG + DB tossed in coins and made wishes. I set my hands on the rim and lean over to look into its depths when something flies at my face with such velocity, I lurch backward, stumble over a rock, and land flat on my bottom.

The terrifying something flaps its wings with a shrill screech and lands on a low branch hanging over the well's mouth. I glare at it, my heart pounding, my breath ragged. It peers at me over its sharp beak, like it knows about the other bird from last night, like I'm to blame for the slow, agonizing death of its brother.

I scramble to my feet and wave my hands.

With a loud caw, it flies off, along with a flock of others I hadn't noticed before. They cry at the sky in high-pitched unison, and when they're gone, there's nothing but quiet.

I tilt my head.

No, not quiet.

The complete lack of sound.

Alarmingly unnatural, because nature is never silent. Nature always has at least something to say, something to whisper. The only sound right now is my own panting.

A gust of wind tears up the path. So strong, the branches groan and sway. It rips leaves from limbs. Strands of hair from my ponytail. It roars through the trees like an angry beast coming. Coming for me.

I pivot on my heel and run.

I sprint like the wind is chasing me. Like it's going to grab me. Like it has matted fur and massive claws and gruesome fangs and it's going to get me. I stumble into a clearing and whirl around, expecting to see it.

The *Nachtdier*.

The Night Beast.

But there's nothing.

Just the trees, standing straight and still.

The wind is gone.

The sun is shining.

Birds chirp.

Squirrels scamper.

A bee buzzes nearby.

I set my hands on my knees and laugh at my ridiculousness. Just like last night, I allowed my imagination to go as feral as these grounds. With a shake of my head, I turn around to see what I've stumbled upon.

Headstones.

My breath goes still. I stare, open-mouthed, unable to believe what I'm seeing. This isn't just a clearing. This is a graveyard, with fourteen, no *fifteen* headstones.

I creep toward the nearest one.

Daniel Vandenberg, 1912 - 1993.

He died two years before John and Maureen and their teenage children vanished without a trace. I fumble for my phone and take more pictures. I turn the camera to the headstone beside Daniel's.

"May I ask what you're doing?"

I spin around.

A young man leans against a tree with one dark eyebrow quirked in amusement.

My pulse stutters. I have no idea how long he's been watching.

5
THE FAMILY GRAVEYARD

He's the kind of person you might see on the cover of a magazine, with flawless bone structure and eyes so blue they match his oxford shirt. His dark hair is thick and neatly styled, with one rebellious lock falling over his quirked eyebrow. But even that looks intentional, as though his imperfections have been meticulously arranged. The corner of his mouth curls into a crooked grin as he stands there at the edge of the clearing, leaning against a tree like an exquisite painting, every stroke designed to draw the eye exactly where he wants it to go.

I'm so caught off guard by his presence, it takes me a minute to register how intensely he's staring. At some point, his languid demeanor has shifted, only I'm not sure when. I'm not even sure how. He hasn't moved. He's still leaning against a tree, his attention traveling upward—from my second-hand running shoes to my wind-tousled hair—with such fervor, my cheeks turn warm.

I tuck a loose strand behind my ear, trying to get my voice unstuck, when he steals my line.

"Who are you?" he asks.

"Who are *you*?" I retort. This is a private estate. A *gated* estate. People aren't allowed to just come inside.

He smirks impishly. "My name's Rafe."

"Well, *Rafe*, this is private property."

"Vandenberg," he finishes.

The surname hits me between the eyes.

Vandenberg.

I blink several times. "But I—I thought you weren't coming until tomorrow."

"That would be my cousin, Jude. And his mother. Or rather, his stepmother." He leans forward slightly, and says in a low, conspiratorial voice, "I don't think he's very fond of her."

A cousin.

My sleuthing never mentioned a cousin.

"Your turn now," he says, his arms still crossed.

"I'm Selah." I lift my chin, annoyed by the flood of heat in my cheeks and the pounding of my heart. "Selah Whitlock. My father is the new groundskeeper. We just moved into the guest house."

"Ah," he says. "Interesting."

"Why is that interesting?"

He cocks his head and continues to stare in a way that makes breathing difficult. When it becomes obvious he's not going to answer, I fold my arms, too, and just as I'm searching for a quippy reply, I remember the shadowed figure I saw in the window yesterday. "When did you get here?"

"Yesterday afternoon. I figure Yale can wait. But the 200th celebration of a town that owes its existence to my ancestors? That only comes, well, every two hundred years."

"You're here for the festivities?"

"Amongst other things." He lets the cryptic words hang in the air with a slightly amused, slightly condescending smile. He uncrosses his arms and prowls toward me like a predator on the hunt. With my heart galloping the way it is, I feel every inch the prey.

The closer he comes, the more gorgeous he gets. High cheekbones. Well-defined jaw. A faint cleft in his chin. When he strolls past, he smells as expensive as he looks.

I turn my head to track his movements—my muscles tense, my breath shallow.

He stops at a tombstone and sets his hand on top of it.

Amos Vandenberg.

The star of the reenactment.

The town's very own hero.

"He was an amazing man, Uncle Amos." The words are respectful. Deferential, even. But there's a wicked gleam in his eye, and that whisper of a grin, like he's privy to some kind of secret that is both awful and delightful. He resumes his prowl, winding his way in and out of the tombstones.

I fix my attention on his shoes.

Patent leather.

Much too expensive to be wearing on a walk through the woods.

"Did you follow me here?" I ask.

I expect him to deny it. Scoff at the accusation. Instead, his barely-there grin widens into a wolfish smile. The gap between us shrinks until he's standing so close, I'm leaning back on my heels, tilting my head to look him in the eye. His are even bluer up close, not a trace of any other color in them. Rimmed with eyelashes as dark as night.

His attention dips to my lips. "Would you like it if I had?"

My body is trapped. Stuck like my breath. My heart a caged bird as he brings the tip of his pointer finger beneath my chin and dips his mouth toward mine. Like he intends to kiss me.

I lurch backward. "What are you doing?"

His eyes remain fixed on the spot where my lips once were. He stays like that for a frozen second. Then he blinks lazily and cocks his head, as though perplexed by my rejection. Sure, the guy is drop dead gorgeous. But that doesn't give him liberty to go around kissing strangers.

"Seriously," I say, voice rising. "What were you trying to do?"

"Have a little fun?"

I take another step back.

The audacity.

The entitlement.

The sheer arrogance.

It's all so ... outrageous.

"I can assure you, I'm not that kind of girl."

My words make his expression go expressionless. Completely deadpan, like an invisible switch has been flipped. He studies me for a drawn out moment. "You look like someone."

"Excuse me?"

"You look like someone," he repeats.

When he makes no attempt to elaborate, I lift my eyebrows in clear agitation. "Who?"

"A girl I ... sort of know."

"Well, I'm not her."

"Obviously."

"Don't follow me again."

"You're a guest on *my* property," he says, sliding his hands into his pockets.

A retort lashes across my tongue. I'm not a guest. I live here, too. But even if I were a guest, that doesn't give him the freedom to follow me or kiss me. I swallow the words. Rafe Vandenberg could very well have a say in my father's job. As much as I might want to bring him down a peg or two, I want to stay here more. I clench my teeth to keep the retort inside.

He looks amused, and maybe a little disappointed. Like he would have enjoyed a verbal spar.

My phone dings.

Grateful for the interruption, for an excuse to look away, I slip my phone from my pocket to check the screen. The time comes as a shock.

It's five past noon.

I was supposed to be in the basement of Evermore Books, recording an episode for the podcast with Twig five minutes ago.

6

INTENSE ENCOUNTERS

Of all the places in Foggy Hollow, my least favorite is Foggy Hollow High. It has nothing to do with the institution of learning and everything to do with the building itself. For a town so steeped in history and lore, our high school resembles a factory—an industrial-looking concrete block with boxy windows, gray lockers, and cheap desks marked with doodles from decades of students who probably felt as trapped as I do. Tacky motivational posters line the walls, all stamped with our mascot. The phoenix, a brilliant bird from ancient mythology. Yet somehow, here, it's been reduced to lame looking stock art.

Today, though, a different vibe hangs in the air.

A new classmate has injected our Monday doldrums with an arousing energy. The first bell hasn't even rung yet and the student body is wide awake.

I'm in an alcove off the main hallway with Naomi Kapoor and Harper Mahoney, the third and fourth members of my four-person friend group. Naomi and Harper have been best friends since Hickory Grove Elementary. Twig and I bonded with them in junior high gym class, mostly over our shared ineptitude with all things sports. Naomi's parents are from India, making her one of the few students of color in Foggy Hollow—a second connection between her and Twig. A third is their shared expertise in robotics. Harper comes from a big family and shops secondhand like me. We both have speaking parts in this year's reenactment. At the moment, Twig's missing from our usual foursome, which is probably for the best, given our current fixation.

"He is absurd," Naomi says in a low voice.

"More like unreal," Harper adds.

The three of us are staring at the profile of Jude Vandenberg as he opens his locker. Perfectly tousled golden hair. Dark, brooding eyebrows. Full lips. And a lean, athletic frame dressed in clothes that scream old money. I tried catching a glimpse of him yesterday, when he arrived just before sunset in a black Mercedes Benz driven by a chauffeur, but all I got was a very distant, mostly obstructed view.

A pair of freshmen boys mosey past.

Naomi shifts. "I can't believe you get to live with him."

"I don't live *with* him."

"You share an address."

"Different mailboxes. Separate roofs."

But Naomi isn't listening. Neither is Harper. They're too busy gawking as Jude removes a binder from his bag. He's pushed up the sleeves of his Ralph Lauren quarter zip pullover, highlighting tan forearms and a leather wristwatch.

For a brief moment, I consider telling them about Jude's cousin, Rafe the Rake. But something tells me that particular encounter would give them both an embolism. It nearly did Twig, and he had zero interest in Rafe's good looks.

Jude hitches his backpack over his shoulder and shuts the locker. Every eye follows him as he walks down the hallway—in *our* direction—with his brow drawn low, a muscle in his chiseled jaw ticking ever so slightly, like he's annoyed to be here.

He passes Lainey Sikes, a notorious drama queen who thrives off theatrics. She catches Kate Calloway's attention across the hall and fans her face like she might swoon. Kate giggles. Lainey's boyfriend, Griffin Tate, doesn't look so amused. He glares after the new guy, his chest puffing like a bull in rut.

Meanwhile, Sterling Bogaard comes around a corner into Jude's path, but avoids collision with a quick step to the side. Sterling walks the halls with his face locked in permanent discomfort, like he's being forced to mingle with the commoners. One might think he'd be glad to have another of his pedigree. Strength in numbers and all that. Instead, he watches Jude like a wary jackal.

Jude strides closer, paying no attention to any of it.

I pinch Naomi's elbow and mutter under my breath, "Stop staring."

She gets the hint. Perhaps a little too enthusiastically. She grabs our arms in an attempt to feign conversation only to knock Harper's phone from her hand.

It clatters to the ground.

Jude's attention flicks in our direction as Naomi and Harper bend over to retrieve it.

Our gazes collide.

And—*oh*. His eyes aren't just brown. They're the color of late autumn leaves dappled in sunlight.

A flush creeps up my neck, because he's not looking away. His gaze remains locked on mine as he passes, steady and unflinching. There's no hint of amusement. No wicked gleam. No cocky smirk. He may be as gorgeous as his cousin, but something tells me they are very different.

The first bell rings, shattering the moment.

Jude looks away, leaving me to stare at his retreating back, heart pounding as Harper and Naomi stand up straight, having no idea what just happened.

To be honest, I'm not sure I do either.

I don't catch another glimpse the rest of the morning. But I do hear plenty of whispered conversations—in class, in the hallways, in the girls' bathroom.

It's getting ridiculous.

I grab a cafeteria tray and slide it along the metal lunch counter, where steam curls from unappetizing food options.

"Has anyone actually talked *to* him?" I ask, snagging a slice of pizza. "The poor guy's being treated like some weird mixture of Messiah and leper."

Twig hands me a chocolate milk and grabs himself a yellow Powerade. "I still can't believe his cousin tried to kiss you."

I swipe my student ID at the cash register. "Me neither, but I can't fault *him* for something his cousin did."

Twig swipes his ID, too.

We stand together, holding our trays aloft. The cafeteria is a large, open room filled with round tables, some crowded, others empty. A few students loiter on the edges, leaning against beige walls while voices hum and trays clatter and backpacks thud against industrial carpet. A cacophony of sound interspersed with the occasional burst of laughter, usually from Lainey.

In the midst of the organized chaos sits the man of the hour. He doesn't have a tray or a lunch box. Just a steel thermos, the contents of which he mindlessly stirs while reading from his book. He sits by himself at a table, but he might as well be the center of gravity.

I tip my mouth toward Twig. "If we had superhuman hearing, how many of these conversations do you think would be about him?"

"If I had to make a bet, I'd say all of them."

I twist my lips to the side. Beneath all that obscene perfection, he's just another student, stuck in this cafeteria, forced to breathe the same air as the rest of us. I glance left, toward our usual table, and make eye contact with Harper. The moment I square my shoulders and turn toward Jude's table, her eyes go buggy.

"Selah," Twig hisses, following sheepishly. "What are you doing?"

"Being hospitable," I hiss back.

All eyes follow our approach. By the time I set my tray in front of the seat beside Jude, a hush has fallen.

I stick out my hand. "Hi, I'm Selah. I live in your carriage house."

He looks up from his well-worn copy of *Macbeth* and blinks at my outstretched arm, ribbons of steam curling from his thermos. Coffee, by the looks of it. Probably some super expensive, French blend his stepmother brought with them from Europe. When it becomes obvious he has no interest in shaking my hand, I pull out the chair and sit. If he recognizes me as the girl he made intense eye contact with earlier, he doesn't let on.

"Did you know actors won't say that name in a theater?" I nod at his book. "They call it 'The Scottish Play' because the production is supposedly cursed."

"If you believe in that sort of thing," he says.

"Oh, I relish that sort of thing." I open my chocolate milk. "But I guess we're not in a theater, so we should be safe. This is my friend, Twig."

Jude quirks an eyebrow.

"Spencer," Twig says, his voice cracking mid-syllable as he drops awkwardly into the seat next to mine.

"But everyone calls him Twig."

Except his family.

And my dad.

Twig stuffs his mouth full of mystery meat.

Jude stirs his coffee.

I take a drink of my milk and resign myself to being the carrier of this conversation. "So, you're a fan of tragedies?"

"I'm a fan of classic literature."

I crane my neck to catch a glimpse of his schedule, which sits on the other side of his thermos. We share a class. U.S. History, final period. "Well, then," I say, "I'm happy to report AP Lit will be right up your alley. You missed *Of Mice and Men*, but you got here right on time for *The Scarlett Letter*."

Both classics.

Both tragic.

"If the trajectory continues, we'll be reading *The Bell Jar* by the end of the semester. Mrs. Cannery loves herself a depressing tale." I take a bite of my pizza.

Jude continues brooding.

I had hoped this little meet and greet might act as a sort of olive branch, an apology on behalf of my classmates. We *are* capable of treating him like a normal person. At the moment, he's not making it easy.

"So," I say, throwing my voice into a lower register, "what kind of literature do you enjoy, Selah?" I tilt my head in the other direction and speak from the opposite corner of my mouth. This time, in my normal voice. "Oh, so nice of you to ask, Jude."

He narrows his eyes.

"If we're sticking with Shakespeare, I'd have to go with *The Tempest*." Magic. Spirits. Strange happenings on an island. It's definitely my cup of tea. "If we're straying from the playwright, I'd probably go with *The Legend of Sleepy Hollow*."

"Small-town folklore," Jude says.

"And a headless horseman." I take another bite of my pizza. Mostly to keep from verbalizing another defining feature of the classic—*mysterious disappearances*. That seems to strike too close to home where Jude Vandenberg is concerned.

I set my elbows on the table. "We should carpool."

"What?"

"Carpool. Here, to school."

"Why?"

"We live on the same property. Might as well use it to decrease our carbon footprint."

He doesn't respond.

"I met your cousin," I say.

Twig coughs. I think my declaration made him choke on his Powerade. It definitely changed something about Jude's demeanor. I'd love to read into it, but the bell rings. He rises to his feet like he can't get away fast enough.

"See you in history," I say.

For a second, I think he's going to leave without acknowledging me at all. But then he caps his thermos and our eyes connect all over again.

It comes with a jolt.

A zinger of heat.

A strike of lightning.

Like his gaze and mine are live wires touching.

His golden brown eyes smolder with something like intrigue, like he feels it, too. But then Twig coughs some more, and Jude walks away.

7

A COMMON MISCONCEPTION

I'm the first to arrive to eighth period. Normally, I find a desk at the end of a row, closest to the door. Quicker to escape that way. Today, I consider moving one seat in, a maneuver that would increase my odds of sitting next to a certain someone. But that would make me just as ridiculous as every other girl tittering in the bathroom.

I sit in my normal seat.

Harper arrives next. When she slides into the empty desk next to mine, I scold myself for the twinge of disappointment. "Oh my goodness, Selah. Tell me everything."

It's the first time we've seen each other since lunch.

She scoots her desk closer. "What did you talk about? What did he sound like? What did he smell like?"

"*Smell* like?"

"Expensive cologne. I bet you anything."

I roll my eyes. "I tried to talk to him about books. He wasn't very chatty, to be honest. He sounded like a human, and he smelled like one, too."

Better, actually.

On both counts.

But I'm not spinning Harper into any more of a tizzy than she already is. Nor am I telling her that at any moment, Jude will be making an appearance. Instead, I turn our conversation toward the reenactment on Friday. Harper is playing the role of Annabelle Doorn, the mayor's daughter. Over the next minute and a half, as the desks slowly fill and Harper and I chat about rehearsals this evening, I don't look at the door once.

Nor do I need to.

The whispers rippling through the room makes his arrival obvious. By now, only two desks remain—one in the front row on the opposite side of the room, another behind Harper. All eyes track the new guy as he takes the closer seat. Harper sits ramrod straight, her eyes going buggy all over again.

The bell rings.

Mr. Langley steps inside and shuts the door.

Usually, the energy in class is low. By and large, Langley isn't known for bringing history to life. He rambles his way through lectures while his students play on their phones or stare into the middle distance with vacant expressions. Today, however, the arousal that has permeated the building condenses here, in Room 216.

Langley writes the words *Salem Witch Trials* on the board. One would think such a fascinating topic would make his basset hound eyes sparkle just a little, but alas, they remain dull and droopy as he meanders through the lesson. Meanwhile, my notes are a chaotic mess. In all caps at the bottom of the page, I jot the words *Podcast idea. Salem! Witches!*

"Hysteria consumed the town," Langley continues. "People turned on their neighbors, paranoia spread, and by the time it ended, twenty individuals had been executed. What can this time period teach us about human nature?"

His question blends so monotonously into the rest of his lecture, I don't think anybody but me realizes he's invited engagement. Carter Muldoni stifles a yawn. A handful of girls aren't even facing front, but have positioned themselves in a perpendicular manner so they have a better view of Jude.

Nobody volunteers.

Nobody pays any attention at all.

Until Langley calls on the new student and the whole class snaps to such attention, you could hear a pin drop.

Jude lounges back with his long legs stretched in front of him, one ankle crossed over the other, idly twirling a pen around the tip of his thumb, a picture of quiet disinterest. He hasn't opened his notebook. It's closed beneath his worn copy of *Macbeth*. "It teaches us the dangers of archaic, uninformed thinking," he says, hardly missing a beat. "And how quick we are to blame evil for things we can't yet explain."

Langley looks pleased. "Care to elaborate?"

"You said the hysteria began when two girls started having fits. It was likely Lyme's disease, an affliction they didn't yet know about. So they blamed evil, pointed fingers, and innocent women were burned at the stake."

"The women in Salem weren't burned," I blurt.

All the attention swivels from Jude to me as the clock on the wall ticks into the silence.

"And the men," I continue. "There were some men. Nineteen were hanged. One was pressed." The thought makes me shudder. "None of them were burned." I know this thanks to Maggie Henshaw, who takes major offense with historical fallacy.

Napoleon wasn't short!

The witches weren't burned at the stake!

"That's a common misconception," I say.

Jude's eyes narrow beneath his brooding eyebrows, and I wonder which part of the statement bothers him more—*common*, or *misconception*?

"I mean, I get why it's a misconception. That's how they

executed witches in England, and burning is more dramatic. If I were writing the story, I'd probably go with that, too."

"You're disappointed they were hanged?" Jude asks.

"Of course not."

"But burning would've made for a better story?"

"I'm simply saying that's probably why the myth stuck. Stories last longer when they leave an impact. Burning leaves a big one."

"So ... factual accuracy is less important than turning history into entertainment?"

"That's not what I said."

"It's what you implied."

I let out a short laugh. "You're the one who got it wrong in the first place."

"A victim of dramatics, I guess."

Warmth rises in my cheeks.

"I don't know the intricacies of the Salem Witch Trials," Jude says. "I've never made a point to study them, but I stand by my original point. Human nature loves to blame evil, when in actuality, it was undiagnosed sickness and mass hysteria."

"You don't think evil was involved even a little?"

"Is it ever?"

I blink several times, dumbfounded by his take. "You don't believe in evil?"

"I take it you do," he says with a bit of an eye roll, like *I'm* archaic and uninformed.

I set my elbow on the back of my chair. "I'm not saying those women were actual witches, but I absolutely believe in evil." People were tortured. Innocent lives were taken. Power was absolutely abused. If that's not evil, what is?

Jude gives his pen a disinterested twirl.

"If you don't believe in evil, then how do you explain a guy like Ted Bundy? Or Adolf Hitler?"

"Chemical imbalances in the brain?"

I open my mouth, a ready retort on the tip of my tongue, but Langley gives his throat a loud clear, pulling the focus back to himself. I hadn't noticed, but the class's attention was pinballing between me and Jude like spectators at a tennis match.

"Yes, well," Langley says, smoothing his notes. "You've both touched on some fascinating points ..."

The droning resumes.

But I'm no longer taking notes. I'm too distracted by the prickle on the back of my neck. When I peek over my shoulder, Jude is staring. And for the first time today, a ghost of a smile tugs at his mouth.

I stand before the manor's imposing entrance, staring at the brass knocker—shaped into the likeness of a hollow-eyed beast. With a tangle of awe and nerves, I lift the ring hanging from its fanged mouth and let it fall with a sharp knock.

I take a step back, tugging at my sleeves. The oak doors are a masterpiece, intricately carved with angelic imagery. Lichen speckles the archway above them. On either side, stone gargoyles stand sentry, their features long since eroded.

Hinges groan as the doors open.

Mr. Tulane appears on the other side dressed like Alfred Pennysworth, his hair neat, his eyebrows wild, and while I should look at him, I can't help but crane my neck to look past him, inside the home where the Vandenbergs disappeared. Even with an obstructed view, I can make out the double staircase in the grand foyer, spiraling outward before coming together on the second floor.

"Good afternoon, Miss Clara."

My attention jerks from the massive chandelier so quickly, I give myself whiplash. "What did you just call me?"

He blinks his protuberant eyes as footsteps sound behind

him. Jude strides toward us. Instead of inviting me in, he joins me outside with a terse nod at Tulane.

I point dumbly at the doors. "He called me Clara."

"What?"

"Mr. Tulane just called me Clara."

And Clara is my mother's name.

"Are you sure he didn't say Sara?" Jude asks.

"Why would he call me Sara?"

"The same reason he calls Isabel Sara. I think it's the name of his niece." Jude crosses his arms. "What are you doing here?"

The curt question is nearly as jarring as Tulane's strange greeting. Apparently, his ghost-of-a-smile in class was a one-off. Or maybe my imagination. Like hearing Clara instead of Sara. I shake off the cold welcome. "I wanted to invite you to the reenactment on Friday."

"The reenactment?"

"*The Burning of Foggy Hollow, a Living History*. It's this whole thing we do in town square every year, and it just so happens to feature your great, great, something-or-other grandfather." I rock onto the outer edges of my combat boots, ankles tilting outward. "This year, he's being played by Harrison Locke, who is Twig's sister's boyfriend."

Jude furrows his brow.

"You should come. It's an ode to our town's history. And in this particular instance, something really *did* burn. Not witches. At least, none that we know of."

He gives me nothing.

Certainly no ghost of a smile.

I press onward. "There's a ceremony afterward, where we light lanterns in honor of the people who died, and set them sail down the river. Most of the town gathers at The Silver Lantern to send them off, but I like to watch from the covered bridge on—"

"I'm not interested," he interrupts, the clipped tone of his voice landing like a slap. "In the reenactment, or being used for fodder."

"Fodder?"

"For your podcast."

Heat blooms in my cheeks.

"I Googled you." He pulls his phone from his pocket and shows me the screen. *Accounts of the Uncanny* is the top search result, along with our two most popular episodes. Both feature the cold case.

"You're obsessed with my family," he says.

"No, I'm obsessed with all things strange and mysterious. What happened to your family fits the bill."

"We're not a circus."

"I never said you were."

"Entertainment though, yeah?"

I open my mouth.

But he gives me no opportunity to reply. "Look," he says. "You found a way to live on this estate. Which, kudos to you, that's impressive. It doesn't mean we're going to carpool. Or be friends. Or discuss literature at lunch."

He steps inside his home, but before he can shut the doors in my face, I press my palm against one of them. "I have no idea what life was like for you wherever you lived before, but you should know that being rich and good-looking doesn't excuse poor behavior."

He glares at my hand.

I glare back. "And co-hosting a podcast about the uncanny in a town that provides plenty of content isn't a crime. Of course the Vandenberg cold case would be featured. A family of four vanishing into thin air is pretty uncanny, if you ask me. I wasn't inviting you to the reenactment to get fodder. I was inviting you because I was being nice. And friendly. If you don't know what those words mean, I suggest you *Google* them, too."

Without waiting for his retort, I turn on my heel and march

away. Apparently, I was wrong. He's a lot more like his cousin than I thought.

Jude the Jerk.

And Rafe the Rake.

Both may be beautiful, but they really need to work on their manners.

8

THE LANTERN CEREMONY

I peek out from behind the curtain, which has just enough girth to conceal the smoke machines positioned stage left and stage right. Twig runs the one across from me on stage left, looking—as his mother said—a little peaked. He releases a burst of smoke as performers in period attire flee across the stage.

Torches line the edge of town square, their flames flickering against brick storefronts. The grassy plaza is alive with spectators watching the performance unfold. Mayor Ridley sits front and center, dressed in his well-worn blazer with his phoenix lapel pin. He's surrounded by the entire board of the Foggy Hollow Preservation Society, not to be confused with the Foggy Hollow Historical Society.

The former is made up of wealthy, well-connected, socially prominent individuals who look down their noses at the latter, which consists of my boss, Maggie Henshaw, and her partner in crime, Walt Jensen. What they lack in donations they make up for with tenacity and duct tape. I scan the crowd for them now, but can't find either.

Behind me, a stagehand rolls out a replica of the old schoolhouse, where Mercy Bogaard once taught. My moment in the spotlight is quickly approaching. I adjust the sleeves of my cotton dress, double check the tie of my apron, straighten my bonnet, and run my hand down the length of my long plait.

Twig releases more smoke.

Kate—AKA, Ida Vandenberg, wife of Amos Vandenberg—screams on stage.

And I catch sight of Rafe, who I haven't seen since our encounter in the graveyard. He stands on the periphery of the crowd, next to a statue. Torchlight flickers across his features, sharpening the angles of his face.

His attention isn't on the stage.

It's on me.

Pulse jumping, I shift into shadow.

Harrison Locke's voice booms across the square. "Miss Bogaard, the fire's coming fast! You must find your father and get to safety!"

I run onto the stage, trying to lose myself in the role—a school teacher who single-handedly saved the lives of sixteen children. But Rafe's attention is distracting, his stare so unwavering its borderline inappropriate. As the scene plays out, it becomes obvious. He's not watching the performance; he's watching *me*. A fact so flustering, I fumble my big line.

Instead of saying, "If this is to be my last night, let it be one of courage, not fear." I replace *fear* with *fate*, which never happened in rehearsals. By the time the performance is over and the curtain call ends, I'm ready to march out onto the lawn and give Rafe Vandenberg a piece of my mind.

But he's gone.

And Twig is getting sick in a garbage can.

He suffers from migraines. Bad ones. Sometimes, they make him throw up. Last fall, he got one so severe, he had to miss Hollow Horror Night at the drive-in, when they played the first three *Nightmare on Elm Streets* back to back to back.

This year, it looks like he's going to miss the lantern ceremony.

Harper and Naomi invite me to join them downtown, where the lanterns are launched. But I like watching them drift downriver. Which leaves me on my own, wandering through the stands and stalls in Willowmere Park, no longer in period attire. I've changed into my street clothes—a Nirvana tee under an oversized flannel, black leggings, and a pair of white hightop Converse All-Stars.

Night has fallen. Fog rolls thick over the Blackwillow River, where the branches of weeping willows dip into its currents. The scent of roasted nuts, warm cider, and kettle corn mingles with the cool air. From atop the covered bridge, a lone violinist plays haunting Appalachian folk songs.

People claim their spots with lawn chairs and blankets. Small children run around wielding paper lanterns and sparklers. The Boathouse's outdoor patio is hopping with patrons and servers. I prefer to sit along the river's stone wall, thirty yards or so past the bridge, where I can let my feet dangle above the water and watch the lanterns arrive like glowing specters through the fog. The magical sight never ceases to take my breath away.

I pass a local writers group as they take turns reading poetry by candlelight, and catch a stanza of a young woman's piece. "What is a lantern but borrowed fire? What is a life but borrowed time?" The contemplative question hits just the right note. I'm *feeling* contemplative. Which I suppose is an appropriate mood since the *Procession of Lights* isn't meant to be a celebration, but a reverent ceremony.

At the local beekeeper's booth, I purchase two honey caramels wrapped in wax paper for Twig. They're his favorite. At the Blackberry Bramble Wagon, I buy a pecan tart for myself. I pass by the *Wish Upon the River* stall, where you can buy a smooth stone for a dollar, write a wish upon it, and toss it into the dark waters. There's a DIY lantern stand. I have two from years past, both carved with stars and moons. And next to it is the Reflection Table, where people can write letters to lost loved ones, seal them inside envelopes, and set them to sail inside their newly made lanterns.

I take a bite of my tart, thinking about my mother and all the things I would tell her if I could, when a low voice rumbles in my ear. "Nothing says 'honoring the dead' like setting fire to paper and polluting the river."

I turn around.

Rafe.

He stands behind me looking offensively handsome, the top two buttons of his shirt undone and that lock of midnight hair falling across his eyebrow again. He tosses a small stone into the air and catches it in his palm. "Does the EPA know about this, or ...?"

"The lanterns are biodegradable."

"Well, that's a relief."

People meander past us.

I step off the path. "What are you doing here?"

He steps with me, his gaze teasing with a dash of puzzlement, like there's something about me that stumps him. I can't imagine what. Surely I can't be the only girl to have rejected his advances.

"Are you going to accuse me of following you again?" he asks.

"If the shoe fits."

His attention drops to my sneakers before slowly sliding up my body in a way that makes me want to cover myself. "As much as I would *love* to follow you around, I'm here for my family." He nods toward The Boathouse's patio. "Networking dinner with the Everlys. We're schmoozing."

I spot Henry and Cosette, a formidable couple in their sixties. Cosette is president of the Foggy Hollow Preservation

Society. The couple sit across from a woman I assume is Isabel. She's too far away to make out her features, but not so far away I can't tell that she's perfectly arranged—hair, outfit, makeup.

Jude sits beside her.

He's not attending to the dinner conversation, either.

He's watching *us*.

Me and Rafe.

"I'm pretty sure they want Isabel's money," Rafe says. "And since Isabel wants the honor of hosting the ball—"

My attention snaps to his face. "The masquerade ball?"

"Something about a hunter's moon ...?"

"It's not going to be at town hall?"

"Not if Isabel gets her way. I, for one, think she should. This isn't any old year, after all. This is Foggy Hollow's bicentennial. Such a milestone deserves to be special, don't you think?"

I don't object.

The Vandenberg Estate playing host to the Hunter's Moon Masquerade Ball? The idea makes me want to swoon. For a myriad of reasons. Namely, I'd finally get to go inside the place. A breeze ruffles my hair as I take another bite of tart.

"So," Rafe says, "where are we watching the lanterns?"

"We?" I wipe a crumb from my lip. "Shouldn't you return to your dinner?"

He waves his hand dismissively.

My attention returns to the patio, where Isabel tips her head back and laughs. Jude's chair is empty.

"You did a fabulous job, by the way."

I peer at Rafe.

"Playing Mercy Bogaard. The whole thing was *so* realistic. It almost felt like I was there." He smirks when he pays the compliment, like it isn't a compliment at all, but a tease. He's making fun of me. He's making fun of all of us.

I glare. "You were staring."

"Isn't that what you're supposed to do at a performance?"

"You were staring at me and only me."

His smirk widens into a grin.

"It was rude. And distracting"

"You find me distracting?"

"I find you off-putting, if I'm being honest."

He sets his hand against his chest, like I just shot him. "Well, if we're being honest, the fact that you find me off-putting is rather fascinating."

"Why would that be fascinating?"

He tilts his head like he's trying to decide whether to let me in on his secret. Then he looks past me and gives the stone another toss. "I was wondering when you'd join us."

I turn around.

It's my new classmate—the one I've spent the latter half of this past week avoiding. The mere memory of our last encounter makes me want to hide under a pillow. I scolded him. Like, actually scolded him. And I'm pretty sure I called him good-looking in the process.

My stomach pools with heat.

"Rafe," Jude says, flat and clipped. When he turns to me, I expect the same cold greeting. Surprisingly, his expression isn't hostile. It's more ... concerned? "Selah," he says, his voice a little husky.

A kaleidoscope of butterflies take flight.

Before I can reply in kind, he turns to his cousin. "I thought you wanted to join us for dinner."

"I thought it would be more interesting," Rafe replies.

"So you decided to bother her instead?"

"Bother? Come now, Jude. You wound me. I saw a pretty girl all alone and thought I'd keep her company. It's not like you were volunteering. Watching, yes. Staring, a little." With a dip of his chin, he leans closer. "A small word of advice? Selah doesn't like staring."

The torchlight along the path reflects in Jude's eyes. They

burn like fire. He stands there with his jaw clenched, his shoulders squared—a picture of measured restraint. Controlled stillness. He's a carefully coiled snake. Any sane person would sense the danger and dial it back.

But Rafe?

His smirk widens into a grin as he shifts his weight and bends toward my ear. "And Jude doesn't like fun. Not even a little."

I lean away from him.

"But he's not without hobbies. He plays the piano beautifully. That prestigious boarding school of his instilled a proper appreciation of the arts, which I find sorely lacking among the youth these days." Rafe lifts a finger. "Speaking of the arts. I've been meaning to show you a portrait. Painted by our most honored ancestor, Ezra."

I gape. Ezra Vandenberg predates Amos, who rebuilt Foggy Hollow after the fire. Ezra was his father, and a town founder. "You have a painting by Ezra Vandenberg?"

"Not just any painting. This one was his magnum opus. The girl he captured was quite a beauty." His attention moves down my body, then flits up to my face. "I think it would capture both your imaginations."

I eye him warily.

He's navigated this conversation into strange territory, and he was very clearly navigating. Intentionally steering the ship. Judging by the expression Jude wears, Rafe's the only one who isn't lost.

A loud *boom* bursts through the night.

A cannon.

The signal that the lanterns have been launched.

"We better go find our seats." With a wag of his dark eyebrows, Rafe gives the small stone in his hand another toss, then saunters away. Leaving me and Jude to stare after him, wondering what in the world he's up to, and why.

9
A PUZZLING OBSESSION

Despair.

The word clangs like a gong as I scramble to make sense of my surroundings. I'm standing inside a house that's gone blurry at the edges. Low, dulcet conversation seeps through the ceiling above me, too muffled to understand. Everything is a wisp. Corporeal in nature. Like if I tried touching something, my hand would sink straight through.

But the despair?

It's as clear as crystal. As heavy as sandbags. Shrouding the hallway like a cold, suffocating blanket. Beside me, a young man sits on a bench with his face in his hands, a tricorn hat resting beside him. He wears a jacket, a waistcoat, and knee length breeches with stockings and shoes with square buckles. His shoulders heave as he weeps.

Somewhere farther away, a woman wails.

And that dread?

It grabs me by the throat.

I want to flee. Run. Sprint far and fast away. But the despair won't let go. It drags me forward, into a room with sitting chairs, a paneled fireplace, and exposed wooden beams. And hanging from one of them is a young woman in a yellow taffeta dress. Her honey blond hair falls in ringlets around a face that has gone puffy and blue. Her eyes are open and bulging. Her neck bent at an unnatural angle as she swings from a rope.

A scream tears up my throat.

I turn to run, but someone grabs my wrist.

Rafe Vandenberg stands beside the fireplace, shaking his head sorrowfully. "What a shame," he says with a tut, and while the words are true, there's a gleam in his eye that make them more sinister than somber.

I yank free and race out the door into the bright, blinding sun. It bathes the front lawn of the Vandenberg Estate in white.

A gust of wind blows through the trees.

"Seeelaaaah."

The breathy whisper spins me around.

And then, right by my ear …

"Come find me."

I jerk upright in bed, lungs heaving, pajama top damp with sweat as my heart beats against my sternum.

Thud, thud, thud.

Blurry sunlight pours through the window and spills across the hardwood floor. I swipe wisps of hair from my face. I haven't heard my mother in eight years and yet somehow I'm positive, it was *her* voice in my dream.

Thud, thud, thud.

This time, it isn't my heart.

It's the door.

I climb out of bed on wobbly legs, grab my robe, stuff my arms inside the sleeves one after the other, and pull my hair loose. As I head down the stairs, I gather it into something less like a bird's nest. The digital clock on our stove reads 8:03 a.m.

Thud, thud, thud.

"I'm coming," I mutter, cinching my robe tight.

I'm not sure who to expect. An impatient delivery man with

a postal emergency? Whoever it is should know that 8:03 a.m. on a Saturday morning is an ungodly hour to be pounding on front doors. I yank mine open with a hefty dose of exasperation.

It isn't a delivery man.

It's Jude Vandenberg, his back outlined by the morning sun. At the sound of the door opening, he turns around, and one thing is crystal clear.

He does not look amused.

<hr>

"How long have you known Rafe?" he asks.

The question spins me around.

I'm having a hard enough time processing his presence, never mind the strange inquiry. I pull my robe tighter, very aware that I haven't brushed my teeth. Or gone to the bathroom. Or put on a bra.

He pulls at his jaw. "Honestly, I don't get the joke, but I feel like I should warn you to stay away from him."

I set my hand on the doorknob. I don't love the feeling of confusion, and right now I'm gobsmacked with it. "What are you talking about?"

"The portrait."

"What portrait?"

His brow puckers.

I lift mine impatiently.

"You don't know?" he asks.

"Know what?"

He stares at me, his gaze intense. And yet, it's different from Rafe's. With Jude, I don't so much feel like I'm being undressed as x-rayed. Like he'd rather see my bones and my guts than what I look like under this robe. Finally, he seems to reach a decision. "I need to show you something."

"Okay."

"It's in my bedroom."

In his bedroom.

Which is *in his house.*

Which would put *me* in that manor.

Confusion morphs into excitement.

I hold up two fingers in request for two minutes. As quickly as possible, I use the restroom, brush my teeth, splash my face, put on deodorant, ditch the robe and pajamas for a pair of black leggings and an off-white hoodie. I top it off with a bit of lip gloss and a spritz of body spray. I hurry down the stairs, slide my feet into a pair of loafers, and join him outside, where the sun has chased most of the fog away.

He looks exasperated, like I just spent thirty minutes curling my hair instead of a meager five engaging in basic hygiene. He turns toward the manor.

I follow him up the cobblestone drive.

Dad has made impressive progress over the past week, but after thirty years of neglect, it's only a drop in the bucket. I take in the weeds, the overgrown hedges. "Are you really going to host the masquerade ball here this year?"

"If Isabel has her way," he answers, his pace unfaltering, his attention fixed forward.

"You don't like the idea?"

"I neither like nor dislike it."

I lengthen my stride to keep up with his. "It's only a month and a half away. Less than, actually."

Jude doesn't respond.

"That's not a lot of time to prepare. The upkeep alone on these grounds is a full time job. What my dad's doing now isn't upkeep. It's ... " I glance over my shoulder at the overgrown garden on the southeast lawn, with a half-crumbled stone arch and an enormous twisted tree, its dead branches tied with faded ribbon—for what reason, I don't know. "Resuscitation."

He stops in front of the tiered fountain in the courtyard, once the *piece de resistance*, now weathered and dry except for rainwater that's puddled in the basin. "Do you have a point, or do you just like to talk?"

"This may come as a shock to you, but talking is a relatively normal thing to do when in another's company."

He glowers.

"But I also have a point."

"Which is?"

"If the ball is going to be held here, my dad's gonna need some help."

"I'll talk to Isabel."

With that, he climbs the stone steps.

Suddenly, we're at the entrance, and I feel like I need a minute. A reverent pause. Some way of commemorating such a momentous occasion. A text to Twig, at the very least. But Jude just pushes the doors open and walks inside. He reaches the staircase before realizing I'm still stuck on the threshold.

With a shaky exhale, I step inside.

The marble floor is a deep charcoal veined with silver. Wrought-iron sconces cast long shadows down midnight blue walls patterned with gold filigree. To my right, a pair of double doors open into the ballroom. To my left, a matching pair remain closed. Two staircases spiral upward, and in the center hangs a massive chandelier that is both beautiful and ominous.

Jude gives his throat a loud clear from halfway up one of the staircases. I hurry to catch up, trying to take it all in. Every detail. Because what if this is my only opportunity? But before I can blink, we're in the upper hall.

I set my hands on the railing and look down into the foyer below, picturing the estate in all its former glory. Filled with people in extravagant gowns, ten Mr. Tulane's smartly dressed in black tuxedos with tailcoats, their white gloved hands balancing silver trays arranged with hors d'oeuvres and flutes of champagne. I can hear the music, the tinkling of crystal, the hum of conversation and laughter.

"Are you coming?" Jude asks, his voice tinged with impatience.

The back wall is lined with floor-to-ceiling windows. A corridor stretches into each wing, and there are two sets of double doors—one to the left and one to the right. Jude moves to the set on the left. He pushes them open and steps inside.

We've reached his bedroom.

Grand in size with a fireplace and a mantle, a pair of sitting chairs on either side of a table, a luxurious armoire, an antique desk, and an opened door that gives way to the tiled flooring of an en suite bathroom. French doors lead to a private balcony. There's a glass of water and a book on his nightstand. At some point last week, he'd exchanged *Macbeth* for *Crime and Punishment* by Fyodor Dostoevsky.

He gestures agitatedly toward the bed, which I've been visually skirting up until now. It feels very intimate, looking at Jude Vandenberg's bed—a king-sized four poster with hunter green bedding ever so slightly rumpled. And there, resting on top, lies a portrait. From my purview in his doorway, I can't make it out. I can only tell that it's large with a thick frame, heavily carved and covered in gold leaf.

I approach slowly, almost reverently, and it takes a minute to process what I'm seeing. A portrait of a young woman painted long ago. She wears a white dress with delicate short sleeves and a scooped neckline. A silver locket rests in her décolletage. It's carved with a symbol that strikes a familiar cord. Her rich auburn hair is fashioned into springy curls that frame her face. Which is ... *my* face.

It's *me* in that painting.

A fact that makes my mind short circuit.

I try to say something—to utter words, questions, accusations of my own—but my tongue fumbles every attempt.

Meanwhile, Jude stands there, studying me intently.

Finally, I manage a simple, albeit breathless phrase. "I don't understand."

"Nor do I."

I take a few steps closer, eyes narrowing at the girl's lips, drawn slightly upward. They are my lips. The exact shape and shade. "Is this a weird joke?"

"That's what *I* thought, remember?"

"This is the painting Rafe was going on about? The one by Ezra Vandenberg?"

His magnum opus.

Jude sweeps his hand toward his bed with a terse exhale. "When I arrived last night, there it was."

"Is it authentic?"

I can tell he wants to say no. Or he's not sure. His attention lowers to the portrait. He scrutinizes it like his own intensity might conjure errors, mistakes. Anything that could elude to a counterfeit. Rafe had this commissioned to mess with us. He's playing a very expensive, very bizarre prank. "From what I can tell?" When he looks up at me, the shadows beneath his eyes resemble faint bruises. "It's authentic."

Silence falls.

There's nothing but the echoing tick of a clock somewhere outside his room.

Jude drags his hand down his face. "Are your ancestors from Foggy Hollow?"

"No. I mean, I don't think so. We moved here—me and my dad. From Ohio."

"What about your mom?"

"She was born in Missouri." I lean forward to get a better look at the silver locket, carved with a delicate symbol that is unnervingly familiar. An inverted tear drop inside an open circle, like a halo unfinished. "I feel like I've seen this before."

"The locket?"

"The symbol." I look closer. "But I'm not sure from where."

"I wondered if you would show it to her."

Jude and I turn in tandem.

Rafe leans against the doorframe with his arms casually crossed, one corner of his mouth tipped infuriatingly upward. His words come back to me—something he said in the graveyard when we first met.

You look like someone.

"This is who you were talking about. The girl you *sort of know*." I put air-quotes around the phrase.

"Good memory. And yes. I've never officially met her, but I've had this painting for so long, it feels like I sort of do, you know?"

"Who is she?" I ask.

"That is the million dollar question."

"Where did you get it?" Jude asks.

"It's been handed down through the generations. I'm not sure how it ended up on my side of the family. Technically, your side created it."

Jude stares at him.

"Your lineage descends from Ezra. My lineage descends from Ezra's younger brother, Raphael. I'm named after him, actually." Rafe tosses a glance at the painting. "You really don't know anything about this portrait? Your father never shared the story?"

"Obviously not," Jude replies, his jaw tight.

"I suppose, with him passing when you were so tragically young, he never got around to it." Rafe saunters into Jude's bedroom with his hands in his pockets. "As the story goes, Ezra came home from the Revolutionary War consumed with a woman who wasn't his wife. For decades, he painted her obsessively, but could never quite capture her likeness. Until he did. He had it framed, and then he died. As you can imagine, his poor wife wanted to destroy the thing. His son, Amos, objected.

And it has passed down through the generations ever since. We're lucky such an exquisite work of art didn't burn in the fire."

I stare at the painting.

At the portrait.

At *me*.

"She really is a stunning beauty," he says. "I can see why my dear uncle was so consumed. It was originally titled *Portrait of a Lady Unknown*. But eventually, it garnered another name."

He doesn't say the name.

He's waiting for me or Jude to ask, which is obnoxious.

And yet, I can't help but take the bait.

"What was it?"

"*Ezra's Obsession*." His icy blue eyes dance as he prowls toward us. "Last night, it became obvious my dear cousin needed an assist. He couldn't stop staring. But he wouldn't do anything about it, either. And I thought, I know just the thing that will help."

Tension radiates off Jude in waves.

I look from him to the portrait to Rafe, who's drawn so close, he's like a taunting devil in my ear.

"Who was this woman?" he asks, sliding one hand over Jude's shoulder, his other over mine. "And why does she look exactly like you? It's quite a mystery, isn't it? I found your podcast, Selah. I know how much you love mysteries. Perhaps the two of you can solve this one together."

10

HATRED ALL THE WAY DOWN

"Any information about a family painting would be in the personal archives," Jude says.

Our footsteps echo as I follow him further into the library, toward a life-sized portrait of Amos and Ida Vandenberg hanging over a commanding fireplace. On either side, spiraling staircases climb to balconies above. Overhead, angelic frescoes decorate the ceiling. Not the kind familiar to the Sistine Chapel —all soft pastels and cotton-candy clouds. These are dark. And moody. An underworld caught in a moment of divine reckoning.

I should be awestruck. This is the Vandenberg library, after all. The crown jewel of the west wing. But all I can think about is that portrait.

Rafe might be a royal jerk. A smarmy creep. But he wasn't wrong. Ezra Vandenberg painted *my* face hundreds of years before I was born. This isn't just a fascinating mystery. It's a fascinating mystery involving *me*.

I must solve it.

We reach the staircase farther away.

The steps creak beneath our weight.

The air grows thick with the smell of musty books.

At the top, Jude reaches past me toward the light switch and I catch a subtle note of his cologne— a luxurious scent that has no business smelling so good. Dusty bulbs flicker to life inside a cobwebbed chandelier. While the light is minimal, it's enough to see that this is more than a simple balcony. It's a proper research space with a long table and rows of shelves crowded with leather-bound tomes, a collection vast enough to chronicle centuries. I pull out the nearest one. The cover is stamped with gold lettering.

Vandenberg Correspondence, 18th Century

It contains letter upon letter written in faded cursive on pages made of thick parchment, yellowed and warped by time. Many are dated *before* the Revolutionary War.

"How did these survive the fire?" I ask.

"The original home sustained damage, but most of the records remained intact." Jude removes one of the tomes and brings it to the table like a man determined to find logic.

Meanwhile, my mind is spinning with one fantastical explanation after another.

"What do you know about doppelgängers?" I ask.

"As a literary device?"

"As an actual phenomenon."

He doesn't look up. He just turns a page like the idea isn't even worth his consideration.

I grab a tome for myself and sit across from him. "They're almost always associated with bad omens. Evil shadow-selves. Ghostly doubles. I don't feel particularly evil or ghostly."

"You're talking nonsense."

"Don't you think the situation warrants it?"

"According to Rafe," he replies, his jaw tightening over his cousin's name, "Ezra came back from the war consumed with a woman nobody knew. Which means he probably had an out-of-town mistress. If I had to guess, she was a relative of yours."

I set my elbow on the table. "How would that explain our *identical* resemblance? No genes are that strong."

He ignores my objection and turns another page.

"Okay. Let's say you're right. Your ancestor Ezra had an affair with my ancestor, some lady *unknown*. What are the odds, statistically speaking, that our paths would cross two hundred something years later?"

"I'll take them over doppelgängers."

Of course he would.

Just like he'll take chemical imbalances of the brain over the reality of evil.

I narrow my eyes at the top of his head as he pores over the archives in front of him.

For the past few years, Twig and I have made it our mission to prove the supernatural. We always thought we'd do so by capturing the Woman of the Woods on camera. But maybe there's another way. Maybe this is it. Maybe somewhere in all these towering bookshelves, I'll find the proof we've been looking for. Something supernatural is going on here. And Jude Vandenberg will have to eat his skepticism.

With a thrill of anticipation, I open the volume.

I dive in with the enthusiasm of a kid on Christmas morning, expecting to unwrap all the gifts I've ever wanted. Only to discover a bunch of socks. The reading turns out to be frustratingly dull and hard to decipher. So much squinting, only to learn about crop yields and estate repairs and land disputes. Thank-you notes for dinner parties that sadly, are every bit as generic and mundane as thank you notes today.

"Not as riveting as you expected?"

I look up.

Jude's watching me with a touch of arrogance. Like he wanted these letters to be boring. I flip a page with unnecessary force. "Can I ask you a question?"

"Sure."

"Why are you so against the idea that something beyond logic could be at play here?"

"Why are you so eager to believe something supernatural is at play here?"

My mind turns to my mother.

Disappearing in fading pixels.

Swallowed up by a black hole of a monster.

"Do you honestly believe in the stuff you talk about on your podcast?" he asks.

My eyes snap to his.

The last time we broached the topic of my podcast, things didn't go so well. And the memory of Rafe mentioning it is still fresh. It felt like a taunt, a more subtle rendition of *I've been watching you*. He was messing with me. And now here I am, sitting at a table across from Jude, who isn't backing down. He's waiting for me to answer. This wealthy, refined, ridiculously gorgeous boy, his expression taut and slightly condescending. But there's something else, too. A trace of hunger in his eyes. Like some repressed piece of him doesn't just want to know, but wants to believe, too.

"I believe in the possibility," I say.

He arches his brow. "You believe in the possibility of cryptids?"

"There's been plenty of sightings."

"None of them confirmed."

"Because once they're confirmed, they're no longer cryptids." I fold my hands on the table. "Not too terribly long ago, people thought the okapi and the Komodo dragon were mythical creatures."

"Okay, then. What about vampires?"

"Thirteen percent of Americans believe in them."

"Where did you get that number?"

"Twig."

He rolls his eyes. "Time travel?"

"Definitely possible."

"Haunted dolls?"

"I'm not saying I'm a believer, but if you dared me to spend the night inside of Bogaard Antiques all by myself, I'd probably say no."

He scoffs.

"Do you believe in God?" I ask.

The question seems to catch him off guard.

He leans back in his seat, his hands resting on either side of the volume in front of him. There's a thin leather cord tied around his left wrist, which is tan, and much sexier than any wrist ought to be. "I don't know."

"Can you concede in the possibility of God existing?"

"Saying no to that would make me sound really arrogant."

This time, *I* roll *my* eyes. "Just answer the question."

"Fine. I can concede in the possibility."

"Then can't you also concede in everything else that would come with God?"

"Vampires and haunted dolls?"

"A supernatural world. One we can't see. One that *transcends* logic."

He taps his finger against the table, as though considering my words. Judging by his expression, I'm pretty sure he thinks they're ridiculous. "What's your theory, then?" he finally asks.

"About the painting?"

"About my family."

Now *I'm* caught off guard.

We stare at one another for a drawn out moment—like a game of chicken. I hold his gaze, refusing to look away first. "You want to know what *I* think happened to your family?"

He inclines his head in a gesture of concession, as if to say, *Have at it.*

I don't know where to begin. The Vandenberg cold case is the most fascinating cold case I've ever encountered. A prominent, wealthy family of four vanishes without a trace. One minute, they're sitting down for dinner. The next, they're gone, food still on their plates. Jude wants to hear my theory, but I don't have a theory. Just a collection of intriguing facts. I point some of them out, starting with John, the shady patriarch.

"He was known around town for his volatile personality. According to inside sources, he was pretty controlling, especially when it came to his children. And there were some rumors of embezzlement and blackmail."

Jude's eyes narrow, as though contemplating this new-to-him information. "Enough to get his family killed?"

"There was never any physical proof that anyone *was* killed. No blood. No bodies. No smoking gun. The only lead police had to follow came from John's brother, Luke."

"My grandfather," Jude mutters. "What was the lead?"

"He told authorities to look into a cousin named Thomas, Rueben, or Frank." I watch him process the accusation, taking in the slow furrow of his brow. "Do you know them?"

He shakes his head, but then he says, "Thomas is Rafe's dad."

The back of my neck prickles.

"I've never met him, but after my grandfather died, Rafe offered condolences on his father's behalf. He said his name was Thomas."

"Do you know anything about Reuben or Frank?"

He shakes his head again.

I gaze at the archives—there are so many—and I wonder what secrets they hold, what stories they tell. "It's a strange tip, isn't it?"

"Accusing a cousin?"

"The wording." I look at Jude. "He said to look into *a* cousin, but then he gave three names."

"You don't think it was a typo?"

"Probably." And yet, the dissonance has always nagged at

me. Like maybe there's something there and we just haven't put it together yet.

"Did anything come of it?" Jude asks.

"Not that I know of. There was nothing more about it in the investigation, anyway. At least not in the parts Twig and I had access to. There was some suspicious stuff about the teenage daughter though."

"Suspicious how?"

"She got into a fair amount of trouble. Once, she was arrested for indecent exposure." My face flushes, which is dumb. It's not like *I* was the one caught swimming naked in haunted waters. "She went skinny dipping in the quarry."

Jude clears his throat. He flips a page of the tome in front of him, then straightens in his seat. "Look at this," he says, turning the volume toward me.

It's a charcoal sketch of a young woman titled *Molly*. She isn't the subject of Ezra's portrait. She doesn't look like me at all. But there is something slightly familiar about her face. It's signed by Ezra. And in the upper right corner?

The same symbol from the locket I'm wearing in that portrait.

I scratch my chin.

Jude turns the page in search for more information. Who is Molly? And what does this symbol mean? Judging by his furrowed brow, there's no more information to be found. When he reaches the end, he snaps a picture of the sketch with his phone and exchanges the tome for another.

Meanwhile, I skim a letter written in 1784, addressed to Ezra's wife. Halfway through, my eyes come to a screeching halt.

There, on the page, are words about the painting.

"My Dearest Elizabeth," I read aloud.

Jude comes around the table to look over my shoulder.

"I have received your most recent correspondence and must confess that its contents have troubled me deeply. The accounts you share of your husband's behavior are most distressing. To hear that he has gone so far as to label his own nephew a 'demon' is beyond comprehension. Such words betray a most unsettled mind, and I fear his long-standing enmity toward his brother has now, most unfairly, been cast upon Raphael's son.

"Moreover, your mention of the *portrait*," I continue, emphasizing the word, "that continues to consume his every waking hour raises further concern. This fixation of his can no longer be endured. I earnestly entreat you to urge him to seek the counsel of a learned physician. There are men of science who specialize in ailments of the mind. Surely, such men might offer him some relief or, at the very least, sound guidance. Given the present state of affairs, I fear this may be your only true recourse.

"Please know that my thoughts and prayers are with you during this trying time. May we soon see Ezra restored to the amiable and worthy man we once held in such esteem. With deepest affection, your doting sister."

I flip to the next page, hoping for more. Something about the subject of his fixation. Who was this girl in the portrait, consuming Ezra's every waking hour? Unfortunately, the letter that follows is from a merchant discussing the procurement of bed linens. I flip several more pages, disappointment sinking into the pit of my stomach.

"That's it," I say, turning around.

Jude is right there, leaning over me with one hand curled over the back of my chair, the other set on the table, so close I can smell peppermint on his breath, see specks of gold in the brown of his irises. His attention dips to my lips. And the same thing that happened in the hallway on his first day of school, then later in the cafeteria, happens all over again.

A jolt of searing heat.

He uncurls his hand from the back of my chair and stands straight, creating space between us.

But the air is warm and tightly drawn.

I return to the letter, my heart beating erratically. "Sounds like Ezra didn't like his brother very much."

"It's hatred all the way down," Jude says.

The intriguing words draw my attention.

He leans against the banister, one arm crossed over the other, his thumb pressed against his bottom lip.

"What do you mean?" I ask.

"The long-standing enmity. My grandfather obviously didn't like his cousins, and my father made a point to keep me away from that side of the family. I never understood why." His eyes darken. "Until I met Rafe at my grandfather's funeral a few months ago."

"Did something happen?"

"Nothing specific. He's just ... not a good guy."

No, he isn't.

I think about the first time *I* met Rafe.

"He tried to kiss me."

Jude's gaze jerks to mine. "He tried to *kiss* you?"

I laugh awkwardly, my cheeks burning with red hot, mortified flame. Because what in the world possessed me to blurt that?

"When?" Jude asks.

"The first time we met. In the graveyard last Sunday. I was out for a jog, and somehow he was there, too. I'm not sure if he was following me or what."

Oh my gosh, Selah.

Stop rambling.

Stop it right now.

But I keep going. Verbal diarrhea. And with each word, his expression tightens all the more.

The coiled snake is back, ready to strike.

I pull at the collar of my hoodie, looking for a conversational exit when Jude's phone vibrates against the table.

The screen lights up, flashing the time.

I hop out of my chair like a hot potato. I reach inside the front pocket of my hoodie. But my phone isn't there. I left it in my bedroom. I set my hand on top of my head. "I was supposed to meet Twig a half hour ago."

Like Cinderella fleeing the ball at midnight, I hurry down the spiral staircase. I don't lose a shoe. And Jude doesn't chase after me. But as soon as I'm outside, I can't help but feel the disappointment of a spell that's been broken.

11

THE LOCKED TOME

Twig and I have had a long-standing date every Saturday at noon in Maggie's basement, where we brainstorm, research, outline, record, and edit episodes for the podcast. Today, I'm late. And I don't mean fifteen minutes late like last Saturday, either. I mean egregiously late. Like, *we should be wrapping up by now because my shift starts soon* late.

I jog across the street to Evermore Books, a two-story brick building on the square. The second floor is home to Maggie's impressive compilation of historical records, accessible by appointment only. The first floor is the book shop, a haphazard maze of mismatching shelves stuffed with mostly used books, many of which have handwritten notes tucked inside. My all time favorite? A hastily scribbled note in all caps that warned, "Do not read after midnight." I found it inside *The Haunting of Hill House* by Shirley Jackson, and Maggie was right. I really shouldn't have read it after midnight.

Breathless and windswept, I rush past the storefront window, which boasts, among other things, a taxidermy raven with beady eyes. The bell on the door jingles as I let myself in.

Twig is bent over the counter, chatting with Walt while the resident black cat, Poe, tries to nuzzle his way between Twig's folded arms.

"I am *so* sorry," I say, rushing toward them, "but I promise when I tell you what I've been up to, you will forgive me."

Twig responds with such an emphatic sneeze, his glasses slide to the end of his nose. He's allergic to cats, and Poe never leaves him alone. "It's not a problem," he says on the cusp of another.

Walt shoos Poe off the counter. "Yes, because being an hour late isn't a problem at all."

"Fifty-four minutes late," Twig corrects, followed by a third sneeze. He grabs a tissue and blows his nose. "Which, in the grand scheme of things, isn't the end of the world."

Walt harrumphs. He's a retired journalist who loathes tardiness. Back in the day, he worked for the Foggy Hollow Gazette as a hard-nosed beat reporter, investigating scandal and corruption in local politics.

The FHPS hates him.

I plop a paper bag from Tudor's next to the cash register. "I bring a peace offering."

Walt digs inside and removes the wrapped biscuits. He tosses one to Twig and takes the other for himself.

"I've been chatting with your friend here about Dante's comet, set to make its appearance over our town in thirty-nine days, ten hours, and ..." He checks his wristwatch. "Forty-four minutes." Walt shoots me a wink. When it comes to time—or any measurement at all, really—Twig is nothing if not exact.

"And brightest on Halloween night," I say, a smile stretching across my face. "What are the chances?"

"Point zero eight percent," Twig replies around a mouthful. He's already unwrapped his food and taken a giant bite. He swallows it down. "That's the probability of a random individual being alive when the comet returns, *and* its peak visibility occurring on Halloween Night."

My smile widens. "Point zero eight percent."

"What a time to be alive," Walt says.

Indeed.

I turn to my friend. "You have your appetite back, I see."

With a nod, he scarfs the rest of the sandwich, then brushes biscuit crumbs from his hands. "So, what had you running late?"

I shoot a glance at Walt, then look back at Twig with wide, excited eyes. "Let's go downstairs and I'll catch you up."

Walt gives another harrumph. "Top secret stuff, huh?"

I grab Twig by the elbow and pull him toward the stairs. "Enjoy your biscuit, Walt," I call over my shoulder. "Share a bite with Poe!"

Descending the steps of Maggie's bookstore always makes me feel like I'm Mike from *The Goonies*, sneaking into the basement of the Fratelli's restaurant with a map I found in my attic. The staircase is narrow with a single overhead bulb flickering uncertainly against the stone walls. At the bottom, the air is damp and cool. We sit in chairs salvaged from upstairs and do our work at a large, scarred wooden table, where wires snake across the surface and connect to microphones and sound equipment. In the shadows, old wooden crates sit like silent sentinels, their contents a mystery.

Twig plugs in his laptop. "I have to be at robotics in forty minutes."

I slap my forehead with my palm, feeling a fresh wash of shame. In several short weeks, Twig and Naomi will be leaving me for one of the most important competitions of their lives. Last spring, their robotics team was extended an exclusive invite to attend the Future Innovators STEM Symposium at Carnegie Melon University. The three-day conference will be culminating in The Catalyst Cup, and if their team wins, every member will get a ten *thousand* dollar scholarship toward their college education. They've been up to their ears in prep work, and yet, never once has Twig showed up this late on a Saturday.

"I am such a jerk," I mutter.

"You aren't a jerk," he says. "You just tend to lose track of time, especially when you're wrapped up in something fascinating. So ... what had you fascinated?"

I tell him everything. The tense encounter between Rafe and Jude at Willowmere Park last night. Going *inside* the manor so Jude could show me something in his bedroom. And then the portrait itself—*Ezra's Obsession*.

"She looked like you?" Twig says.

"She was *identical* to me."

"Did you take a picture?"

"I didn't have my phone. But even if I did, I don't think snapping a pic would have gone over too well."

I tell him the rest—the story behind the painting, the symbol on the locket my doppelgänger was wearing, and how we found it again, on the sketch of Molly. I tell him, too, how both were familiar. Somehow, I've seen them before—Molly and the symbol.

"What did it look like?" he asks.

I grab a pad of sticky notes along with a nearby pencil and draw a simple sketch. "Do you recognize it?"

He shakes his head.

I lean back in my chair. "I don't know, Twig. I feel like something big is going on."

"What do you mean?"

"The timing of everything. The Vandenbergs have been MIA from Foggy Hollow for the past thirty years, and now they're back. This portrait shows up. Dante's comet is on its way. The last time it made an appearance, Ezra was alive. It all feels connected somehow.

We sit and stare at one another, our podcast long forgotten, when the bell jingles upstairs and footsteps echo overhead, followed by a greeting that's muffled but unmistakably Maggie's. If anyone in town is going to recognize a symbol on a locket from the early 19th century, it'll be her.

Twig and I race each other up the stairs.

Maggie Henshaw is a painfully thin, hawkish woman in her late seventies who has mousy gray hair and dresses in layers, even in the summer. Maxi skirts on bottom. Cardigans and scarves on top with bizarre accessories, like preserved insects encased in brooches or a necklace made from a tiny bird skull. She's never without her journal, which is stuffed with hand-written notes, to-do lists, and loose scraps of paper. She has the kind of voice you have to lean in to hear, yet she's always telling me and Twig to speak up.

We find her and Walt bickering in one of the narrow aisles.

"Maggie, you have *Frankenstein* shelved next to *The Federalist Papers*."

"They were published in the same era," she replies, "and they both start with F."

"Maggie," Walt says.

"What?" she barks.

"That's insane."

"It's not insane. It's chronologically intuitive."

"No customer looking for *The Federalist Papers* is going to search for it next to a horror novel."

No customer is going to look for *The Federalist Papers*, period. But I keep the sentiment to myself. It will only exacerbate the bickering. The two of them act like an old married couple. One of their favorite topics to argue about is the way in which Maggie organizes her shop, which is, admittedly, terribly confusing to customers.

"I have a question," I say, giving the sticky note a wave as I join them in the post Revolutionary War, pre-fire section. "Have either of you seen this symbol before?"

"Never," Walt declares while Maggie pats inside her pockets and mutters something about her reading glasses.

"They're on your head," Walt says.

She brings them to the end of her nose and inspects my rendering. When she's finished, she turns to me with her unblinking stare. "Why do you want to know?"

"I saw it on a sketch and I'm curious." It's best to keep it vague. Maggie gets very irritated with strange and mysterious things. Not because they frighten her or even because she doesn't believe in them. Sometimes, I think she might. She just doesn't like how easily they overshadow history. History, to Maggie, is the most important thing in the universe.

"Well," she finally announces. "I recognize it."

"You do?"

She waves at us to follow, then heads toward the reading nook, where a faded velvet armchair and a rickety side table sit beneath a floor lamp that almost always flickers. The area is boxed in by shorter shelves, the kind you might find in the children's section of a library. The books in this section aren't for sale; they're for looking. She bends over, removes a large book from a bottom shelf, and places it in my hands. The thing is hefty, and looks like it belongs with the Vandenberg family archives. A proper tome made of leather. And there, on its dusty cover, is the symbol embossed in gold.

"It's locked," Twig says.

He's right.

Its pages are sealed shut with a sturdy metal lock.

"Where's the key?" I ask.

"If I had to guess, somewhere inside that estate you're so obsessed with. This book was donated to me in 1995, along with several other volumes."

"By who?"

"Denis Tulane."

My mouth drops open.

Maggie waves her hand in my direction like one shooing away a fly. "We are acquainted."

I stare incredulously. She knows more than anyone how hard Twig and I have tried to get an interview with Denis Tulane, and all this time, she's known him? "Why didn't you tell us?"

"Because the last thing Denis needs is a couple kids bugging him about that disappearance. He's been pestered enough. The man deserves some peace."

Walt lifts his eyebrows imperiously. "Why would this gentleman donate a locked book without also giving you the key?"

"Who knows and who cares," Maggie replies. "My favorite thing about this book is that lock."

I blow on the cover, sending up a small cloud of dust. "What does the symbol mean?"

"I haven't the faintest idea."

"Do you want to know what I think?" Walt asks.

"No," Maggie replies.

"I think it's probably something religious. Lots of old groups used to carve their beliefs into things. Cults. The Knights Templar."

Maggie blinks at him. "Did you just lump the Knights Templar and cults into the same category?"

"The entire lot of them were executed on Friday the Thirteenth. That sounds pretty cultish to me."

Maggie's thin frame puffs with indignation. She's so wound up, she doesn't notice the mischievous wink Walt shoots at me and Twig. "Walter Jensen," she scolds. "You know very well the Knights Templar were not killed on Friday the Thirteenth! They were arrested."

Poe meows and weaves figure eights around Twig's ankles.

He sneezes.

I take out my phone and snap a picture of the dusty tome while Maggie and Walt argue. The next time I see Jude, I'm going to show this to him. And maybe together, we can find the key.

12

WHAT MAGGIE
DOESN'T KNOW

I don't receive an early morning wake up call from Jude on Sunday. Just Dad, poking his head inside my bedroom a little after eight to make sure I'm awake for church.

For the past seven years, we've gone to St. Oswald's nine o'clock service. Twig's family goes, too, and while he finds it a touch boring, more of an obligation than a spiritual practice, I've always enjoyed church. Especially St. Oswald's, with its natural lighting, wood-beamed ceilings, and free-standing panels of stained glass. I love the tradition, the liturgy, the stories.

It's a place where the uncanny permeates everything. From that giant wooden cross on the altar, to the eucharist placed in our hands, and the Apostles' Creed we recite afterward. The Holy Trinity. Hypostatic Union. The very nature of God—omnipresent and omniscient? I love that Pastor Tim doesn't scramble about, trying to make sense of these grand mysteries. He embraces them. Calls them sacred, even. Then spends the rest of the hour encouraging us to love and serve.

Today, however, I can't quite settle into it. I keep thinking about Jude and the look on his face when I told him Rafe tried kissing me in the graveyard. If ever I could take back my words, those would be the ones.

When the service ends, Twig and I run errands for Mrs. Calloway, who's been the Volunteer & Logistic Coordinator on the Phoenix Parade committee ever since I moved here seven years ago. Over the course of those seven years, Twig and I have become her unofficial errand-runners. We drop off flyers at local businesses for sponsorships and donations. We post signs soliciting volunteers. We take t-shirt inventory for float crews and parade day helpers. And when we're done, we explore more of the Vandenberg grounds.

Dad lets us take his Bronco around the eastern perimeter, where twisted trees cast long shadows over the dirt road. In the northeast corner, we discover a motor house—a more recent addition, by the looks of it, with steel garage doors and clerestory windows that let in the light but protect privacy. John Vandenberg was a known auto enthusiast, so I can only imagine what kind of collection might be hidden inside.

We don't run into Jude or Rafe, but we do have an epic encounter with some turkeys. A rustle of leaves stops us both in our tracks. We tilt our heads toward the sound like a satellite dish honing in. Then comes a cluster of strange, guttural noises. Twig silently pulls out his phone and starts recording.

We creep forward, thrumming with excitement, only for a flock of wild turkeys to explode into flight, flapping and screeching like feathered banshees.

After recovering from our near heart attacks, we fall into hysterical laughter and play the video on repeat. We'd been so convinced we were on the cusp of paranormal discovery, Twig had been ready to fetch our proton pack.

For the next ten minutes, we take turns concocting fake episode titles for the podcast.

Paranormal Poultry.

Cryptids with Tail Feathers.

Fowl Play in the Fog.

Sasquawk: The Mystery Screech of Foggy Hollow.

Eventually, Twig ditches me for his robotics team. I spend the rest of the evening trying really hard not to think about Jude, but failing miserably. What is he doing inside that giant manor? Poring over more tomes, researching by himself? And if so, has he found any more references to the portrait? We parted ways mid-scene, loose ends galore twisting in the wind. I'm eager to tie some of them down.

By the time Monday morning rolls around, I've worked myself into a tizzy of curiosity. I hurry into school ready to bombard him with questions, only to discover he's playing hooky. He's not in the hallways. He's not in the lunchroom. And he's not in eighth period history class, either.

That night, I curl up in my window seat and pretend to do homework. But really, I gaze out my window toward his, illuminated against the dark. Every so often, there's the vague impression of movement, but never his outline.

Is the portrait still in his bedroom?

Has he been studying it, and by proxy, studying me?

The thought is like a space heater in my belly.

When he's a no-show on Tuesday, disappointment curdles into irritation.

"What if I imagined it?" I say to Twig as we move through the lunch line. "What if everything I told you in Maggie's basement was one giant fever dream?"

Twig selects a Jello, rejecting the idea with the shake of his head.

"You weren't there, though, Twig. I have no witnesses. For all we know, I could be going mad like Jack Torrance from *The Shining*."

"Or Teddy Daniels from *Shutter Island*."

I set a small bag of baby carrots on my tray. "Oh my gosh. I'm Teddy Daniels. And Jude is my Rachel Solando."

Twig chuckles.

"No, seriously. What if I'm not even here? What if I moved to Illinois with my dad, which broke my brain, and now I've conjured this elaborate fantasy where I'm not only living on the Vandenberg Estate, I'm the focal point of the family's obsession."

"It's a good fantasy," Twig says.

I heave a sigh, feeling irrationally abandoned.

This is an alluring mystery. An intoxicating riddle. I'm itching to dive in headfirst and hunt for answers. Meanwhile, Jude has gone AWOL.

"I just don't get how he's so ... *uninterested*." I swipe my lunch card, then come to such an abrupt stop, Twig runs into me from behind.

It's him.

Jude.

He's here, in the cafeteria, sitting in the same place he sat the first day of school. He's attracting the same amount of attention, too, looking as tortured and standoffish as ever.

Maybe even more so.

I motion for Twig to follow, and before I can second guess what I'm doing, I'm already halfway there. He doesn't notice my approach. He's too caught up in *Crime and Punishment*, staring at the pages like a man reading his own fate.

"Hey," I say, setting my tray on the table.

He looks up, and there's something on his face that wasn't there before. A dark purple bloom on the ridge of his jaw like a storm cloud under his skin.

I drop into a seat. "What happened?"

A hint of color rises along his cheekbones, faint but undeniable. "It's nothing."

"That isn't nothing. It looks like you got into a fight."

"I didn't," he says tersely.

But my imagination has run wild. I'm already picturing him

and Rafe coming to physical blows. Over *me*. I quickly dismiss the thought. It reeks of narcissism. I've gone and put myself in the center of Jude's life, and there's nothing to suggest I'm even on the periphery.

He dog-ears his page—which would make Maggie holler—and glances up at Twig.

I give my friend a look like *sit down already*.

Twig lowers himself into the seat on my left.

I fish my phone from the pocket of my slouchy cardigan and pull up the picture I took of Maggie's book. "Look what I found."

Jude tosses my screen an annoyed glance, quickly followed by a giant double take. He leans closer, his attention flicking to Twig before returning to me, and I'm caught off guard by his nearness. Maybe not as close as he was on the balcony of his library, but close enough to make out each one of his dark eyelashes.

"Where's it from?" he asks, separating himself a little.

"Evermore Books. I drew the symbol and showed it to my boss, Maggie Henshaw, and she showed me this book. It was donated from *your* estate, by Denis Tulane."

Jude casts another glance in Twig's direction.

"I told him about the portrait," I say. "And everything we found when we were researching in your library."

His countenance goes very, very dark.

He doesn't like that I've told Twig.

But what's a girl to do? Of course I was going to tell my best friend.

"You don't have to worry. It's not like we're going to do a podcast episode about it."

"Aren't you?"

"Of course not."

Jude drags his hand along his bruised jawline. "I think we should drop this."

"What?" I practically come out of my chair, garnering the attention of several people sitting at the table next to ours. I lower my voice. "Why—because I told Twig?"

"Because we don't even know what we're looking for."

"The identity of Ezra's obsession."

"She's his mistress."

"You can't honestly still think that."

"Why not?"

"If she was simply his mistress, why is there this mysterious symbol? What's it doing on the locket and that sketch?"

"Maybe they had an illegitimate kid together, Molly is their daughter, and the symbol is your family crest."

"I don't have a family crest."

"That you know of."

I hold up my phone with the picture of the tome. "And this? What's the symbol doing on this?"

"What's inside?"

"We don't know."

"You can't tell from the picture," Twig says, "but it's locked."

Jude's eyes spark with interest.

I grab onto it for all I'm worth. "Pretty strange, don't you think?"

But he only shakes his head. "I shouldn't have shown you the portrait."

"Of course you should have. It's a painting of *me*."

"Someone who looks like you," he says in a tone tight with aggravation. "Rafe is up to something, and whatever it is, he's trying to pull you into the middle of it."

My attention shifts to his bruise. "Is that why you want to drop this, because of Rafe?"

"You should stay away from him."

"I don't plan to go anywhere near him. I just want to pull on the string."

Jude quirks his eyebrow.

"You know that scene from *The Goonies*? Where Mikey finds a string and he starts to pull it up?"

"I've never seen *The Goonies*," Jude says.

"Doesn't it lead to a booby trap?" Twig asks.

I ignore the interjections. "Right now, we've picked up a string. I don't know where it leads. I only know that I have to follow it to the end. Don't you want to follow it with me?"

Jude's knee begins bouncing under the table.

I can tell he wants to say yes.

I set my elbow next to my tray. "You should come to Evermore after school. I'll be there until seven. At least let me show you the book."

The battle rages.

I'm desperate for curiosity to win.

"I can't after school," he finally says. "I have ... obligations."

Something tells me if I were to wait for some elaboration on these cryptic obligations, I would be waiting in vain. "When are these *obligations* wrapping up?"

"When your shift ends."

"Then why don't I bring the book to you?"

Twig almost spits out his Powerade. He manages to get the drink down, then pats his chest. "Sorry," he says, coughing some more. "Wrong pipe." He wipes his mouth with his napkin and looks at me like he has opinions.

"Just say it," I tell him.

"Maggie isn't going to let that book out of her shop."

"What Maggie doesn't know won't kill her."

Twig frowns.

Honestly, I'm not a fan of the idea either, but it isn't like I'm going to steal the thing. I'll return it first thing tomorrow. "She won't even know it's gone, Twig. I promise." I turn away from his disapproval. "Meet you at seven fifteen?"

"Sure," Jude says.

We spend the rest of lunch period in silence.

Twig, nervous.

Jude, brooding.

Me?

Wondering how the heck I'm going to get such a giant book out from under Maggie Henshaw's nose.

13
THE SCENE OF THE CRIME

I did not prepare myself for Jude Vandenberg in business attire. So when he answers the door in perfectly tailored trousers, a crisp white dress shirt, and a slim black tie loosened at the collar, I'm a little caught off guard. It's a distracting ensemble, one he wears entirely too well. I picture him at his prestigious boarding school, striding through an ancient stone courtyard somewhere in Europe, looking effortlessly put together while his classmates fuss with their blazers and ties.

He invites me in.

I step inside with my head on a swivel—this time, less out of obsessive curiosity and more to avoid ogling him.

"Is that it?" he asks.

I clear my throat and hand him the tome, taking excessive interest in the mahogany paneling that runs partway up the walls. I managed to smuggle the book out of Evermore inside my backpack while Maggie was upstairs in her office, clacking away on her typewriter.

Jude takes the book in both hands. "Tulane donated this?"

"In 1995, according to Maggie."

The date isn't lost on either of us.

It's the year the Vandenberg four vanished.

He slides his thumb over the lock. "Let's go find him."

"*What?*"

"He might know where the key is."

Protest bubbles up my throat. I have no idea how acquainted Mr. Denis Tulane and Maggie are. For all I know, they talk on a regular basis. What if he mentions the book being here, with me?

But Jude isn't asking permission.

Our footsteps echo as I follow him into the west wing corridor. Towering lancet windows line the exterior wall. The waning daylight cuts through their narrow panes, creating bands of light and dark along the marble floor. They rise up the opposite wall, where statues stand inside arched alcoves, half bathed in gold, half swallowed in shadow.

Here in the Vandenberg manor, even the hallways are extraordinary.

"I think he's in the kitchens," Jude says as we turn a corner.

I glimpse a regal sitting room through a set of opened doors to my left. We pass a set of closed doors to our right before reaching the dining hall.

My skin erupts in goosebumps.

Here it is.

The scene of the crime.

The room where it happened.

I stand on the threshold, taking it all in—a massive table with throne-like chairs, a fireplace at the far end, French doors that open to a terrace, and windows on either side. They aren't narrow and pointed like the ones in the hallway. These are wide and arched, with an open view of the back lawn, where golden pink sky melts into lilac purple. The house casts a wide shadow, turning the orchard into a darkening sprawl of tangled branches and overgrown grass. I spot Dad near the far edge, a lone figure moving methodically, his pruning shears flashing in the fading light.

"Are you coming?" Jude asks.

But I can't answer.

I can't move.

My feet are stuck in the entryway.

I've studied the investigation so thoroughly, pored over every detail I could get my hands on, it's almost as if that thirty-year-old scene unfolds before me now. The family sitting down to dinner. Perhaps a terse conversation over Lily's most recent rebellion, plates and silverware clinking. Then, something ... *horrible*. Maureen calls for help, but it's too late. There's panic and chaos and pleading as the horrible, mysterious something descends.

"Selah?"

I blink several times, my attention returning to the present moment. I focus on Jude, standing there with Maggie's tome in hand.

"I feel like Oda Mae Brown," I say.

"Who?"

"Whoopi Goldberg."

He looks at me blankly.

"From the movie *Ghost*?"

Still blank.

"You've never seen it?"

"Should I?"

"It's only one of the best films of all time. Whoopi Goldberg plays Oda Mae Brown, who claims to be a medium, only she's a total fraud. Between you and me, I think most of them are."

"Careful," he says. "Your podcast listeners might hear."

"They already know."

"So, *not* between you and me, then."

But I hardly register the comment.

I'm too busy looking around at more of the room. An

impressive sideboard with clawed feet spans the length of one wall. A pair of matching candelabras stand atop it on either end. Above, a gilded mirror reflects the sun's lingering glow.

What has it seen—that mirror?

If I could look into its depths, if it held actual memory, what would it show me?

"If she's a fraud," Jude says, "why do you feel like her?"

"She *was* a fraud. Until Sam—he's the ghost—starts speaking to her."

"Is a ghost speaking to you now?" he asks, more than a little dubiously.

"Depends on your definition of ghost." I look up at the crystal chandelier, where delicate cobwebs shimmer like spectral threads. "Do you think past events can leave behind an imprint?"

"An imprint?"

I look at him and immediately regret the decision, as I am flummoxed by his appearance all over again. Seriously, couldn't he have changed into some sweats?

He slides his hands into his pockets and quirks one perfectly brooding eyebrow.

"There's this theory in paranormal circles called the stone tape theory," I say. "Basically, an intense event can leave a lasting impression on a location. Energy gets trapped, causing the event to be replayed over and over. Like a residual haunting."

"Let me guess. You believe in this theory."

"I don't know." I close my eyes, ears perked, as though the candles might whisper their secrets. "I can almost hear them sitting down to dinner. Their meal gets interrupted. Then the phone call to 911."

When I open my eyes, Jude is staring at me like I'm something novel. An impossible puzzle. A book he'd really like to read, only it's written in a foreign language.

"It's like this space is caught between worlds. This big thing happened here. Nobody knows what, exactly. But the room does. It's a bridge between the living and the vanished." My goosebumps multiply. The moment has grown serious. And spooky. I shake it away and flash Jude a self-deprecating smile. "Like Oda Mae Brown."

"Well, *Oda*," he says, "let's find Denis, shall we?"

Right.

Because we're here, now, to chase down a different mystery. One that is separate from the Vandenberg cold case.

He slides open a discreet door beside the fireplace. I hurry after him, through the butler's pantry, into the kitchen. There's an iron stove and a brick oven and a long wooden table. Above it, copper pots and pans hang from a rack. Further back, in the scullery, Mr. Tulane washes dishes in a deep stone sink, his suit coat folded neatly on the workbench behind him.

When he sees Jude, he shuts off the water. Then does a double take at the sight of me, like *he's* the medium and *I'm* the ghost. Maybe he keeps looking at me this way because he's seen the portrait, *Ezra's Obsession*. Or maybe he's just wary of me in general, given my persistent, enthusiastic requests for an interview.

Jude shows him the book. "Do you remember donating this? It would have been thirty years ago."

"To the historical society, yes."

"Do you know where we could find the key?"

Mr. Tulane dries his hands on a towel. "All the items I donated came from storage on the third floor. If there is a key, I imagine it would be somewhere up there."

14
FORGOTTEN THINGS

Jude strides toward a hobbled apothecary desk while I set my sights on a wardrobe, its imposing stature making up for its lackluster condition.

Third floor storage is ripe with neglect.

Cobwebs stretch between exposed rafters. Sheets hang over mystery items like moth-eaten ghosts. Dust covers everything else like peach fuzz—old trunks, broken furniture, forgotten heirlooms.

My fingers itch to explore.

I open the wardrobe's doors and let out a soft exclamation. It's full of clothes straight out of the nineteenth century. Hardly believing my eyes, I pull a dress free—a dusty rose ball gown made of silk and lace, its skirt cascading in layers of tulle. The bodice is stiff with boning, and the fabric smells of old perfume and cedar wood. "I can't believe this is up here."

Languishing in the dark.

I lift it higher, but Jude barely looks. He's too busy prying open the many small drawers of the apothecary desk, one after another.

I hold the dress in front of me, admiring my dingy reflection in the mirror on the inside of the wardrobe's door. I imagine waltzing in the ballroom during the Hunter's Moon Masquerade Ball. Wearing *this*. I sway a little, then exchange the dress for a midnight blue cloak made of velvet, trimmed with fur. I drape it over my shoulders. "Are there smelling salts in those drawers?"

Jude casts me a distracted glance. "Smelling salts?"

"In case I swoon?" I give a twirl.

A cloud of dust billows around me.

"These clothes should be on display in a museum." I shuffle past a collection of Edwardian era menswear, imagining Jude in a black tailcoat with satin lapels and a cravat. He'd look like a gothic hero.

"I don't mean to rain on your fashion parade," he says, wresting open another drawer. "But I don't think you're going to find the key in there."

"You never know. It could be hiding in one of these pockets." I reach inside several to no avail, then force myself to turn away from the wardrobe, cloak still fastened over my shoulders. Jude is right. We came here for a specific reason.

I set my hands on my hips and give the room another scan. "If I were a key, where would I be?"

A broken mirror rests against the wall. Beside it, a child-sized rocking chair with peeling paint.

I give it a tilt with my shoe.

It rocks in a mournful, rhythmic groan.

"Have you ever seen *The Changeling*?" I ask.

"With George C Scott?"

His response surprises me. *The Changeling* is one of the more obscure horror films of the 1980s. It doesn't involve a rocking chair, but it does involve a wheelchair with *very* similar vibes.

"My roommate was into classic horror," he says with a

shrug. He shuts the last drawer of the apothecary desk. "He never introduced me to *Ghost*, though."

"*Ghost* isn't horror. It's romance." I grab a sheet beside me and tug it upward with a flourish. There's an oil painting underneath—a portrait of an elderly woman with eyes that seem to follow me as I sway back and forth. "Do you miss it?"

"Miss what?"

"Your boarding school. Your life there. Your roommate."

Jude inspects a bookshelf stacked with old children's literature. Picture books from a bygone era. "My roommate was preferable to Isabel."

And Rafe, I'm sure.

But he doesn't mention him.

He opens a small book with a gray cloth binding. *The Tale of Peter Rabbit* by Beatrix Potter. "I miss the challenge. And the opportunities."

"Like?"

"Cambridge." He snaps the book shut.

I fold the sheet and hang it over the mirror's frame. "Is that where you want to go for college?"

"It was the plan. Not sure they admit many students from Foggy Hollow High, though."

Probably not. But then, no student at Foggy Hollow High has ever been a Vandenberg. I fiddle with the cloak's clasp—hooking it, and unhooking it, then hooking it again—feeling a bit defensive for this town I love. "What other opportunities did your school offer that Foggy Hollow can't?"

"Fencing. Archery. Equestrian training."

"You have stables."

"*Empty* stables."

"So fill them," I say with a shrug. "And continue on with your equestrian training. Or, teach me archery. I'll be Little John to your Robin Hood."

Jude frowns.

Maybe he's not planning to be here for much longer. So what would be the point in filling his stables or teaching me archery? Or finding a key, for that matter. And yet, he searches like a man absorbed, his attention on a vintage suitcase. He pulls out a porcelain doll with no eyes.

"You want this for your podcast?" He holds it up with a crooked grin, the first real smile I've seen on his face. And heaven help me, Jude Vandenberg has dimples.

"That is horrifying," I say, pulling up another sheet. There's an old phonograph underneath, perched atop a three-legged parlor table. And beneath it, a wooden crate full of vinyls. "Holy motherlode."

I pick up the crate, set it on a nearby trunk, and flip through the albums, reading each artist aloud. "Glenn Miller. Benny Goodman. Nat King Cole."

The floor creaks.

Jude stops behind me, so close I can feel his warmth, smell that delectable cologne. He reaches past me to flip further back. "Beethoven," he says, his voice right next to my ear. "Puccini."

I swallow hard.

"David Bowie," he reads next. "*Scary Monsters and Super Creeps.*"

"Now that's a title I can get behind." With a smile, I continue flipping where Jude left off. Fleetwood Mac. Rolling Stones. And then ...

"Stevie Nicks!" I pluck the album from the rest. "My mom loved her."

As soon as the words are out, my cheeks catch on fire. I just brought up my mother. In the past tense. A faux pas that turns Jude's attention into something acute and curious, as weighty as the cloak over my shoulders.

"You live with your dad," he says.

"Yep," I say back, searching for an outlet so we can plug in the phonograph to see if it works. I move aside a taxidermy fox and a velvet-upholstered chair chewed by mice.

"So ... where's your mom?"

"That's the million dollar question," I say, all false bravado. "She took off when I was nine. At least, that's what my dad says. And Dr. Penny."

"Dr. Penny?"

"My therapist. After my mom left, my dad was worried about me, so I had the privilege of sitting on her couch for awhile." I brave a look, and discover Jude standing very still, watching me—shadows beneath his eyes, that bruise along his jaw, his tie loose and ever so slightly crooked.

"I had a dream before she disappeared. The night before, actually. She got swallowed up by a black hole. Dr. Penny said it was trauma, manifesting itself in sleep. My mom was troubled. She grew up in foster care. And somewhere along the line, she became an addict. Her presence in my life was pretty unstable, so Dr. Penny's diagnosis makes sense, I guess. It's just kind of weird, because after that dream, I never saw or heard from her again. Not a phone call. Not a card or a letter. She just ... vanished."

Jude is looking at me like something has clicked into place, like suddenly he understands why I am the way I am. Annoyed, I scoot the parlor table closer to the outlet I've found. "What about *your* parents?"

"They're dead," he says.

My heart twists.

Jude plugs in the phonograph's cord and flips the switch. The turntable comes to life with a quiet crackle.

It still works.

He sets the vinyl into place, lifts the lever, and lowers the needle.

Music fills the room.

The witchy aesthetic combined with Stevie's ethereal voice

has a smile whispering across my lips. For a moment, Jude and I stare at one another. And I want to tell him I'm sorry. That his parents are dead. That he had to move away from his boarding school. That he's stuck here with a stepmother he doesn't seem to like very much and a cousin he likes even less. But before I can get any words out, he rubs the back of his neck and opens a nearby trunk.

It's filled with old books and journals and several random odds and ends, including a crystal ball with a dead spider inside. I remove it and set it aside, then pick up one of the books—*The Great Gatsby* by F. Scott Fitzgerald. There's a stack of letters underneath, bound in twine. "They're addressed to Enoch," I say.

"My one-eyed uncle." Jude picks up a gold pocket compass and flips it open.

"Your one-eyed uncle?"

"Great, great uncle, if you want to get technical. He died before I was born, but my dad told me stories. His stuff must have been sent to the estate after he passed."

A tube made of leather rests at the bottom of the trunk, spanning its length. I pull it out, take off its tarnished brass cap, and remove a long roll of aged parchment from inside. It resists unrolling, stiff from years in its cylindrical case. But as it slowly unfurls, breathing fresh air for the first time in decades, names and dates begin to appear.

We have just uncovered a Vandenberg family tree.

Andreas & Catherine Vandenberg
of the Dutch Republic
Emigrated to America, 1742

Elizabeth &
married 1776
Foggy Hollow, W.Va
died 1817

Ezra Vandenberg
born 1731
died 1807
Foggy Hollow, W.Va.

Raphael Vandenberg &
born 1735
died 1809
Winchester, England

Susan
married 1761
Winchester, England
death unknown

Ida &
married 1815
died 1867

Amos Vandenberg
born 1777
died 1828

Raphael ii Vandenberg &
born 1762
Winchester, England
death unknown

Jane
married 1790
Winchester, England
death unknown

Ruth
born 1816
died 1832

Gabriel &
born 1816
died 1890

Agatha
married 1843
died 1890

Raphael iii
born 1791
death unknown

Edward
born 1792
death unknown

Catherine
born 1794
death unknown

& **Beatrice**
married 1867
died 1890

Lucian?

Reuben?

Frank?

Thomas?

Esther
born 1868
died 1890

Deborah
born 1869
died 1890

Isaiah &
born 1872
died 1930

Margaret
married 1908
died 1930

Enoch
born 1910

Daniel &
born 1912
died 1993

Rose
married 1931
London, England
died 1940

& **Dorothy**
married 1946
died 1988

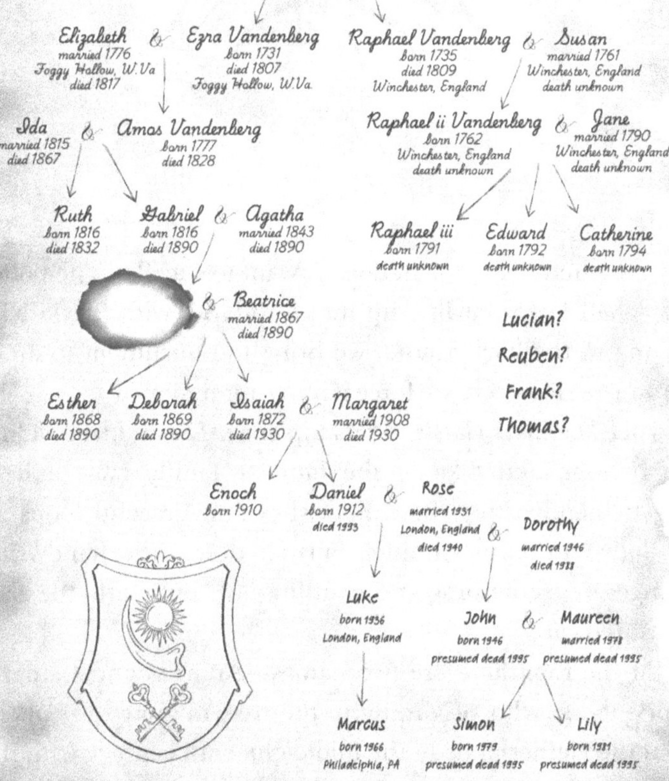

Luke
born 1936
London, England

John &
born 1946
presumed dead 1995

Maureen
married 1978
presumed dead 1995

Marcus
born 1966
Philadelphia, PA

Simon
born 1979
presumed dead 1995

Lily
born 1981
presumed dead 1995

Compiled by Isaiah Vandenberg, Anno Domini 1890
Continued in faithful record by Enoch Vandenberg

15

A FAMILY TREE

The hefty parchment doesn't want to stay flat. The bottom half keeps curling up into a roll. So, with Stevie Nicks playing in the background, we bring the document to an old drafting table, where we force it into submission.

I set *The Great Gatsby* on its top edge, *The Maltese Falcon* on the bottom, and take in the familiar family crest and the elegant handwriting. Bold flourishes and graceful loops, the ink faded to a rusty-brown. Further down, the handwriting changes to something more utilitarian, but with the same measured care.

At the top, there are two names—Andreas and Catherine Vandenberg, who, according to the tree, migrated to America from the Netherlands in the mid eighteenth century with their two sons, Ezra and Raphael. At the bottom, there's a postscript. *Compiled by Isaiah Vandenberg, Anno Domini 1890.* Underneath it, in that utilitarian scrawl, *Continued in faithful record by Enoch Vandenberg.* And smack dab in the parchment's center is a blackened scorch mark.

Jude brushes his finger over the spot.

The missing name is surrounded by other Vandenbergs whose identities remain intact. The scorch mark had a wife and three children, one of whom was Isaiah, the original author of the tree. I take in the brittle hole with its charred edges, an open wound in the family's past, and wonder why. What offense would erase a person so violently?

I do a quick count of the generations descending from Ezra's line. There are eight including himself, with Simon and Lily—the teenage siblings from the cold case—at the bottom. On Raphael's side, I count only three, each one with increasingly less information.

A symptom of Ezra and Raphael's long-standing enmity, perhaps? Or maybe it's simply the natural fallout of so much distance, for at some point in time, Raphael moved to Winchester, England, where he married, had children, and died. Whatever the reason, the original author of the tree stopped keeping track of Raphael's lineage. Under the third generation, a foursome of disconnected names is scrawled in Enoch's hand. A question mark follows each one, as if he knew of their existence, but didn't know where to place them.

Three of the four set off a chorus of bells in my mind.

"Lucian. *Reuben. Frank. Thomas,*" I read.

Jude looks at me.

"The tip your grandfather gave to the police. He said to look into a cousin named *Thomas, Reuben,* or *Frank.*" I point to each name in turn, because here they are.

Thomas, Reuben, and Frank. Vandenberg men on Raphael's side of the family. I want to park here, discuss this, but Jude has already moved on, his gaze fixed on another.

Marcus Vandenberg, of the eighth generation. Born, 1966 in Philadelphia. There's nothing about either of his marriages— not to Jude's mother, or Isabel after her. Enoch must have passed away before Marcus's first marriage, but after the disappearance of John, Maureen, Simon, and Lily, because their information *is* recorded.

Presumed dead: 1995.

Stevie Knicks stops singing.

Her voice had been unobtrusive in the background. Now, there's nothing but the soft crackle of the needle as it drags through a vacant groove, along with the creaks and groans of a house too big to settle.

"We should get back to looking for the key," Jude says, leaving the family tree behind, stretched wide between *The Great Gatsby* and *The Maltese Falcon.*

He opens a different trunk.

As discreetly as possible, I snap a picture with my phone. I can't help myself. I have to show Twig.

We search for an hour more before I receive a text message from Dad.

> School night, kiddo. Whatever you're doing, time to wrap it up.

The key is nowhere to be found.

Jude grabs a bobby pin from one of the apothecary drawers and, despite my objections, tries to pick the book's lock. When the lock refuses to budge and he suggests we bust it open, I put my foot down. "I have to return this in the same condition or Maggie will murder me in my sleep."

"Don't you want to see what's inside?"

"Of course, but not if it means incurring Maggie's wrath." Or losing my job. I slide my phone into the back pocket of my jeans, thinking quickly. Perhaps, a little desperately. Our lunchtime conversation, when Jude all but ordered a cease and desist on our search for answers, has me spooked. Whatever headspace he was in then, I don't want him going back there now.

"What about the sketch of Molly?" I ask.

"What about it?" he replies.

"She has to be connected to the portrait in some way, right? Why else would the same symbol be on both of them? We have her name, and a general time period of when she lived." If Ezra sketched her, she had to have been alive when Ezra was alive. "If anyone would know anything about a young woman named Molly living here in the 1700s, it'll be Maggie. And maybe, if we find Molly, we'll learn more about the portrait, too."

<hr>

I walk in the door with *The Great Gatsby* in hand, on loan from Jude. I close the screen door quietly behind me and muffle a sneeze. On the walk home, I was struck by a string of them. Perhaps wearing that dusty cloak for so long wasn't the smartest idea.

Inside, Dad is stretched out on the recliner. A *Seinfeld* rerun plays on the television. There's an open can of Coors Light on the end table. I can tell from here that he's fallen asleep. A fairly common occurrence. All that manual labor makes him tired, but he refuses to retire to his room when I'm still out. His bed—he likes to say—is only for sleeping when he knows I'm in mine.

I tiptoe closer.

His dark hair is still damp from his shower. His skin is a deep tan from days spent outdoors, grooved with deeper lines than most guys his age thanks to all that sun. And probably my mother. My attention moves to his left hand. He still wears his wedding ring, even all these years later. I pick up the beer can, which is half-full. He only ever has one, and usually forgets to finish it. I dump the remainder down the drain and put the can in the recycling, then grab a blanket off the couch. I'm just about to cover him when I'm overcome by another sneeze—so suddenly, I have no chance to muffle it.

And I am a notoriously loud sneezer.

Dad opens his eyes.

"Hey," he says in a crackly voice. "How was your day?"

"Good. Yours?"

"My day was good."

We nod in unison, as if to say *glad to hear it*.

"Want me to shut off the TV?" I ask.

"That's all right. I'm gonna finish this episode, then head up to bed."

I'm not fooled. Dad wasn't watching *Seinfeld*. He was *pretending* to watch *Seinfeld* so he could wait up for me. He's a good man, my dad. Quiet. Hardworking. As patient as the day is long. A walking green flag, really. I glance again at his wedding ring. In all my years, I've never heard him say one negative thing about Mom. And in all my memories of her, she never said one negative thing about him, either. In fact, she used to tell me he was the one thing she got right. The one thing she was proud to give me.

A really great dad.

I kiss the top of his head. "Night, Pops."

Upstairs, I brush my teeth and wash my face. I change into an oversized t-shirt and pajama bottoms, then settle into my window seat with *The Great Gatsby* in my lap, gazing at Jude's illuminated bedroom window when movement below catches my attention. A figure, prowling around the side of the home. I narrow my eyes, trying to get a better look, but everything is dark and foggy and another sneeze grabs hold, followed by two more.

In their wake, I'm struck by a bout of dizziness. The kind you get when you stand up too fast, only I'm not standing, and my neck is suddenly warm. I unlock the window and push it open, inviting in the crisp night air, fanning the collar of my shirt as I refocus my attention. But I find nothing.

Did I imagine it?

My phone dings with a message from Twig, asking how everything went.

I send him the picture I took of Jude's family tree, along with a reply:

Look what we found in an old trunk!

A few seconds later, he texts back.

Twig: Frank, Reuben, and Thomas?

Me: IKR!?

I pull up the picture and zoom in on the names. A connection to the cold case, stumbled upon in a search for answers about a portrait of *me*. Two confounding mysteries.

My phone dings.

Twig: Scorch mark is intense. Who got annexed?

Me: No idea.

There's a beat of nothing, then a scrolling ellipse.

Twig: What happened in 1890?

Unsure what he's talking about, I look at the picture. I zoom in, studying the dates—really having to focus, too, like I'm in sudden need of reading glasses. I find the date in question. 1890, listed several times over. A year of death. Whatever happened wiped out every Vandenberg alive at the time except for the author of the tree, Isaiah. Unless, of course, his scorch-mark of a father was still alive.

My phone dings.

> Twig: And 1930?

I search some more and find a second shared death. This time, only two. Isaiah and his wife both died in 1930.

Ding.

Twig sent an image. A screen shot of a Wikipedia page. Railway accidents from the 19th century. To make things extra clear, he highlighted one in particular. *April 1890, a train derails en route to New York, killing dozens, including several members of the prominent Vandenberg family of Foggy Hollow, WV.*

Ding.

> Twig: Can't find anything about 1930.

Ding.

> Twig: Selah.

> Me: What??

> Twig: 1832 ... Ruth Vandenberg

I stare at the name, unable to believe I missed it until now.

Ruth Vandenberg was featured in *Episode 8: Cryptid Craze.* And here she is, listed on Jude's family tree. I didn't notice her because she hardly takes up any space at all. She's nothing but a side note. Now that I really look, all the Vandenberg daughters are side notes. None of them are listed as married with children. Each of them died at a tragically young age, including Ruth Vandenberg in 1832. She perished alongside her friend, Violet Underwagon. The two girls were found dead in the woods. Mauled to death by a wild animal, or was it the *Nachtdier*?

I try to focus on my phone screen, to find something about Isaiah and his wife's death in 1930, but the search results keep blurring in and out of focus. I no longer feel warm. I feel cold. And clammy.

I shut the window and shoot Twig a text.

Chat 2morrow

I shut off my phone before he responds and crawl into bed and under the covers. With my teeth chattering, I fall into a fitful sleep.

16
SICK AS A DOG

I sprint through the woods, lungs burning, heart racing as branches scratch and claw at my face and arms. I look over my shoulder—at the rabid, snarling beast in close pursuit— and a vine grabs my ankle. I fall flat on my face with a loud *oomph*. I scramble to my feet and keep running. I don't look back and I don't stop until I burst into a clearing.

Two bodies lay in the grass.

There's blood.

So much blood.

And a young man, rocking back and forth, weeping in despair.

I turn to flee.

But Rafe is there, blocking my way.

Fear turns to anger.

"You punched Jude."

His smirk curls into a grin.

I wind back and clock him in the jaw. He grabs his chin. His nostrils flare. His chest heaves. His skin grows fur. He tips his head back and howls at the moon as his body morphs into the monster. *The Nachtdier*. His eyes glow red, and he pounces.

I lurch upright in bed, my sheets drenched in sweat, my stomach a ball of fire that hurls up my throat. I cup my hand over my mouth, fall to the floor, and grab the garbage bin next to my desk just in the knick of time.

Dad finds me.

His strong arms scoop me up. He places a cool rag over my forehead as I slip into fevered dreams.

I'm dancing in a candlelit ballroom, the faces of the guests blurred like melted wax. I'm tumbling down the stone well and there are crows at the bottom. They peck at my arms and my legs. I stand in the hallway at school with Twig, who holds a lighter in one hand, the Vandenberg Family Tree in his other.

"We have to erase all of them," he says, touching flame to parchment.

Hooves clop on cobblestone.

A horse whinnies outside.

My bedroom door opens.

A gaunt man in a dark coat and cravat steps inside carrying a black medical bag. His eyes are sunken, his cheekbones sharp as he comes to my bedside with a mournful shake of his head.

He opens his bag.

An assortment of tools glint from inside. He pulls out a glass jar. The dark water churns sluggishly. Sinuous black forms writhe within. "We must draw the fever out."

I bat my hand listlessly.

The doctor is gone.

The sickness remains.

My body is fire but I can't stop shivering. My teeth chatter. My stomach rolls. My bones hurt.

I'm standing in the ruins of St. Fortuna's. The Woman of the Woods is with me, her long raven hair cascading down her back. I want to see her face. I want to speak with her. Ask her who she is and why she haunts this place. But she keeps dancing out of reach. I can't get to her. Then the ground opens up beneath me and I'm falling, falling, falling.

Into a dungeon with coffins.

One creaks open.

A whisper rises from within.

"Seeeeelaaaaaaaaah."

The voice is familiar and feminine.

"Come find me."

My eyes flutter open.

I lie in bed, my sheets still drenched. Or maybe drenched again? I try to move my tongue but my mouth is Sahara Desert dry. Sunlight pours through my window. Birds chirp outside. The clock on my bedside table reads 10:58 a.m. There's a bottle of Pedialyte on my bedside table. A digital thermometer. And a bucket. With a grimace, I rise up to peek inside. Thankfully, it's empty.

I sink into my bed.

I feel like a wrung out rag. A bowl full of limp noodles. It takes all my strength to sit up and grab the Pedialyte. I take sips at first, then long draws, until the bottle is empty and my tongue is no longer sandpaper. My body, however, feels like it's been through war. Even reaching for my phone hurts.

The screen lights up.

It's Thursday!

I've been incoherent for over twenty-four hours. With a million missed calls and text messages, most of them from Twig.

Dad pokes his head inside my bedroom. When he sees me sitting, his tired eyes brighten. "Hey, there." He comes all the way in. "It's good to see you up."

"I wish it *felt* good."

Dad chuckles a little, then runs his hand through his hair, which sticks up in the back. "Can I get you some more Pedialyte? Maybe something to eat?"

I grimace.

The mere mention of food makes me queasy, but if I want to get some modicum of energy back, I should probably try to eat. We agree on toast and a Gatorade. He helps me to the bathroom, where I set my hands on either side of the sink and behold my reflection. I bear an uncanny resemblance to the physician from my dreams. Pale face. Sunken eyes. Hollow cheekbones.

I move like a sloth as I brush my teeth, shower, dry off, and dress in fresh clothes. By the time I'm back in my bedroom, Dad has changed the bedding and fluffed my pillows. There's a bottle of white Gatorade on my bedside table, along with a plate of toast and a sleeve of saltine crackers, a bottle of Tylenol, and a television remote.

Dad comes in behind me carrying the set from downstairs.

"Dad," I say.

"In case you get bored." He sets it on a TV tray and plugs in the cord. "Will you be able to see it from your bed okay?"

"I'll be able to see it just fine."

He nods, his hands resting on his hips. "Well, I have a lot of work to catch up on, so if you're feeling better ..."

I tell him I'm fine and thank him. He drops a kiss on my forehead. I crawl back into bed with my phone and sink against the pillows. I drink some of the Gatorade. I force down a few bites of toast. Then attend to the messages I've missed.

There are two from Walt. One's from him, and the other is from him on behalf of Maggie, who doesn't own a cell phone, because *why in tarnation would I want to make myself constantly available?* There's two from Naomi, three from Harper.

The rest are from Twig.

Wednesday, 8:16 a.m.: Hey. Where are you?

Wednesday, 8:31 a.m.: Must talk ASAP. Text me when you get here.

Wednesday, 8:32 a.m.: Dug this up last night.

The message came attached with a link. When I click on it, I'm taken to an old blog post titled *Forgotten Crimes of West Virginia*. There's a small paragraph dedicated to a bank robbery in 1930. In Foggy Hollow. Isaiah Vandenberg and his wife are listed among the victims.

I return to my messages and continue scrolling.

Wednesday, 9:24 a.m.: I'm at DEFCON 2 here, Selah. One more hour and I'm calling in the National Guard to report an alien abduction.

Wednesday, 10:12 a.m.: Okay. So Mom says you're sick. Hope it's not too bad. Talk after school?

Wednesday, 5:32 p.m.: Thinking of you. Feel better soon.

Thursday, 7:04 a.m.: Any better? Proof of life?

Thursday, 8:23 a.m.: Mom says you're still sick. I have robotics at four, but I'm stopping by after school to make sure you aren't actually transitioning into a vampire. If you're going immortal, I'm going with you.

This makes me smile.

There's one final message at 8:25 a.m.

P.S. Will bring homework.

The time is now 1 p.m. I take two Tylenol and munch on some saltine crackers as I pull up the picture I took of the Vandenberg Family Tree. I try to do some research, but there's little to no information online and my eyes are sore. I'm dying to talk to Maggie, who would know all about the train crash in 1890 and the bank robbery in 1930. I ring Evermore Books, but there's no answer. I'd email her, but I don't think she has one of those either.

Walt does though.

A phone, too. Hence, his text messages.

And he used to work for the *Foggy Hollow Gazette*.

I send him my request.

> Hey Walt, I'm looking for information regarding a train crash near Foggy Hollow in 1890, as well as a bank robbery in 1930. I'd get myself to Maggie's archives, but I'm still under the weather. Can you help?

I hit send and stare at the screen, like Walt is attached to his phone and might send an immediate response. But there's nothing. No *read* receipt. No scrolling ellipse.

With a sigh, I turn on the television. I open Amazon Prime, where I have a collection of fantastic movies at my disposal. In light of Twig's reference to the immortal, I select *The Lost Boys*. Right around the time Michael lets go of the train tracks and plummets into the fog, I begin to doze.

An hour and a half later, my phone dings.

Walt has replied.

And he has delivered.

I skim the pair of headlines.

Bank Heist Ends in Bloodshed; Prominent Businessman Slain in Crossfire.

Express Train Plunges from Tracks; Multiple Dead, Many Injured.

I zoom in on a grainy black-and-white photograph of a wealthy-looking family standing shoulder to shoulder, and read the caption below.

The Vandenberg family, photographed earlier this year at their estate in Foggy Hollow, West Virginia. All but Mr. Isaiah Vandenberg perished in Thursday's fatal derailment en route to New York City.

Also among the deceased was Miss Helena Pisel, a young woman traveling in the family's company. Sources close to the family confirm she had been engaged in a quiet courtship with Mr. Vandenberg, the family's sole surviving heir.

Poor Isaiah.

I swipe to the bank robbery article. There's no picture, but there is a list of the deceased, which includes Isaiah. He escaped death in 1890 only to meet an untimely demise forty years later, alongside his wife, and a young woman who was betrothed to their son, Enoch. Enoch survived, but lost his left eye.

Jude's one-eyed uncle.

That's how Enoch became one-eyed. He was injured in a bank robbery, which stole the life of his parents and his fiancé. Before him, his father lost everyone he loved in a train crash. And before them? Young Ruth Vandenberg was killed alongside her friend in a supposed animal attack.

"Yikes," I whisper.

Downstairs, the front door opens.

A familiar voice calls from below.

"Selah? Your dad said I could come up."

After a beat, footsteps sound on the stairs.

Twig peeks inside my room and smiles. "A queen on her throne."

"A sickly queen," I reply.

He holds up a thermos. "I come bearing gifts. Homemade soup from Mom. And schoolwork. Most of it's on Google Classroom, but I brought you the new chem packet so you don't flunk out while you're recovering, and your copy of *The Scarlett Letter*. Mom had to bribe the custodian to let us inside your locker." He sets his gifts next to my half-eaten toast. "You look fairly normal."

"Not like a vampire, then?"

He asks to see my teeth.

I bare my fangs, then show him the articles Walt sent.

He scans them with interest, then lets out a low whistle. "That's a lot of tragedy to befall one family."

My mind turns to Jude and the sad, lonely way he stared at his father's name. Both of his parents are dead. I make a mental note to do some sleuthing. How, exactly, did they die?

I can tell Twig wants to stay and discuss the findings further, but robotics is calling and he must go.

"Oh," he says, stopping at the door. He reaches into the pocket of his jeans. "I almost forgot. I'm supposed to give you this."

He hands me a slip of paper.

There's a phone number on it—the handwriting neat and slanted.

"It's from Jude," he says. "He, uh, came and found me in the hallway after school."

"What did he want?"

"To know where you've been. I told him you were sick, and he gave me his number to give to you."

I look down at the slip. "He wants me to call him?"

"Looks like it." Twig gives his fingers a snap, then claps the palm of his left hand over the fist of his right. "I'm glad you're lucid, Selah. Try the soup. It's really good."

When he's gone, I twist off the lid and take a sip, and of course, he's right. Mrs. Calloway has always been a phenomenal cook. I rest against my throne of pillows, sipping the soup, twirling the slip of paper until Dad returns with another bottle of Gatorade. Happy with what he sees, he excuses himself to the great outdoors, determined to squeeze in as much work as possible before twilight chases the sun away.

I turn on *Harry and the Hendersons*—a feel-good movie about a cryptid who isn't a murdering, ravenous monster. I vaguely recall a fevered dream about the *Nachtdier*. A weeping boy and two girls and Rafe, turning into a werewolf.

Outside, a chainsaw buzzes in the distance.

The sky is soft, the shadows long.

And Jude Vandenberg gave me his number.

Biting my lip, I type a hasty message into my phone and hit send.

> Hi. It's Selah. Twig gave me your number.
> Sorry I've been AWOL. Sick as a dog.

I stare at the screen, expecting nothing. If Jude replies at all, it will probably be later this evening, or sometime tomorrow. But a scrolling ellipse appears.

I sit up straight.

> Jude: Hey. Sorry you've been sick.

I stare at the words, unsure how to reply. Normally, I'd pride myself in sending something smart and quippy, but my brain is full of fog. I think I should suggest we visit Maggie, as previously planned, but then ... what if he already met with Maggie? It's not like he needs me to make introductions.

The scrolling ellipse returns.

> Jude: Will you be at school tomorrow?

I can't fathom it. Untwisting the Gatorade bottle was hard enough. Walking through the halls with a backpack? No way. But I'm tempted all the same. Simply because he asked.

> Me: Unlikely. But I am feeling more human.
> Good enough to meet at Evermore after
> school, if you're up for it.

I hit send with a grimace, dreading his response. I'm sure he already went to Evermore without me. Or maybe he wants to drop the string again.

Jude: Can I call you?

My heart takes off, an aggressive hammer inside my chest.

Me: Sure

A moment later, the X-Files theme song fills my bedroom, giving me zero time to prepare. I accept the call and say hello, hoping I don't sound as out of sorts as I feel.

"Hey," he says, his voice soft in my ear. "I'm glad you're feeling better."

I'm thrown for a loop. Not by his words so much as his tone —gentle, and concerned. Like Jude Vandenberg has been worried. About *me*. "Me, too. I had some pretty gnarly dreams while I was in the thick of it."

"About haunted dolls?"

"No, but there was a cryptid. And I punched Rafe in the face."

A short pause ensues.

I close my eyes and tap my forehead with my fist.

Stupid, stupid Selah. Why did you bring him into the conversation?

But Jude only chuckles. "I would have enjoyed seeing that."

And just like that, all my anxiety melts away.

I bite back a smile.

Jude is different on the phone.

Less guarded, somehow.

"So ... Maggie's tomorrow? Or did you give up on me and go there already?"

I hold my breath.

I really hope he didn't.

The mystery of the portrait is a once-in-a-lifetime mystery. I want to investigate it with him.

"I haven't been to the historical society. But we don't have to go tomorrow. It can wait until you're feeling better."

"I think I'll be fine. I'm already feeling loads better than I did a few hours ago." I can hold my phone up without sweating, anyway. "But if, you know, something changes, I have your number now, which was brave of you. I can bug you whenever I want."

"And I have yours. So I guess … same."

The smile I've been biting back can no longer be repressed. Was Jude just flirting? He certainly doesn't sound like he's eager to get off the phone.

I climb out of bed, taking a blanket and a pillow with me, and make myself comfortable in the window seat. I look at his bedroom window and imagine him in there, talking on the phone. With me. I want to tell him about the research I've done —about the train crash and the bank robbery—but that would require a confession. I took a picture of his family tree without permission. I'm trying to figure out how to get out of this corner I've painted myself in when he speaks.

"I found the identity of the scorch mark."

I sit up straighter. "Who?"

"Elijah Vandenberg. I found a record of his birth in 1844, and his marriage in 1867. But there's nothing in our archives about his death. So I took a visit to the family graveyard."

He pauses.

It's a charged beat.

Perhaps he's thinking of me in the graveyard. And Rafe, trying to kiss me in the graveyard.

"He doesn't have a headstone," Jude says. "His wife does. All three of his children do. But not him."

"You think he was buried elsewhere?"

"I don't know. But I did some research. And I kept coming back to a particular scenario that would make sense."

"Which is?"

"Back then, there was a big stigma around a certain kind of death. So much so, anyone who died that way was often left out of family records."

"Suicide," I whisper.

"He would have been denied a proper burial."

And most likely erased from a family tree.

There's another pause. This one isn't charged or awkward. But thoughtful. Almost intimate. I imagine Jude stretched long on his bed, staring up at his ceiling, messing with his hair.

"I have a confession," I blurt.

He's quiet on the other end.

I squeeze my eyes shut. "I took a picture of your family tree."

"Oh." It's not a mad *oh*. It's not even a surprised *oh*. If anything, he sounds a bit relieved, like he was worried my confession was going to be something worse.

So, I dive in.

I tell him about the train crash and the bank robbery. He knew vaguely about the latter and nothing about the former. I forward him the newspaper articles and listen as he reads them out loud, lulled by the hypnotizing timbre of his voice. When he finishes, we talk. At first, about the tragedies, then about Elijah—born into Antebellum America, married after the Civil War. What might have compelled such a man to suicide?

But then, the conversation shifts, and we're talking about *Harry and the Hendersons* and *The Lost Boys* and *Ghostbusters*, and my deep and abiding love for all things supernatural pop culture in the 1980s. I sit in the window seat as twilight turns to dark, telling him about *Tales from the Crypt*, which is campy and gruesome and delightfully over-the-top, and somehow, I'm back in bed while he downloads my favorite episodes, and we watch them together.

Over the phone.

Dad brings me more soup. Twig left a whole pot in the fridge. And we go on talking and watching and laughing.

We don't say goodbye until midnight.

<h1 style="text-align:center">17
THE HISTORICAL SOCIETY</h1>

I hold a penny in my palm and waffle between two wishes: *Return the locked tome without incurring Maggie's wrath* or *find the identity of Molly*. I can't tell if my fingers are tingling from nerves, anticipation, or the idea of seeing Jude.

I wish for luck, a vague request that feels like cheating, and toss the penny into the fountain. Water ripples through my reflection. I'm still pale, my eyes a bit shadowed, but I'm not the spectral of death I saw in the bathroom mirror yesterday. It helps being outside in the sunlight, dressed in clothes that aren't pajamas.

I set my backpack on a bench across from a statue poised in the center of a flower bed, and sit down. I twirl the stud in my left ear and watch the bees buzz, getting drunk on the last nectar of the season. All day I've been antsy. Waiting for the afternoon. Now it's here and it feels like the bees are buzzing in my hands.

"Hey."

I twist in my seat.

Jude stands behind me with the sun at his back. He's dressed in a suede jacket over a tan polo and wears a pair of aviator sunglasses, his dark golden hair slightly tousled from the day.

My throat goes dry.

"You look good," he says.

"You're a liar," I say back, smiling at the ground as I come to my feet and slide the strap of my backpack over my shoulder. "But since I'm pretty sure I almost died from norovirus, I'll take what I can get."

A breeze ruffles his hair as he taps the rolled-up sketch of Molly against his palm. "I've been thinking about *Tales from the Crypt*."

"Oh?"

"Recovering from nightmares, actually."

My smile grows as we turn in tandem toward Evermore Books.

"How did you discover this show?" he asks.

"I found a box set at a thrift store when I was like, eleven." We cross the street. "As soon as I laid eyes on the Crypt Keeper, I knew I had to have it."

"So, while most girls your age were watching dance trends on TikTok ..."

"Twig and I were digging up a VHS player from his basement, and the rest is history. I fell in love."

"With a skeleton in a bowtie."

"What can I say? I'm a sucker for a man with strong bone structure."

A smile teases the corner of his mouth.

"Admit it," I say, giving him a bump with my shoulder. "You had fun."

"I had ... an experience."

"Well, prepare yourself for another." We've arrived at Evermore Books with its taxidermy raven in the window. "Maggie's an icon."

As I tug on the door's handle, Jude grips the frame over my

head, so close behind me I can feel his warmth, smell the subtle note of that intoxicating cologne.

My stomach flutters.

The bell jingles.

And I force myself to move.

Maggie isn't at the front counter. Just Poe, who meows his greeting next to an abandoned cup of tea.

Looking left, then right, I seize the opportunity. With a nod at Jude to follow, I speed-walk to the reading nook, unzipping my backpack and pulling out the unwieldy tome as I go. Just as I'm about to slide it into its spot, a familiar, raspy voice makes me jump.

"Good afternoon."

I twirl around, book in hand.

Maggie peers suspiciously as she stirs her tea, a fresh cup curling with steam. Today, she's wearing a velvet choker and a black and white hair scarf patterned with moths and crows. A pair of reading glasses hang around her neck; another is perched atop her head.

I hold the tome aloft. "I was just showing this to Jude."

Maggie turns her suspicious gaze upon him. A lesser man might cower beneath her unblinking stare. Jude doesn't even fidget.

"The new Vandenberg boy," she mutters. "You and your stepmother have been spending an awful lot of time with that preservation society."

"Regrettably."

It's the perfect response—one that brings a twinkle to Maggie's eye.

I make official introductions. When I'm done, she nods at the rolled-up sketch in Jude's hand. "What's that?"

"Something we wanted to show you," he says. "A sketch of a woman. We're hoping to find out who she was. According to Selah, you're our best hope."

He gives her the sketch.

Maggie hands him her tea. She puts on her glasses—the pair hanging around her neck—and unrolls the paper. Her attention pauses briefly over the symbol drawn in the upper right corner, same as the one on the cover of the book. But then she catches sight of Ezra's signature and the symbol is completely forgotten.

"A Vandenberg original," she says in a breathless whisper, a tremor taking hold of her hands. "Young man, do you have any idea how valuable this is?"

"I could take a guess."

"Ezra Vandenberg was a prolific limner, but much of his work was burned in the fire."

"He was a prolific what-er?" I ask.

"Lim. Ner," Maggie replies. "A portraitist. Three of his pieces hang in town hall."

"They do?"

She looks at me dully. "Selah Whitlock, you mean to tell me you've never noticed those paintings in town hall?"

"Of course I have, I just didn't realize they were painted by Ezra." The portraits in question feature our town heroes, the same three men who have their own statues in the square— Amos Vandenberg, Kit Bogaard, and Alexander Doorn.

Maggie brings the sketch to her bosom. "A relic such as this belongs in a museum."

"If you can tell us who that woman is," Jude says, "you can have it for yourself."

She makes a strangled noise, then adjusts her glasses as if his offer is a visible thing, and she wants to make sure she's seeing it correctly. When his expression remains utterly sincere, she releases a loud bark of laughter. "*Tell you who she is*? My dear boy, I will write a dissertation if it means I get to keep this."

She peers down at the graphite strokes, muttering Molly's

name several times over. "A pretty girl Ezra Vandenberg sketched. Simply a subject, or was she more?" She peers a bit longer, as if considering her own question.

"What do you think about the symbol?" I ask. "It's on the sketch, and this book."

She casts a look at the book in question, still in my hand. "It is curious, isn't it?"

"We'd like to open it up," Jude says. "See what it says."

"Do you have a key?" she retorts.

"I could break the lock."

Maggie lets out an indignant huff. "Absolutely not."

Then, quite decisively, she pushes up the sleeves of her cardigan and tells us to keep up.

Jude and I follow her to the back of the store, me with the locked tome, him with her teacup.

We climb the rickety staircase that leads to the second floor —an unevenly shaped room with Maggie's small office straight ahead and the rest, a playground for the curious. The space is lined with shelves crowded with obscure ledgers, incidental records, and old newspaper archives. Featured on one of the wood-paneled walls are the same three men who hang in town hall. Not grand portraits, but smaller silhouettes—hand cut black paper set against aged parchment—arranged inside elegant oval frames.

Maggie marches to the shelves and Jude strolls past the displays, three exhibits dimly lit beneath hanging bulbs. The first, a model of Foggy Hollow as it was in 1822, set beneath a cracked glass case. The second, artifacts from the fire, including a list of people who perished, a piece of blackened stained glass from St. Fortuna's Church, a charred jewelry box from the original Bogaard Estate, a warped horseshoe from the blacksmith's forge, and a half-burned prisoner's boot from the old jail house.

At the third and final exhibit, Jude stops.

This one features his family and their mysterious disappearance thirty years ago. He studies each item. Maureen Vandenberg's pocket planner, marked with appointments that would later be cancelled. A sketch of a man with no face, signed by Lily Vandenberg, placed into evidence but later removed under unknown circumstances. And most peculiar of all, a Vandenberg clock that stopped two minutes after Maureen dialed 911. I watch as Jude takes in the newspaper article titled, *No Bodies, No Clues - Just Questions*, written by our very own Walt Jensen in the spring of 1995.

"Hey Maggie," I call, my eyes still on Jude. "Have you ever heard of a painting called *Ezra's Obsession*?"

He gives me a sharp look.

This wasn't part of our plan.

But I don't know why not.

Or why I haven't thought to ask her sooner.

"Of course I have," she says, removing a leather-bound album from one of the shelves.

"You've seen it?" I ask.

"That would require a time machine now, wouldn't it?"

"What do you mean?"

"*Ezra's Obsession* was burned in the fire."

Jude and I exchange a look.

Ezra's Obsession wasn't burned in the fire.

It's currently in his bedroom.

"I do, however, have a related artifact." She sets the album on a long, solitary table and hobbles into her office. When she returns, she holds a folio wrapped in linen, tied with faded twine. She places the folio on top of the album and carefully begins unwrapping it.

Jude sets Maggie's teacup aside.

I do the same with the locked tome.

There are two items inside the folio. On top is a note written in Maggie's handwriting.

Unproven fragment from Ezra Vandenberg's personal journal. Acquired in 1973 with donation of salvaged fire artifacts.

She shuffles the note aside to reveal a clear sleeve underneath—protection for a brittle piece of parchment dated 1807. The handwriting matches Ezra's.

"Maggie," I exclaim. "Why isn't this on display?"

"I wouldn't dare expose it to light, and we can't definitively say Ezra wrote it. If I put it behind glass, people will call it gospel."

I pick up the sleeve.

"The dates coincide, you see." Maggie taps the time stamp written on top of the parchment. "By all historical accounts, Ezra Vandenberg finished the portrait in question on this very day."

I read the short, cryptic entry while Jude looks over my shoulder.

Finally, I have captured her, and yet I know not who she is.

Balm or blight.

Beacon or burden.

A blessing sent to end my suffering, or a promise that it shall endure.

I recall the mysterious revelation written by my own hand in the year of my son's birth, and I wonder if she is the one to whom it refers.

The back of my neck tingles.

I know not who she is ...

I turn the sleeve over, like there might be more on the back. But there isn't, and my thoughts have spun into a whirling dervish.

"*A blessing sent to end my suffering*," Jude reads. "Did Ezra suffer?"

"Only as much as any tortured artist with wealth, status, and no known ailments. There was a rift in the family, which I'm sure didn't help his sense of suffering."

"Between him and his brother?" I say.

"Raphael," Maggie replies with a nod. "According to all accounts, the two were estranged."

Hatred all the way down.

"There were rumors of madness, too," Maggie continues. "But those centered around the portrait. Hence, the title. Ezra's *Obsession*." She emphasizes the second word. "Most limners didn't go around painting figments of their imagination."

"Is that what she was?" I ask.

"If I had to guess, I'd say she was a lover."

Maggie's conclusion irks me.

So does the smug look on Jude's face when she says it.

"Then his own words don't make any sense," I say. "If the subject of *Ezra's Obsession* was a lover, why would he write *I know not who she is*?"

"Like I said, he was a bit touched in the head. And, if he was having an affair, he wouldn't very well record a confession, would he?"

"It was his private journal."

"His *supposed* private journal." Maggie's attention slides to the charcoal sketch, her eyes brightening. "Is this what you're after? You believe this woman was the subject?"

No, actually.

She's not the subject.

I am.

It takes every ounce of will power to bite back the words, to shrug along with Jude like neither of us know.

Maggie takes back her artifact.

But I'm not ready to move on.

I want to examine the words. Dissect them with Jude.

Instead, I barely have time to snap a picture before she returns the journal fragment to the folio and heads back to her office. I open my mouth, but Jude gives his head a curt shake, like now isn't the time to talk about anything.

When Maggie returns, she opens the album she retrieved from a shelf. Its leather binding creaks in protest.

A registry of ball guests have been written in elegant cursive. Not for the Hunter's Moon Masquerade Ball, but its predecessor, Foggy Hollow's Yuletide Ball.

"The fire took a great deal," Maggie says, flipping toward the front. "But not everything." She runs a reverent hand down the column of names. "Plenty of archives like these were kept in stone cellars. Fireproof and damp as death. And thank the heavens, too. Otherwise, we wouldn't have any public records at all before 1822."

She turns to the very first register—December 23, 1758.

The inaugural Yuletide Ball.

She slides her finger down the list, then comes to a stop.

Miss Molly Ludwig, escorted by Mr. Ezra Vandenberg.

My eyes go wide. "That has to be her, right?"

Maggie's already on the move, muttering *Ludwig* under her breath as she marches toward an old-fashioned card catalog. She pulls open the drawer labeled with an L and starts shuffling through the cards.

I join her, watching as she bypasses *Lovell, Nathaniel*, who—according to the card—drowned in the Blackwillow River in 1792. Then *Lowry, Esther*—a milliner who crafted elaborate hats for the town's elite. Then *Ludwig, Peter*—a reverend who advocated for temperance and moral reform. On the improbable chance that Maggie has alphabetized wrong, she flips past Peter to *Lyle, Eleanor*—a midwife who delivered all the town's babies from 1872 through 1888. She turns back to *Ludwig, Peter* and removes his card.

It lists his wife, Greta Ludwig. Along with his two children, Gideon & *Molly*. The card contains six reference numbers.

We chase after each one.

The first leads to an obituary for the wife, who died in childbirth in 1739. The second leads to the *Temperance Proclamation of 1756*, authored by the reverend, who publicly condemned local taverns for promoting vice, drunkenness, and moral decay. The third leads to the guest list that mentioned Molly. The fourth, a collection of his sermons from the 1770s. The fifth, a *Public Petition to the Magistrate in 1779*, urging town officials to shut down a boarding house of ill repute. The sixth and final reference, Reverend Peter Ludwig's obituary, published in the *Foggy Hollow Gazette* in the summer of 1781.

I read the last few lines aloud, "He is preceded in death by his beloved wife, Margareta Ludwig. He is survived by his esteemed son, Gideon Ludwig, and a devoted congregation who mourn his passing yet take solace in the promise of his eternal rest." I look up with a furrowed brow. "It doesn't say anything about Molly."

Maggie rubs her chin, as though pondering the curiosity.

I stare hard at the symbol drawn in the corner of the sketch.

"What about town hall?" Jude asks. "There might be some information there."

"You'll find nothing more than birth, marriage, and death records," Maggie says, her disdain evident. She doesn't loathe town hall to the degree with which she loathes the FHPS, but she certainly isn't a fan of the impersonal way in which they handle history—*they drain all the life and blood out of a thing!* I'm sure there's also some jealousy involved, given their legal right to archives she'd rather have in her possession.

"But if she got married," I say, "there could be more to find here. Under a different surname."

"That is a possibility," Maggie concedes. "Unfortunately, it's a possibility that will have to wait until Monday. Town hall is already closed."

Jude looks at his watch, and sure enough, the time is 4:38 p.m. Town hall locked its doors eight minutes ago.

<hr>

We step outside, the bell jingling behind us as we turn toward the square, in the direction of our parked cars—Dad's Ford Bronco for me, a dark gray BMW for Jude.

"Well, at least we got some clarity." I curl my thumbs under the straps of my backpack. "The symbol isn't a family crest. Which means we can eliminate your theory."

Jude slides on his sunglasses. "How do you figure?"

"Molly wasn't an illegitimate love child."

"Ezra was courting her," he says.

"Exactly," I say back.

"So maybe the symbol represented his affection." Jude and I pause at the curb as a minivan drives past. "He loved Molly, just like he loved the woman in the portrait. Who could still very well be one of your ancestors. Or maybe she's not an ancestor. Maybe she's just a lookalike."

"Jude—"

"I did some research. On doppelgängers."

My jaw drops.

"Not the supernatural kind. The biological kind. Twin strangers. They're rare, but they exist."

"According to Ezra's journal fragment, the woman he painted *didn't* exist. He, himself, didn't know who he was painting. How do you explain that?"

"The same way Maggie explained it. Ezra struggled with

mental illness. Maybe he forgot she existed. Maybe he lost her, and the grief of it drove him insane."

I take a deep breath, grasping for patience as we cross the street. "At what point does your obsession with logic turn into something illogical?"

"It's no more illogical than *your* theory. Which is what, exactly? He painted *you*?" He pushes a short huff of breath from his nose. "How is that possible? And why?"

"I don't know, but I think those answers could be found in this mysterious revelation he mentioned in that journal fragment. He said it was written by his own hand in the year of his son's birth. And he suspected it was about me."

"Selah," Jude says, both syllables filled with exasperation.

"Fine, not me. The girl in the portrait who looks exactly like me. He thought I—*she* might end his suffering."

"The man is dead. His suffering has ended."

"But the painting is still here." I stop and face him, my hand held up to my forehead like a visor against the sun. "I know I sound crazy. But the portrait *is* crazy. And yet, it exists. I don't know about you, but I have to know why."

18

UNLUCKY IN LOVE

On Saturday, Jude travels to Charleston to meet with his family's legal team regarding matters of the estate.

Twig and I finish editing our latest podcast episode, then spend an additional hour planning the finale of our second season. Afterward, I meet Naomi and Harper at The Lucky Penny. We peruse the racks, try on a few things none of us need, then grab ice cream at Frozen Joy.

The whole time, they pummel me with questions about Jude. I keep the answers vague, which frustrates them to no end. It's better than going into detail. If I did, they'd probably side with him, insist the portrait must have a logical explanation, and that would send me over the edge.

On Sunday morning, I go to church with Dad. I keep checking my phone, an annoying compulsion I can't seem to control. I saw Jude return last night in their black Mercedes Benz. I stayed up for an hour later than I should have, waiting for him to text or call.

He never did.

I slide my hands beneath my knees as a gentleman in front of me yawns. Pastor Tim spent the hour talking about impossible things, illogical things—life through death, glory through suffering—and nobody scoffed. Nobody even batted an eye.

After the benediction, we filter through the exit—Mrs. Calloway and Kate in front, Twig and me in the middle, Dad and Mr. Calloway taking up the rear. We shake Pastor Tim's hand, then step outside to weather that's cloudy and chillier than it ought to be in September. I pull my jean jacket tight when Twig gives me a nudge with his elbow.

I follow the direction of his nod, and my breath catches in my throat.

Jude sits on a bench outside St. Oswald's. Not on the seat, but atop its backrest with his boots on the bench and his elbows on his knees. He's wearing dark jeans and a dark wool overcoat with a high collar. He holds a book, and while he's too far away to make out the title, I can tell he's moved on from *Crime and Punishment*.

His eyes meet mine.

I run my hand through my hair, then excuse myself from Dad and the Calloways. As I approach—perhaps a smidge too eagerly—I can't help but smile at his latest literary selection. *The Turn of the Screw* by Henry James. "I'm rubbing off on you," I say, nodding at his book.

Jude looks down at it, as though only now realizing he holds a book at all, then gets right to the point.

He found another reference to the portrait.

"Is it the revelation?" I ask.

"No," he says, glancing past me—toward Twig and my dad, who are watching us with varying degrees of wariness.

We decide to take our conversation inside The Cobbler, a retro diner with the best pie in town. It's located on the square, between Hallowed Grounds Cafe and Flicker and Foam Emporium—too long of a walk from St. Oswald's. And so, for the first time ever, I climb into Jude's BMW.

He's quiet on the drive, his hands tense on the wheel.

He opens the door for me at the diner, and I'm glad to step inside where it is warm and familiar. There's a long counter on one side and a row of red leather booths on the other, with black and white checkered flooring in between.

A waitress named Gemma stands behind the counter chatting with the cook through the service-window. When her eyes land on Jude, they follow him like a hungry cat. We head down the aisle, toward the booth farthest in the back, next to the jukebox and a hidden hallway leading to the restrooms.

Gemma wastes no time.

She joins us, jutting her hip and clicking her pen as she asks what we'll have to drink, her drawl thicker than usual. I order a ginger ale. She gives me a clipped *mm-hmm* before turning her ravenous eyes upon Jude. I resist the urge to roll my own. Gemma graduated from Foggy Hollow High two years ago, and I'm almost positive she lives with her boyfriend.

He orders a coffee without giving her a second glance.

"I went to the cemetery this morning," he says once she leaves, grabbing a menu from behind the condiment caddy.

"The town cemetery?"

He nods. "I was looking for the Ludwigs."

"And?"

"I found all of them but Molly."

"Do you think she moved away?"

"If she got married, maybe. But why wouldn't she or her husband be mentioned in her father's obituary?"

"Maybe they left the faith, and he disowned them." Based on the small amount of research we did on Friday, he seemed like the sort of guy who would do such a thing. "Or maybe she got pregnant out of wedlock. Or committed some other sin he considered egregious."

"Like Elijah?"

The question hits hard.

I stare back at him, considering the possibility when

Gemma returns with our drinks. Jude doesn't order any food. I think about doing the same—my appetite still spotty—but then I'm struck by a sudden and profound craving for apple pie.

After I order, Gemma lingers. "Are you sure I can't get you anything to eat? You strike me as a pecan pie kinda guy ... rich, smooth, just the right amount of sweet. I could bring you a slice. Or I could bring you something better."

This time I *do* roll my eyes. Her innuendo is as subtle as a sledgehammer.

"I'm not interested," Jude says, his dismissive tone filled with innuendo of his own.

He's not talking about pie.

Gemma blushes, but gets the point.

She leaves with a pout.

I take a drink of my ginger ale, not entirely sure what to do about his theory regarding Molly Ludwig. A reverend's daughter committing suicide in the eighteenth century? Surely that would be an incredibly rare occurrence. But then I have a memory. A very unsettling memory. Because it's not really a memory at all, but a dream I recorded in my journal. A young woman hanging from a rope, wearing a yellow dress with a hoop skirt and a matching petticoat, her long hair in ringlets.

Just like Molly in Ezra's sketch.

Unsettled, I tug at the sleeves of my jacket. "You said you found something about the portrait?"

Jude removes a letter from his coat pocket and slides it across the table. I pick it up and read the date at the top— March 9, 1833, addressed to Amos Vandenberg's wife, Ida. The mother of Ruth Vandenberg, who died in an animal attack.

I take a reverent breath and begin reading.

My Dearest Sister Ida,

Your last letter was both a comfort and a sorrow, for it assures me of your well-being, and yet, the news of dear Gabriel grieves me beyond expression. To have lost, in that single, dreadful attack, both his cherished twin and the young lady to whom his affections were so tenderly bound, oh, Ida! How much sorrow can one heart endure? Young love is a most violent affliction, and few recover from it unscathed.

But this new distress, his departure for Winchester! I can scarce comprehend it. That he would leave everything familiar, everything dear, to cross the sea in such a fragile state. What business could possibly require his presence in England now, in the midst of his grief? Pray tell it is not the painting that compels him.

Ezra's portrait was lost in the fire, was it not? How strange for Gabriel to insist otherwise. Stranger still is his belief that Raphael the younger stole it. Does he truly insist Amos laid forth such a charge at the end of his days? I was ever under the impression that your husband and his cousin were of the best accord, despite the old quarrel between their fathers. Could Ezra's madness have unsettled Amos's mind, and now poor Gabriel's as well?

I do hope I do not trouble you with such talk. Forgive me if I have been too bold in my musings. My concern for you and your son weighs heavy upon my *heart, and I should very much like to hear from you soon. If you should hear from Gabriel, pray urge him to write as well. Until then, know that you are ever in my thoughts and prayers.*

With steadfast love,
Your devoted sister

By the time I'm finished, Gemma has already come and gone with my pie.

I stare down at the looping cursive on the page. I've studied Jude's family tree enough by now to connect several dots.

Ezra was the father of Amos, and Amos was the father of Gabriel, whose twin sister, Ruth, starred in Episode 8, *Cryptid Craze*, along with a girl named Violet Underwagon. According to this letter, Violet was more than Ruth's friend. She was the girl Gabriel fancied.

Raphael the younger would be Raphael II, Amos's first cousin. Despite the feud between their fathers, they must have gotten along. So perhaps it wasn't hatred all the way down, after all. But then something must have gone south between them, because Amos made accusations in his final days, and whatever he said was enough to convince his son, Gabriel, that Raphael II had stolen Ezra's portrait before the fire.

After the vicious death of his sister and the girl he loved, Gabriel set sail for Winchester, England. Which is also on the family tree. Raphael married in Winchester. Raphael II was born in Winchester. He married there as well and had his three children.

It's a lot to keep track of, and I make a mental note to write everything down when I get home. I unwrap my silverware and pick up my fork. "He must have gone to Winchester to get the portrait back, right?"

Jude hands me a second letter, this one hastily written and much shorter than the first. "I found them together."

Dear Mother,

I write only with tidings of disappointment. My errand has come to nothing. Raphael II was nowhere to be found in Winchester, nor any account of the Vandenberg name. The journey has been fruitless and I shall return home at once.

Your loving son,
Gabriel

"No account of the Vandenberg name." I look up. "What does that mean?"

Jude's leg starts bouncing under the table. "I have no idea."

"I wonder why he stole it," I mutter, cutting off a bite of pie with my fork.

I read the letters again, frowning as I go. Struck anew by the tragedy of it all. The animosity between Raphael and Ezra is described like some sort of hereditary disease, an inevitable infection passed from father to son. But what caused the original rift between Ezra and Raphael to begin with? Could grief have been a trigger?

Ezra lost Molly, possibly by suicide.

Gabriel lost Violet and his twin sister in an animal attack.

After him, the misfortune only deepened.

Isaiah lost Helena Piesel, the girl he was privately courting, along with his entire family in a train crash.

Enoch lost his betrothed, his parents, and his left eye in a bank robbery.

"The Vandenberg men weren't very lucky in love," I mutter, cutting off another bite.

Jude takes a drink of his coffee, his brow tightly knit, like he's spent the past twenty-four hours thinking the same thing.

"Hey," I say.

He drags his hand down his face, then looks up at me. "Rafe keeps talking about you."

"What?"

His leg bounces faster.

"What do you mean?" I ask.

"I don't know. It's like he's baiting me. Saying things."

"What kind of things?"

Jude drums his finger on the handle of his coffee mug, clearly agitated. I try not to press, but morbid curiosity rises like flame on the tip of my tongue. If Rafe is talking about me, I want to know what he's saying. But then I look at Jude—really look—and he's clearly miserable.

"Just ignore him," I say.

"That easy, huh?"

"It's the best way to handle a jerk. Seriously, he isn't worth your time."

It's true.

Rafe is a giant jerk. And while I may have thought the same about Jude a few weeks ago, I couldn't have been more wrong. "What *is* worth your time, however, is pie from The Cobbler."

I lift my fork, waving it back and forth with a perfectly-sized bite on the end. "Do you want to try some? It'll cheer you up. Pie from The Cobbler cheers everyone up."

"I'm good, thanks."

I scoop the bite into my mouth, lifting my eyebrows in an attempt to entice him.

He chuckles softly, then rotates his coffee cup. "I've been thinking about your idea the first time we met."

"You're gonna have to refresh my memory. I have a lot of ideas all the time, and they sorta jumble together."

He smiles a little, the crease between his brow losing some of its edge, and it's the most tortured, beautiful smile I've ever seen. If I were Ezra Vandenberg, I'd paint it a thousand times over until I captured it perfectly. My own personal obsession.

"To carpool," he says.

"Oh."

"I'd be up for it, if you still wanted to—you know—decrease your carbon footprint."

19
BIRTHDAY WISHES

I sit on the bench in the Midnight Garden, playing with a fallen ribbon. I rub the delicate fabric between my fingers and stare at the pond, no longer choked with fallen leaves. Its dark, glassy surface reflects the twisted silver tree behind me. Several of its limbs are still tied with ribbon like the one in my hand. I wonder what they were tied for? Protection? Remembrance? Wishes?

If I could make a wish right now, what would it be about? The portrait, which remains a mystery? Or perhaps it would be about the boy I've been investigating the mystery with.

More than a week has passed since Jude and I convinced the grumpy clerk at town hall to help us dig through old records. We found Molly's registration of birth in a bound ledger from the 1700s. After that, the trail went cold. There was no record of marriage, no record of death. It's possible such records were lost in the fire, but we found a record of her father's death, and her brother's, too. If those survived, it seems like Molly's would have as well. We even checked different sections just to be thorough—land deeds, wills, taxes. It was to no avail. After Molly Ludwig attended the Yuletide Ball with Ezra Vandenberg, it was as if she vanished into nothing.

Just like the Vandenbergs.

Just like my mother.

Or, possibly, Elijah.

Was Molly the girl from my dream? I've read my journal entry a thousand times, but I haven't shared it with Jude. Over the past eight days, as we've sifted through his family's sweeping archives—letters and journals sorted by century but rarely in order—I've kept this morsel of information to myself. If he's still operating under the assumption that the subject of *Ezra's Obsession* is one of my relatives from the past, he's not going to accept the idea of me having dreams about tragedies long ago.

I twist the ribbon around my thumb.

Early evening sunlight filters through branches, casting shifting shadows along the cobbled path. Mushrooms and bloodroot bloom between the stones. But the thick tangle of weeds has been cleared away. Several days ago, the news became official. The Vandenberg Estate would host this year's Hunter's Moon Masquerade Ball. Upon the announcement, Dad acquired a three-man crew and they've been getting the grounds into tiptop shape ever since.

The smell of autumn weaves through the crisp evening air.

It's the eve of October.

The best month of the year.

But I feel restless and out of sorts.

Jude and I have been carpooling to school. Eating lunch at the same table. Sitting next to one another in U.S. History. And I've discovered none of the adages hold true.

When it comes to Jude Vandenberg, proximity and exposure haven't dulled his appeal.

The shine hasn't worn off.

The magic hasn't faded.

Familiarity has not bred contempt.

On the contrary, every moment with him is kindling, fueling a fire deep down in my abdomen that sometimes burns so hot, I feel like I might crawl out of my skin if he doesn't touch me already. But he never does. He doesn't even reach, leaving me to wonder if the things I feel are completely lopsided. But then, what about the wounded expression he wore when he dropped me off this afternoon? I failed to mention the significance of today, and he caught wind of it after school. Would he have looked so hurt if I was just some girl he was doing research with?

"What a sad little picture you make Selah Whitlock."

I look up from the ribbon.

Rafe has stepped out of the shadows, impeccably dressed as always, twirling a small clover between his fingers. He sits next to me on the bench. "Clutching your ribbon like a love-struck maiden."

I ignore him.

I wasn't lying to Jude in The Cobbler last Sunday. When it comes to Rafe, this really is the best course of action.

He leans close. "Funny, isn't it? You sitting here, thinking about him. Him somewhere in there, thinking about you."

I stare resolutely at the pond.

"Wondering why he hasn't swept you off your feet yet?"

My spine stiffens. How in the world could he possibly know what I've been thinking?

"He's probably brooding about it. My poor, lonely cousin does love to brood. Tell me, sweetheart, do you think he's being moody and mysterious, or is he just hot and bothered?"

I turn and glare. "What do you want?"

"I want to help. You're pining. Jude's pining. But you must remember, the poor boy has spent the last six years attending an all-boys boarding school." Rafe shudders, like the very idea is torture. "I'm not convinced he knows what he's doing. Which means you might have to make the first move. Or ..." He crawls his fingers along the backrest of the bench and extends his arm long behind me. "We could help him along by making him jealous."

He nips my ear.

Actually *nips my ear*.

With his teeth.

My response comes like a reflex.

I slap him across the face.

Then I surge to my feet, my palm stinging.

Rafe rubs his cheek, and I remember him from a fevered dream, turning into a werewolf. Thankfully, when he removes his hand and looks up at me, his eyes aren't red. They're as blue as ever, sparkling with that infuriating amusement. He cocks his head slightly, examining me in that way he often does. Like I'm a puzzling riddle, and he isn't used to being stumped.

"Ouch," he says, his lips curling into a pout.

"Why was your car at the football game on Friday?" I ask.

He gives his eyebrows a wag. "Were you looking for me?"

"What would compel you to attend a high school football game in Foggy Hollow?"

"I think the better question is, what *wouldn't* compel me to attend a high school football game in Foggy Hollow?" He stands with a devilish grin, hands me the clover, and leans close to my ear again. "Happy birthday, sweet Selah. I hope you get everything you wish for."

With that, he strolls away.

When he's gone, I look down at his gift.

It isn't just a clover. It's a four-leaf clover. Only it's not green, but yellow with curling leaves.

A lucky charm on the brink of death.

Dad and I step inside the Calloway's split-level home, immediately engulfed in the glorious scent of homemade chili and cinnamon rolls. He claps Twig on the shoulder, then follows his nose up the short flight of stairs to the main floor. Twig looks down at me with a smile. "You've been obsessed with Mexican food lately, right? Maybe some tamales?"

I swat his arm. "Don't you dare."

He laughs as we join the others in the kitchen. Compared to our former trailer home, it always felt so big. But in actuality, the Calloway kitchen is small and cozy, separated from the dining room by a bar counter lined with mismatching stools. On one side, Mrs. Calloway moves about, an impressive multi-tasker. On the other, their well-loved dining table, already set with a basket of cornbread, sits under the glow of a hanging light.

Dad gives Mrs. Calloway flowers.

She gushes over the grocery store bouquet, then asks Kate to put them in a vase while she stirs the chili simmering on the stove and flips the bacon sizzling on the griddle. The kitchen is a war zone of food. My birthday dinner has turned into a smorgasbord of oddity, with the same standard main dish, and a growing collection of random sides.

It started innocently enough.

On my twelfth birthday, over a meal of chili and cornbread, Twig casually mentioned I like my chili with cinnamon rolls. On my thirteenth birthday, cinnamon rolls joined the fare. That also happened to be the year I was obsessed with Red Lantern, a hole in the wall sushi bar that was never destined to succeed in a town like Foggy Hollow. But man, did I do my best to keep it afloat. Twig made another innocent comment, and lo and behold, there was a tray of sushi from Red Lantern on my fourteenth birthday. At this point, Twig had caught on, and—being an avid fan of bacon—made a more strategic comment. Last year, Kate joined the fun and insisted I couldn't live without egg rolls.

Mrs. Calloway asks her children to set the table, but not me. The birthday girl isn't allowed to lift a finger. So I sit on one of the stools while Kate and Twig move in and out of the kitchen and Dad and Mr. Calloway talk about cars and the weather and the grounds at the Vandenberg Estate.

I find myself gazing at their refrigerator, an explosion of quirky magnets and motherly pride. There's Twig's official invite to the STEM symposium at CMU, along with the science fair ribbon he won in middle school. There's Kate's spelling bee certificate from fifth grade, a playbill from her last show, and a team photo from cheer camp. There's also a car repair schedule for Mr. Calloway's shop, a rotary magnet, and a family photo from their trip to Gatlinburg last spring. Twig towers over them all. Carl, Kelly, Kate. And Spencer—the only one without a Cuh name. Unintentional, for sure. But just one more way in which he feels *other*. No matter how much they love him, he can't quite escape it.

Mrs. Calloway hands him a sushi platter from Kroger.

"Ah," Twig says. "The finest sushi in all of West Virginia."

"I'm not about to make it myself. You know how nervous I get about raw fish. The last thing I want is for anyone to get sick on Selah's birthday."

"Mom," he says, completely deadpan. "It's imitation crab meat."

Mr. Calloway grabs a beer from the refrigerator. "Hey Spence, you know why crabs don't share their food, right?"

He waits a short beat, his eyebrows raised as he holds back the punchline.

We stare at him warily.

"Because they're all a little shellfish!"

Groans ensue.

Mr. Calloway laughs.

So does Dad, which is something I don't often see. I enjoy seeing it now, despite this ache inside I can't quite shake. You would think I'd relish my birthday. But it always comes with a bout of melancholy. It's a somber holiday, like Good Friday at St. Oswald's, only Dad and the Calloways try really hard to make it festive. The thing is, my birthday makes me think of Mom. Is she alive out there somewhere? And if she is, is she thinking of me—her peaceful pause? As soon as I was born, did the demons latch back on?

I set my chin in my hand.

When I was little, before she left, she'd wake me up on my birthday with a playful roar and declare the time had come for a wild rumpus. That same night before bed, she'd read me her favorite story. *Where the Wild Things Are* by Maurice Sendak. Sometimes, her voice would catch a little at the end, when Max returned with his dinner waiting for him, still hot. She'd smooth down my hair, her fingers smelling of nicotine, and she'd whisper, "Dinner will always be waiting for you, too, Selah."

Back then, I thought it was a promise.

She might leave sometimes.

But she'd always come back.

She'd always take care of me.

Now I know she was never talking about her.

She was always talking about Dad.

He catches my attention, wrinkles in the corners of his eyes. Worry lines. Laugh lines. Both, I guess. Because that's what love does.

Mr. Calloway sneaks a slice of bacon, dodging his wife's playful swat. He picks up the plate of egg rolls and tells everyone to move into the dining room. He sets the plate on the sideboard between the pot of chili and a gift bag. They really shouldn't have. And yet, they always do. Usually a new candle or some fun smelling soaps from Flicker and Foam. Mrs.

Calloway comes in with party horns—the kind that roll out when you blow into them. Kate brings the bacon. And with a clatter of dishes and silverware, everyone digs in.

Conversation starts with a bit of housekeeping. Parade float construction begins this weekend, and Mrs. Calloway wants to make sure the trailers are up to code—a task for her husband and son. With it being the bicentennial, there will be more floats than usual this year, so they'll need to make two stops: the fairgrounds, where floats have always been stored pre-parade, and the back lot behind the high school bus barn.

Once that's settled, she shifts her attention to our podcast. Mrs. Calloway wants to know all about the twelfth and final installment of season two, which drops tomorrow. When that runs its course, the men dive into last Friday's football game.

Dad tears off a piece of cinnamon roll. "That fourth-quarter fumble really cost us."

"Griffin Tate's got an arm, but he sure did fold under pressure."

Kate dips her egg roll into a puddle of sweet and sour sauce. "I don't think he was folding under pressure so much as nursing a broken heart."

"What do you mean?" Mrs. Calloway asks.

"Lainey broke up with him last week."

Mrs. Calloway's face visibly falls. "But they've been together for so long."

"I know. It was a total blindside. He planned this elaborate proposal to the masquerade ball and carried it out at cheerleading practice. But she rejected him in front of everyone. Then she made a huge scene by breaking up with him right before the game."

Mr. Calloway releases a low whistle.

Mrs. Calloway frowns. "That doesn't sound like Lainey."

Kate quirks an eyebrow. "Causing a scene?"

"Well, not that part. She's always had a flair for the

dramatic. But she's never been cruel. Breaking up with Griffin before such a big game feels a bit cruel, doesn't it?"

"More than a bit," Mr. Calloway mumbles.

"Apparently, she's seeing a college boy."

I drop my spoon. "Who?"

Kate wipes the corner of her mouth with a napkin. "That's the question. She's being super vague about him. She just keeps bragging to me and Harrison about how he goes to Yale."

Mr. Calloway helps himself to some more bacon. "From QB one to Ivy Leaguer, ay? Gotta hand it to the girl, she's got taste."

My mind hums.

It's Rafe.

It has to be Rafe. He told me himself he was taking a sabbatical from Yale, and now he's seeing Lainey Sikes? This must have been the reason he went to the football game. To watch Lainey cheer.

"Speaking of love lives," Kate croons. "Did your boyfriend get you a birthday present?"

"Boyfriend?" Dad says.

Kate gives her egg roll another swirl in the sauce, her eyes meeting mine with a friendly tease. "Jude Vandenberg."

"He's not my boyfriend," I say, a little too emphatically. I could kill my cheeks for how hard they're blushing right now. "We're not even dating."

"You eat lunch together every day."

"Twig eats lunch with Jude every day, too, and they're not dating."

"Jude doesn't look at my brother like he looks at you."

My face goes even hotter.

Kate shoots me a wink. "Okay, fine. Did your *friend*, Jude Vandenberg, get you anything for your birthday?"

"He couldn't have," Twig says. "Selah didn't tell him it was her birthday."

I kick him under the table.

"Why wouldn't you tell him?" Mrs. Calloway asks.

"Because," I say with a shrug. "It's just ... another day."

"Nonsense," Kate declares, slapping the table. "This is the overture to the great production that is another year of Selah Whitlock's magnificent life. A tale of mystery, adventure, and, most importantly ... the strangest assortment of food you will ever find."

Everyone laughs as Mr. Calloway lifts his beer with a hardy *Hear, hear!* Then they blow their silly party horns.

"To Selah!" everyone choruses.

It's a ridiculous moment, but a happy one, too. And for just a little while, the ache in my chest relents.

20

ACCOUNTS OF
THE UNCANNY

SEASON 2, EPISODE 12
SUPERNATURAL OR SUPERNOVA?
OCTOBER 1, 2025

SELAH: Welcome, seekers of the strange. We're coming to you from good ol' Foggy Hollow, where the weird never sleeps and we wouldn't want it any other way. Today, we're wrapping up season two with a doozie of an episode. But first, we've reached October. Which means ...

TWIG: Spooky season has officially arrived.

SELAH: In my humble opinion, it is the best time of the year, and there's no better place to experience the vibe than right here in our town.

TWIG: We kick things off with a bonfire at the quarry, where the water is said to be bottomless and has swallowed entire things whole.

SELAH: Boats, cars ... bodies. For those brave enough to try, swimming across it will make you a Foggy Hollow legend.

TWIG: Next up is Hollow Screen Horror Night at the drive in.

SELAH: If you miss it again this year, I will cry.

TWIG: They're playing all three of the original Poltergeist movies. There's no way I'm missing that.

SELAH: The weekend before Halloween, we take a brief pause from the spooky festivities to honor our town's history. Not its birth, but its rebirth. This year will be extra special because we're celebrating our bicentennial.

TWIG: In 1822, our town mysteriously combusted into flame. If this sounds intriguing to you, check out season one, episode five, *Inferno Without a Spark*. Suffice it to say, lives were lost and the damage to property was unimaginable. Most towns like ours would have perished after such a devastating tragedy, but not us. Three years later, we emerged like a phoenix from the ashes, and every October we celebrate with our very own holiday.

SELAH: A two-day event that begins on a Friday, with a parade and a festival and best of all, no school.

TWIG: Followed by the Hunter's Moon Masquerade Ball on Saturday.

SELAH: Usually it's held at town hall, but this year the event is taking place at the one-and-only Vandenberg Estate, and you all know how we feel about that estate.

TWIG: In case you don't, check out season one, episodes ten through twelve.

SELAH: Last up is the crown jewel of October itself— Halloween. Your town might feature haunted houses and a pumpkin patch. Ours has its own Wraith Walk, a self-guided tour featuring Foggy Hollow's creepiest haunts.

TWIG: The boarded up train tunnel is terrifying.

SELAH: Not as terrifying as The Night Beast Feast, the very spot where two girls were killed in 1832. Authorities say by a wild animal. Others, the *Nachtdier*.

TWIG: Listen to season one, episode eight and decide for yourself.

SELAH: For local teens, the night culminates in a costume party to end all costume parties. The location is, as always, top secret. I'm not allowed to say it on air. But I can say that this year will be extra special. Because of ...

(*A drumroll sounds.*)

TWIG: Dante's Comet.

SELAH: Which means, we're done with the preamble, folks. Let's get to the show, shall we? It's time to grab your flashlight, keep your wits, and tune in for another ... uncanny account.

(*An eerie electronic motif plays, pulsing with an unsettling rhythm. The music fades into a lingering, uneasy silence before the hosts continue.*)

SELAH: I think I'd like to start with a number. Point zero eight percent. Tell us about this number, Twig.

TWIG: It's the probability of being alive to witness Dante's Comet, *in tandem* with its brightest night occurring on Halloween. You won't need a telescope. You won't even need binoculars. This thing is going to be very visible.

SELAH: Dante's Comet only comes once every two-hundred-sixty-eight years, and the last time it appeared, something big happened. Listen carefully as Twig reads two eye-witness accounts.

TWIG: The first is taken from the journal of Minister Dirk Van Buren on April 18, 1757. *Near the midnight hour, a light as brilliant as the noonday sun did consume the heavens. The sky was set aflame. Many fell to their knees. Women wailed, babes shrieked, and even the cattle did flee in terror. Surely, this was an omen of judgment. The Lord hath set a sign before us, yet its meaning remains unclear.*

This next one was sent from Captain Tobias Hargrove to Colonel Wexley of Fort Cumberland. *Sir, the men and I were camped three miles east of the Blackwillow River when the night did turn to day without warning. The flash lasted but a moment, yet in that instant, the trees cast shadows as if it were midday. The men stood in arms, fearing the end, yet no end came. A fiery ball was seen in the heavens, but it did not fall, rather, it vanished, as though swallowed by the stars. I have sent scouts to search for signs of an impact. If this be an enemy weapon, we must prepare for war.*

SELAH: These are only two of many accounts regarding an event we Foggy Hollowans refer to as *The Flash of 1757*. Allow me to set the scene.

It is the mid-eighteenth century. Foggy Hollow was a relatively new, but thriving settlement, a close knit community of Dutch immigrants who left New Jersey for more fertile lands. The forests stretched vast and unbroken, the river ran dark and deep, and the mountains loomed like shelter from the wider world.

By day, the settlers worked. Men toiled in the fields. Women spun wool and baked bread. Children either helped or ran free. But by night? The darkness was absolute. No streetlights. No glow of towns or cities. Just flickering candlelight behind cabin shutters and the night sky. These people lived on the edge of the unknown. God-fearing and superstitious, their faith and their fear were inextricably linked. So imagine for a moment, what it must have been like to see a ball of fire in the sky.

TWIG: By 1757, people had observed Halley's Comet multiple times throughout history. While scholars and astronomers might have recognized the ball of fire for what it was, under-standing amongst the general public was lacking. Comets were still viewed as omens, often associated with disaster, war, or divine judgment.

SELAH: Dante's comet was met with widespread fear. Most people saw it as a harbinger of doom. A warning from God. This mystery in the sky left the whole town on edge. So you can imagine what it must have been like when the night erupted in light. No warning. No explanation. Just a blinding, brilliant flash that turned midnight into midday. Nobody knew what it was. Nobody knew what it meant. We still don't today. But that doesn't mean there aren't theories. The most predominate being a lightning strike plus mass hysteria, the whole thing blown way out of proportion. However, there were no reports of storms of any kind on the day in question. One would think if lightning were involved, somebody would have mentioned a storm.

TWIG: It could have been a meteor exploding in the atmosphere. But if this were the case, such an explosion would release an immense amount of energy. The Tunguska Event in 1908 and the Chelyabinsk Meteor of 2013 are great examples to look at here, and they both came with a sonic boom and damage on the ground.

SELAH: So you're saying an exploding meteor would create sound.

TWIG: Exactly. According to reports in 1757, there was no sound at all. No damage, either.

SELAH: What about some kind of crazy solar storm, or aurora borealis?

TWIG: It's possible, but unlikely. A solar storm would happen across entire regions, and yet, there are no records from surrounding settlements corroborating this event. Not to mention, auroras don't flash like lightning. They shimmer. They roll like waves. This was a single, massive burst. So unless this was some kind of unknown atmospheric phenomenon that happened only over Foggy Hollow, that leaves us with ...

(*A dramatic orchestral sting plays: dun-dun-duuuuun!*)

SELAH: Supernatural explanations.

TWIG: What are your theories, Selah?

SELAH: I have two. First, it could have been just like Minister

Van Buren said. An actual warning from God. Maybe it was about the fire. I mean, if that's the case, it came four and a half decades early, but a day is like a thousand years and a thousand years is like a day and all that jazz.

TWIG: Okay, what's your second theory?

SELAH: As cliche as it might be, it has to be said. Extraterrestrial visitors.

TWIG: ET phone home.

SELAH: Ugh, don't talk about that movie. It's so sad. Anyway, those are my theories. Let's hear yours.

TWIG: I have three. The first is time travel.

SELAH: Great Scott!

TWIG: Doc Brown and his DeLorean aside, hear me out. What if settlers glimpsed a scene from the past or the future—a tear in the space time continuum?

SELAH: A flash of daylight from an entirely different day.

TWIG: Exactly.

SELAH: I like that theory. What else ya got?

TWIG: Mass possession.

SELAH: Yikes.

TWIG: It could have been an attack on the mind. A supernatural entity broadcasting a message directly into the settlers' brains. Which would make the flash not a real flash, but a shared hallucination.

SELAH: Courtesy of the aliens.

TWIG: My third and final theory is similar to your God theory. The flash could have been some sort of celestial being descending from the heavens.

SELAH: Like an angel?

TWIG: If your glass is half full. Or a demon, if your glass is half empty.

SELAH: I'm building a theory off your theory. What if the Great Flash wasn't something crashing down, but something *waking up*?

(A high-pitched, maniacal cackle of glee fades into eerie silence.)

TWIG: Definitely food for thought.

SELAH: So what about this year's comet?

TWIG: By the time this episode airs, it will be twenty-one days, thirteen hours, and sixteen minutes from making its first appearance in the sky. But don't count on noticing anything unless you have a telescope. It'll grow steadily bigger and brighter until Halloween night, when you won't be able to miss it. I recommend a pair of sunglasses, just in case another flash makes an appearance.

SELAH: I can't wait!

TWIG: Well, listeners, this officially ends our second season. We'll be back in November with season three, which promises to be our best yet.

SELAH: But first! I would be remiss if I didn't wish my co-host and his robotics team good luck at the prestigious Carnegie Melon University for the Catalyst Cup in nine days. All five of you are brilliant brainiacs, so I'm calling it right now. You're gonna bring home the gold, and if I'm wrong, I'll go on record saying The Flash of 1757 was a giant hoax.

TWIG: You do realize we're going to be surrounded by fellow brainiacs, right? The brightest minds from around the country will be there.

SELAH: But you're the brightest of them all, and you can't convince me otherwise, Twig. My bet's on you.

TWIG: Well, that's a wrap, listeners. Thanks for joining us on this journey into the unknown.

SELAH: As always, stay curious and never stop wondering!

21

ROTTEN BLOOD

Jude's BMW idles in a fog that swirls and shifts like a dancing troupe of pale ghosts. October has arrived like a whole mood.

I open the passenger door and slide inside, unsure what to expect. Thankfully, the wounded young man from yesterday is gone. Jude looks at me over the top of his sunglasses with a heartbreaking grin. "I got you a belated birthday gift."

He hands me a leather-bound journal with the initials I.V. stamped in the lower right corner. Isaiah Vandenberg, original author of the family tree, son of the scorch mark, survivor of the train crash. A man who was born into the Gilded Age and died just after the Roaring Twenties. The journal itself is nothing novel. We've looked through many just like it.

What's new is Jude's excitement.

"Check out March third," he says.

I thumb through the pages. Each entry is short and to the point. The year is 1927, which means Isaiah only had three more left to live before he would die in the same bank robbery that would leave his son, Enoch, with one eye.

I stop on the entry in question and begin to read out

loud. "My second-born son, Daniel, is lost to me. Led astray by his wretched cousin, lured into vice and ruin. Can blood be evil? Lucian sought to tempt me in my grief …"

My voice trails off.

Lucian.

One of the disconnected names on Raphael's side of the Vandenberg Family Tree. Followed by Reuben, Frank, and Thomas, names given to the police by Jude's grandfather in the Vandenberg cold case.

I look at Jude.

He nods for me to keep reading.

"Lucian sought to tempt me in my grief. Now his son, *Reuben*, has ensnared mine. My wife weeps. Enoch rages. I am powerless."

I look at Jude again. "Reuben."

Jude reaches across the console to turn a few pages. "Read this one, here."

The entry is marked April 5, 1927.

"Daniel has returned. I am certain something dreadful befell him in his time away. He speaks little and refuses to say what transpired. But he has severed ties with Reuben, and for that, I am grateful. I can only pray that in time, he will find his way back to himself."

I turn back to the previous entry and blink at the page.

Can blood be evil?

The question makes my skin prickle.

"Remember those letters in Enoch's trunk?" I say. "They were bound together with twine? I think they might have been from Daniel."

Enoch's younger brother, who was briefly led astray by Rueben.

We're getting nowhere with the portrait.

Perhaps we can get somewhere with this, a clue in the cold

case. A mystery that captivated my attention from the moment I moved to town.

Jude shifts into drive. "Let's look at them after school."

It's raining outside. It's been raining most of the day—a dreary drizzle that ran down the window panes at school, and now runs down the window panes on the estate's third floor.

Last time I came here, I got horrendously sick afterward. I don't actually believe it had anything to do with the dusty cloak I donned for the majority of my visit. Even so, I give the wardrobe a wide berth.

Jude and I remove the bundle of letters from Enoch's trunk. Sure enough, the vast majority are from Daniel, Enoch's younger brother. We divvy them up in search for more information about their wretched cousin, Rueben.

Jude settles into a regal, high-backed armchair. He sits in the shadows with his ankle crossed over his knee, skimming one correspondence at a time. Meanwhile, I set up camp near the window. I sit on the floor in a child's pose, propped up on my elbows as I read the letters I've spread across a rug beneath the dim, gray glow of a dreary afternoon.

Raindrops patter the roof.

"What are you doing this Friday?" I ask, shifting my weight as my attention moves to a different letter.

Jude lowers his stack.

"There's a bonfire at the quarry. It's an annual tradition. A sort of kickoff to October. You should come."

"Why?"

"Because it'll be fun. An opportunity to socialize with the local teens. A chance to make some new friends."

He quirks his eyebrow.

"And I'll be there."

"Well, then. If you'll be there."

I can't see his mouth, but I think he might be smiling.

With a flutter in my chest, I smile back.

Then I return to the letters, and come to a quick halt.

"I found something," I say, sitting up on my knees, holding the correspondence between my hands. It was written from Daniel to Enoch on March 12, 1960.

"Enoch," I read. "A man named *Frank* has come to Foggy Hollow, claiming to be Reuben's son, the ruthless cousin we cut out of our lives decades ago. Now I find myself facing the same helpless grief our father must have felt.

"Frank is doing to my son what his father once did to me— leading him astray, poisoning his mind, with the same charm and the same wicked pull. The similarities are uncanny. So much so, I have begun to fear I'm losing my mind. God help me, Enoch, I can't help but wonder if Frank is a demon. I have enclosed two photographs. You were always the rational one. Look at them and tell me—what do you see? Please write as soon as you can. Daniel."

I look at Jude.

He looks back at me.

Then together, we return to Enoch's trunk in search of the photographs. In the midst of looking, we come upon a piece of parchment that escaped our notice last time.

A sketch of the locket.

Jude turns the paper over, as if he might find the artist's signature on the back. But there is no signature. It's just a piece of aged parchment with the exact same locket from *Ezra's Obsession* drawn in graphite.

We keep digging until the trunk is empty.

There are no photographs to be found.

A demon.

I sit back on my heels. "What do you think Daniel saw in the photographs—devil horns?"

Jude shakes his head, every bit as stumped as myself.

I think about his grandfather's tip to the police. We have stumbled upon two of the names—Rueben and Frank.

Both of them, corrupters.

Bad apples.

Rotten fruit.

Can blood be evil?

Suddenly, it's very clear to me why Jude's father warned him to stay away from that side of the family. I want to give Jude the same warning now.

I can still feel the nip of Rafe's teeth against my ear. The sting of my palm after I slapped him. I keep the memory to myself, and say instead, "I think Rafe is seeing Lainey Sikes."

"What?"

"Last night, Kate said Lainey broke up with Griffin, and apparently, she keeps bragging about dating a college boy who goes to Yale."

Jude's expression darkens.

"You really think he'd be interested in Lainey?"

"I have no idea what interests Rafe," Jude says, picking up the sketch. "We should show this to Tulane. The locket could be a family heirloom. Maybe Denis has seen it before. Maybe he knows where it is."

22

ERRATIC BEHAVIOR

Jude thinks Tulane might be in the conservatory, so we descend the spiral staircase inside the east wing turret. When we reach the bottom, the sound of raised voices greets us.

Jude pulls me to a stop.

The door is ajar, allowing us to see a sliver of the unfolding scene. Isabel faces off with Rafe, the two of them surrounded by exotic plants as rivulets of rain run down the glass walls.

The first time I saw Jude's stepmother, I thought her a beauty. Then I met her up close and realized it was a trick of her meticulous grooming. In actuality, her face is too narrow, her lips too thin, her nose like a beak. A combination of features that could either be described as striking or off-putting, but certainly not pretty. At the moment, her cheeks have gone blotchy pink. She stands like a frightened deer with her hand pressed against her clavicle.

She's covering a necklace.

Rafe faces away from us. I can only see his back, but I can tell from his posture that for once, he isn't being playful or coy.

There is nothing cryptic about the anger radiating from him now. It's as obvious as Isabel's fear.

As quick as a viper, he grabs Isabel's arm so hard, she gasps.

"Rafe," she pleads. "You're hurting me."

I move toward the door to stop him, but Jude wraps his arm around my waist and pulls me into shadow.

"Tell me where you got this," Rafe demands.

"In the family safe," Isabel whimpers.

"Liar."

"I'm not lying. It was part of Maureen Vandenberg's collection."

"This," he curls his hand around her necklace and yanks it toward him, eliciting another gasp as she's pulled forward, "was not part of Maureen Vandenberg's collection."

I want to move.

Crane my neck.

See if the necklace is the locket.

But I also don't want to move.

Maybe not ever.

Not when I can feel the tautness of Jude's muscles, his breath against my ear, his hand on my hip, his beating heart against my back.

"Please, Rafe. I'm only telling you what Denis told me."

Rafe lets the necklace go.

Isabel stumbles backward and I catch a glimpse of a glimmering ruby pendant resting just above her décolletage. It's not the locket, but it is familiar. I recognize it just like I recognized the symbol, only this time, I know where it's from. I can still remember it—holding a little boy, shielding his body as sirens blared and bombs rained from the sky. I was wearing that necklace in a dream. I wrote about it in the journal on my nightstand.

"I was only going to borrow it," Isabel says tremulously. "For dinner tonight with town council."

Rafe steps closer.

Isabel flinches, but his touch is gentle as he brushes his knuckles down her cheek.

She sniffs. "I promise I would never do anything to upset you."

"Of course you wouldn't," he says. "Which is why you will give me the necklace now."

She looks up at him, crestfallen. Hesitant. But then her attention drops to the ground. She turns obediently and lifts her hair. Rafe unclasps the necklace, his lips so close to her neck, he's practically kissing her skin. "I never want to hear you mention this necklace again, do you hear me?"

She nods.

He curls his fingers around the pendant. The chain dangles from his fist. His face is a mask of mutiny as he turns on his heel and storms away.

As soon as Isabel flees, we make our decision.

Jude and I follow Rafe.

Down the corridor and into the ballroom where his footsteps echo. We catch a glimpse of his polished boots as he exits through a set of doors on the opposite side. We hurry after him on quiet feet, into the antechamber opposite the foyer, out into the gloomy afternoon, where the hedge maze stands center-stage—a horticultural masterpiece that has consumed Dad's attention as of late. Rafe is striding around it, toward the woods beyond.

The sky rumbles.

There's no time to converse. No time to consider. Rafe's moving too fast. We follow him into the woods, down a shadowed path where the rain is a soft drizzle misting through the trees. Rafe doesn't stop until he reaches the small clearing with the well.

We hunker behind a tree, watching as he yanks a stone from the well and removes a small pouch from behind it. He pours three gemstones into his palm. One is red, like the ruby necklace. He compares the two, and whatever he sees sends him into a rage.

Rafe roars at the sky.

Birds take flight.

I flinch.

Jude's hand circles my wrist—a silent reminder to stay still, stay quiet as Rafe hurls the gems into the trees. He crumples the pouch in his fist and stalks away.

My pulse pounds like a drumbeat beneath my skin, so frantically I'm positive Jude must feel it. Heat blooms where his fingers touch my wrist. Very slowly, he lets go, and I exhale a breath I didn't know I was holding.

"What was that about?" I ask.

Jude wipes the rain from his face with his palm. And then, as though reaching an unspoken agreement, we get out our phones, turn on our flashlights, and search for the gemstones. It takes awhile, but eventually we find them—a pearl, a triangular onyx, and a diamond-shaped ruby the same shape and size as the one Isabel wore.

Jude picks up the stone Rafe removed from the well.

"I dreamt about it," I say, the disembodied words escaping without any premeditation. They drift from my lips and hover in the air.

He looks at me.

"The ruby necklace Rafe took from Isabel. I was wearing it in a dream. There were sirens and bombs. I was holding a little boy, using my body like a shield. There was an older couple there, too. With British accents."

He stands very still—his hair dark from the rain, his face pale—as though carved from marble. "That's real?" he finally says. "What you just said?"

"Why wouldn't it be?"

He scrubs his palm down his face again, and when his hand comes away, he looks disturbed. Almost angry. "My great grandmother died in The Blitz. She saved my grandfather when he was only four." His eyes meet mine. "By shielding his body with her own."

The sky rumbles—low and long.

I close my fist around the gemstones.

Somehow, I am the subject of *Ezra's Obsession*, a portrait painted centuries before I was born. And now, I'm having dreams of Vandenberg tragedies centuries after they died.

I have no idea what's going on. But whatever it is, I think it's time to show Jude my journal.

"Hey kiddo," Dad says as I close the door behind me. He's looking inside the refrigerator with his back turned. "The rain chased me inside. Are you up for an early—dinner?"

His voice hiccups on the tail end of his question as he shuts the refrigerator door and spots not just me standing in the entryway, but Jude and me, wet from the rain. I can practically see the cogs in his brain turning, trying to catch up with the situation. I'm sure last night's dinner conversation is powering at least one of those cogs.

Kate called Jude my boyfriend.

Dad grabs a couple kitchen towels from a drawer. He hands one to Jude, the other to me while I make introductions and they shake hands.

"I'm, uh, just gonna show him something in my room," I say, patting my neck dry.

Dad looks uneasy, like a man navigating unchartered territory. It's not like I haven't had a boy up in my room before. But somehow, Twig in my room feels very different from Jude in my room.

I give Dad a reassuring smile. "We won't be long."

We slip off our shoes and head upstairs.

The soft patter of rain has turned into a downfall. It pounds against the roof and blurs the grounds outside my window.

I grab the journal from my nightstand with more bravado than I feel, and when I turn around, I catch Jude surveying my room. He looks from my daybed, decorated with vintage throw pillows from The Lucky Penny, to the handmade lanterns hanging from the window, to the modest collection of books standing at attention between mismatching bookends on my writing desk, to the Magic 8 Ball and the clamshell trinket dish on my dresser. His attention lifts to the pinboard above it, tacked with photographs. Polaroids mostly, taken at the Hunter's Moon Masquerade Ball two years ago, when Harper went through her photography phase.

Jude sets the kitchen towel next to my new autumn-scented candle from the Calloways and examines the one photograph that isn't a polaroid, but a glossy 4x6. A picture of toddler me, sitting on my dad's knee, holding tight to my mother's hand, like I knew even then that if I let go, she'd slip away.

I open to the journal entry in question and hand it over.

The longer he reads, the deeper the furrow in his brow gets.

When he finishes, I point him to another entry. One I've read so often, I have it memorized. A young woman in a yellow taffeta dress, her hair in ringlets, hanging from a noose. By the end of it, his face is pale, his jaw tight, his hair dark and damp against his forehead. "You don't think this was about ...?"

"Molly Ludwig?"

His attention returns to the entry. Namely, the date of the

entry. I recorded it before we researched Molly. Before we even found the sketch of her in the family archives.

I wring the towel in my hands. "Jude, I really don't think the subject of Ezra's portrait was a relative of mine. Or some coincidental twin stranger he loved and painted, either."

For the first time, he doesn't argue.

23
BONFIRE AT THE QUARRY

On clear nights, the quarry looks like a black mirror framed by jagged cliffs and tall pines. In October, fog hovers over the water like a ghostly veil, making tonight's challenge all the creepier.

I stand with Twig, Naomi, and Harper near the bonfire with my hands tucked into the front pocket of my hoodie. Flames crackle and pop. Music pulses in the background, layered with laughter and the low buzz of multiple conversations unfolding at once. My attention keeps sliding to the parking lot in the distance.

Naomi nudges me with her shoulder, her sleek black hair glowing in the firelight. "Who do you keep looking for, Selah?"

I roll my eyes.

But inside, my stomach has tied into a knot. Jude has been distant ever since I showed him my dreams. He left my room abruptly, and for the past two days, he's been unusually busy with family obligations.

"Are you ever going to tell us what's going on between you two?" Harper asks. "Twig, do you know? I feel like you have to know."

I dagger him with a look.

He gets the hint and pleads the fifth.

But even if he didn't, what would he say? I don't think he could explain what's going on between Jude and me any better than I could, even if we have been brainstorming possibilities the same way we would for a podcast episode. Exhaust all logical explanations, then dive into the supernatural ones. But this time, we're stumped. It's one thing to sit in Maggie's basement as third-party observers, commenting on a strange and uncanny mystery. It's quite another to find myself embroiled in the center of one.

The only thing we've confirmed is what we've always suspected—Rafe is definitely up to something. What that something has to do with the gemstones he chucked into the woods or the ruby necklace he nearly tore off Isabel's neck, we haven't the faintest clue.

Before Naomi and Harper can press any further, Brady Keller stumbles into our conversation. He drapes one arm over my shoulders, his other over Naomi's, the smell of beer clinging to his breath. "Whadaya say, ladies? Are you gonna make tonight legendary?"

"I'm good keeping tonight ordinary, thanks," Naomi replies.

Brady turns to me, his eyes unfocused.

"Sorry, Keller," I say. "I'm staying dry."

He looks at Harper, who gives her head an adamant shake. He completely ignores Twig. I'm about to say something when Twig catches my eye and shakes his head, a nonverbal *drop it*. Brady moves on to the group beside us and a burst of cheers erupts near the water's edge. Someone's about to take the plunge. The crowd shifts to get a better look, but I turn back toward the parking lot.

And there he is.

Emerging from the fog like a dream, his hands tucked

inside the pockets of his leather jacket—halfway zipped, collar popped, breeze ruffling his hair.

Harper squeezes my arm.

I shake her off as he joins our half circle, firelight casting flickering shadows along his jawline. He greets Twig, Harper, and Naomi. Then me.

"You came," I say.

"Someone said it would be fun," he says back, his autumn eyes sparkling.

More cheers erupt. This time, beneath a copse of Hawthorn trees. Caleb Briggs has gotten down on one knee to ask his girlfriend, Brynn Alcott, to the Hunter's Moon Masquerade Ball. She replies with a playful *maybe*, then releases a delighted shriek as Caleb throws her over his shoulder and marches toward the water, like he's going to toss her in.

Jude uses the moment to ask if I'd take a walk with him. We leave the warmth of the fire, away from the drunken laughter and the silly behavior, Naomi and Harper's attention hot on my back.

We walk along the shoreline, fog drifting at our feet. Jude keeps his hands buried in his pockets. I do the same. But every now and then, our elbows brush, and each time, a current of heat zips up my arm.

"Sorry I've been MIA," he finally says.

"You don't have to apologize."

"I feel like I do." He rubs the back of his neck. "I just—I don't know what to think about any of this, let alone what to say."

Neither do I, honestly.

My thoughts drift to the portrait—what it means, how it came to be. We're no closer to answering those questions than we ever were. Sometimes, I find myself wondering if its only purpose was *this*. Bringing me and Jude together.

"Do you believe in fate?" I ask him.

"No," he replies.

"That's a confident answer."

"I'm not a fan of inevitability."

"You want your choices to matter."

"Don't you?"

"Of course," I say. Like discovering a mystery and pulling on the string. The portrait may have brought us together, but it didn't have to keep us together. It was our choice to pick up the string, to follow its path, to be here now. Wasn't it?

"Alright, Whitlock," Jude says with a sigh. "Let me hear it."

"Hear what?"

"Your theory. About these dreams."

"For a while I was contemplating reincarnation. Like, what if every time I die, my memories are erased but I'm born again into the same body? It would explain how Ezra painted the portrait. My path crossed with his in a past life. These dreams could be memories from past lives seeping into my current life. But then I realized that can't be true, because in that scenario, your great grandmother would be my doppelgänger, too. She's not, though. I found a wedding picture in Maggie's archives and there's no resemblance."

"Selah." Jude pulls me to a stop. "This is crazy."

"I know."

His eyes smolder with frustration. "Aren't you bothered?"

I mull over the word.

I'm stumped.

Fixated.

Fascinated.

Enthralled.

Bothered, though?

"No," I say.

He lifts his brow—and with it, a lock of errant hair—then

repeats the words I said to him moments earlier. "That's a confident answer."

I smile. "Yes, well, in case you've forgotten, I co-host a podcast about really weird things. Weird is kind of my jam."

A flicker of amusement pulls at the corner of his mouth.

"I don't know," I say. "I think eventually, we have to come to terms with the fact that not everything in life can be explained. And honestly, wouldn't it be a pretty boring world if it could?"

Water laps against the rocky shore. Music thumps in the distance. And Jude Vandenberg stares at me like I've said something profound. Then, he bends over to pick up a stone. With a flick of his wrist, he sends it skimming across the water in perfect arcs before it disappears into the fog.

"Show-off," I mutter.

He grins.

"Was this one of your extracurriculars at boarding school?"

"Oh, yeah. Rock skipping is a noble art." He skips another just as gracefully as the one before it. "Very old world. Very elite."

I laugh, then try it myself.

My rock hits the water with a pathetic *kerplunk*.

"That was tragic," he says.

"Show me how it's done then, Captain Skipper."

His smile widens, bringing out a pair of dimples so deep they should be illegal. "The key is finding the right stone. You want one that's smooth and flat." He toes the ground, finds one worth inspecting, then hands it to me.

Our fingers brush, and I'm impossibly aware of the space between us. Or rather, lack of space between us. I peek up at him, and it's as if the night itself has pulled tightly around us. The air is electric, a live wire about to snap. And I think this is it. He's finally going to make a move.

Laughter douses the moment.

Lainey Sikes stumbles through the fog, held upright by Rafe. My already racing heart thuds all the more aggressively as I behold the pair of them—proof that he's her college boy.

"Don't stop on our account," Rafe says, leading Lainey closer. "We love a good slow-burn romance, don't we, Lain?"

My muscles tighten.

Lainey laughs some more, the sound cut short by an inebriated hiccup. "No slow burn for us, thank you. Have you seen this guy, Selah? Could there be a more gorgeous specimen? And he goes to Yale."

Rafe smirks. "She really likes that I go to Yale."

Can blood be evil?

The question echoes in my mind.

I want to tell Lainey to run. Far and fast away. Griffin Tate might be a bit of a tool, but he's an absolute catch compared to Rafe Vandenberg.

Beside me, Jude has closed up shop, his shutters drawn. The only sign of life is the muscle ticking in his jaw ... where a bruise once was.

I narrow my eyes at Rafe. "Is your grandfather named Frank?"

He cocks his head. "All that alone time the two of you have been spending in the family archives, and it turns out, you really are just doing research."

"Did you know that Jude's grandfather thought Frank and your father might have something to do with the disappearance of John, Maureen, and their children?"

"Selah." Jude says my name low, like a warning.

Rafe waves him off. "Let the lady speak, Jude. I'm fascinated to hear what she's thinking. In fact, I'm fascinated to hear what the two of you have learned in all this research you're doing."

"Your lineage isn't great," I say.

"Ah, my lineage. The black sheep of the Vandenbergs. Every family needs a villain, don't they? It's so much easier than looking in a mirror." He dusts a speck of lint off his coat sleeve, like he's bored by the subject. "Tell me, have you learned anything more about the portrait?"

I glare at him.

"It's odd, don't you think? Painting someone over and over again, decade after decade. Surely he would have written about such an obsession. And yet, there's nothing in his journals. One might think those particular volumes have been hidden."

"Are you looking for them?" I ask.

"Are you hiding them?"

"Why would we hide them?"

"Oh, I don't know. Perhaps you came across some valuable information and you want it for yourself."

Lainey has been trying to follow the conversation, but her eyes can't seem to focus. "I'm bored," she whines. "And thirsty."

Rafe snaps at a group of teens nearby.

One is Brady Keller, who staggers toward us.

"Lainey wants to swim," Rafe tells him.

"No, she doesn't," I shoot back.

"Oh, but she does," Rafe insists. "Don't you Lainey?"

Lainey looks up at him like a drunken puppy eager to please. "You think I should?"

"Absolutely. I think you should show everyone how it's done. Let them see what legends are made of."

Lainey has begun bobbing her head enthusiastically. "Yeah," she says, "I wanna do it." She starts removing her shirt like she's going to jump in right here, right now.

Rafe stops her with a grin and sends her away with Brady. I'm about to object, to go after them—Lainey Sikes is nowhere near sober enough to swim in the quarry. But Rafe takes my elbow. "Where are you off to, sweetheart?"

Jude takes an aggressive step forward. "Get your hands off her."

"Oh, but she wants my hands on her. Don't you, Selah? I

make your blood boil, which is just another way of saying I make you hot. The beginning of a different sort of love story. Enemies to lovers, perhaps?"

Jude's hand curls into a fist, but I grab his arm and step between them. "Don't," I say, gathering his attention. Getting him to look at me, not his awful cousin. And when he finally does, he looks every bit as dangerous as Rafe ever has. "Please. Let's just go and stop Lainey."

Some of the tension in his shoulders lets go.

I give his arm an encouraging tug.

With a terse exhale, he agrees and comes with me.

"You should let her do it," Rafe says behind us. "If she makes it across, she wins. If she doesn't ... well, I guess that makes me the winner."

I whirl on him.

Two quick steps, and *I'm* in his face. I want to claw out his eyes. Scratch off his skin. Because what an awful, rotten thing to say. Instead, I play his game. Blood might be pounding in my ears, but I act calm. Unbothered. My head tilted, mouth curled in a smirk. "What's up with the ruby necklace, Rafe?"

His blue eyes flash.

Finally, I've hit a nerve.

"Aw, is play time over? It's not fun, anymore?" I draw my lips into a pout. "What were you hiding in the well? It sure made you grumpy."

His nostrils flare. For a second, he looks terrifying. Like the young man from my dream, right before he turned into a were-wolf. But I refuse to back down. I square my shoulders, lift my chin, and stare him in the face.

Jude takes my hand.

Noticing, Rafe gives his eyebrows a smug lift—one that reminds me of our Midnight Garden conversation. I don't know if I'll ever forget the feeling of his teeth on my earlobe.

"I'd be careful if I were you, Selah. You don't want your

boyfriend here paying the price for your rash words. I'd have a fun time tormenting him, too. Just like my father had fun, and my grandfather, and my great grandfather." He leans in. "You just poked the bear, sweetheart. I'd really think twice before doing it again."

With that, he turns and saunters away.

24
HOT AND COLD

Jude drives us home in silence.

We left after making sure Lainey didn't get in the water. She was stubborn about it, too. Belligerent even. Until finally, Jude convinced her to take a drive with Kate and Twig, who would get her home safely.

A lump has lodged itself in my throat, and I'm not even sure why. Because of Rafe, and his callous dismissal of Lainey's safety? Because of the things I said to Rafe that I shouldn't have? Because of his ominous threat before he sauntered away? I bite the inside of my cheek to keep the tears at bay.

Jude slows to a stop in front of the carriage house.

I tug at the sleeves of my hoodie, then say in a rush at the same time as Jude, "I'm really sorry."

We laugh a little nervously.

His hand comes off the wheel in a gesture for me to go first.

"I'm sorry for telling you that would be a fun time." I twist my fingers in my lap. "It really wasn't a fun time."

"I'm sorry for my cousin's behavior," he says.

"You're not responsible for Rafe's behavior."

"No, but I can still be sorry for it."

"He's such an awful person. A legitimately awful person. I didn't think I was capable of hating anyone as much as I hate him, but I really hate him. I can't believe he was going to just—"

"Can we not talk about Rafe right now?"

Heat crawls up my neck.

Jude winds his hand around the back of his.

The lump returns. I'm pretty sure he's annoyed with me, and I don't blame him. I'm letting Rafe live rent free in my head, which is—I'm sure—exactly what Rafe wants. And the last thing I want is to give Rafe Vandenberg anything he wants.

"Will you go to the ball with me?"

My thoughts short-circuit.

I glance at Jude, positive I heard him wrong. "What's that?"

He smiles a half-smile full of self-deprecation, and my insides turn to putty. "I wanted to know if you'd go to the masquerade ball with me."

"I usually go with Twig."

"Oh," he says.

"I don't mean—I was just—commenting. Thinking out loud. I *usually* go with Twig. But that doesn't mean I *have* to go with Twig. I would feel a little bad about ditching him, but I—"

"It's okay, Selah," he says. "You can go with Twig."

"I don't want to go with Twig."

He blinks at me, confused.

I'm being very confusing.

"Can we try this again?" I ask.

His half-smile returns. He bites it back. Tucks it in one corner, where one of his dimples makes a faint appearance. With a dramatic breath, he shifts in his seat so he's facing me, and I swear, I fall in love with him for playing along. "Selah Whitlock, would you grant me the immense honor of escorting you to the Hunter's Moon Masquerade Ball?"

"I don't know."

His eyes narrow roguishly.

"I'm just saying, if we're being old-fashioned about this, you should probably ask my dad for permission first."

Jude unbuckles his seatbelt. He grabs the door handle, like he's going to get out and ask my father's permission right now. With a laugh, I take his arm and pull him back into his seat.

The live wire returns, crackling in the cab of his BMW.

I tuck my hair behind my ear with a noticeable tremble in my fingers. "Of course, Jude Vandenberg. I would love to go to the ball with you."

The morning air is crisp as I jog my usual loop. I cut around the stables, the grass tipped with silver. The season's first frost always feels magical, but even more so here on the Vandenberg estate. Sunlight filters through a scatter of gold and crimson as I turn down the wooded trail that takes me toward the manor.

The whole time, I've barely felt the ground.

Last night, Jude asked me to the ball and I'm still floating. For once, I didn't dream about fires or monsters or bombings. I dreamt of pleasant things. Happy things. *Attractive* things.

A smile breaks across my face.

I'll need a dress. Something period-appropriate. My mind wanders to the wardrobe on the third floor. I imagine donning that gorgeous gown. I imagine Jude in a dark coat and gloves, a cravat at his neck, looking at me the way he did last night.

I burst through the woods. Ahead, the backside of the manor rises from the fog like a gothic dream. I follow the path, which curves around the hedge maze, and to my delight, I discover I'm not the only one awake this early on a Saturday morning.

Jude sits alone on the terrace with a book and a mug of coffee, bathed in golden sunlight like a brooding Adonis. His hair is damp, as though from a recent shower. And as I approach, I notice he's not reading a book after all, but one of the leather journals we've been poring over as of late.

"Hey," I say, smiling as I come to a stop, my breath escaping in puffs of white.

He looks up, and for a slip of a second, it's like watching a candle catch flame—a warm, delectable spark. But then, just as quickly, the flame flickers and dies. A shadow creeps across his face.

"Hey," he says back.

I step onto the terrace, feeling uncertain. "Do you usually get up this early?"

"I couldn't sleep," he says.

"Me neither." Only something tells me our sleepless nights were very different. I couldn't sleep because I was too giddy to sleep. Jude, on the other hand, looks haunted. Or, shoot. Maybe regretful? My chest tightens at the thought, the warmth from my run evaporating.

He avoids eye contact as I stand there awkwardly, pulling at my sleeves, stretching them over my hands. I nod at the journal. "Find anything new?"

He taps the porcelain handle of his coffee mug. "I was thinking about what Rafe said last night. It is strange that he didn't write about the portrait."

"He did, though. Maggie has the proof in her office, remember?"

"That's just one mention. Written on the day he finished. What about all the decades he toiled?"

"He might have written more. There are whole years unaccounted for. Journals that were lost in the fire."

"Maybe. But we have quite a few. And aside from that one scrap Maggie has, there's nothing. Don't you think he'd write about the object of his obsession as much as he tried to paint it?"

I'm not sure. I've read plenty of Vandenberg journals by

now, and the menfolk weren't exactly verbose when it came to their inner thought life.

"I want to show you something," Jude says, finally meeting my eye. "It's up in my room."

———

In the upper hall, Rafe steps out of Jude's bedroom.

Jude and I come to a stop.

"What were you doing in my room?" he asks.

"Looking for you," Rafe says, far too casually. He gives Jude a once-over and clucks his tongue. "My, my. You look like hell, Cousin. Trouble sleeping? Insomnia got you down? It does seem to run in the family."

"What do you want?" Jude asks.

"I wanted to check in. Things got a little dicey last night, and I've been thinking—there's no reason for all this hostility. Whatever drama our ancestors stirred up doesn't have to be ours. Water under the bridge, right?" Rafe extends his hand.

Jude doesn't shake it.

"Well, just know there's no hard feelings on my end." He slides his hands into his pockets and turns to leave, then stops short. "Oh, I almost forgot. Isabel wanted to know if you got the job done."

"What job?"

"Securing a date to the ball. I know you're not thrilled about going, but you are a Vandenberg, after all. Certain obligations come with the territory."

A wave of heat rushes up my neck. Obligations? Is that why Jude asked me—not because he wanted to, but because Isabel was pressuring him with obligations?

"After everything she's done to bring the event here," Rafe continues, "her one and only son can't very well show up stag."

"I'm not her son."

He holds up his hands in mock apology. "*Step*son, mea culpa. Anyway, with the Founders' Descent being reinstated, the FHPS is pressuring her to make an announcement, so I was just checking in." His attention slides to me, the girl with the face on fire, and his eyes brighten with an understanding that looks every bit as contrived as his apology. "Ah, so you *have* secured a date. What a perfect picture the two of you will make. The Vandenberg heir with a local girl on his arm. It's almost like ... history repeating itself."

He shoots us a wink. Then he strolls to the staircase and leaves.

By now, the fire in my cheeks has spread to my ears. Maybe even my forehead. "What's the Founders' Descent?"

Jude rubs his jaw. "It's an old tradition. Founding family members of a certain age are formally introduced, along with their dates. Then they open the ball with a dance. I should have mentioned it last night."

"What kind of dance?"

"An English country dance. Apparently, it's a Foggy Hollow original. The steps aren't complicated, but there will be a couple rehearsals to get them down. If you aren't comfortable, I understand."

I'd be more comfortable if he'd look me in the eye. As it stands, he's making a concerted effort to look anywhere but, leaving me to assume *he's* the one who isn't comfortable.

"Do you regret inviting me?" I ask.

This does the trick.

His attention snaps to mine.

"Because if you do, I'd rather just go with Twig."

"Of course I don't," he says.

"Okay, then," I reply. "Let's go see what Rafe was up to."

Inside Jude's room, nothing strikes me as out of place. But something must strike him, because he crosses to his desk in a few long strides and rummages through a stack of journals.

"Two are missing," he says, moving the journals aside. "So is a photograph I found of my great grandmother wearing the ruby necklace."

Jude shuffles through more papers. "And the sketch of the locket." He strides toward his wardrobe and yanks it open, revealing a row of neatly hung jackets and pressed shirts. He reaches past them, and with a relieved exhale, removes *Ezra's Obsession* with care.

Seeing it again—seeing *me* again—is every bit as jarring as the first time.

"I wish we knew what he was up to," Jude says.

"Me, too."

Whatever it is involves the ruby necklace, and those gemstones. And now, the locket. Because why else would he take the drawing?

My attention returns to the portrait. "I think we should move it."

"Where?"

"My bedroom. It'll be safer there than here."

"And if your dad sees it?"

"I'm not going to hang it on my wall, and he isn't a snoop." I pull at my sleeves. "You said there was something you wanted to show me?"

Jude grabs one of the journals. He opens it, flips to the middle, and shows me what he sees—a gap, like several pages have been removed.

Outside, a car door slams shut.

We move to Jude's window.

Down below, the family car idles in the circular drive. Rafe hands a suitcase to the chauffeur, then slides into the back seat.

Jude and I look at one another.

A few moments later, we find Isabel in the conservatory, thumbing through mail with a glass of something far too strong for the morning.

"Is Rafe leaving?" Jude asks.

"For a stint," she says, barely looking up. "Family matters to attend to."

I think of his father, Thomas.

Then Frank and Rueben.

Are they still alive?

"Where is his family?" Jude asks.

Isabel gives her hand a vague wave, like it doesn't concern her. Like it shouldn't concern us, either. "Somewhere in England."

25
A HIDDEN STASH

My mouth splits wide with a yawn as I plop my bag on top of my writing desk. I've worked the evening shift at Evermore every day this week. A favor to Maggie, who was struck by the same hellish bug that visited me a month ago. Walt took care of her while I took care of Evermore, and finally after school today, she returned with a vengeance and told me to take the weekend off.

I didn't protest.

The week has wrung me dry.

Funny how I can go a whole month of school without any homework at all, then *bam*! Tests, papers, projects, oh my. On Tuesday, I had a quiz in Probability & Statistics. On Wednesday, I had to convince my peers that paranormal investigations deserve scientific legitimacy in a five minute persuasive speech. Yesterday, I had a test in chemistry I'm pretty sure I bombed. And tonight, before the clock strikes twelve, I have to submit an essay exploring themes in *The Scarlet Letter*.

Not to mention, float building for the parade has officially begun. After Maggie dismissed me from my shift at Evermore, Harper and I spent two hours spray painting cardboard feathers for the Phoenix Float, and now I fear my palms might be permanently stained red.

Exhaustion drags at my eyelids as I remove my Chromebook and settle into my seat, slightly jealous of Twig and Naomi, who finished all their schoolwork early and are currently in Pittsburgh having the experience of a lifetime.

I shoot Twig a text.

> How was day 2? Are you in heaven? Leaving me for CMU forever? OMG Twig, r u going to change ur life's ambition from ghosts to robots!?

Yesterday morning, the student body lined the main hallway to cheer on the robotics team as they left for this most prestigious honor. The memory of Naomi's game face and Twig's smile makes me smile now. Those guys made their exit looking like the Ghostbusters on a mission.

With a roll of my shoulders, I force myself to focus. I cannot bomb this essay, too. But the Vandenberg manor might as well be the sun, pulling my attention like gravity. All the windows are dark. Everybody is gone. Jude is with Isabel at a fundraising event with the snooty members of the FHPS. Tulane was leaving as I was arriving. And Rafe's been MIA all week.

Somewhere in England according to Isabel.

I open the top middle drawer of the writing desk and remove three gemstones from inside. Rafe discarded them like they were counterfeit. But they aren't. Jude had them appraised. Together, they're worth more than Dad's Bronco. I'm keeping them here, along with the portrait, in case Rafe decides he wants them back. Whenever he comes back. We don't know when that might be. And Lainey Sikes has become a burr in Jude's side.

Sometimes I wonder if I have, too.

This past week hasn't gone at all as I hoped or expected it

might. I thought his invitation to the ball would be a turning point in our relationship. Instead, he's erected an invisible wall between us and I have no idea how to knock it down.

On Monday, Dad drove me to school. Jude didn't show up until lunch, and for a second, I thought maybe he had norovirus, as well. He was pale, with shadows under his eyes. He insisted he felt fine; he just didn't sleep well. He avoided eye contact when he said it, a pattern that would continue for the remainder of the week. A pattern that would have led me to confront Rafe if he were here. Was he following through with his threat at the quarry? Was he tormenting Jude in secret?

Jude has certainly looked tormented.

But of course, this could have nothing to do with Rafe, because Rafe is gone.

I give my head a rattle and flex my fingers over the keyboard of my Chromebook. "Focus, Selah. Focus."

Themes of *The Scarlet Letter*.

Guilt. Hypocrisy.

I'm overcome by another yawn. I cover it with my fist and set my elbow on the desk.

Isolation. The nature of evil.

I rest my chin in my hand, eyelids drooping.

Sin ... and judgement.

The sound of laughter echoes down the hallway. I chase after it, the tail end of a night gown whipping around the corner and out of sight.

"Seeeelaaaah."

The whisper floats through the dim light of the corridor. The voice is achingly familiar.

I lift my foot to take a step when the voice speaks in my ear, "Come find me."

My chin slides off my hand.

My head jerks up.

My eyes fly open.

The cursor blinks on the screen.

And light flashes in the periphery of my vision.

It comes from the manor.

A window is illuminated on the second floor.

Only nobody's home.

At least, nobody's supposed to be home.

I lean closer, trying to place its location when a figure steps into the frame. Slowly, the shadow turns and stares.

I duck, heart pounding in my ears.

When I'm brave enough to look again, the window is dark. Like I imagined the whole thing.

The next morning, I knock on Jude's front door. Tulane answers. He insists Master Jude is still sleeping, but halfway through the excuse, Master Jude descends one of the staircases. To Tulane's credit, Jude is still dressed in sleep wear—gray henley, flannel pajama pants, a matching robe, and old money slippers.

Bowing, Tulane excuses himself, leaving us alone in the giant foyer. Me, just outside the doors. Jude, still on the stairs.

"Is Rafe back?" I ask.

He runs his hand over the back of his hair, which is tousled from sleep. "Not that I know of."

"You went to the fundraiser last night?"

"Yes," he says, drawing out the word, the tail of it lilting upward so it sounds more like a question than a statement.

"And Isabel?"

"She's the one who insisted on dragging me along." Jude tilts his head. The shadows beneath his eyes are worse than they've been all week. "Why are you asking?"

"Someone was here while you were gone. A light came on

in one of the windows, and it wasn't Tulane. I saw him leaving in his car when I was pulling in."

Jude's eyes narrow.

"Were there workers here? A cleaning crew, maybe?"

"No," he says.

"Are you sure?" They'd had their fair share as of late. A revolving door of cleaners and repairmen, getting the manor in tiptop shape for the ball. The one I'm supposed to attend with Jude, who—despite what he said—very likely regrets inviting me.

I'm tired of feeling angsty about it.

With a roll of my eyes, I invite myself in. I sweep past him, up the stairs, through the upper hall, into the west wing corridor, which is lined with portraits. Vandenbergs of the past. I don't stop until I'm standing in the doorway of a large, empty bedroom.

"What are you doing?" Jude asks, stopping beside me.

I creep inside, floorboards creaking underfoot, and come to a stop in the same spot the shadowed figure stood. I can see my bedroom window perfectly. With my light on, a person standing here would very much be able to see me sitting there, in the window seat.

I turn to Jude. "Someone was in here last night."

"Are you sure?"

"I'm positive."

He rubs his jaw, looking slightly uncomfortable.

"What is it?" I ask.

"Nothing, it's just ... this was Simon's bedroom."

Goosebumps crawl across my skin.

Simon's bedroom.

The moment feels as poignant as the time I first stood in the dining hall. I'm Oda Mae Brown all over again, summoning Simon's ghost. I take a step and the floor creaks differently.

Enough to make me stop, back up, and step again. The sound is decidedly altered.

Crouching down, I give the floorboard a rap with my knuckles. It sounds solid. I move to the next. It sounds solid, too. Then another, the one closest to my foot, and it doesn't sound solid at all. It sounds hollow. I knock again to make sure, and yes, it's definitely hollow.

With the tip of my fingers, I reach between the crack and pry the floorboard up. It lifts easily, like it's been waiting all this time, begging to be opened.

And underneath ...

"*Great Scott*," I whisper, reaching inside the long, narrow compartment as Jude joins me.

We've uncovered a hidden stash.

The first item is a large Bible, one that looks too old to belong to Simon Vandenberg. I set it aside and pull out two items underneath—a pack of cigarettes in a black and red box that smell of clove and a half-empty bottle of Hennessy. "Looks like Lily wasn't the only one with a rebellious streak."

"A sixteen-year-old who drank cognac and smoked Djarums?" Jude quirks an eyebrow. "He was definitely going for a certain aesthetic."

I remove a stack of CDs. Smashing Pumpkins. Nine Inch Nails. Radiohead! I flip through them with increasing enthusiasm.

"Don't you have a shirt like that?" Jude asks, pointing to the Smashing Pumpkins CD.

"Siamese Dream," I reply. "It's only the most powerful listening experience of all time."

It also happens to be my mother's favorite. These bands are from her era. Which is probably why I got into them, too.

My attention returns to the hiding spot, where two more items are hidden, and I experience a jolt of excitement. Because one is a disposable camera. With undeveloped film. Pictures Simon would have taken.

The question is, why would he hide them?

The cigarettes and the liquor bottle make sense. The CDs, too, if his parents were against alternative rock. But a camera? What would compel him to hide a camera? There must be something about the pictures he didn't want anyone to see. And suddenly, my thoughts are racing. My blood, humming.

"We could get this developed," I say.

It could be evidence.

Newly uncovered evidence.

Jude reaches inside the narrow compartment and removes the last item—a small, hardcover book made of burgundy leather with scuffed corners, held shut by a brass clasp. He opens it. Someone wrote with black ink on the inside cover in handwriting so compact it's intense. There's a quote and postscript.

"I desire the things that will destroy me in the end," I read. "Sylvia Plath."

And underneath:

Property of Simon Vandenberg.

We just found his private journal.

26

THE RIFT

January 3, 1995

I couldn't stay in the house yesterday. Lily and Father were at it again, fighting like always. I wasn't sure where to go. The diner and the cafe downtown are always so crowded. I decided to slip into the library.

There was a girl there I've never seen before, tucked in the back corner with her head buried in The Great Gatsby. An assignment from her school, most likely. And yet, she was reading that book like she meant it, like she might fall head first into the pages. I wanted to say something. I wanted to introduce myself. But I left like a coward.

Today, I went back and there she was

again. Same corner, same book. Still, I said nothing.

January 7, 1995

I did it. I introduced myself, and she was better than my wildest imagination. A true original. She saw my book, The Picture of Dorian Gray, and teased me for it. Then she said, "It sure took you long enough to introduce yourself."

For once, I didn't trip over my words. I looked at her book and I asked if I should call her Daisy. I kid you not, her whole face lit up. She stuck out her hand and she said, "Hi Dorian, I'm Daisy Buchanan. It's lovely to meet you." I think I might have met the girl of my dreams.

I look up from Simon's journal, lost for a moment. Stuck on something but unable to pinpoint it. Like a strand of hair tickling the back of my arm, only it's so thin I can't find it.

Dorian Gray.

Daisy Buchanan.

DG.

DB.

"The initials!" I exclaim, excitement coursing through my veins. "I found a set of initials, carved into an old carriage in the stables. Inside a heart. DG + DB."

Dorian Gray.

Daisy Buchanan.

From *The Great Gatsby*.

"They must have belonged to Simon, and this girl." With my mind abuzz, I flip the page and keep reading. Entry after entry, she fills the page. Entry after entry, he is utterly infatuated. And intense. Exactly what you'd expect from a boy drinking cognac, smoking Djarums, and reading *Dorian Gray*— a book about a doppelgänger and a cursed portrait, a connection that isn't lost on me or Jude. I read quickly, ferociously, unwilling to skip or slow down. Because in three months, then two, then one ... Simon Vandenberg will disappear.

In an entry marked March 12, I come upon a phrase written in all caps.

"*The air tore open*," I read aloud, my breath catching in my throat. "It's the only way to explain it. A slit of a doorway, floating in space. It opened right there in the hedge maze. It's the only thing that could have distracted me from her beauty. Daisy took my hand and we stepped through. We were there in the maze. And yet, it wasn't the maze. It was something more than the maze. I don't have words to explain. Only to say that we ran into Lily. She was crying. Daisy tried to comfort her, but she couldn't see us. Nor could she hear us. Not even when I yelled her name. It was the strangest thing I've ever experienced. Somehow, we found our way back out again. I'm so glad Daisy was with me. If she hadn't been, I would think myself crazy."

I look up, eyes wide. "The trapped teens!"

Jude has no idea what I'm talking about.

So I tell him the story.

Season two, episode two on *Accounts of the Uncanny*. In 1998, a pair of teens trespassed onto the Vandenberg property. This was before Tulane moved back into the home. And they went missing for two whole days. When they finally showed up, they told police they'd been there the whole time, but nobody could see them and everything was strange looking. "The girl refused to do an interview with us, but the guy agreed. He chalked it up to being high. But what if it had nothing to do with drugs? What if they went through this same doorway?"

"Oh my gosh." I bring my hand to my mouth. "What if this is it? What if this is what happened? This doorway opened, the whole family went inside, and they got trapped. Holy crap, Jude, what if they're still in there?"

I don't give him time to answer. I return to the pages, where Simon's handwriting becomes more compact, more frenzied. His words bristle with fear, longing, and confusion as the doorway appears again.

He and Daisy argued before it happened—angry words, slammed doors. But then, suddenly, they were kissing. Like they knew the end was near. Like they were trying to hold on to something already slipping away. That's when it opened. They went inside and it was a frightening place. An evil place. With shadows and monsters and everything off kilter.

He hates it, but Daisy has grown obsessed with the doorway. With this other world.

Then I reach it.

The final entry.

Written one day before they vanished.

April 12, 1995

We found it again. The doorway. Daisy calls it The Rift. She says she can feel it when it's near. This time, we were playing pool in the billiard room, trying to escape the tension. The house has been seething with it lately. Low-level. Constant. Like a storm brewing just out of sight. But there was no escape to be found.

And I started to wonder if the tension wasn't in the house at all ... but in me.

That's when the air above the table began to shimmer. Daisy beckoned me to come with her. I didn't want to, but I couldn't let her go in by herself. So in we went. This time, we weren't alone. Something was following us. A dark entity lurking in the shadows. Then we heard my parents arguing in their bedroom. I thought it was about Lily. But it was about me. And Daisy. They don't like her. They said awful things about her. Daisy heard all of it.

I hate them for what they said. I hate them entirely.

I make a beeline to the last known place the rift was open—the billiard room. A masculine retreat with the lingering scent of old cigars. I search every nook and cranny like a woman on a mission. I don't even know what I'm searching for. A secret button? A lever to pull? By Simon's account, this rift just magically appeared at random. But still, I search. And when I find nothing, I move into the dining hall.

Jude silently follows.

"I saw someone in the window in Simon's room, which brought me to Simon's room." The goosebumps on my arms might very well be a permanent fixture, growing in quantity and size. "It was almost like the figure was leading me to that loose floorboard. It couldn't have been Simon, could it? If he's stuck inside the rift, I don't think I'd have been able to see him."

I move to the sideboard and start opening drawers.

The way Simon described it, the doorway leads to another dimension. Superimposed over ours. And the last time they ventured inside, a dark entity was with them.

I think about the town of Foggy Hollow, riddled with strange phenomena. The Woman of the Woods. The Night Beast. The Flash of 1757. The Fire of 1822—an eruption of unexplainable flame that devoured a whole town. What if this rift is the reason? If Simon and Daisy could go in, what would stop forces on the other side from coming out?

My goosebumps quadruple.

I open more drawers, searching like my life depends on it. A full believer with zero doubt. Zero skepticism. Fully primed for something just like this.

Jude, not so much.

"He was high," he finally says. "They both were."

I turn to face him.

He stands in the entryway, still holding onto the Bible like he forgot to put it down. "Simon Vandenberg had to have been on drugs. Just like the trapped teens in your podcast."

But I'm not listening to his objection.

I'm too distracted by the behemoth book in his hand.

"Why would Simon hide that under his floorboard?"

Jude looks down as though only now realizing what he's holding. A Bible, which isn't something a teenager would typically hide. Not like cigarettes and alcohol, anyway. Slowly, Jude opens the cover and his eyes widen.

I can see why from my spot next to the sideboard.

Two spaces have been hollowed out where the pages should be. I come closer to make out their shape. One is circular. The other, a narrow, oblong cavity with a rounded, clover-like shape at one end, a small rectangle at the other.

Jude traces the shape. "It looks like it could fit one of those old-fashioned skeleton keys."

We exchange a look, and I can tell the first thought that

pops into my head pops into his. The locked tome from Evermore Books. But if this carved-out cavity did hold a key, it seems like it would be too big for that lock. Jude runs his thumb around the circular cavity. The pages are carved in concentric circles like a curved object fit inside. Something with a small notch at the top.

"The compass from Enoch's trunk," he says.

This time I follow him—not to the third floor, but to his bedroom. I watch as he opens the drawer of his bedside table and removes the gold pocket compass.

It fits perfectly inside the Bible.

27

TIME OF DEATH

Jude sits at his desk, searching on his MacBook for a photo lab that can develop thirty-year-old film. Behind him, I pace in the gloomy sunlight spilling through his arched windows.

The only photo lab in Foggy Hollow is at CVS, and they stopped developing film on site years ago. We'd have to mail the camera to a central lab with a turnaround time of seven to ten days. I can't wait seven to ten days. I'm dying to know what's on these pictures *right now*.

My phone dings.

> Hey … r u almost here with the glitter bins?

My stomach drops.

The text is from Harper, who's at the fairgrounds. I'm supposed to be there, too. With the glitter bins. I promised Mrs. Calloway I'd grab them from the high school. Instead, I'm here—wrapped up in something from which I can't possibly disentangle. I shoot her a quick apologetic reply as Jude leans back in his chair.

"The closest one's in Greensboro," he says.

"North Carolina?"

"It would be a four-hour drive one way." He taps his desk. "If we left now, we'd get there by two. One hour to develop the photos. Home by seven. It's not awful."

I want to say yes.

More than I've ever wanted to say yes before.

But I have a prior commitment.

"I can't be gone all day. I promised Mrs. Calloway I'd help with the floats."

Jude looks disappointed.

He wants the film developed, too. But for a different reason. I think it might show the rift, maybe even a few shots of Daisy Buchanan. If we can identify her, maybe we can find her. And possibly, interview her. Jude halfway agrees. He thinks Daisy's on the film, too. Only instead of traveling through a rift, he suspects she'll be getting high with Simon.

"It's weird that she was never mentioned in the investigation," I say, more to myself than Jude. "Two of Lily's friends were interrogated. You'd think they'd do the same with one of Simon's. But the report made it sound like he didn't have any friends at all."

"Maybe Daisy Buchanan wasn't any more real than this rift," Jude says.

"You think she could have been a figment of his imagination?"

He looks at me ruefully, for he has unwittingly made a connection from one mystery to the other. The portrait and the cold case. Both involve a mysterious girl nobody seemed to know.

Jude picks up the camera. "Maybe we ought to take this to the police."

"Why would we do that?" I ask.

"It's evidence, isn't it? Undeveloped film hiding in one of the victim's bedrooms, along with a journal written at the time the family disappeared."

He's right, of course.

It is evidence.

But I give my head an adamant shake.

If we submit this to the police, we'll never see it again. They'll read Simon's journal, draw the same conclusion as Jude, and toss it into an evidence locker where it will languish in perpetuity. They might develop the pictures, but they certainly won't share them with us.

I *need* to see these pictures.

Not in seven to ten days, either.

I resume pacing—thinking, thinking, thinking when a thought strikes. "The photography guy!"

I snap my fingers a few times, trying to drum up his name. "Mr. Evensby, maybe? He taught a photography workshop last winter at our school."

Organized by Mrs. Calloway.

I had to work, but Twig went.

I shoot him a text, then bite my thumb nail and keep pacing.

A moment later, Twig replies.

> Len Ebely?

I text him back.

> YES! That's him. Do you think he'd have a way to develop film from a disposable camera?

I stare at the scrolling ellipse.

> I'm 87% sure he has a dark room in his basement. What are you doing with a disposable camera?

Will fill you in later! Enjoy the symposium! Kick
butt tomorrow!

I pocket my phone. "Run a search for *Len Ebely, Foggy
Hollow*."

Jude types the phrase into his laptop and hits return.

Two results load at the top.

An Etsy shop, and a website.

Jude clicks on the website.

It's minimalistic with a simple header and a small portfolio, along with a short bio and contact information that includes an email address and a phone number.

Even though it's a Saturday morning, I give him a call.

He answers after the second ring.

"This is Len."

"Hi, uh, Len? My name is Selah Whitlock. I'm a junior at Foggy Hollow High. My good friend, Spencer Calloway, took your photography workshop last winter. I wanted to go, but I couldn't make it because of a previous obligation."

Jude leans back in his chair, looking slightly amused by my preamble.

"I remember Spencer," Len says. "What can I do for you?"

"I was wondering ... well, I found this disposable camera, and I'd really love to have the film developed. But there's no photo lab here in Foggy Hollow that develops film, and the nearest place is in Greensboro which is a four hour drive. I was wondering if you had a way to do it?"

"A disposable, huh? How old?"

"The mid 1990s." 1995, to be exact. But I'm wary of giving him the year. To someone born and raised in Foggy Hollow, it would stick out like a sore thumb. According to Len's bio, he's lived his whole life in this town.

"I'm not sure how well the pictures will turn out, but I could give it a try. Do you want to drop it off?"

Twenty minutes later, Jude is parking along Maple Grove Road. Len Ebely's small, weathered home hides behind a magnificent tree with leaves like fire. Past the tree, we find a sagging front porch and a single car garage, currently open with no car. Instead, Len stands in front of a worktable wielding a welder as sparks fly, the electric sizzle of scorched steel drowning out the sound of leaves crunching underfoot as we approach.

As soon as Len spots us, he stops. The torch extinguishes. He lifts his protective mask onto the top of his head and there he is, a middle-aged white man with wheat-blonde hair and a matching scraggly beard.

"You came fast," he says, pulling off his work gloves.

After brief introductions, Jude hands him the camera.

Len turns it over in his hand. "These were popular when I was a kid."

"Do you think the film will develop correctly?" I ask.

"It looks in decent condition. The pictures might turn out foggy, but I guess we won't know until we try."

I wipe my palms on the thighs of my jeans. What if the photos do turn out, and Len comes upon an incriminating picture? What if he goes to the police and Jude and I get arrested for obstruction of justice? What if we're dragging poor Len Ebely into a crime scene? The questions keep spiraling, but I hold my tongue. Why open a can of worms if it doesn't need to be opened? These could very well be benign photographs. But then, why hide the camera?

"Any idea when they'll be done?" Jude asks.

"I've got some projects to finish up here, but I should be able to get around to them tonight or tomorrow. I'll give you a call when they're ready."

Jude nods, cool as a cucumber, and shakes Len's hand.

I stuff my own inside the pockets of my jeans, positive their clamminess will give us away. I don't exhale until we're back in Jude's car.

"Now we wait," he says, turning his key in the ignition.

"My favorite," I reply with a heavy dose of sarcasm.

My phone vibrates.

The message is from Mrs. Calloway.

I text her back, letting her know I'm on my way.

Then I look at Jude, an idea dawning. One that might make the wait a little less painful. "On a scale of one to ten, how good are you with glitter?"

The sharp wail of a newborn cuts through the room. A nurse places a slick and wriggling child on the mother's chest. She cries, too. Only hers is a much different sound as the nurse gently cleans the baby's skin and covers him with a warm blanket.

The father is there, too. Right by the woman's side, sliding a small cap over a crown of dark, downy hair as the baby's cries subside into adorable grunts and whimpers. Huddled together, beholding their child with wonder and awe, the man's eyes fill with tears. He kisses the mother's sweaty brow.

"I love you," he says, like he's never said it before. She looks up at him like she's never heard it before, her eyes dewy, too. They come together in a kiss as the baby coos between them.

All is right and happy and perfect.

Until it isn't.

Without any warning at all, the woman goes limp.

Alarmed, the man taps her cheek. "Rebecca? Rebecca, wake up."

Her head lolls.

The man shouts for help.

The nurse rushes back into the room, noticing what the man has not. Blood. So much, it soaks the pad and the bedding beneath her. She hurries to the emergency call button and says, "Rapid Response in Labor and Delivery, Room 204. Heavy post-partum bleeding."

The man continues to call for his wife, like she simply needs to wake up.

Wake up, Rebecca. Wake up.

The nurse scoops up the baby and places him inside a plastic basinet as a medical team rushes inside with a crash cart.

The man begins to panic.

"Sir, we need space to help her," another nurse says. "You will need to wait outside."

"But my wife, what's happening to my wife?"

He's ushered out of the room without an answer.

The baby is, too.

The door swings closed but it doesn't shut out the sound. Horrible, urgent sound. A tornado of noise and voices, shouts and commands, and then, the worst sound of all.

A flat, monotone beep.

No more movement.

No more commands.

Just a hollow voice that says, "Time of death, 4:24 p.m."

The baby lay alone in the basinet, cooing obliviously. Unaware of the man who has collapsed onto his knees. Somehow, I'm there in the hallway, looking at the child, swaddled in a blanket, wearing that tiny cap—not hospital issued, but hand knit with love and care. Stitched with a name.

Jude.

I lurch awake with a loud gasp.

It's dark.

The middle of the night.

I'm not in the hospital.

I'm in my bed.

The red digits of my bedside clock cast an eerie glow upon my journal, and my stomach knots with dread.

Somehow, I know.

That dream wasn't just a dream.

28

THE LAST PHOTOGRAPH

When Len Ebely calls after church, he doesn't sound alarmed or suspicious. He doesn't ask any worrying questions. He doesn't demand to know who the camera belonged to. He just says the photos are done and we can come get them anytime.

I stare out my kitchen window waiting for Jude to pick me up—memories from yesterday's float building and last night's dream, along with the prospect of seeing these photographs, coalescing into a jumble of nerves. By the time Jude pulls to a stop outside, it takes every ounce of restraint to walk at a normal pace.

I slide into the passenger seat and quickly pull the belt across my lap—a safety precaution, sure. But also a necessity. Like if I don't anchor myself in place, I might float off the seat. Not until I'm properly buckled do I dare a look at Jude.

His gaze lifts to my hair.

"What?" I say, flattening my palm over the crown of my head, where every so often, a cowlick misbehaves.

"It's nothing. You just have, well ..." He reaches across the console, and with a touch so light I can barely feel it, he teases something free.

A speck of glitter twinkles on the tip of his finger.

We share a smile.

"I think my hair might sparkle for eternity," I say, picturing Jude with his sleeves rolled up, a hammer in hand. He didn't have to help me pick up the glitter bins. He didn't have to stay and build floats, either.

But he did.

And when a glitter fight erupted, he didn't stand on the sidelines, either. Brooding Jude Vandenberg joined the fray, and somehow, his arm ended up around my waist, both of us laughing at the absurd amount of glitter in my hair.

My smile widens at the memory.

Jude's gaze dips to my lips.

And the playful vibe melts into molten lava. The heat is too hot to take. Breaking eye contact, I tuck a strand of hair behind my ear and give my throat a nervous clear. Effectively dousing the moment in cold water.

Jude shifts his car into drive.

I curse my cowardice.

And my own morbid curiosity.

Because I know what I'm about to ask. I can feel the question rising within me. No amount of self-control will tamp it down.

I fidget with the strap of my seatbelt. "Hey, Jude?"

He glances at me as we ease to a stop in front of the gate.

"What happened to your parents?"

For a moment, he looks stricken.

And I want to take it back, strike it from the record—this question that badgered me throughout the entirety of church.

But I can't rewind time.

The question has been asked.

The gate groans opens, and I think he's going to plead the fifth. But then he turns onto the street and says, "My dad died of pancreatic cancer when I was ten, shortly after he married Isabel. He didn't tell me until after the wedding, but I think he knew before. Sometimes I think I'm the reason he married her. So I wouldn't be alone." He scoffs at the irony. As soon as his father died, Isabel shipped him off to boarding school, absolutely alone.

"And your mom?" I ask.

"She died when I was born."

I may have braced myself for the answer, but it still comes like a wallop—an aggressive hit that knocks the world off kilter.

Jude doesn't notice.

His grip is tight on the wheel, his attention fixed steadfastly on the road. "She died in labor. Or I guess, shortly after labor."

He looks at me, then, and whatever he sees must be alarming. His foot comes off the gas pedal. "Are you all right?"

I don't answer.

I can't answer.

My breath is stuck.

"Selah?" The car slows to a near stop.

I tell him I'm fine. Everything's fine. He can keep driving. Then I set my trembling hands on top of my knees and take a shaky breath. "I'm sorry," I say. "It's just ... that's really sad."

It's true.

But it's not the full truth.

I can't bring myself to tell him that.

It's one thing to dream about long-ago tragedies in his family's past. It's quite another to dream about him and his parents.

"Yeah, well. I was just a baby, so ... " He lifts his shoulder, like not having memories of his mother means he's not allowed to grieve his mother.

My breath gets stuck all over again.

He drives on, and I slide my hands beneath my knees, like burying them might bury the memory. Of that tiny little cap. Of the baby all alone in the plastic basinet. Of the woman, bleeding out on the delivery table, and the man, falling to his knees in the hallway of a hospital.

I can't stop picturing it.

It plays on a loop in my mind until we reach Len's house.

This time, his garage is closed. So we stand on the sagging porch and ring his doorbell.

Len answers holding a manilla folder with the words *35mm, Oct 12, 28 exposures* written on the front in neat script. "I'm sorry to say, only a few turned out decent. Most were either blank or warped. It could be light damage, or age." With a shrug, he hands me the folder. "I guess that's what old film will get you."

"What do we owe you?" Jude asks, reaching for the wallet in his back pocket.

Len waves him off. "Don't worry about it. It didn't take long, and like I said, there's not much there."

We thank him and return to Jude's car.

He drives us to a nearby park and cuts the engine.

I open the folder in my lap.

There's a tissue-thin sheet between each photograph. The first several are blank. The ones after, warped. But are they warped because the film went bad? Or are they warped because they were taken in a different dimension?

Jude and I lean over his console, studying each one with care.

The light bends strangely. Straight lines appear fragmented. The perspective is off, and each one has a hazy, unnatural glow. Anytime we come to a photograph of a person, the face is blurred, like the subject moved too fast to catch. One is entirely black, except for a pair of off-centered glowing red pinpricks that give me the heebie-jeebies.

I shuffle past it, quicker than the others, to the first photograph that's come through.

Simon Vandenberg, smiling as he reaches for the camera,

like Daisy had taken it without his permission and he was objecting, but flirtatiously. I stare at this boy, frozen in time, shortly before he would vanish, and I wonder if Len Ebely knew who this was when it came through in his dark room. There's a second picture of Simon from a different angle, his attention cast downward.

Then I shuffle to the final image and a gasp tumbles from my lips.

Simon must have reclaimed the camera and turned it on Daisy. He snapped a picture of this girl he met in a library and traveled with through a supernatural doorway. This girl he so obviously loved. The mysterious Daisy Buchanan.

Only she's not a mystery any more.

I may not have seen her face in years, but I would recognize it anywhere for its strong resemblance to my own.

Daisy Buchanan was my mother.

I sit on Dad's recliner waiting for him to come home, my mind unable to process. There's the picture in my hand and everything it means on one side, and all that I thought to be true on the other.

Like my nightmare when I was a little kid. A trauma dream. The monster wasn't real. According to Dr. Penny, it was a visual representation of my mother's addiction. I tried to save her from it, but I wasn't strong enough. Addiction won. But what if it didn't? What if that dream I had so long ago was every bit as real as the dream I had about Jude's mother?

A gust of wind pushes against the window panes. I haven't bothered with the lights, and the day is cloudy. So when Dad steps inside, it takes him a minute to notice I'm here, sitting in the dark.

"Hey," he says. "What are you doing over there?"

I don't move.

Dad grabs a soda from the fridge and cracks it open. "Everything okay, kiddo?"

"Mom lived here," I say.

"What's that?"

"She lived here, in Foggy Hollow."

Dad cocks his head.

"And you didn't tell me," I say.

"Selah, sweetheart, what are you talking about?"

I stand from the chair on shaky legs and hold out the photograph. "She lived here, and you lied about it."

He said we needed a fresh start.

But this was never about a fresh start.

He was chasing her ghost. While getting me therapy.

"Selah, I don't understand what you're ..." But before he can finish, his attention snags on the picture, and his words slide into oblivion. He takes the photo from my hand. "Where did you get this?"

"Simon's bedroom."

"Who's Simon?"

The question cracks through the numb shell around my brain, and out from the fissure leaks a tremble of indignation. I can't believe he lied to me.

"Vandenberg." I jerk my hand toward the manor. "This whole time I've been obsessed with the cold case and you didn't think I'd want to know Mom was friends with him? That they were—"

More than friends?

Simon certainly thought of her as more than a friend.

But Dad just stands there, blinking at the photo. "You got this from Simon's bedroom?"

"From a disposable camera. Jude and I found it under a loose floorboard."

"This picture was on that film?"

"Yes."

He sets his hand on top of his head, his wedding ring forever in place.

I narrow my eyes at it. "Did we move here because of her?"

"Selah, we moved *away* because of her."

My father isn't a good actor. He doesn't lie, which is part of the reason this came as such a shock. How could he keep this from me? But now it seems he hasn't. Now, I think he's just finding out for himself.

He shakes his head. "Are you sure this isn't some sort of mix-up?"

"It's not a mix-up," I say. "He wrote about her in his journal. They hung out together before he vanished."

Dad sinks onto the sofa, truly dumbstruck.

"What are the chances?" he finally asks.

It's a rhetorical question.

And yet, if Twig were here, he'd probably know. I'm sure they're smaller than point zero eight. Still, Dad grapples for logic. For an explanation. Because my father is a logical guy who thinks most things can be explained. After all, I never had a prophetic dream when I was little. That was a trauma dream. Induced by my drug-addicted, here-again-gone-again, deeply troubled mother. Soon enough, Dad will come to terms with this new tidbit of information, and he'll chalk it up to wild coincidence.

But not me.

Never me.

My mother lived here.

She went through some doorway between dimensions. She stepped into something supernatural.

I think about the other night.

Before I saw the light turn on in the manor, I dozed off and had a small snip of a dream. I was chasing someone down a hallway. And that someone whispered my name. In a voice that sounded an awful lot like my mother's.

Come find me.

My skin prickles.

What if it didn't just sound like her? What if it *was* her? What if she's been here this whole time—stuck on the other side, trapped with Simon and his family? Maybe this is why I've always felt such a strong connection with Foggy Hollow.

My mother is here.

And she's trying to get out.

29
FRESH DIRT

I run my fingers along the carving.

 DG + DB

Dorian Gray.

Daisy Buchanan.

Simon Vandenberg.

Clara Green.

I press my nose into the sleeve of her denim jacket, like the faded scent might conjure her tangible presence. Is she the reason Simon had that collection of CDs in his cubby hole? Clara Green loved alternative rock, so she introduced the genre to the tortured boy who drank cognac and smoked Djarums. Did they smoke them together? Was she standing here with him when he carved these initials inside this heart?

I think of her disappearing in fading pixels. My desperation as I tried to put her back together again. The spidery tendrils that gathered into a black hole and sucked her inside.

Could it have been the rift?

Simon disappeared in 1995.

My mom disappeared much later.

After she married Dad.

After they had me.

If the monster was real, how did it get to her? And why did it wait so long?

A gust of wind makes the barn doors groan. I leave the carriage uncovered and wander through the woods, hair blown this way and that, numb to the chill until I reach the graveyard.

I wander from tombstone to tombstone, pausing at Isaiah Vandenberg's. He lost everyone he loved in a train crash. And afterward, he was tormented by a cousin named Lucian, who spawned Rueben and tormented Daniel, who spawned Frank and tormented John, who spawned Thomas. Did he torment Simon? Did these bad apples have something to do with the disappearance?

Or was it the rift?

And what did my mother know? What did she see when she was here, at the Vandenberg Estate?

I stop at Ruth Vandenberg's gravestone and run my hand over the top. Was she killed by a wild animal or a monster that slipped through a tear between worlds? I keep wandering, further back in time. To Amos. His wife. His mother. And then

...

My breath catches.

Ezra's grave is different. There's no grass. No moss or leaves. Just raw earth—scattered soil, dark and clumpy. As though someone has dug up his grave.

When I knock on the front door, Jude answers, his hair looking as disheveled as my own, as though he'd spent the day raking his hands through it.

After seeing my teenage mother in a photograph that came from Simon's bedroom, I clammed up. I shut down. I left him in the lurch, and now I'm back and breathless, and he looks relieved, like he thought I'd gone and jumped in the Black-willow River.

"Someone dug up Ezra's grave," I blurt.

"What?"

"His grave," I repeat. "There's fresh dirt where the grass should be."

Before Jude has a chance to reply, Mr. Tulane steps into the foyer dressed in his butler attire. And something in my brain fires, a connection I'm surprised I haven't thought of until now. He was here when my mother was here, and not too long ago, he called me by her name. Not Sara, as Jude assumed. But Clara. My ears weren't playing tricks on me after all.

"You called me Clara," I say to him.

"You look just like her," he replies.

Jude goes very still.

I step around him and show Tulane the photograph that has rocked my world.

He takes it with a fond smile. "Miss Clara and Master Simon were good friends."

"But then ... why wasn't she in any of the police reports?"

Twig and I pored over that investigation. At least, the parts we could get our hands on. There was not a single mention of Clara Green, not even an anonymous female friend of Simon's. Lily's friends made the report. John and Maureen's friends made the reports. Why not my mother?

"I don't think anyone knew of their friendship outside of the family. Master Simon didn't go to the public high school, and Miss Clara was new to town."

"But you knew."

He nods.

"So, why didn't you say something?"

"Because Miss Clara had nothing to do with it. I spoke with her that very evening, in the produce aisle of Kroger. She was a kind young lady, and she made Master Simon very happy. I saw no reason to drag her into the mess when the loss itself was devastating enough. And besides, she left town shortly after."

"Who was she staying with?"

"Samuel and Marlene Abner."

"Do they still live here?"

"Of course. They no longer foster children, but for a time, they were a revolving door for the parentless. I was upset when they sent Miss Clara away. I worried a great deal for her, and did for many years, until she came back to visit."

I blink at him. "Came back?"

"Why, yes. Five years ago, I believe."

"Clara Green came here five years ago?"

Tulane nods.

The air in my lungs goes still. "What did she want?"

"It seemed to me she was looking for closure."

"How long did she stay?"

"It was a brief visit. I'd say no more than an hour."

"Did you see her leave?"

"I walked her to her car."

I gape at him. And then, with a gasping inhale, I turn on my heel and leave. Like doing so might defrost my lungs. Get them going again. I hurry away, grabbing at my neck, trying to breathe. I rush past the fountain, down the cobbled drive, when Jude calls my name. I don't know when the tears began. I only know that when I face him, my cheeks are wet.

"She came to see *him*?"

The question seems to cause him as much pain as it causes me.

I wipe at my face. "Why wouldn't she come to see me?"

"Maybe she didn't know you were here," he offers.

I shake my head. If that's true, then the theory I've been building, the hope I've been harboring—that my mother isn't just here, but has gone to great lengths to draw me here to her —falls to pieces. If she visited Tulane five years ago and left that same day five years ago, then she couldn't have drawn me here at all.

My throat closes up again. "I have to go."

"Selah." Jude takes my arm.

Not roughly, like Rafe.

But gently, with all the tenderness in the world. He places Simon's journal in my hand with the picture of my mother tucked inside. "You should have this."

30

PIECES OF THE SAME PUZZLE

I toss and turn and doze a little. But slumber eludes me. So I stare at the ceiling through the dark, listening to the sounds outside my window. The creak of tree branches. The rustle of leaves. The dull clank of the iron gate as the roof groans over-head. Somewhere further away, a train horn echoes through the hollow—a drawn out, lonely sound.

I can't stop thinking about her, living in this town. Friends with Simon when the Vandenbergs disappeared. Then sent away.

Why?

Why did they send her away, and why did she come back five years ago? And why did she make an effort to see an old man from her past, but none at all to see her daughter or her husband?

Maybe Jude's right. Maybe she had no idea Dad and I lived here. And maybe that should make me feel better somehow.

But it doesn't. Not even a little.

Because in some small, honest, private part of my brain, I've always imagined her keeping track of me. Paying attention to my whereabouts. Following my endeavors. Maybe even listening to my podcast? If she didn't know I was living in Foggy Hollow then she never bothered to look me up, and somehow, that hurts more than any of the other possibilities my imagination has conjured.

I blink at my ceiling.

Maybe she didn't know.

Maybe she did.

Maybe it's better thinking she's dead. Easier to believe she isn't out there at all, than to believe she is, choosing to stay away.

I turn on my side.

Questions and scenarios tumble about like clothes in a dryer. I wish I could shut off my brain, but it refuses to settle.

I turn onto my other side.

The clock reads 5:18 a.m.

With a huff, I sit up in bed and kick off my covers and wave the white flag. Insomnia has won. Fighting it this late in the game feels futile. With my elbows on my knees, I rub my eyes with the heel of my palms. When I look up, my attention settles on the bottom drawer of my writing desk where I keep the memory box and two of her favorite books—one became a bedtime story birthday tradition, and the other brought me and Twig together in fourth grade.

I pad across the creaky floorboards. I pull open the drawer, remove the box and the birthday book, turn on my lamp, and settle back into bed. I open the story about the boy in the wolf suit and flip through the pages, stopping on the one where love sounds like hunger, and the monsters beg Max to stay. She always read this page best, with her arm pulling me in extra tight. And I wonder, was my mother a wild thing? Or was she Max, and the wild thing was me, begging her to stay?

I set the book aside and open the box, beholding the collection within. Faded postcards written in guilt. The letters, too. I take them out, searching for clues in the tear-stained words. Something—*anything*—that might reference Simon Vandenberg or this rift they traveled through. I find nothing but apologies and empty promises.

But there is the front page of a *National Enquirer*, a magazine she could never quite resist. In hindsight, it almost feels like a clue. I read the headline—*Vampire Baby Born in Idaho, Doctors Baffled*—while imagining another. *Family Disappears Through Inter-dimensional Portal, Girlfriend Left Behind*. Did she believe these wild stories? Was she searching for one similar to her own?

I move aside the sour cream container and the empty pill bottle and the Chinese finger trap, my intention set upon the photographs.

But those intentions are thwarted.

I freeze, staring down into the box where rosary beads have tangled with the antique necklace she was always wearing. A skeleton key on a chain. I pick it up and measure the weight of it in my palm—this thin, oblong object with a handle like a clover and a small rectangle on the end that engages with the lock.

I snag my phone and take a picture.

Not thinking of the time, I text it immediately to Jude.

Insomnia must have gotten the best of him, too. Because as soon as the picture goes through, a scrolling ellipse appears on my screen.

***

The house is asleep, wrapped in a hush as I follow Jude through the east-wing corridor lined with looming marble statues. He speaks in a low voice, as if not to disturb them. We're less inclined to run into Isabel in the east wing, he tells me. When she wakes up, she'll head to the dining hall where Tulane will bring her coffee and breakfast. We slip inside a room I've never been in before.

Jude closes the doors behind us.

Moonlight shines through the large recessed window, gleaming off the polished surface of a grand piano. On the opposite side of the room stands a tall, ebony harp with silver inlays. In between is a Persian rug, a settee, a pair of Victorian arm chairs, and a claw-footed coffee table. A gilded mirror hangs above the fireplace, reflecting the soft glow of lamplight near a fainting couch. Dark paneling, damask wallpaper, and medieval tapestries pull everything together, making the room as gothic and elegant as the rest of the home.

Simon's Bible sits on the coffee table. Along with the pocket compass. Next to it, a silver tray with a steel thermos, a bowl of sugar cubes, a mini pitcher of cream, and two porcelain mugs.

"You made coffee?"

"I figured you might need some."

"You figured right," I say, sitting on the settee.

Jude sits, too, and pours me a cup. I say yes to cream and sugar, then take the mug between my palms, glad for its warmth. Once he has his own—no cream, no sugar—I reach inside the pocket of my puffer vest and take out the skeleton key.

I open the Bible and just as we suspected, the key slides into place—a perfect fit.

I try to make sense of the items. My mother had the key, which she must have gotten from Simon. Simon had the Bible, which he hid under his floorboard. And the compass came from Enoch's trunk. Three pieces of the same puzzle, only they don't form a clear image.

"I went to the graveyard," Jude says.

I look up at him.

"You were right. Ezra's grave was disturbed."

His words are alarming.

Unsettling.

Certainly worth discussing.

But my brain can only hold so many disquieting things at once, especially when it's this tired. I take a few sips of coffee. It's smooth and decadent, perhaps the best coffee I've ever had. Outside, birdsong begins—a few isolated chirps as the dark indigo sky gives way to a dusky gray.

I set the mug on the table. "I showed my dad the picture."

"What did he say?"

"He didn't know she lived here."

He looks skeptical.

"I believe him."

His skepticism grows.

It annoys the crap out of me. "And no, I don't think it was a coincidence. Obviously something supernatural is at play here, which isn't a shock. I never believed the Vandenberg cold case was a typical crime. I've never believed this town was a typical town. Now we have proof. Simon and my mother traveled through some sort of portal. Ezra painted a portrait of me. And I'm reliving past events in my sleep."

"They could just be dreams."

I look at him disbelievingly.

"Dreams don't always have to mean something," he insists.

My disbelief expands into incredulity. How can he think my dreams are just dreams? "Jude."

But he's agitated.

Visibly agitated.

A muscle in his jaw tick, tick, ticks away.

I could ask him why, access my curiosity. Instead, I double down. "All last night, I kept thinking, how could my mom have been here before me? But she wasn't here before me. I was here first. In the freaking eighteenth century, somehow a figment of

Ezra Vandenberg's obsession. Then my mom showed up, and Simon just happened to run into her at the library? He and his family vanish. My mom's sent away, only to disappear years later, but first she leaves me this?"

I pick up the key. "She used to wear it all the time. Why would she leave it behind? Now you're here, and I'm here. With that portrait under my bed and a journal full of dreams about your family's past on my nightstand. I'm sorry, Jude, but I think it's much easier to believe something supernatural is at play than to think this is all one insane coincidence after another."

He shoves his hand into his hair and curls it into a fist, his eyes a storm.

"Why are you so angry?" I ask.

"Because I'm having dreams, too."

His heated response leaves me speechless.

I sit there for awhile, blinking at him as a clock ticks in the hallway.

"What kind of dreams?" I finally ask.

"Bad ones." His voice is clipped. "They started after that night at the quarry."

When he asked me to the ball.

He drags his hand down his face. "They're all a little different, but there have been some common themes." His knee begins to bounce. "The portrait always catches on fire, and you always die."

I stare at him, not sure what to say.

When his eyes meet mine, they are haunted and pained. "It's always me. I'm the one who kills you."

Understanding dawns.

The shadows under his eyes. Not sleeping well. It's been these dreams. He hasn't regretted asking me to the ball. He's worried he's going to hurt me. "Jude, those dreams aren't real."

"You just said they mean something. According to you, these are all pieces of the same puzzle. So where do my dreams fit, Selah? You're dreaming of the past, and I'm what—dreaming of the future?"

His knee is really going now—an agitated jackhammer. Without thinking, I place my hand on top of it, as if doing so might still his worries.

His tortured eyes meet mine.

And the air in my lungs goes hot and shaky. "You're not going to hurt me, Jude. You're not—"

Rafe.

But I stop myself before I say it.

"I'm not worried about your dreams. Not even a little."

My words pull at some invisible thread. They unravel his anger, showing it for what it's always been. Fear. Because for all his bluster about logic, he *is* worried about his dreams. More than a little.

His gaze drops to my hand.

"You're not afraid?" he asks, his voice low.

My heart gallops. It pounds in my ears, in my throat, in my knees. I can feel it pulsing in my neck. I swallow. "It's not fear I'm feeling right now."

He sits there, leaning back against the settee, as still as a statue except for his hand, sliding closer to mine.

Our fingers touch.

It's barely a graze, but heat pools deep in my abdomen. His attention dips to my mouth, then lifts again to my eyes. His are dark and fathomless. And I'm drawn like a moth to flame.

I lean closer, closer ...

A chime clangs through the room.

My galloping heart careens.

The clock chimes a second time. A third. A fourth. Each metallic gong echoing through the room, the halls, the home. My body.

Outside, the Midnight Garden is no longer a shadowy blur. It's begun to take shape—wrought iron benches, frost-covered moonflowers, that twisted tree. A chorus of birds chirp as the dusky sky melts into ribbons of peach.

Jude clears his throat and picks up the key, which has slid onto the velvet cushion between us. He peers down at it. "Think this could unlock the book at Evermore?"

It seems too big, but it's the only lock we know to try.

31
RETURN OF THE RAKE

Maggie greets us with a look of utter bewilderment. She's unused to teenagers banging on her front window this early in the morning. She's hours away from opening, and we've just interrupted her favorite part of the day. I know her well enough to know her routine. She arrives around seven. She feeds Poe. She sorts books that have lost their way. She brews herself a cup of lavender tea. Then she heads up to the second floor and drafts letters to long-dead historical figures on the typewriter in her office. It's her way of conversing with the past, she says, to which Walt rolls his eyes.

When she swings the door open, she clutches her planner like someone clutching their pearls. "What in the name of Amos Vandenberg do the two of you want this early in the morning?"

Poe meows in the doorway.

"I'm sorry, Maggie, but we *really* need to check something."

She scowls, and while I'm ninety-five percent certain she would tell any other person to scram, she invites us in with a harrumph.

We don't waste time. We make a beeline for the locked

tome, but the key doesn't fit. It's too big. While I suspected as much, disappointment settles all the same. Judging by the look on Jude's face, he feels it, too.

"Still obsessing over this book, I see," Maggie says. "What do you think's in there, anyway—a summoning charm for that ghost lady you're always chasing?"

Jude lifts the tome. "Can I have this?"

Maggie harrumphs again.

"I gave you that sketch of Molly," he says.

"In exchange for her identity," Maggie replies, pointing her bony finger at him. "Not that tome."

Jude tucks the book under his arm. "Okay, then. Name your price. What'll it take to get this?"

She narrows her eyes.

"A portrait from our collection? There's a giant one of Amos and Ida hanging in our library. It might be hard to get it up those stairs, but I'm sure we could figure something out."

"You're not serious."

"I'm very serious."

She studies him some more in that unblinking way of hers. "You're telling me, in exchange for that book, you'd be willing to part with, say, some of those letters and journals the pair of you have been poring over these last few weeks?"

"Let us make copies first and I'll throw in the seal stamp Amos used on the rebuild plans after the fire."

She leans forward slowly, her eyes locked on his. "You have that stamp?"

"In our study. Top drawer of his original writing desk."

Maggie wets her lips like a cat who's cornered the canary. She doesn't need anymore convincing. The two of them shake hands, and no sooner is the deal struck than Jude starts prying at the lock.

Maggie's delight turns to horror.

She protests as Jude makes his way to the front counter in

search for something that might break the book open. He tries a letter opener, but that doesn't work any better than his hands.

"There's a toolbox in the basement," I say, my blood humming with anticipation. Because one way or another, we're getting inside this book.

A moment later, we're descending the stairs into Maggie's dungeon as she pursues with continued protest. "What in tarnation has come over the pair of you? Destroying a book? You might as well join the censors and pitch it into the flames."

"We want to read it, Maggie. Not destroy it," I say, grabbing a hammer from the tool box. I hand it to Jude, who sets the book on the scarred, wooden table where Twig and I record our podcast. Maggie watches, aghast in the shadows, as he bangs on the steel lock.

Once.

Twice.

The latch finally busts open.

He drops the hammer onto the table and all three of us, even scandalized Maggie, surge forward to see what's hiding inside. I expect answers. I expect clarity. Finally, all the confounding puzzle pieces will come together to form a picture that makes astounding sense. Instead, we find nothing more than a gothic children's tale, complete with macabre illustrations.

Still, I devour it, page after page, written in old English, eager for some sliver of insight. But it's just a fable about two fallen angels—Dante and Seraphina—undone by their own love. Power hungry and jealous, they drag mortals into their affairs in an attempt to wrest the upper hand. The tragic tale ends in Dante's eternal slumber and Seraphina's eternal madness, trapped in a fiery rock that streaks across the night sky every 268 years.

The origin story of Dante's comet.

While it would have been interesting under different

circumstances—a treasure worth sharing on *Accounts of the Uncanny*—right now, it's a giant letdown. There's nothing at all about the symbol. Not one mention of Ezra or his obsession. Not a whiff about a rift between worlds. Nothing to suggest this book has anything to do with the portrait or Molly or me or any of the Vandenbergs at all. All my hope and anticipation crumbles. We're no closer to solving these riddles than we ever were.

"Why are the three of you acting so out of sorts?" Maggie asks. "What mystery are you trying to solve this time?"

Jude cocks his head. "The *three* of us?"

"The two of you, and that cousin of yours. Why is he so suddenly curious about family heirlooms? He showed up yesterday and—"

"Wait," Jude interrupts. "Are you talking about Rafe?"

"Do you have another cousin?"

Jude and I exchange a look.

"He was here yesterday?" I ask Maggie.

"He showed up just before close. I was of half a mind to tell him he should go ask that preservation society he's so fond of, but it turns out, he's a very charming young fellow."

Charming?

Maggie doesn't find people *charming*. And even if she did, surely she'd see right through a guy like Rafe. I must admit, I'm disappointed.

"What did he want?" I ask.

"He had a necklace with him. A giant ruby necklace. He wanted to know if I knew anything about similar necklaces belonging to the Vandenbergs, only instead of a ruby, they would have been made of—"

"Onyx and pearl."

"Why, yes. He also wanted to know if I knew where Molly Ludwig was buried."

Molly Ludwig.

My mind spins.

Rafe is back.

When did he return, and why isn't he making his presence known? Did he disturb Ezra's grave? And now, is he looking to disturb Molly's? What does he want with these gemstones?

"What are the three of you after?" Maggie asks.

Jude and I exchange another look.

If only we knew.

32
LIKE A TATTOO

Samuel and Marlene Abner live in a white clapboard house with green shutters on the outskirts of town. Jude and I step onto their front porch, where wind chimes catch the breeze and two rocking chairs creak like a pair of ghosts having a visit.

The hour is nine. AP Lit started thirty minutes ago, which means soon, or already, Mrs. Calloway will see my unexcused absence and begin to worry. Maybe she'll call my father and he'll worry, too. But I can't help it. There are answers to find. Not in that locked tome, perhaps. But maybe here, in this modest home that housed my mother for several months once upon a time.

Jude knocks as I read the wooden plaque above the door. *As for me and my house, we will serve the Lord – Joshua 24:15.*

The door opens.

An elderly woman appears on the other side. She wears a paisley house dress, her white hair pinned back in soft curls. With cautious warmth, she opens the screen door, which groans in protest, and studies me longer than she studies Jude.

"Hello," I say, working hard not to fidget. "You're Mrs. Abner, right?"

She nods curiously.

"My mother was Clara Green."

When I say it, I don't know if it'll mean anything. If, as Tulane said, the Abners were a revolving door for the parentless, then perhaps they don't remember Clara Green. She was one of many foster children they took in through the years. But Marlene presses her hand against her sternum with an audible gasp, and it becomes clear that she absolutely remembers my mother.

She opens the door wide to shake my hand. Hers is soft, her skin a bit papery. She ushers us inside a home that is trapped in time. Not from centuries past, like the Vandenberg manor. This is more 1970s, with floral wallpaper and gingham curtains, worn carpet, and faded linoleum. In the living room, there's a couch with crocheted doilies. Hanging above it, a framed needlepoint of the Serenity Prayer.

Her husband, Samuel, rises slowly from an armchair—tall but stooped, wearing a pair of carpenter jeans and suspenders over a button-down shirt. Marlene introduces me with a softly-spoken, "This is Clara Green's daughter," and when Samuel shakes my hand, his is calloused. They invite us to sit. Marlene offers us tea or water.

Jude and I politely decline.

"We've had many foster children through the years," Marlene says, sitting in the chair opposite her husband. "But we remember Clara well. I must say, you look very much like her."

I'm unsure how to respond to this. I'm unsure what to say at all. I'm a bit stuck on the fact that my mom lived here, in this house. The television is off. It's small, set inside a wooden cabinet. Beside it, stands a bookshelf filled with well-worn Bibles, devotionals, and what appears to be a collection of Christian romance novels.

"How is your mother?" Marlene asks.

"I'm not sure," I reply. "I haven't seen her in a long time."

The woman frowns. "I'm sorry to hear that."

I stuff my hands beneath my knees. "Did she visit you, by chance—around five years ago?"

Marlene and Samuel exchange a look of puzzlement.

"No," Marlene says. "We haven't seen her since the social worker took her away."

Took her away.

It's a different story from the one Tulane told.

I lean forward. "Do you mind if I ask ... could you tell us about her friendship with Simon Vandenberg?"

The couple share another glance, this one less puzzled, more uncomfortable. Like they'd rather not discuss her friendship with Simon Vandenberg.

Samuel clears his throat. "We didn't know much about it, if we're being honest."

"Clara was only with us for six months," Marlene adds. "She was a very quiet girl. Beautiful, but private. She kept to herself mostly. We thought she was spending her time at the library. It was only later, after the disappearance, when we learned she'd been spending so much of it with Simon."

"Because she told you?" I ask.

"Oh, she told us alright," Samuel replies.

I look at him quizzically.

"She went a little crazy, if you want to know the truth."

"Samuel." Marlene says, her tone gentle but reproachful.

"What do you mean, she went a little crazy?" I ask.

"Well," Samuel continues, "she kept insisting she knew where Simon was. The rest of his family, too. She kept—" He stops, his brow furrowing, like he isn't sure he should say any more.

"She kept what?"

"We don't want to upset you," Marlene says.

"It's okay. I already know she was troubled."

They exchange a third look, resigned this time. Marlene takes up the story. "Well, she kept insisting they found some sort of ... doorway? She was very adamant, and it was all very upsetting. We tried to help her, but she refused to let it go. Every day got a little worse, until she was in near hysterics. In the end, social services thought it would be best for Clara to start fresh somewhere new and they took her away."

"Do you know if it helped?" I ask.

"I'm afraid it didn't. She was eventually admitted into a *facility*." Marlene says the word delicately, but I can read between the lines. My mother was put into a psych ward. I can't help but wonder for how long. "We were very sad to hear it. She was such a good student, your mother. Very smart. Pretty as can be. She loved reading."

"Did she go to the high school?" I ask, realizing it quite suddenly. Unless Marlene home-schooled her foster children, or sent them to Blackwillow Christian Academy, which could certainly be a possibility if they were given financial aid, she would have gone to Foggy Hollow High.

"Well, of course." Marlene smiles. "All of our foster children did."

Jude and I return to school at the beginning of third period.

Mrs. Calloway buzzes us inside the front office looking every inch the mother hen. "Selah, I've been worried sick. I called your father, and he said you were dealing with something." She turns from me to Jude. "I marked you absent as well, dear. And left a message with your mother."

"Stepmother," Jude says.

"Yes, I'm sorry. Your stepmother." Mrs. Calloway turns back to me. "Selah, what is the matter? It's not like you to play hooky."

I tell her. The non-supernatural parts, anyway. About my mother living here, being a student here. Friends with Simon Vandenberg. When I finish, Mrs. Calloway looks properly shocked.

I slide my hands into the pockets of my puffer vest. "We just went to speak with her foster parents—Marlene and Samuel Abner."

"I remember the Abners," Mrs. Calloway says. "Up until a few years back, they were always enrolling new students. They fostered your mother?" She asks the question as she types into her computer, and I can tell by the light in her eyes that she's found something.

The transcripts of Clara Green, perhaps.

"For six months," I say. "Then she was sent away after Simon and his family disappeared."

Mrs. Calloway swivels her chair to look from the computer screen to me. "Selah, sweetheart, that's a lot to take in."

"I haven't told Twig yet," I say, squirming a little as I do. It's not like me to keep things from Twig. "I thought I'd fill him in tonight, after dinner. It's too much to explain over the phone."

Twig comes home later this evening. The team took fifth place in the Catalyst Cup, an impressive finish, really, considering the competition. Mrs. Calloway invited me to join them for dinner to celebrate. Naomi, too. Which means I'll have to catch him up after she leaves.

Mrs. Calloway nods kindly, then starts writing us both a pass.

I fiddle with the skeleton key inside my pocket. "Can I see her transcripts?"

She stops writing. I think she would give me anything if she could. But even I know this is too big of an ask. "I would love to give you more information about your mother, but I can't give you her transcripts. That would get me fired." Even as she says it, she looks conflicted, like she might bend the rules just once. She taps her finger against the laminate desktop, her lips pursed. Then she scoots her chair back. "But there is something we could try."

Jude and I follow her down the hall, into Foggy Hollow's uninspired library.

She walks decisively to a shelf near the front, which contains all the yearbooks from years past. Mrs. Calloway removes one with a spine that says *Class of 1995*.

The year my mother attended.

She sets it on top of the waist-high shelf and opens to the index, searching for Green, Clara. Her finger stops on the name, and I'm excited to see there are three page numbers. Mrs. Calloway gives my shoulder a squeeze, and, understanding that Jude and I might want some privacy, excuses herself to the main office.

I blink down at my mother's name, proof that she's been here this whole time. A part of this school. She walked these halls. Sat in these classrooms. Gazed out the windows, daydreaming of Simon and the Vandenberg estate and probably, the rift. With a shaky exhale, I turn to the page listed first. Her yearbook picture. In it, her nose is sun-kissed, her ears pierced, her eyes not so haunted. I capture it on my phone, then turn to the next page listed in the index. This one, a short write-up about the high school's first poetry club, with Clara Green listed as one of its members.

"She wrote poetry," I say, more a question than a statement.

I didn't know she wrote anything.

I capture this, too, then turn to the final page, this one a collection of pictures taken at a pep rally. In one of them, my mother smiles tentatively with a group of girls. I stare at her face, as mesmerized as I've ever been, when Jude points to her clavicle. She's wearing a v-neck shirt. Her collarbones are pronounced like my own. And what he has noticed takes my breath away.

The symbol.

A tad grainy, but unmistakable.

It's not etched on a locket. Or sketched in some corner. It's right there, beneath her left collarbone, like a tattoo on her skin.

After school, I show my dad the picture, zooming in on the mark in question.

"That was her birthmark," Dad says.

We're standing in the rose garden in the back lawn, to the right of the hedge maze.

"A birthmark?"

He lifts his ball cap to wipe his forehead with the sleeve of his flannel. The temperature is mild, but the sun has come out, and my dad's a hard worker. "I thought it looked more like a tattoo, but she always said it was a birthmark."

So then, this explains it. Why the symbol has always struck a familiar cord. I must have seen it on my own mother, a "birthmark" on her skin. This mysterious mark has become a web of gossamer, connecting one mystery to the other—the portrait and the cold case, confirming what I've already begun to suspect. The two aren't separate mysteries at all, but one.

"You doing okay, kiddo?" Dad asks.

When I look up at him, his eyes are concerned.

"I know this is a lot to take in. A really bizarre coincidence, if you ask me. Moving here, of all places." He rubs his chin. "You know I'm not much of a believer when it comes to all that supernatural stuff. But with the way you took to this place, it always felt like, I don't know. Fate. I would hate for this discovery to ..." His words fall away with a frown.

To *what*, I wonder.

Undo me?

Send me back to therapy?

Dad looks so stressed. And for just a moment, I'm tempted to show him everything. *Ezra's Obsession*. The drawing of the locket with my mother's "birthmark" drawn in the corner. Her visit to Tulane five years ago. Simon's journal entries.

I try to imagine what he might say. How he would respond. And I know, deep in my bones, it would be too much. Especially when he's already wrestling with worry. And perhaps—a flare-up of grief?

"I'm okay, Dad," I say with a smile. "It's kinda cool, if you think about it. I'm going to school where she went to school. I'm friends with a Vandenberg, just like she was."

I'm laying it on a little too thick. Saying the wrong words, probably. Mom didn't have a happy ending in Foggy Hollow. Her best friend disappeared, and she was sent away, and eventually admitted into a *facility*. I wonder if Dad knows about the psych ward. I'm afraid to ask. So I just kiss his cheek and tell him not to worry.

A couple hours later, I'm sitting in the Calloway's dining room, listening as Twig and Naomi tell us everything about their time at CMU. When dinner is over and Naomi goes home, we slip into his bedroom, and I tell him everything that happened while he was gone. The whole truth and nothing but the truth. He's not upset that I didn't tell him sooner. He understands why I didn't want to get into it on the phone.

That night, exhaustion steamrolls me.

I'm asleep before my head hits the pillow.

I have dreams.

In one, I'm standing in the dining hall. A man is yelling, pounding his fist against the table. A young man yells back, his face red with anger. A woman cries for them to stop, please stop, while a teenage girl fumes in silence. The very air in the room seems to feast on their emotion. It shimmers and darkens, then turns into the same terrifying black hole that sucked up my mother. I watch in horror as it does the same to John and Maureen, Simon and Lily.

It sucks them right off their seats and swallows them whole.

33
REHEARSALS

As the week deepens into the middle of October, the season arrives in full force, with pumpkins on porches, leaf bags on curbs, and Halloween decor in every window. The Monongahela forest has become a tapestry of blazing red, golden yellow, fiery orange, and deep green. The days grow shorter, the parade floats come together, and sweater weather is here to stay.

Twig's been busy helping his dad at the auto shop, so I spend most of my free time with Jude. We're still digging through his family archives, though the search has grown tedious and muddled. What are we even looking for anymore? Clues about the portrait? Evidence of rift encounters? Another link between the two? Jude's focusing on the symbol, which we found on my mother, and the gemstones, since we're racing Rafe toward a finish line neither of us understands. I keep an eye out for Ezra's revelation, written the same year his son was born.

Honestly, I've grown bored with the library. I much prefer our other endeavor—searching for keyholes. AKA, an excuse to explore the manor. There's so much to discover, from secret passages to hidden hallways used by servants long ago. The basement has been the creepiest by far—a labyrinth of stone corridors with walls that sweat.

According to Tulane, no one's gone down there in years, aside from the occasional trip to the cellar, which is dark and musty and lined with barrels of aged wine and whiskey. So it's interesting, then, to run into Rafe nowhere near the cellar. More interesting still to find him looking on edge, like it's been days since he's had a proper meal or a decent night's sleep. It gives me a boost of morale. A glimmer of hope. Whatever he's up to, it must not be going well.

On Friday evening, I take a break from the Vandenberg mysteries to help Mrs. Calloway. Twig and I sit at his kitchen counter, stapling together parade packets. When we reach the end, Jude calls.

He invites us over.

Not only has Twig been dying to get inside the manor, he's been dying to use our EMF meter inside the manor, an idea that has Jude rolling his eyes so hard, his irises practically disappear. So when he extends the invitation, I know he's doing it for me.

Twig jumps off the stool like it's a hot stove.

We head over with our proton pack.

And what transpires has both of us losing our minds. The meter jumps wildly between low and high frequencies. One minute, it emits a long, shrill tone as if detecting a massive, constant field. The next, it falls silent without any input change at all. The LED lights remain stuck on red. It doesn't matter which room we're in or what level we're on.

Jude thinks the meter must be broken.

But later that night, Twig sends a video of it working just fine in his bedroom. Along with a million-and-one follow-up texts.

Ding, ding, ding.
One after the other.
The readings defied physical law.
Magnetic pulses don't appear in short bursts.
They don't reverse polarity.
Electromagnetic fields are supposed to be consistent. Directional. With a clear source.

> Selah. It's coming from everywhere and
> nowhere.

In the morning, he sends more. Charts. Graphs. Screenshots. And what can I say, other than *Foggy Hollow's always been strange.* We devoted an entire podcast episode to it. Our town has a long history of lost signals, weird static, and phantom broadcasts. Radios patching into distorted sounds. Dropped calls. Glitchy electronics. Phones that pick up disembodied voices. EMF meters don't act normal in Foggy Hollow.

But last night was something else.

The results were fascinating, creepy, and ultimately ... unhelpful. The rift could be hiding in any of the rooms. Which makes sense, I guess. According to Simon's journal, it opened in multiple places.

The real question is:

How did it open?

And why?

The questions circle in the back of my mind as I grip the cool balustrade of the ballroom's balcony and gaze toward the ceiling, where crystal chandeliers hang in perfect line, casting fractured rainbows across the polished parquet flooring.

Isabel and her entourage of cleaning crews and preservationists have been busy preparing for next weekend, and it shows. There's not a cobweb in sight. Everything looks bright and new, so much less frightening in the daylight than it had the night before.

Jude, on the other hand, stands like a closed book at the bottom of the staircase. His face unreadable. His posture refined. His features drawn. His hair perfect.

As though sensing my stare, his eyes lift to mine, and for just a moment, the closed book cracks open a smidge. The look makes my pulse jump as erratically as the EMF meter.

Beside me, Lainey leans over the railing to get a better look at Rafe, who looks much improved from our last encounter. I tug her back before she tumbles head over feet and plummets to her death. The last thing this estate needs is another tragedy on its hands.

Next to Rafe and Jude, Mayor Ridley converses with Miss Eloise Applewhite, Foggy Hollow's very own retired ballerina turned drill sergeant. She's on the masquerade committee and is walking us through our first rehearsal, starting with the Founder's Decent, followed by the opening dance.

The men stand at the bottom. The women at the top. As per tradition, each man will walk halfway up the staircase while the woman descends. He will meet her on the landing and escort her to the dance floor below. At the moment, Miss Applewhite and Mayor Ridley are trying to decide the order in which the couples will be announced.

They settle on the mayor going first, even though his connection to the founding families is a significant stretch. Apparently, his wife is second cousins twice removed from Marvin Doorn—an out-of-town math professor who has agreed to ride in the parade but has no interest in staying for the ball. Mayor Ridley gladly stepped in to take his spot.

Isabel and her escort, Everett McBride, go next. Everett is a Foggy Hollow transplant. He moved from Alexandria after retiring early from a lucrative antique and estate appraisal business. Isabel hired him to catalog the estate's historical items under the pretense of preservation.

Jude isn't fooled.

He thinks she's hunting for valuables.

As I watch them reach the bottom of the staircase, Rafe catches my eye with a smirk. I turn up my chin as Miss Applewhite announces Camilla Bogaard, escorted by her husband, Ignatius Bogaard. Then their son, Sterling, escorting Becca Lynn Parker, a mousy girl who has always tried very hard to fit in with the popular crowd.

"Miss Selah Whitlock," Miss Applewhite calls next. "Escorted by Jude Vandenberg of the Vandenberg Family."

I'm tempted to rush.

Hurry to Jude.

Especially when he's looking at me like that.

But Miss Applewhite had been very clear, and very stern, about how we are supposed to walk. *Like a wedding march, ladies. Not a sprint.* She'd been eying Lainey when she said it, but I might've been just as guilty.

With one hand on the railing, I force myself to walk slowly. With poise. Taking care not to trip. Even if my heart is doing its best impression.

Jude meets me on the landing, his footsteps quiet and precise, his eyes never leaving mine. He extends his arm in perfect form. I slide my hand into the crook of this elbow. His shirt is smooth beneath my palm, the fabric taut over the shape of his bicep.

Together, we descend.

"What are you doing after this?" I ask in a whisper from the corner of my mouth.

"Whatever you're doing," he says back, his voice low.

I bite back a smile. "Floats at the fairgrounds."

"More glitter, huh?"

"Maybe some paint."

"We could continue our research afterward."

"It's a date," I say as we reach the dance floor.

Jude's hand moves to the small of my back and butterflies take flight—a whole kaleidoscope of them.

We stop next to Sterling and Becca Lynn and watch Rafe meet Lainey halfway up the stairs.

"He's unraveling," Jude says, his voice even lower.

"What do you mean?" I ask.

"He came home last night about an hour after you and Twig left. Went straight to the study. I heard him slamming cabinets, opening drawers. He poured himself a scotch, drained it pretty fast, then hurled the glass against the wall."

I peer at Rafe with fresh suspicion.

He's desperate. That much, we know. Why else would he have dug up Ezra's grave? The question is—*why* is he desperate? What's so special about these gemstones? Who would have planted fakes? And what does it have to do with the larger puzzle at play?

When the twelve of us are assembled, Miss Applewhite takes her place at the head of the ballroom, her posture arrow-straight. "The Waltz of the Hollow was first danced by lantern light during the Yuletide Ball of 1758."

I think of young Ezra with Molly Ludwig. Jude must be thinking the same thing, because his eye catches mine.

"It was said to have bound the town's founding families in rhythm and ritual. After the fire, when the Hunter's Moon Masquerade Ball replaced the Yuletide Ball, the dance remained and was given its name. It's designed for three couples. Which means we'll have two sets of dancers: the older generation ..." She gestures to the grown-ups. "And the younger generation."

Great.

Our set includes Rafe.

Miss Applewhite gives her hands a sharp clap. "Two lines,

please, facing your partner. Ladies on one side. Gentlemen on the other."

We shuffle into place. And as she launches into a long-winded monologue about the historical significance of this particular dance, my eyes drift to the fireplace. It's adorned with an impressive carving of a fallen angel—wings outstretched, one hand reaching skyward, the other dragging something unseen into shadow.

The exact spot where Twig's EMF meter went particularly berserk.

Music plays from the bluetooth speaker on the ground by Miss Applewhite—graceful and lilting, in three-quarter time. She speaks over it, positioning Rafe and Lainey as the lead couple in our set. Jude and I are second. Sterling and Becca Lynn, third.

"Now, we bow and curtsy to begin."

Across from me, Jude bows, a lock of hair falling over his brow, and everything else—Rafe, the gemstones, the rift, last night's experiment—disappears.

"We begin the dance with a circle of six," Miss Applewhite calls. "Three couples, hand over wrist, circling left—*your other left, Mayor Ridley*—and then right again. Think of it as a brief alliance. Don't get attached."

My skin crawls as Rafe's hand circles my wrist. We turn clockwise for eight counts, then counterclockwise for the same.

"Return to your places now. Second and third couple, do try to look elegant while doing absolutely nothing. You'll get your turn soon enough. Top couple, take hands."

Rafe and Lainey come together, passing between me and Jude, Sterling and Becca Lynn—four steps in, four steps out.

"Now cast off and progress!" Miss Applewhite cries, modeling the move in dramatic fashion.

Jude and I become the new lead couple. I anticipate coming together, taking his hands.

But no.

Miss Applewhite tells us to move diagonally.

Becca Lynn gets Jude.

I have to take Sterling, whose palms are clammy, his lips moving as he mouths the steps in rhythm.

Miss Applewhite continues calling commands, leading us through the dance, and only once does she yank on my shoulders. "Posture, darling. You're dancing, remember. Not hauling potatoes."

Poor Sterling gets the brunt of her critique.

Mayor Ridley takes a close second.

She keeps pointing out Jude, and begrudgingly, Rafe, whose only mishap was intentional.

"The hand goes here, Mr. Vandenberg. Any lower and I'll put you under etiquette review."

Lainey bursts into laughter.

It's as if the Vandenberg cousins already know this dance. It's as if they've danced it at a thousand balls before this one. Jude leads with quiet authority. And I quickly realize ...

The Waltz of the Hollow might be modest, but somehow, it's more arousing than anything I've seen on our high school dance floor. It's a study of anticipation and longing. The rush of coming together, only to be separated much too soon. Brief touches that are never enough, stirring up a cauldron of warmth that could drive a person insane. And all the while, Miss Applewhite insists upon *eye contact, eye contact, eye contact*! By the time the rehearsal ends, I feel as though Jude has seen into my soul, and there's a fire in my cheeks I'm not sure will ever go away.

"Dress rehearsal will be on Thursday," Miss Applewhite announces. "Please make sure your attire is finalized. Mrs. Tibbs has informed me that she is very busy with parade costumes, so if you plan to use her for alterations, do be considerate and contact her sooner rather than later."

It occurs to me that I don't have any attire at all. I've been preoccupied with other things.

Everyone breaks.

I expect Rafe to linger, to say something cryptic. Instead, he makes a hasty exit with Lainey.

I watch them go with narrowed eyes.

If only we knew what he was up to.

34
HIDDEN SCANDAL

After float building, Jude and I head to the family archives only to be chased away by a team from the FHPS. We retreat to the study, a private room behind the library, accessible via a paneled door that blends into the wall like part of the wainscoting.

I sit at the commanding desk of Amos Vandenberg, which we've already checked for keyholes. I imagine him here in quiet retreat, the stone fireplace crackling behind him, the tall windows before him offering a view of the hedge maze and part of the orchard as he dips his feather quill into a silver inkwell to draft his mostly boring letters.

Outside, the orchard is nearly unrecognizable. Rows of trees with thinned branches, now pruned and shaped, boast a few stubborn apples and pears. The grass between is neatly trimmed but scattered with leaves, a mixture of russet and buttery yellow. Early evening sunlight pours through the windows, casting Jude in an angelic glow. He sits on one of two leather armchairs with a chess table in between, tinkering with the gold-plated pocket compass.

"I don't know what business they have in the library," he says. "We're opening the east wing to the public, not the west."

"Does it bother you—the changes she's making to the estate?" Which is, in actuality, *his*. Held in trust by Isabel until Jude turns twenty-one, or twenty-five, or thirty. I don't really understand the particulars of his inheritance. Only that it will be released to him in stages upon his twenty-first birthday.

He shrugs and sets the opened compass on the chess table. "If it keeps her occupied and away from me, I don't particularly care."

I pull the chain of a green glass banker's lamp and a warm pool of light spills over the items on the desk. An elegant fountain pen in a carved wooden stand. A tarnished, antique inkwell. And a glass ashtray without cigarettes or residue, as if Tulane cleaned it after John Vandenberg vanished.

"This compass spins like it's drunk," Jude says.

"Given the readings we got last night, I'm not sure it's the compass."

"I tried it at the fairgrounds. It didn't work there, either."

I open the desk drawers and find nothing revelatory. Paperwork mostly—mortgage statements, tax receipts, a property survey from 1991, timesheets for the former groundskeeper and the housekeeping staff. There's a Foggy Hollow phone directory, circa 1994. Estate letterhead. And a leather rolodex. I flip through the handwritten contacts. Landscapers, home repairs, pest control, a family physician, a list of lawyers, and interestingly, *Walter Jensen, reporter*.

"So, are you brave enough to survive Hollow Screen Horror Night tonight?" It's finally here, and the forecast looks perfect. "There's nothing quite like *Poltergeist* outside in the fog."

"Isn't that something you and Twig do together?"

"It is, but you're welcome to join. Ten bucks will get you three movies and a full tub of popcorn."

He frowns.

"Do you have something against popcorn?"

"I have something against third wheels." He turns the compass one hundred eighty degrees. "And since I'm already taking you away from him for the ball, maybe I should let him have this one."

Let him have this one.

It's an interesting turn of phrase.

"You know we're just friends, right?"

"I know *you* think of him that way."

"He thinks of me that way, too."

Jude looks doubtful.

I can't help but laugh. "Trust me when I tell you, Twig thinks of me as a sister. If he has non-platonic feelings for anyone, my bet's on Naomi. But she despises horror movies, which makes me question Twig's taste." I set my elbow on the desk and twist the gold stud in my ear. "Are you sure you don't want to come?"

He seems to consider for a moment, and I hold my breath. The prospect of sitting next to him at night, surrounded by fog while a scary movie plays on the big screen makes my skin prickle.

"Isabel scheduled a dinner with the Bogaards. I should probably attend."

Disappointment hits hard. The tantalizing prospect of Jude beside me in the dark, our arms touching, is replaced by Jude and Sterling at the Bogaards' dining table, sitting stiffly across from one another.

"You sure you're not just sick of me?"

"If that were the case, I wouldn't have spent the afternoon building floats for a parade I don't care about." He holds my gaze. "And we wouldn't be here right now, either."

A flush creeps into my ears.

With a shaky breath, I look away first, returning the rolodex to the bottom right drawer. I slide open the shallow one in the center.

It's filled with the standard office supplies—pens, pencils, paperclips, pushpins—along with a pack of playing cards, a matchbook from The Cobbler, return address labels, and a tin of long-expired mints. I try to open the tin, but the lid is stuck. When it finally pops off, tiny mints scatter everywhere. I gather them into a pile, then reach toward some strays in the back of the drawer, when the ring on my finger snags on something.

I pull the drawer open a little farther and notice a faint separation in the back corner. I press on the spot and the bottom shifts downward, like there's space underneath. Curious, I peel up the corner. It's a false panel, and it lifts easily, revealing a hidden compartment where two letters rest side by side.

"*Great Scott,*" I whisper.

"What is it?" Jude asks.

"I found something." I set the false panel aside and pick up one of the letters. It was written on September 7, 1822, four short days before fire would consume the town. Jude has come to his feet. He stands behind me, reading over my shoulder.

My Dearest Amos,

I ought not to write. A thousand times, I have told myself so. But here I sit, pen in trembling hand, compelled by a heart that refuses to yield.

You are not mine. I have known this from the first. And yet, the moments we have shared, stolen though they were, have rendered this truth more cruel than ever.

I dream of a different life, one in which our love is not forbidden. But such dreams are cruel compan-ions. I wake each morning to a reality I cannot bear.

You are bound in marriage, however loveless you claim it to be, and you have children who shall carry your name. What have I but fleeting moments, and a longing that grows with each passing day? Tell me, Amos, can any solace be found in so hopeless a circumstance?

Forgive me this letter. I shall not write again.

Yours in secret,
Florence

My heart pounds as I reach the signature.

Florence ...

Why does it strike such a familiar note?

Florence?

The recollection snaps into place.

Florence!

It comes like a shout, a cry in my mind, a memory of another dream. Smoke and flames everywhere as a man yelled for a woman with this very name.

Jude reaches past me to pick up the second letter, much shorter than the first. He clears his throat and reads it out loud. "Dear Father, I pray you will forgive me and the Lord will still take me. Is it a sin to protect those I love? I know of no other way to stop this curse. Please tell Isaiah everything. Yours most sincerely, Elijah."

Elijah.

The scorch mark on Jude's family tree. A man with no record of death, nor a headstone to mark his grave.

Have we just come upon his suicide note?

"To stop this curse?" Jude says, repeating the line. He turns the letter over, like there might be an explanation on the other side. But of course there is none. With a shake of his head, his troubled eyes find mine. "What curse?"

35
POISONED

I sit in the center of Twig's bed with my stomach in knots, working my way through a bundle of letters dated from 1770 to 1800 while Twig shares an erratic playlist on Spotify. So far, there's been jazz, grunge, blues, and rock. He keeps looking at me expectantly, like he's waiting for me to pick up on the punchline, but when Amy Winehouse starts singing after Kurt Cobain, I'm truly stumped.

"They're all members of the 27 club," he finally says.

"The what club?"

"*Cursed* musicians. Winehouse, Cobain, Joplin, Hendrix, Morrison. All of them died at the age of twenty-seven under mysterious circumstances."

Ah. I nod wisely.

Ever since last night, when I told Twig about Elijah's reference to a curse in his suicide note, my tall friend has been struck with inspiration for an episode. He already has a title picked out—*A Chronicle of Curses*—and spent a good chunk of Hollow Screen Horror Night recounting the string of eerie coincidences and tragic events that occurred on set during

Poltergeist, a movie believed to have been just as cursed as these poor musicians.

My mouth splits with a yawn.

Lack of sleep is catching up with me. Thankfully, we have a shortened school week ahead of us. In-service tomorrow, which means I get to sleep in on a Monday, along with our very own town holiday on Friday. Normally, I would be giddy. The Phoenix Parade. The Harvest Festival. The Hunter's Moon Masquerade Ball. A trifecta of pure whimsy. Instead, I can't kick this bout of anxiety. Perhaps watching *Poltergeist* until two in the morning wasn't the smartest idea.

Mrs. Calloway knocks on Twig's half-opened door and sticks her head inside with a bright smile. She holds up a big bowl of Muddy Buddies, which is one of my favorites. She's been extra motherly ever since she pulled up my mother's transcripts, but couldn't show them to me. She sets the bowl on Twig's desk and tells us to enjoy.

I drop the stack of letters into the box and flop back onto Twig's bed. I grab the eyeball off his nightstand—which isn't really an eyeball, but a stress ball that only looks like an eyeball—and toss it toward the ceiling.

Catch and toss.

Catch and toss.

Four dreams.

Molly Ludwig, hanging from a rope. Rose Vandenberg, dying in The Blitz. Jude's mother, bleeding out on a delivery table. And a woman named Florence, perishing in the fire.

All women.

All dead.

All involved with Vandenberg men.

Then there's my mom, and the dream I had about her.

Twig scoops up a cup of the powdered, chocolatey Chex mix. "We could cover King Tut's tomb. The Hope Diamond."

"Macbeth," I offer, recalling the book Jude was reading the first time we met. I give the eyeball another toss. Was it me, or was he noticeably different after yesterday's discovery? He hasn't texted or called today—not once. And we're approaching dinnertime.

"James Dean's car," Twig says.

"James Dean had a cursed car?"

"It's how he died. Car accident in a Porsche he nicknamed Little Bastard. Afterward, a whole bunch of weird stuff happened with the salvaged parts, including deaths and severe injuries."

"We could cover the Kennedy's," I say.

They're supposedly cursed. I did a report on them in the seventh grade. The more I think about it, it really is surprising we haven't done an episode on curses already. I catch the eyeball and set it back on Twig's nightstand. I grab myself a cup of Muddy Buddies and continue reading the letters, determined to get through this box so I can knock on Jude's door tomorrow morning and ask for another.

I try to focus as I read a letter addressed to *My Dear Cousin*, written by a woman named Drusilla Voorhees of Woodbridge, New Jersey. One run-on sentence in, it becomes clear that *My Dear Cousin* is Ezra's wife. The tone is warm and chatty. The content, dry as toast. Drusilla's youngest daughter is recovering from a fever, and she is proud to report that she has successfully transplanted her tulip bulbs.

I shuffle to the next, a letter addressed to Ezra Vandenberg from a business associate in Baltimore regarding shipment delays.

Thrilling stuff, truly.

I shuffle again and find another letter addressed to *My Dear Cousin*, only this one is written in a masculine scrawl, and is much shorter than Drusilla's. Two sentences in, all traces of boredom have vanished.

My Dear Cousin,

I am deeply saddened to hear of my uncle's continued hostility. I believe my father would gladly bury the hatchet, but Ezra's hatred will not be thwarted, and now I find myself its recipient.

The tragic death of your dear Lydia is sorrow enough, but to accuse me of harming her! How could I, in Winchester! I hate to even suggest it, but might his obsession with this curse have led him to poison Lydia?

Do give my warmest regards to your mother, Elizabeth.

Yours sincerely,
Raphael

By the time I reach the end, I'm gripping the letter in both hands.

His obsession with this curse.

The phrase blurs in and out of focus.

According to the last line, this letter was written to a young Amos, and the sender was his cousin, Raphael II. A girl was poisoned. Amos's *dear* Lydia. Ezra must have accused his nephew. Young Amos must have told his cousin about his father's accusation, and in response, the younger Raphael cast his suspicions upon his uncle. Because of his obsession. With a curse.

I'm on my feet, tapping Twig on the shoulder. I thrust the letter at him.

My mind is no longer sleepy. This discovery is as rejuvenating as two cans of Red Bull. Another mention of a curse, and a bread crumb we can follow.

A girl named Lydia was poisoned.

The next morning, Twig and I show the letter to Maggie.

"They must have been romantically involved, right? Amos and this Lydia?" I don't wait for an answer. I'm already moving toward the ledger that gave us Molly Ludwig—registries of guests at the Yuletide Ball. If Amos Vandenberg was romantically involved with Lydia, then it stands to reason he would have escorted her to the ball.

Maggie doesn't object, but she doesn't join us either. She stands there rubbing her chin, reading and rereading the words while Twig and I set the ledger on the table and flip to the registry from 1794, which would have taken place before Lydia's death. A thrill of excitement sparks in my finger when it runs into his name—*Amos Vandenberg*. Only he didn't escort a girl named Lydia. In 1794, young Amos escorted Eleanor Doorn. I flip back a page, to the registry taken in 1793. There's no mention of Amos at all.

"They couldn't have gone in 1795," I say disappointedly. "She was already dead by then."

Maggie has climbed onto a step stool. She stands on tiptoe, reaching for a shelf lined with volumes of *The Foggy Hollow Gazette* bound by year. Despite the devastating fire in 1822, her issues span as far back as 1788. If not for the Bogaard's obsession with preservation, the first four decades of the paper's existence would have been lost. Thankfully, the family kept personal copies of each issue.

Maggie's fingers stop over a cracked leather spine three inches thick. "Here we are—Gazette, 1795." She removes it from the shelf and steps off the stool. "If a young woman named

Lydia was poisoned to death and the Vandenbergs were involved, I can guarantee you it would have been headline news in the Tittle Tattle."

"The what?" Twig says.

"*Tittle Tattle from the Hollow*. A gossip column that ran weekly from 1790 to 1811. It was revived briefly in the 1840s, but lacked the same pizzazz. The original was always teeming with scandalous tidbits, let me tell you." She sets it on the table with a look of warning. "Gentle hands now. These pages aren't spring chickens."

Carefully, I open to the front page of the first edition. The pages are brittle. The script is faded. The margins, small and tight. There are no headlines. No images or illustrations. Just long paragraphs. My eyes are crossing already when Maggie reaches past me and turns to the centerfold. "Page two is where you'll find local announcements." Her bony finger moves left to right. "But if you want the real tea, you'll head over here."

To page three, a roundup of softer news. Community events, poems, philosophical musings, and, sure enough, *Tittle Tattle from the Hollow* with its own tagline—a *weekly whisper of this and that, plucked from parlors, pews, and porch steps alike.* I skim the first one. A shocking tale of an impertinent young man's public proposal at Assembly Hall, which not only disgraced his intended's family, but descended into fisticuffs to the great distress of ladies present.

I give a low whistle. "The nerve of the guy," I say with more than a little sarcasm.

"Public proposals were quite scandalous back in the day, Selah," Maggie says. "Especially if this fellow didn't ask for permission first. By the sound of the rapscallion, I doubt he did."

The front door jingles downstairs.

Walt calls out a greeting.

Maggie leaves us be as Twig and I take a seat at the table.

We're unsure when Lydia died. We only know it couldn't have been any later than July of 1795. The letter to Amos was dated in early August of that same year and post back then didn't travel quickly, especially if Raphael II was, as he claimed to be, writing from Winchester, England.

But was he, really?

I recall a different letter, one Jude showed me weeks ago inside The Cobbler, written from a grieving young man to his mother. After the violent death of his twin sister, Gabriel Vandenberg set sail for Winchester, England. Presumably, to reclaim the stolen portrait. But according to the letter, Raphael II was nowhere to be found in Winchester, nor any account of the Vandenberg name. Having no idea what to make of this contradictory information, I shove it aside and focus on the topic at hand.

A poisoned girl named Lydia.

Each publication is four pages printed back-to-back on one large sheet folded in half. Deaths are listed on page two. Gossip on page three. We find nothing in January. Nothing in February. Nothing in March or April or May. Not until the second publication in June do we hit pay dirt.

I hunch over the paper. "On the third day of June, Miss *Lydia Mabel*, aged sixteen years, of the River District, passed from this life following a brief and sudden illness. She is survived by her parents, Mr. and Mrs. Jonas Mabel. Burial was held at St. Fortuna's Churchyard on the sixth. The family requests privacy in their time of grief."

"Mabel," Twig says, his eyes meeting mine.

We have a last name.

Together, our attention moves to page three.

Twig reads the column aloud. "A cloud lies heavy over the River District this week, dear readers. Word reaches us that the late Miss Lydia Mabel, a quiet girl of sixteen summers, has departed this life by means most unnatural. The name arsenic drips from certain lips like poison itself, and tongues wag from the market to the magistrate. It is said the girl had caught the eye of a certain heir. A Vandenberg, some say. Perhaps too fine a name to be seen at her door by the light of day. It is known the elder Vandenberg had his objections. Is this a case of a tonic gone astray, or something more sinister?"

By the time he finishes, I'm already opening the M drawer of Maggie's card catalog. I flip through the cards, stopping only when I reach one in particular—*Mabel, Lydia.* "It says here she's mentioned again in the next publication, and one last time in late July."

We turn to the respective columns.

The first focuses on young Amos's suspicious absence from church, Ezra's private meeting with the sheriff, and the rumors swirling over Ezra's open disapproval of the budding courtship. The last takes a significant turn. The author questions Lydia's virtue, dancing around the notion that she may have been with child, and if so, by whom? It seems to me it would have been Amos, but there's no mention of the Vandenbergs at all.

"Another tragedy," I say.

"Involving the Vandenbergs," Twig replies.

The knots in my stomach tie tighter.

I've been keeping a notecard in my bedroom to keep track of them all. With the addition of Florence lost in the fire, I've officially run out of space. But now, here's another.

"If she was poisoned," I say, "there would have been an autopsy report, right?"

Twig and I look at one another, then we scoop up the ledger filled with gazettes and hurry downstairs, where Walt and Maggie bicker behind the counter. The argument cuts short as soon as Maggie sees what I'm holding.

"What are you doing with that down here?" she asks, aghast, like first floor air is more toxic than second floor air and at any moment, the pages will disintegrate.

I set the ledger on the counter and show her what we've found. Walt reads over her shoulder.

"Now that was reporting with a flair," he says with a nostalgic, faraway look in his eye.

"Would there be an autopsy report?" Twig asks.

"A coroner's inquest, if it survived the fire," Maggie says with a scowl. "And that, as you well know, would be in town hall."

My phone dings—a sound that makes my heart leap.

> Did Horror Night live up to the hype?

Finally, a message from Jude.

I told myself I wouldn't reach out to him unless he reached out to me first. Yesterday was radio silence. Today, contact. I can't send my reply fast enough.

> Absolutely! Twig and I are at Evermore. We found another mention of the curse.

I snap pictures. The letter from Raphael II, the notice of Lydia Mabel's death, along with all three mentions in *Tittle Tattle from the Hollow*. I send them off with an invite to join us at town hall. His reply comes five minutes later, when Twig and I are already cutting through the square.

In no time, we're stepping into the cool, quiet foyer, which smells faintly of lemon. We walk past a young receptionist who doesn't look up from her phone, and follow the hand-lettered sign that reads, "Public Records Office." Inside, a fluorescent light buzzes over rows of filing cabinets and labeled boxes. The grumpy clerk sits behind the counter, hunched over his Sudoku puzzle book.

"Hi," I say, my voice full of cheer. Anticipation, too. If Lydia Mabel was with child, surely this information would be in the coroner's inquest.

The older gentleman looks up, his wary eyes moving from Twig to me. "You again."

"Yep, it's me." I smile brightly, determined to catch my flies with honey. I set my elbows on the counter between us. "We're hoping to look at a coroner's report from 1795. It's for a girl named Lydia Mabel. She lived in the River District. The death was ruled a poisoning."

He blinks slowly. "From *seventeen* ninety-five?"

"It may have been filed with the physician's notes or burial permits. Possibly under deaths of interest."

He rubs the bridge of his nose, an exaggerated gesture of long-suffering. "Miss, as you must know, most of those records disappeared in the fire."

I hold up my finger. "Molly Ludwig's didn't."

At least, not her record of birth, anyway.

He bowls past my objection. "And even if it does exist, it'll be sealed up in archives, not open for public curiosity."

"But we're not just curious. It's for historical research. I—we work for the historical society."

"Then let Maggie Henshaw come ask me herself."

The door opens behind us.

Jude steps in—cool and understated, wearing a perfectly tailored coat, the shadows under his eyes extra dark. A fact that makes the knots in my stomach tie tighter once again.

Behind the counter, Mr. Grumpy Pants's demeanor changes visibly. Jude is a Vandenberg after all, and *tittle tattle* on the street says the stepmother is a bully not to be crossed. Never mind Jude himself, who radiates a my-family-built-this-town energy. The man is several decades Jude's elder, but becomes as deferential as Mr. Denis Tulane.

I can't help feeling a mixture of gratitude and annoyance.

The clerk comes to his feet. He unlocks a cabinet, removes a ledger labeled *1770-1799 Coroner's Inquests*. He brings it to the counter and flips to June of 1795. Lydia Mabel's is one of two reports made in that year.

"Those archives sure are sealed up tight," Twig mutters under his breath.

I stifle a laugh.

It took the clerk approximately two minutes to dig this up. The magic word was obviously *Vandenberg*. The three of us lean over the handwritten report, held on the fourth day of June, ordered by the town physician, and investigated by the sheriff. It includes a testimony of witnesses—who found her, where she was found, the description of the body.

The conclusion?

Suspected poison, consistent with arsenic. Murder by person unknown. There's no mention of a pregnancy. But there is mention of a strange birthmark, which is accompanied by a sketch.

With wide eyes, I look at Jude.

But he refuses to look back at me.

He just stares down at the sketch, his face as pale as wax.

The same symbol that marked my mother, marked Lydia Mabel, too.

36

A WALL OF EVIDENCE

The next day, Jude isn't at school.

Each period crawls by at a snail's pace.

By the time U.S. History rolls around, I'm about to come out of my skin. I stare at the clock, bouncing my knee and tapping my pencil to such a distracting degree, Harper gives me an exasperated look halfway through Langley's lecture about the First Continental Congress.

But I can't seem to help myself.

My body won't settle. Neither will my mind. It keeps jumping from one peculiarity to the next. The portrait. The gemstones. My dreams. The loose floorboard in Simon's room. My mother. The mark beneath her collarbone, which leads back to the portrait, and Molly, and now, Lydia Mabel.

After our discovery in town hall, Jude hardly spoke. He snapped pictures of the report, then asked to see the coroner's inquest for Violet Underwagon, who died in an animal attack alongside Ruth Vandenberg in 1832. But there was no coroner's inquest to be found, even though this was after the fire. The whole time, he remained silent and brooding. All in all, I saw him for no more than thirty minutes. He got his information about Lydia, he tried to get more about Violet, then he left.

And he's been ghosting me ever since.

Too bad for him, I refuse to be ghosted.

As soon as the final bell rings, I head straight to the manor. Mr. Tulane answers the door with his trademark bow. I tell him Jude invited me. He doesn't call my bluff, but welcomes me inside. I hurry up the stairs, march through the upper hall, and rap on Jude's door.

A moment later, it opens.

He stands on the other side like a tortured poet on a bender —his shirt untucked, his hair a mess, the shadows beneath his eyes so dark they're like bruises. The look has no right to flatter anyone, and yet somehow on him ...

"Where were you today?" I ask, shifting in an attempt to see past him, into his private quarters.

But he shifts, too, like he's hiding something. "I think you should go."

"Why?"

He drags his hand down his face. His jaw is tight, and when he speaks, his words are, too. "Because something is obviously going on here, and I think it's better if you're not involved."

I blink up at him. "You're joking, right?"

He doesn't answer. He just stands there looking miserable.

"Jude, I've been involved since the day I was born. Two centuries before then, actually."

"Selah." He says my name like it's a torment.

And I've had enough.

I barge past him.

He doesn't stop me. I'll give him that.

Dreary sunlight filters through his windows, illuminating a wall that looks like a murder board in a squad room. It's been covered in paper—copies of pictures, letters, journal entries, newspaper articles, death records.

Without realizing it, I've moved closer.

All the tragedies I've been keeping on a notecard in my bedroom are here on his wall. In chronological order and carefully documented.

Pre-Revolutionary War: Molly Ludwig dies by suicide. There's the sketch of Molly. Or rather, a printed copy of the sketch. The symbol in the corner has been circled in red ink, along with three words written in bold handwriting—*Ezra loved her*.

Post Revolution: Lydia Mabel dies by arsenic. Next to it, he's pinned her autopsy report. The symbol has been circled in the same red ink. Three words have been written in the same bold handwriting—*Amos loved her*.

Fire of 1822: Florence Wessel is one of the victims. He's included the scandalous love letter. It's obvious Amos loved her, too.

Pre Civil War: Ruth Vandenberg and Violet Underwagon die in animal attack. There's the letter about Gabriel grieving not only his twin sister but the girl to whom his affections were so tenderly bound.

Post Civil War: Elijah commits suicide. Jude has made a copy of the suicide note, where he has not just highlighted, but underlined the ominous phrase—*I know of no other way to stop this curse*.

There's the article about the train crash in 1890, including a caption that hinted at a courtship between Isaiah and Helena Pisel, who perished alongside his family. Then there's the article of the bank robbery. Poor Enoch lost not only his parents and his left eye, but Mary Donovan, to whom he was betrothed. There's information about Rose Vandenberg, who died in The Blitz wearing the ruby necklace.

And then my mother.

He's made a copy of the yearbook photograph. On it, he circled the mark beneath her collarbone with the words *Simon loved her* scrawled underneath. Next to her is a photograph of Jude's mother, a woman who bled to death on a delivery table after his father's profession of love.

And there, in the midst of all that evidence, is an item I've not yet seen, plucked from the timeline. A journal entry written by the scorch mark's mother. Dated one year after her son penned his suicide note.

I turn to Jude, who's still standing in the doorway, his hand on the crown of his head, fisting his hair.

"I found it Sunday morning," he says.

November 12, 1873

>It has been a year, one full, ruinous year since Elijah cast off this world, and still, I cannot accept that he is gone. My son. My heart. I miss him with every breath I draw.
>
>At night, I dream of him as a child chasing butterflies in the orchard, his curls golden in the sun. I wake, and the pain of his absence is suffocating. It presses against my chest like stone. So does the shame.
>
>My husband weeps behind closed doors. He prays late into the night. But prayer cannot mend what he has broken. He gave our son poison. This wretched curse. And Elijah believed it. Enough to choose death, convinced it was the only way to protect those he loved. Yet in his final words, he begged his father to pass the poison onto his own son, to warn Isaiah. Pray tell, how would that protect his precious boy? Gabriel will not grant him this request. He says he has learned.

But what good is wisdom earned too late? The blood will forever stain his hands. I will never forgive him.

"To love brings death," he told Elijah, and he dared tell me the same. I wanted to strike him. To scream. If love brings death, then why am I still here? My heart beats on. I am his wife, am I not? So then, he does not love me?

I want to follow my son to the grave. Let Gabriel contend with the wreckage. Only the children keep me here. They are too young to understand the shame they will carry all their lives. Sweet Esther. Precious Deborah. Little Isaiah.

I will not leave them with more sorrow.

But I am forever emptied.

—A.V.

My fingers linger over the phrase "to love brings death." I look again at the evidence Jude has gathered.

Ezra loved Molly, and she died.

Amos loved Lydia, and she died.

Then he loved Florence, and she died, too. The whole town caught on fire.

Gabriel lost Violet.

Elijah took his own life.

He begged his father to tell Isaiah everything, but Gabriel refused, and Isaiah not only lost Helena, but his entire family.

Enoch lost his betrothed.

Daniel lost his wife in The Blitz.

Jude's father lost his mother in the wake of Jude's birth.

And Simon loved my mother only to vanish alongside his family.

All these stories of affection.

Every one ended in tragedy.

To love brings death.

It should fill me with sadness.

Instead, all I feel is anger.

"You think this is an actual curse?" I spin around, indignant. But he's not in the doorway anymore. He's standing right behind me, close enough to see exactly what conclusion he has drawn. I let out a hollow laugh. "You? The cynic? The skeptic? Suddenly now, you're a believer?"

He jerks his hand toward the wall. "Are you not?"

"Of course I am. I've always been a believer. You, on the other hand, have white-knuckled logic like your life depends on it, even when it was completely illogical to do so. But now, *now*, you want to believe in curses?"

"I don't *want* to believe in anything."

I shake my head.

"But the evidence is pretty overwhelming." For a moment, he closes his eyes. When he opens them again, he won't meet mine. He simply walks to his door, his face as guarded as it was the first time we met. "I really think you should go."

37

THE GEMSTONES

Dry leaves skitter across the shingles as I climb out of Twig's bedroom window. The roof outside is flat and large enough to sit comfortably. I shake out the flannel blanket I brought from inside and sit down cross-legged with a small stack of books and a thermos of cider while Twig moves to the telescope mounted on its tripod.

"It's supposed to be somewhere near Cygnus," he mutters. Last night he couldn't find the comet. Tonight, he's determined.

Across the street, a motion-activated skeleton cackles in the fog, its red eyes glowing as Mr. Takahashi rolls his garbage bin to the curb. Above, the sky is clear—a spray of stars and a thin sliver of moon.

Inside, I'm a mess.

The parade is tomorrow.

Dress rehearsals for the ball were tonight. I was supposed to spend the evening in Jude's presence. Some of it, in his arms. Instead, I spent it at the fairgrounds, finishing up floats I no longer care about, doing what I've done for the past two days. Working through the evidence in my mind.

283

I hate that it makes sense.

I hate that Jude is shutting me out.

I throw my head back. "I wish I never would have lifted the false bottom of that stupid drawer."

Out loud, the comment is very random. In my head, it followed a logical train of thought. Thankfully, Twig has known me long enough by now to keep up.

He adjusts his telescope with practiced care. "If death is involved, isn't it better to know?"

"I'm not going to die."

"You've become a skeptic?"

A growl rumbles in my chest. Because no, I'm not a skeptic. Unlike Jude, my belief system hasn't taken a jarring about-face. "I just wish he would talk to me."

"Can you really blame him, though? The guy believes loving you will—"

"He doesn't love me."

Twig casts a doubtful look over his shoulder. "I mean, I've never exactly conducted a field study on love, but I'd say he was at least in the preliminary stages."

A flush blooms in my cheeks. I think about the way he looked at me on the ballroom floor at our last rehearsal. Then later, at the fairgrounds. An innocent touch here. A playful swipe of paint there. The thinnest sliver of space between our arms on the car ride home.

Maybe I was in the preliminary stages, too.

I set the thermos of hot cider beside me and settle the small stack of books in my lap—on the bottom, the no-longer-locked tome, and on top, my journal of dreams. The glow from Twig's bedroom spills softly through the open window behind me, illuminating each entry as I thumb through the pages.

So far, I've dreamt of Molly, Florence, Rose, and Jude's mother. All four, victims of the curse. And two centuries before

I was born, Ezra Vandenberg painted me, looking exactly how I look today.

"Why me?" I say. Not in a powerless, frustrated way, either. My question isn't rhetorical. I want to know the answer. "He painted *me*, Twig." Not Molly or Florence or Rose or my mother. "Then he wrote those strange words on a scrap of journal in Maggie's office, referencing a revelation."

Balm or blight.

Beacon or burden

A blessing sent to end his suffering, or a promise that it shall endure.

Surely, his suffering was the curse. Which didn't die with him, but continued on.

"You think you're the balm," Twig says.

"Is that really such a crazy thing to think? I mean, what if this is my purpose? What if this is the whole reason I'm here?"

"To end the curse?"

"Why not?"

"I don't know, Selah. Something tells me Jude isn't going to risk your life to find out."

And just like that, my optimistic bubble pops. At the end of the day, it doesn't matter what I believe. Jude won't change his mind unless he believes it, too. I picture the manic collage spread across his wall, the tormented look on his face when he answered his bedroom door. Maybe if it weren't for his nightmares—ones in which I die and he's responsible—he wouldn't be so quick to assume the worst. Maybe, if he'd just take one of my phone calls, or talk to me at school, I could get him to see the bright side of things.

I set the journal aside and run my hand over the tome's cover, embossed with the same symbol Ezra painted on the locket and drew on the sketch of Molly. It was found on Lydia Mabel, postmortem. Jude wanted the autopsy report for Violet

Underwagon. No doubt to see if she had the mark, too. If we could get autopsy reports for Helena Pisel, Mary Donovan, Rose Vandenberg ... would they have similar marks? Could Jude get the autopsy report for his mother?

Is this symbol a mark of the curse?

And what does this old English story about two angels named Seraphina and Dante have to do with it?

I rub my eyes.

Sleep has been nearly impossible.

For the past two nights, I've lain awake with a scrambled mind and a heart in tatters. I want to be in the Vandenberg ballroom, dancing with Jude while Miss Applewhite demands *eye contact, eye contact, eye contact!* Instead, I'm here, feeling as hollowed-out as that skeleton across the street.

As if on cue, it starts to cackle again.

I lift my gaze to the stars, searching for Cygnus, a cross-like constellation in the western sky. Somewhere out there, Dante's comet hurtles through space. A fiery snowball? Or an angel unhinged by love?

Twig keeps searching.

I sip my cider and open the fable, trying to distract myself with the illustrations. They mimic stained glass. The colors are rich and saturated, the outlines bold—Seraphina with long raven hair and radiant wings spread across two pages. The handwritten text tells of her three special gifts.

The first: power over darkness and shadow.

I run my fingers across the page. The pad of my thumb brushes over a symbol I haven't noticed before. Embedded in the stained glass design is the outline of a candle with a white body and a black triangular flame.

Just like the onyx.

I turn the page to the angel's second gift: the power to see what is hidden.

This time, I study every panel of glass, carefully searching. Then I find it—an eye with a white circular iris.

Just like the pearl.

I turn another page, to the angel's third and final gift: the power over human hearts. She can stop them. Break them. Seduce them. Start them. And apparently, make them pound, because mine is doing just that as I scan the illustration.

And there it is, over her left wing.

A red heart.

With an outline of the diamond inside.

"Whoa," Twig says. "Selah, come see this."

He must have found it.

The comet.

But I can't look away from the book, because I've found something, too.

"Selah?"

I look up.

He's no longer peering through the viewfinder of his telescope. He's staring at me.

I scramble to my knees and thrust the book at him. When he doesn't take it, I point at the black flame. "The onyx."

I point at the white iris. "The pearl."

I point at the diamond inside the heart. "And the ruby."

"The gemstones," he whispers.

We stare at one another for a disbelieving moment.

"Twig ... is this what Rafe's after? Do you think—are there actual powers tied to these gemstones?"

My mind reels.

Rafe thought he had them. But then he caught Isabel wearing the ruby and threw a bonafide temper tantrum. The question is, why did he hide them in the well? If he thought he already had the gemstones, what was he waiting for?

I stare at the book with the symbol of the curse on the cover.

And inside, the origin story of Dante's comet, which returns every two-hundred-sixty-eight years.

Ezra Vandenberg witnessed it the last time.

Then he painted me, a girl who wouldn't exist until that same comet returned again.

The puzzle pieces swirl.

Closer and closer.

They have to be related.

38

A NOT SO EMPTY THREAT

The marching band rehearses in bursts of music. Snare drums and tenors rattle out a commanding tempo as the fog lifts and golden sunlight spills over the meandering line of floats in the high school parking lot. Silver pompoms sparkle as cheerleaders run through a routine.

I lace up my boots, Mercy Bogaard once again, my insides a tangle of emotion as more parade participants arrive. Sports teams. Civic groups. Local performers. My personal favorite? A mime troupe. But not even their charming absurdity distracts me this morning.

My attention keeps returning to the spot where the Cadillac should be—long and black with sweeping fenders. More relic than vehicle, unearthed from the estate's motor house.

Behind the empty space, Sterling Bogaard sits atop the backseat of a red thunderbird convertible, joined by his great grandmother, Opal, an old woman who looks to be pushing a hundred. A 1948 Chrysler Town and Country is parked behind them, to be driven by Carl, who will be escorting Marvin Doorn, the out-of-town professor.

The Vandenbergs are MIA.

I called Jude twice last night. The first rang and rang. The second went straight to voicemail, making me want to scream. Or maybe cry. I sent him a cryptic text instead, thinking curiosity might tempt him into conversation.

> Just discovered something big. Call me.

It went as unanswered as every other text I have sent him this week. Apparently, the only way I'm going to be able to tell him about last night's discovery will be face-to-face.

Wheels clatter over uneven concrete as I pocket my phone and rub my hands to ward off the chill. Mrs. Calloway approaches, pulling a red Radio Flyer filled with bottled waters, granola bars, and—because she's Mrs. Calloway—a selection of individually wrapped homemade goodies. She passes the wagon to me with profound gratitude, like I'm saving lives instead of handing out provisions.

"I'm happy to help," I say with a smile.

She gives my elbow an appreciative squeeze. The walkie-talkie clipped to the pocket of her coat squawks. She excuses herself with a harried expression and joins the inspector in front of the Phoenix Float—a giant, mythical bird constructed from metal wire and papier-mâché, complete with wings that flap as it rises from the smoke. It's the parade's grand finale. Every year, it's preceded by the marching band and joined by the color guard, who dress in fiery colors and wave red and orange flags.

Right now, though, neither the wings nor the fog machine are working. Not ideal for a grand finale. Mr. Calloway and Twig are on the job, though, which means Mrs. Calloway has no reason to fret. They'll figure out what's wrong and get things up and running in no time.

I pull the wagon to the Dutch float, decked out with tulips, a windmill, wooden shoes, and a sign that reads, "In search of new beginnings." A tribute to our town's heritage. Several people help themselves to drinks and snacks.

The Founder's float is next, featuring Andreas Vandenberg, Tobias Bogaard, and Amadeaus Doorn—played by three overly serious men from the Preservation Society. Then comes the float I'll be joining, a burning building facade with faux flames made of red and orange cellophane blown upward by a pair of electric fans. Torch bearers will march in front and behind. The Aftermath float follows, an ash heap mostly, ridden by kids from junior theater. They descend on Mrs. Calloway's wagon like tiny chimney sweeps, snatching up most of the homemade goodies when at last the Cadillac arrives.

My heart soars.

I quickly look away, needing a second to collect myself. Across the lot, Kate breaks away from the cheerleading squad to join her mother. They give a cheer as the fog machine sputters to life. Twig hops off the trailer and crawls underneath to work on the motor for the wing mechanism.

I take a steadying breath and peek again at the Cadillac.

Only then do I notice.

Jude isn't driving. Instead, Rafe sits behind the wheel. Isabel rides shotgun. I crane my neck, searching for Jude in the back seat.

But he isn't there.

My stomach plummets as Rafe eases the Cadillac into place. He steps out looking like he belongs in one of those black and white perfume ads. He's wearing dark trousers, a white button down shirt open at the collar, a black leather jacket, and dark sunglasses.

He circles around the chrome grille, opens the door, and offers Isabel his hand. She takes it like she's royalty—sliding out in a wide-brimmed hat and a cream-colored coat dress with oversized lapels and gold buttons. It's unnerving, watching them smile at one another when not so long ago, Rafe made her cry out in pain.

Isabel glides toward Mayor Ridley's wife and greets her with kisses on both cheeks. Rafe lingers behind. He leans against the Cadillac, one ankle crossed over the other, a picture of careless charm. Then he lowers his sunglasses just enough to meet my gaze.

He flashes a wicked grin.

Clenching my jaw, I grab the wagon handle and wheel it toward him.

"Selah Whitlock," he says, his grin widening. "Looking dutiful as ever."

"Where's Jude?" I ask.

"He didn't tell you?"

My grip on the wagon handle tightens.

Rafe clicks his tongue. "How rude of him. We'll have to have a little chat about being more considerate."

"Where is he, Rafe?"

"He stayed behind. Isabel was disappointed, of course, but what can she do? He's adamantly uninterested. In *anything*, really. Which has become a problem, hasn't it?" He leans in slightly, his voice dropping. "What's going on between the two of you, Selah? Trouble in paradise?"

I don't take the bait. Instead, I fold my arms and lift my chin. "I know what you're up to."

He arches a brow. "Do tell."

"You're looking for the onyx and the pearl."

This earns a pause.

"The question is why," I continue. "Do they have powers?"

"What would ever make you believe something so dramatic?" he asks.

Oh, I don't know. Perhaps the so-called children's fable that no longer feels like a children's fable. But I bite my tongue.

"I'll tell you what," Rafe says. "I'll divulge what I'm up to if you tell me where you've put the portrait. I've asked Jude, but he keeps pleading the fifth."

"Why do you want it?"

"Sentimental reasons."

"Well, I'm sorry to break it to you, but I don't know where it is."

"You're a horrible liar, Selah."

I lift my shoulder in what I hope is an unbothered shrug.

"You should really tell the truth." He examines his nails. "Lying has consequences, you know. If you keep it up, something horrible might just happen to Jude."

"You know, Rafe, the last time you made a threat like that, you disappeared for ten days. Any chance we could be so lucky a second time?"

His smile fades, but before he can reply, Lainey Sikes makes an appearance. She flings her arms around his neck with a giddy squeal. "Rafe! Oh my gosh, you look amazing." She leans back and pouts her lips. "You told me last night you weren't coming."

"I wanted it to be a surprise. I know how much you love surprises."

Lainey hugs him again, pressing her cheek to his.

Desperate.

Clingy.

Just watching makes my skin itch with claustrophobia.

Rafe whispers in her ear.

She stiffens slightly.

He cups her chin and brushes his lips against hers. "Pretty please? For me?"

It makes me want to vomit.

But apparently, it works on Lainey. Whatever Rafe requested, the public display of affection does the trick. She squares her shoulders and marches away.

I watch her go, suspicion coiling in my gut. "What are you doing with Lainey?" I ask, turning to face him.

Rafe smiles.

"You don't even like her."

"Now why would you go and say something like that? I've become a big fan of Lainey's. She's very useful."

I open my mouth, ready with a retort, but his phone dings.

He lifts a finger as if to say—*hold that thought*—and checks the message. He taps out a slow reply, then slides his phone into his pocket. "So, where were you last night, Selah? Poor Jude had to dance with Miss Applewhite."

My insides drop like a stone. "What?"

"The dress rehearsal. You weren't there."

"Jude went?"

"He was late, and not at all in the appropriate attire. But yes. He came, which is more than I can say about you. Miss Applewhite was in quite the tizzy."

"He's going to the ball?"

"He's a Vandenberg. Of course he's going."

"Who's he going with?"

But Rafe has no time to answer.

Anything he has to say is drown out by a shout that cracks across the parking lot.

Another follows, higher-pitched and panicked. Mrs. Calloway is screaming. Joined by the booming voice of Mr. Calloway. "He's stuck under the wheel!"

My heart lurches.

Twig!

I race toward the commotion, where the trailer has shifted forward, trapping Twig beneath the rear wheel. Mrs. Calloway and Kate are on their hands and knees, frantic, like they might crawl under the trailer to join him.

"One, two, three, push!" Carl commands.

I throw my weight into the trailer with several others. It

lurches forward just enough for Twig to slide free. Mr. Calloway hauls Twig upright. Mrs. Calloway and Kate surround him.

"What happened?" Mayor Ridley demands, pushing his way forward.

"Someone pulled the brake lever," Harrison Locke replies.

Murmurs ripple through the crowd.

"Should we call for an ambulance?" the mayor asks.

"It'll be quicker if I take him," Carl says, his face as bloodless as Twig's, who's wincing and clutching his arm. "Let's go, son. We need to get this x-rayed."

Twig goes with his dad, offering reassurances to his mother, his sister. He gives me a reassuring look, too.

I just stand there, frozen in place, my imagination shifting into overdrive as Carl ushers Twig through the crowd and calls over his shoulder, "Someone will have to drive Professor Doorn in the parade."

They rush past Lainey.

Her eyes are wide.

Wild.

Guilty.

My stomach turns to lead.

According to Harrison, someone pulled the brake lever. And Lainey's eyes are welling with tears as she spins on her heel and runs away.

"It's amazing," Rafe says, suddenly beside me, "how much excitement the simple pull of a lever can drum up. Be careful, Selah. The next one might not walk away."

My heart gallops.

My body shakes.

Rafe slides his hands into his pockets and strolls toward Isabel.

Five minutes later, I stand at the doors of the Vandenberg manor, knocker in hand. But before I can do anything with it, the doors swing open. Jude appears, glancing over his shoulder, looking very much like a man on a mission. Until he catches sight of me and stops dead.

"Rafe just hurt Twig. I think his arm is broken."

Jude's brow furrows. "What?"

I open my mouth to elaborate when the items in his hands distract me. The compass, or at least, two halves of the compass, along with a brittle scrap of paper. "What is that?"

"I took it apart, and this was inside."

He hands me the scrap.

It's fragile in my fingers, like it might crumble if I breathe too hard. On it, someone has written a string of numbers, one stacked over the other. Six digits per line, grouped in pairs, each followed by a symbol. The first ends in N, the second in W.

"These are coordinates," I whisper.

Old-fashioned coordinates. The kind you'd find on an explorer's map from long ago. Degrees. Minutes. Seconds.

I flip the scrap over.

A short phrase has been scrawled on the back.

Beneath the highest point.

"I plugged them in." Jude shows me a map on his phone with a pin dropped in the hills.

A gasp tumbles from my lips.

Because I know that location.

It's the ruins of St. Fortuna's.

39
THE SECRET DOOR

We park at the cemetery and walk the rest of the way, the blue dot on Jude's phone tracking our movement. Clouds have gathered on the horizon. Wind begins to stir. It's almost as if the weather can sense my mood—on edge, wound tight, my insides a snarl. I can't stop thinking about Twig, or how easily that wheel could have rolled over something more vital than his arm.

Beside me, Jude walks with his mouth set, his jaw tense, his hands shoved deep into the pockets of his jacket. He has fixed his attention straight ahead, because heaven forbid it lands on me.

I want to shout at him.

Your cousin did this!

He threatened me by hurting Twig. He manipulated Lainey, who had no control over that trailer. I can't stop picturing Mrs. Calloway and Kate on their hands and knees, frantically calling his name. His legs thrashing as he cried out in pain. Rafe did that. Rafe's responsible for that. And yet, Jude's acting like *I'm* the leper, like *I've* done something wrong. Like he couldn't stand being in that car with me for one more second.

Well, fine.

If my presence is such a horrible thing to bear, I won't subject him to the misery. I lengthen my stride. Mercy Bogaard's dress billows around my ankles as I weave between sunken gravestones, their epitaphs long faded. There must be *something* here worth discovering. Why else would the scrap of paper be hidden inside a compass that was hidden inside a Bible?

A blanket of fallen leaves surrounds the skeletal remains of St. Fortuna's. Honeysuckle crawls up broken archways. Moss creeps over fallen stone. Virginia creeper snakes around blackened support beams that protrude from the earth like a ribcage —blood-red veins over scorched bone.

I step over a crumbled wall, into the footprint of the former chapel. Beneath my boots, faint mosaic flooring peeks through layers of dirt and debris.

Birdsong fills the quiet.

And then my phone.

It dings with a message from Twig.

> Deemed non-urgent. Stuck in waiting room.
> Guy with chest pain got right in. I should have
> exaggerated. Arm hurts like a nutcracker.
> How's the parade?

I type back a quick, slightly deceptive reply, my guilt quadrupling. But what can I say in a text? This is a story I have to tell him in person. I add some extra exclamation points, two heart emojis, and hit send.

"This is supposed to be the spot," Jude says, glancing at his phone. He stands directly in front of an elevated stone base, cracked and covered with ivy.

St. Fortuna's altar.

We search the area, nudging loose stones with our shoes—

looking for what, I'm not even sure. Jude puts the compass back together, but like always, it twitches erratically.

I set my hands on my hips.

The scrap of paper had coordinates. But it also had a clue. "Beneath the highest point," I mutter, more to myself than Jude.

The altar could be the highest point spiritually. But physically? That would've been the steeple. Probably the tallest thing in all of Foggy Hollow pre-fire. I turn in a slow circle until I spot it—a knee-high ring of sunken stone at the far corner, half-buried.

"St. Fortuna's bell tower," I say. "That has to be it."

We hurry forward, and without a word, we start clearing the area. We sweep aside dead leaves and brittle branches. We pull back briars and curtains of ivy, yanking at the clinging vines. We haul away chunks of stone, some so large we have to lift them together. At some point, I remove my coat. We don't stop until we're both dirt-smeared and breathless and all that's left is bare earth.

Beneath the highest point.

Jude and I share a fevered glance. Then we drop to our knees and dig.

The soil is damp. Dirt wedges beneath my fingernails as we tear through roots, our urgency growing, like we're digging toward something crucial. Finally, my knuckles scrape against a smooth, solid surface.

I pause for a moment, my breath catching. Then I dig harder, scooping away the earth until we've uncovered a flat stone slab too symmetrical to be an accident.

"It looks like a door," Jude says.

My phone dings in the pocket of my coat.

I'm sure it's from Twig.

Maybe he finally got a room. Or he had his x-ray. I picture him in a sterile hospital, annoyed about missing the parade—

while I'm here, in this once sacred space, unearthing century-old clues.

Jude brushes away the last of the dirt, exposing seams and edges. Along one of them, a shallow groove has been carved into the stone. Just big enough for a person to slide their fingers beneath.

So I slide mine in and pull with all my might.

The door doesn't budge.

Jude tries next. The tendons in his neck strain. His face goes red. The slab shifts—a centimeter, then an inch. He's lifting it, ever so slightly.

Quickly, I grab a nearby rock and wedge it underneath, holding the stone up so we don't lose progress. We reposition ourselves, side by side on our knees, and slide our hands beneath the propped corner. Together, we try to lift, but we're too close to the ground to get any leverage.

I find a stick in the rubble and try using it as a lever.

It snaps in half.

Jude spots a partially burned beam a few feet away. It's charred on the outside, but when he knocks it against a rock, it holds. He jams the beam into the narrow gap, and slowly, he shifts the slab again, just enough to get my arms completely under it. My back aches as we give one final heave and push the door aside.

"*Great Scott,*" I whisper.

A narrow stone stairwell descends into darkness.

Jude uses the flashlight on his phone, and together, we climb down the stairs. The walls are damp to the touch and lined with sconces—half-melted candles still intact in their holders. The air smells of wet earth and decay and the temperature drops with every step. By the time we reach the flagstone landing, it's cold enough to make me wish I'd grabbed my coat.

We've reached a small antechamber. A cast-iron door looms

before us, set into an arched frame inscribed with Latin. Jude shines his light across the carved words.

"*Quod clausum est,*" he reads aloud, tilting his head. "*Manere clausum debet.*"

"Did you learn Latin at boarding school?"

He eyes the inscription. "That which is closed ... must remain closed."

"That's creepy," I mutter.

He moves his flashlight down the length of the door. The beam glides over a keyhole and comes to an abrupt stop.

I move my hand to my clavicle, over the key I've taken to wearing like a necklace. Just like my mother used to. I slide the chain from around my neck. I fit the key into the hole, just like I've done a hundred times before, in every keyhole we could find.

Only this time ... the lock clicks.

40
A CRYPT

The room is long and rectangular with a coffin in the center.

"A crypt," I whisper.

Only there's no skeleton with a bowtie.

Jude shines his flashlight past the coffin, where a large stone table spans the length of the far wall.

It isn't empty.

We hurry toward it.

A lantern with soot-streaked glass sits beside an inkwell crusted with dried ink. A feather quill lays on a small piece of cloth next to a rolled up scroll secured with a cord. There's a pile of charcoal sketches, a leather-bound Bible so dry and cracked it looks like old bark, and a hand-drawn map that has curled in on itself.

I smooth it straight and take in the familiar geography—the Blackwillow River, the mountains, the forest. Along with historic landmarks, like assembly hall and St. Fortuna's. A bold X marks a spot in what must have once been red ink but has since faded to rusty brown.

"This is in the cemetery," I say, pointing at the X.

Jude shines his light on the annotated words at the bottom. "Where the blood must fall," he reads.

"The compass will lead the way," I finish.

He picks up the charcoal sketches. The first one is of Molly. There's no symbol drawn in the corner. But there is an apology written in Ezra's hand.

I'm sorry I loved you. I'm sorry it killed you.

I want to snatch the sketch from Jude and tear it into pieces. The last thing he needs is more reason to shut me out. Thankfully, he's moving along, shuffling to the next, and the girl isn't Molly. The girl looks more like me. As though drawn from the vague recollection of a dream. Each successive sketch bears more of my likeness. In the final one, I'm wearing the locket.

With a pounding heart, I pick up the scroll. My hands tremble as I untie the leather cord and begin unrolling the vellum parchment. Ornamental script appears, written in more Latin, and there are two symbols at the top—the one that marked my mother, and another just as familiar.

"That's your family crest," I say.

Jude runs his thumb over it. The shield is missing, and the sun doesn't have any sunbursts. But it's the same basic structure.

I finish unrolling the scroll.

A small sheaf of paper slips out, filled with cramped handwriting.

Jude and I stand close as we read the words.

Taken from the Testament of the Watchers, AD 1053

In the beginning, God made the angels. He formed them in light and goodness, that they might serve His will. But many fell from grace, drawn by pride and the lust for dominion. Among these were Dante and Seraphina, glorious in form, terrible in purpose, bound together in a love corrupted by envy.

Dante, seeking to magnify his strength, begat a mortal line in secret, that his power might be increased through the mingling of blood. Unwilling to be lesser, Seraphina did likewise, and forged a lineage of her own.

But when Dante perceived her ambition, he rose up in fury. From her three amulets, wherein her gifts were bound, he did strip of power and sealed it within his tomb. The vessels left barren, he descended into the grave by his own hand.

She doth now wander the earth, awaiting her hour.

When his fire blazeth brightest in the heavens, when the amulets are set within the arch, and the mortal blood of Dante's seed is willingly spilled upon the vault wherein her power was sealed, then shall she rise, more terrible and mighty than before.

Translated faithfully by my hand.

- Ezra Vandenberg, AD 1757

"1757," I whisper.

The last time Dante's comet appeared, blazing bright in the heavens.

Jude's eyes meet mine. He hasn't given me the chance to tell him about the gemstones, about Seraphina's powers. But this does the job well enough.

I open the Bible, half-expecting it to be carved out like the one from Simon's bedroom, only this will have the gemstones inside. But the pages are intact and as dry as fallen leaves. I flip through them, stopping in Lamentations, where three loose pages have been tucked, their edges ragged on one side.

As though torn from a book.

No. A journal.

The first was written the same year as Ezra's translation.

She came to me not as an angel but in the likeness of a woman, fair to behold with a countenance that stirred longing in the hearts of men. She named herself Sara—a maiden with no kin, a damsel in need of saving. Many fell beneath her influence. I alone beheld the truth and would not receive her.

She turned then to my brother. He gave her his heart. I entreated him to reconsider, for I perceived she sought not love but power. She required our blood to reclaim that which had been taken from her. But he would not listen. Or perchance he did, and chose to love her still.

I resolved to destroy her, but every attempt failed. I came to suspect the endeavor an impossibility. That which hath fallen from heaven cannot be destroyed by earth. My only hope was to cast her out. Yet in my attempt, it was my brother whom I destroyed.

In my despair, I struck a bargain with the devil. My brother's life for my heart. I believed I might outwit her.

As she brought Raphael back from death, I moved against her. I opened the tomb and sealed her within. The seal held. Yet what returned to me bore not the soul of my brother, but a shadow of a man filled with bitterness and rage.

He has fixed his hatred upon me, for it was I who imprisoned Seraphina.

"She was real?" Jude says.

It's not so hard for me to believe. But for him? His face has gone a shade paler, casting the shadows beneath his eyes and cheekbones into sharper relief. This beautiful boy, tumbling deeper down Alice's rabbit hole.

Seraphina and Dante.

Not just characters in a children's fable.

But actual fallen angels.

As real as the curse.

I reread the entry, trying to make sense of the implications. Seraphina wanted her powers back. To do that, she needed to open the tomb. To open the tomb, she needed the blood of

Dante's mortal descendants. So she went after Ezra, and then Raphael. Which means ...

"Jude," I whisper.

But I don't have to say it.

He has made the same connection.

If Ezra was a mortal descendant of Dante, then so is he. Which means Jude Vandenberg is part angel. And Rafe is, too.

My mind spins.

My blood pounds.

Here, too, is the reason for the brothers' long-standing enmity. The beginning of the feud. In Ezra's attempt to kill Seraphina, he accidentally killed Raphael, then begged her to bring him back from the dead. She did, and in so doing, he imprisoned her and Raphael came back different.

Jude turns to the second entry, written a year later.

My brother's life in exchange for my heart. I had believed myself spared from her curse, for after I sealed Seraphina away, my heart beat whole.

But no longer.

My dearest Molly. I loved her, and she loved me. Yet somehow, he deceived her. He seduced her. He delighted in her ruin. And in her shame, she died by her own hand. This was no cruel accident. Raphael has ensured I understand as much.

I took from him the object of his devotion. Now he has taken mine. His life for my heart, and mine is lost. Broken. Ravaged.

My brother is no longer the man I knew. He

is a creature remade in bitterness. Seraphina has cursed my blood and corrupted his.

Can blood be evil?

The question reverberates in my mind. It was first penned by Isaiah. A question about Lucian, who had Reuben, who had Frank, who had Thomas, who had Rafe. I picture him whispering to Lainey, and Twig, stuck under the trailer. And I know the answer.

Yes.

Blood can absolutely be evil.

I keep reading.

Raphael is gone now. He departed but recently, setting sail for England and leaving wreckage in his wake. I say good riddance, though our mother weeps.

For her beloved sons, who have become sworn enemies. For his absence, and for the sorrow that has settled in my soul. I have told her I shall not take a wife. I shall not bear heirs. This curse upon my blood shall perish with me.

Jude has gone ghostly pale now as he turns to the third and final page. The entry is written almost twenty years later.

I am ashamed. I am weak. A fool, and worse still, a fool who hath acted foolishly.

I saw her in the house of God, wearing a locket I have seen a hundred times before, though never in waking life. It has haunted my dreams, always upon Seraphina's neck as she drives the blade into Molly's heart. And yet, there she stood, adorned with it.

She told me she purchased it from a traveling peddler, who sold charms and oddments from a wooden cart. In that moment, my reason faltered. The sight of that wretched locket turned my heart to fury. I forgot my vow.

I was drawn in not by love, but madness, and hunger for what once was. I took pleasures where I ought not to have taken. What else could I do but offer her my hand? I would not leave her disgraced, as Raphael left Molly. I would be the better man.

Yet I do not love her. My heart is no longer capable of love. It lies buried with Molly in a grave left nameless.

But now I am afraid, for she is with child. And what if the curse passes to him?

I depart for war in a fortnight. Before I go, I must do all I can to protect the truth. To keep her sealed away forever. I have found the amulets Raphael hid. In their place, I have left clever facsimiles. The key and the compass are hidden within the Word of God. The truth is buried beneath sacred ground. Should my brother return, his depraved soul shall not venture near either.

My mind spins as dots connect with cataclysmic speed. The compass, the key, the Bible. Three pieces of the same puzzle, separated over the centuries, and now, brought back together. By me, a girl Ezra foresaw. And Jude, a descendant of Dante.

I pick up the charcoal sketches, which would later become a painting. And in that painting, the locket was Seraphina's.

She wore it in his dreams.

Then it showed up in his actual life.

I pick up the scroll, eying the two symbols at the top. One, the Vandenberg crest, which belonged first to Dante. The other, the symbol on the locket, which belonged first to Seraphina. It isn't the mark of the curse. It's the mark of the one who cast it. And every time it was triggered, she signed her name.

Then he painted me, wearing it ...

"The revelation," I say. Mysterious words written in his own hand, the year of his son's birth. "What if it's here?"

Jude flips through the rest of the Bible. He turns over the map. He does the same with the scroll. But there's nothing else to be found. The mysterious revelation remains frustratingly elusive.

With the table thoroughly searched, he shines his light on the coffin.

It sits in a low stone recess, its surface warped and split with age. We move closer, as though compelled. And I can't help but think that this coffin doesn't fit. If someone were entombed in here, the crypt would have been written about. But I've never read anything about a crypt under St. Fortuna's.

I press my hand along the coffin's seam and push. The lid groans but doesn't move. I find a crack near the corner and wedge my fingers beneath it. Jude joins me. We pull and yank, and with a splintering sound, the wood gives way.

Just as I suspected, there are no bones inside.

But there is a jewelry box.

A domed walnut chest.

Slowly, I lift the lid.

And there it is.

Resting in the upper tray on a velvet cushion. The locket. My heart pounds as I pick it up. It's cold to the touch. Heavy, too. I try to open it, but it's locked tight. And for just a second, it pulses violently in my palm.

With a gasp, it clatters to the floor.

"Are you okay?" Jude asks.

"I-I'm fine," I say.

He picks it up, and for one panicked moment, I want to shout at him to stop. Don't touch it. But he's too quick. And nothing happens.

The locket is silent and still.

I lift the upper tray to investigate the compartment beneath. And there they are. The two items Rafe has been searching for —the onyx and the pearl.

Not clever facsimiles.

But Seraphina's amulets.

Empty vessels without any power.

Except to open the tomb.

With Vandenberg blood.

Under the light of Dante's comet.

Finally, Rafe's finish line has come into view.

We know exactly what he's up to.

41
THE QUESTION IS WHY?

Clouds swirl overhead as Jude and I work together to slide the stone slab back into place. By the time we're through, the temperature has dropped and the sky is spitting.

Thunder rumbles.

A gust of wind rips through the ruins.

I slide my arms into the sleeves of my coat and fish my phone from the pocket. The screen lights up with a slew of missed messages.

Half a dozen from Twig and two from Dad.

The parade's over. He wants to know where I am and why Mercy Bogaard never appeared on the Fire of 1822 float. Also, severe thunderstorms are approaching. The festival's postponed. Could I please let him know I'm okay?

I type out a quick reply.

> All good, Dad! Sorry to worry you. Something came up with a friend and I had to help. Will be home soon. XOXO.

I hate being dishonest, but I hate worrying him even more. A vague half-truth is the best I can do.

I scroll through Twig's texts as lightning flashes in the distance and Jude covers the door with detritus—dead leaves and sticks and chunks of smaller stone.

> 10:12 a.m.: Fracture confirmed. Sling acquired. Ortho scheduled for next week. Zero stars. Would not recommend.

> 10:54 a.m.: Pain meds: engaged. Recliner: activated. Boredom: reaching critical mass. Parade update: conspicuously absent? Requesting field report.

> 11:11 a.m.: Gnarly storms inbound. Mom says festival is postponed. I'm beginning to suspect your battery has passed from this life to the next.

> 11:37 a.m.: Ground control to Major Tom. Come in, Major Tom. Your phone is ringing, which means the battery is intact. Mom says you weren't in the parade and your dad called. Storms about to go full apocalypse. Do you copy? Over.

I shoot him a text every bit as vague but slightly more truthful than the one I sent my dad.

> Sorry for going AWOL. Went on side quest. Too much to explain. Will call when I can.

I drop the phone into my pocket.

Jude finishes camouflaging the door.

"I'm going to find the tomb," I announce.

"What?"

"According to the map, it's right over there." With a pair of fallen angels locked inside.

I don't wait for permission or protest. A fork of lightning splits through the clouds as I turn toward the cemetery and go.

"Selah," Jude calls.

I keep going.

He catches up. "We need to get indoors."

I only walk faster. "We know what he's after now," I say over the wind. "Rafe wants to open the tomb. The question is—why?"

Does he think Seraphina will share her powers with him if he lets her out? Is this some foolish duty, passed down from one rotten generation to the next? Or does he simply want to unleash chaos?

Lightning flashes.

Thunder booms.

And the sky opens.

Rain falls in a deluge.

Jude begs me to stop. We can find the tomb later. But I'm done with later. After so many dots connecting, with the picture finally coming into focus, I need to see it whole. "Maybe we'll find more answers at the tomb."

"Selah." He grabs my arm.

I jerk free, blinking away the rain that's falling in my eyes. "Nobody's making you come with. If you're so worried about the storm, then go."

But he doesn't go.

And we're almost there.

I can see the map in my mind. I know exactly where I'm headed—the oldest corner of the cemetery. We reach it soaked to the bone. Cold water sloshes in my boots. Strands of hair cling to my cheeks as I stop in front of what should be Dante's tomb.

Only it's not a tomb.

It's a sunken mausoleum, cracked down the middle and choked with ivy. Ezra's translation mentioned an archway, but I don't see anything that even comes close.

I turn to Jude, squinting through the downpour. "The map said to use the compass."

"Selah, this is crazy."

"We're well past crazy! Just give me the compass."

With rain streaking down his face, he pulls it from his pocket and flips it open, shielding it with his hand like a makeshift umbrella. I'm sure it will work. It *has* to work. *Where the blood must fall, the compass will lead the way.* Ezra wrote those words for a reason. But the needle twitches wildly, as useless as ever.

Trees groan.

Branches twist.

Thunder cracks so loud I jump.

The rain turns to ice. It stings like needles as it slices down in sheets driven sideways by the wind.

Jude scrubs his face with his hand. "Selah, *please*. We have to get inside."

Lightning strikes in a blinding white flash.

And for just a second, it's there.

Illuminated behind Jude.

A marble archway carved with three symbols.

The candle.

The eye.

The heart.

I gasp.

He whirls around.

But the light is gone and with it, the vision. Only the broken mausoleum remains.

A tree limb crashes to the ground.

Our phones blare in unison

SEEK SHELTER NOW.

Rain patters against the roof in a soft staccato and runs down my window in rivulets, blurring the night outside. The day's storms have calmed into a steady downpour with the occasional flicker of lightning and the distant rumble of thunder.

The festival has been postponed until tomorrow. The rain is supposed to continue through the night. Power crews are still out, clearing away the debris. There wasn't a tornado—just a dodgy funnel cloud. But the winds were strong enough to tear down tree limbs and damage power lines.

I slip a long-sleeved thermal over my head and tug my hair free, exhaustion settling into my bones. It's as though I've run a mental marathon, and still, I can't turn off my brain.

If only there were a switch.

Something to stop the thoughts.

I remove the skeleton key from around my neck and open the bottom drawer of my desk. I set the key on top of Simon's journal, which sits on top of the shoebox filled with keepsakes, which sits on top of the book my mother read to me on my birthday. I remove Enoch's worn copy of *The Great Gatsby*, which reminds me of my mother now, too. Daisy Buchanan to Simons' Dorian Gray. Maybe reading will help quiet my mind. Maybe losing myself in a story my mother once loved will lull me into peaceful, dreamless sleep.

I turn off the light, turn on my bedside lamp, and crawl beneath the covers. I open the book and flip through the musty pages when something falls loose—a pair of photographs pressed together face-to-face.

I sit up and take them in hand.

The one on top has been labeled in a slanted scrawl.

1927, me and Reuben.

I flip it over.

In black and white, three people sit at a poker table. A very young man, perhaps yet a boy, with a cigarette pinched between his fingers. He leans back in a velvet-upholstered chair too large for him, his posture cocky but not quite comfortable.

And beside him ...

My heart begins to pound.

A man who is *not* a boy, sharply dressed in a pinstripe suit, drink in hand. A woman with a feathered headband and a fringed dress sits on his lap. He smiles at the camera—a familiar wicked grin—like he can see through the lens.

Like he can see through time.

Like he can see me.

My heart pounds harder.

It slams against my sternum as I flip to the second photo. This one is square with a thick, white border—an early polaroid. On the bottom, written in the same slanted scrawl:

Frank Vandenberg, 1960.

This is a candid shot.

Frank Vandenberg didn't know he was being photographed. But his face is captured clearly as he stands on the edge of a familiar terrace, a cigarette between his lips. His posture is elegant. His eyes, detached. And his face—

My blood runs cold.

Here they are.

The photographs Jude and I couldn't find when we searched Enoch's trunk. They've been here this whole time, tucked inside *The Great Gatsby*. Daniel sent them to his brother in a letter, asking if he was going mad. And here is why.

Reuben and Frank don't just bear a strong resemblance.

Reuben and Frank are identical.

One and the same.

My hand curls around my throat, as though the gesture might help me breathe. But my lungs won't cooperate. I stare at these photos, mouth open, throat dry.

Suddenly, the letter Gabriel Vandenberg sent his mother—the one Jude showed me inside The Cobbler—comes into crystal clarity. He couldn't find his father's cousin in Winchester. Nor any account of the Vandenberg name. Which never made sense. If Raphael married in Winchester, had children in Winchester, and died in Winchester, there would at least be an account.

But Gabriel couldn't find one.

Because Winchester was a ruse.

Raphael Vandenberg may have *gone* there, but he never married there. Or had children there. He certainly didn't die there.

The room tilts.

My hands shake.

Rafe isn't *from* a spoiled bloodline.

There never *was* a spoiled bloodline.

Reuben is Frank.

Frank is Thomas.

And Thomas ...

My skin erupts in goosebumps.

Seraphina brought Raphael back to life.

And he's remained that way ever since—the bad egg through history, frozen in time. Torturing first his brother, then his nephew, then his great nephew. All the way down the line.

Why does Rafe want to open the tomb?

Because he's the one who loved her.

Raphael *is* Rafe.

And now, he wants her back.

42
BRAVO, SELAH

The next morning, I walk through fog as thick as soup, the manor a hulking shadow in the gray haze. Not until I reach the fountain does the portico take shape. With my heart pounding and the photographs pressed nervously between my palms, I climb the stone steps.

The front doors fly open.

Just like yesterday.

Only this time, it isn't Jude on the other side with a compass and a brittle sheet of paper. It's Rafe with his car keys. And for just a moment, before he realizes I'm there with him, he looks wild. Unhinged. Terrifying.

My thoughts lurch to our first encounter in the graveyard.

You remind me of a girl I sort of know.

From a portrait painted by his *brother*.

Rafe is Raphael.

And Raphael is Rafe.

He seduced Molly Ludwig. Did he poison Lydia, too? Has he been the harbinger of this curse, a living ghost through the centuries, tormenting Ezra's descendants and killing off innocent women?

Am I next?

His attention lands on me. He stops in the doorway and his charming mask slides into place. "Good morning," he says, the corners of his mouth curling upward like the Grinch. "How's your bestie? Is his arm okay?"

I hide the photographs behind my back, heart revving into overdrive.

Rafe narrows his eyes. His gaze drops to my throat, where my pulse hammers. He tilts his head. "You're afraid of me."

I step back, heels brushing the edge of the stone stair.

"And not just afraid like I-hurt-your-friend afraid." He makes a low sound in his throat—interested, amused—the tilt of his head deepening as he slides his hands into his pockets. "You know, don't you?"

Fear grabs me by the throat.

"You know who I am. Bravo, Selah. Most people don't figure that out until it's too late." He cocks his head in the other direction. "What else have you figured out—the location of the gemstones?"

My gut twists with nausea.

The entryway spins.

I don't want to make eye contact. I'm terrified he'll see the truth if I do.

But Rafe darts forward like a snake. Suddenly, he's right there—mask gone, unhinged once again—gripping my arm with such ferocity, I gasp.

"My brother could have buried those gemstones," he growls. "He could have traveled to the ocean and tossed them in the waves. But Isabel found the ruby in the family safe. A Vandenberg heirloom. If he turned that amulet into a necklace, I can't help but think he did something similar with the other two. Am I getting warm, Selah?"

I try to jerk free, but his grip only tightens. "With all the research you and your boy toy have been doing, something tells me you know exactly where—"

"What's going on?" The commanding question comes from Jude.

Rafe's eyes droop with annoyance as Jude steps into the doorway, concern etched on every line, in every angle of his face.

"We were just having a little chat." Rafe lets go of my arm and straightens his coat.

Jude's concern melts into suspicion. "About what?"

"Tonight. The ball. Her dance card." He gives his dark eyebrows a wag. "If you won't dance with her, I will. You are going to come, aren't you, Selah? It's shaping up to be quite the show. Your friend, Lainey, has a starring role."

He leans close, his voice a blade against my ear. "You keep asking what I want with her. Come to the ball and find out." He tosses his keys in the air, catches them with a flick of his wrist, and disappears into the fog with a soft chuckle that chills me to the bone.

I stand there, frozen.

Terrified.

"What was that about?" Jude asks.

But I can't answer.

I can't hardly breathe.

"Selah." He steps closer. "You're shaking."

I suck in a breath. "He's Raphael."

"What?"

"The reason he wants to open the tomb? It's because *he's Raphael.*"

Jude's brow furrows.

I hand him the photographs. "I found these last night inside *The Great Gatsby*. From Enoch's trunk."

"The pictures from Daniel," Jude mutters.

I watch as he takes them.
I watch as he looks at them.
And I watch as all the blood drains from his face.

43
THE FOUNDER'S DESCENT

I stand on the balcony with my hands on the rail. Below, Mayor Ridley gives the opening speech while a stringed quartet plays softly. Flickering candlelight casts a haunting glow upon masked guests in their formal attire. It feels like I've stepped into history, until I glimpse Twig on the edge of the crowd with his arm in a sling, dressed in a suit that's a little too short and a little too modern.

I set my hand over the bodice of my dress, as though doing so might calm the butterflies in my stomach. The dress arrived this afternoon after the Harvest Festival, delivered in a vintage box with a handwritten note.

You said you didn't have anything to wear. -J

For a moment, I wondered if it wasn't the dress from the wardrobe. But then I pulled it out, and there was nothing faded or moth-eaten about it. When I tried it on, it fit to perfection, a fact that makes me blush even now. Because how could Jude know my size so intimately? I adjust my mask, pearl white with gold filigree, and run my hand beneath my hair, which is half pinned up. The rest falls in loose curls down my back with a

323

few carefully placed tendrils framing my face. All credit to Naomi, who came over with her curling iron.

I look at her and Harper next to Twig, and not too far from them—Mr. and Mrs. Calloway and Dad. After Rafe's ominous words about tonight, I made a quick and definitive decision.

"I'm going," I told Jude. "I'm sorry if that upsets you. I'm sorry if you don't want me there, but I can't sit in my bedroom while people I care about step into danger unknowingly."

He didn't argue.

He didn't even let me finish.

"Obviously, the circumstances have changed," he'd said.

I was going to the ball.

And he was going with me.

Jude stands at the bottom of the staircase in a black coat with a high collar, his gloved hands folded behind his back, his black mask simple but striking. He paints such a flawless picture, it seems obvious that he's part angel. A dead giveaway, honestly. Like I should have known this upon first sight. His looks are quite literally from heaven.

When he looks up at me, the fluttering in my stomach multiplies.

Mayor Ridley receives a round of polite applause. He hands the microphone to Miss Applewhite. She thanks the mayor and begins the Founder's Descent.

"Don't you look ravishing." The words belong to Lainey, who prowls toward me, breathtakingly gorgeous in a blood-red dress and a golden mask. She stops beside me at the railing, toying with a necklace at her décolletage.

It's the ruby.

I nearly choke at the sight of it.

She smiles. "It's gorgeous, isn't it? When Rafe gave it to me to wear, I could hardly believe my eyes."

"Lainey," I say, unsure what to add, my unease curdling to

dread. Whatever role Rafe has picked for her, I'm positive it won't end well. "I don't think you should wear that."

"Of course you don't." She slides the amulet up and down its chain. "You know, you sure do have a lot of nerve sitting on your high horse, trying to villainize Rafe when *you're* the thief."

"What are you talking about?"

"He told me about the onyx and the pearl. It's really rude to hide something that doesn't belong to you, Selah."

"He told you about them?"

"Rafe tells me everything."

I turn to face her fully. "What did he ask you to do at the parade?"

She lifts her chin.

I've never been Lainey's biggest fan. But not for one second do I blame her for what happened to Twig. I didn't yesterday, before I knew who Rafe really was. And I certainly don't now. "He made you hurt Twig, didn't he?"

"He didn't *make* me do anything." Her eyes are glowing, almost fevered. "I don't know what you have against him, Selah, but he loves me."

"Twig broke his arm," I shoot back. "He ended up in the hospital."

It could have been so much worse.

But Lainey only glares, like *I'm* the enemy. "He told me you would do this."

"Do what?"

"Try to turn me against him." She twirls a strand of dark, silky hair, gazing down at the object of her affection. Raphael Vandenberg. A harbinger of evil. A wicked shadow. A beautiful lie who has snared Lainey Sikes in his web.

"What does he want you to do tonight?" I ask her.

"Wouldn't you like to know." With a coy smile, she shoots me a wink. Then she turns and nearly runs into Becca Lynn at the top of the stairs, waiting to be announced.

Lainey's never been mean before. Absurdly dramatic and overly emotional, always. But never cruel. And yet, she looks Becca Lynn up and down, a peacock next to a sparrow, and says in a sickly sweet voice, "You're so lucky you don't care what people think, Becca. To show up in a dress like that on a night like this is just ... so brave of you. Admirable, even."

Becca Lynn's face falls. I can see it behind her mask.

Miss Applewhite calls her name.

She stumbles over the second step.

Lainey laughs, loud enough for Becca to hear.

I turn and glare at her.

She shrugs demurely, then she grins a grin so reminiscent of Rafe, my hands curl into fists.

"I hope you don't mess up the dance, Selah. Having missed the dress rehearsal and all."

Before I can offer a retort, Miss Applewhite's assistant sweeps in with her clipboard in hand and earpiece in place, telling me to stand straight, shoulders back. I'm next.

I come to the edge of the stairs. I set one hand on the railing, the other over my stomach as Jude's eyes find mine and lock into place with an intensity that makes me forget all about Lainey Sikes.

"Miss Selah Whitlock," Miss Applewhite announces, "escorted by Mr. Jude Vandenberg of the Vandenberg Family."

I walk down the stairs to the sound of gentle applause. I don't trip. I don't stumble. I don't take my eyes off of Jude. And I don't breathe until I reach him. He offers his arm. With my hand safely tucked in the crook of his elbow, we descend the rest of the way together.

At the bottom, I'm forced to walk past the *other* Vandenberg, his blue eyes gleaming behind a serpentine mask. His predatory gaze follows me as I walk with Jude onto the dance floor.

Lainey's name is called.

The ruby amulet resting in the dip of her clavicle catches the light and the muscles in Jude's arm tighten.

Lainey and Rafe join us on the floor, the last of the founding couples. The guests gather to watch the opening dance. The stringed quartet begins to play a light and lyrical melody.

With my heart still racing, I curtsey.

Jude bows.

The Waltz of the Hollow begins.

The six of us come together. We circle left. We circle right. I don't look at Lainey or Rafe. Neither does Jude. It's just us—me and him. Even when we come apart, his attention remains fixed on me, and although he's wearing gloves, I can feel the heat of his fingers when the dance brings us back together. We step close, our bodies nearly touching. He turns me in a circle one way, then turns me again in the other. And I have to let go. The dance demands it. I take Rafe's hand with gritted teeth.

The strings rise in cadence, a dance from another century resurrected under flickering candlelight. A melody spun like a spell as Jude and I are drawn together like magnets, like destiny, then pulled apart as we progress down the line and follow the steps. Every departure a heartbreak. Every return sweet relief as his touch lingers and his gaze smolders.

I'm left spinning.

And wanting.

More of him.

All of him.

But then the song ends.

And the crowd claps.

And the spell is broken.

Beside me, Lainey's face is flushed as Rafe pulls her to him. He tells her she looks stunning. Lainey smiles coquettishly then bats her eyes at Jude. "Tell your mom thank you for the mask, by the way. She's the one who lent it to me."

"Isabel isn't my mother," Jude replies.

"Oh, really?" Lainey says, all false surprise.

I want to step on her toe. Lainey knows Isabel isn't Jude's mother. She's made this mistake before. Just like it got under his skin then, it clearly gets under his skin now.

"You're so forgetful, Lainey," Rafe admonishes, his arm sliding around her waist. "Jude's real mother died, remember? Giving birth to you, right, Jude?"

Like a drawn bow, Jude's spine stiffens.

"So technically, you're what killed her." He leans close. "Or I guess it was your father's love. The curse and all. Better be careful with Selah, yeah?" He casts a slow glance toward me, as though checking my reaction as much as Jude's. Then he whirls Lainey around, and with a whisper in her ear, sends her off toward a group of our classmates.

She prowls toward them like a lioness on the hunt.

44

A STORM OF EMOTION

Jude keeps his eye on Rafe while I keep tabs on Lainey.

As the night unfolds, I watch as she flits from the ballroom to the salon to the gardens outside—doling out innocent touches, lingering looks, generous laughter. She even dances with Griffin, her ex. In *front* of his new girlfriend, who bursts into tears and runs away. Rafe looks on with a smirk, like *this* is his plan. To stir up drama by turning Lainey Sikes into a shameless flirt.

When Twig and I step onto the terrace for some fresh air, he tells me Lainey kept pressing him about the gemstones. He swears he didn't say anything, but his cheeks are flushed and he looks flustered.

I'm choosing to believe it's because of the circumstances. We're no longer operating in theoretical territory. The uncanny has permeated our actual life. We've stepped over a major threshold—into a realm of angels, curses, and immortal humans. For a guy as fascinated with the supernatural as I am, this is pretty thrilling stuff.

"Remember Marla Stenson?" Twig says.

I dig around in my brain.

Marla Stenson …

"Didn't we interview her for the podcast? Wait." I snap my fingers. "She's the one who saw an angel standing in line at the DMV."

Twig nods. "I reached out to her today, and she sent me a link to this blog called *Heaven's Battlefield* written by this religious lay scholar named Ezekiel Cotton. A couple months ago he wrote a post about mortal descendants of angels."

"And?"

"He made two basic claims. The first is fairly obvious. They have a strong connection with the spiritual realm."

Obvious, sure. But ironic, too. Jude Vandenberg hasn't exactly lived his life like one strongly connected to the spiritual realm.

"The second is a lot more interesting," Twig continues. "They're able to wield the supernatural."

"What does that mean?" I ask.

"He didn't go into detail, but I thought maybe … objects?"

We stare at one another.

Objects.

Like the gemstones?

Before either of us have a chance to comment on Rafe and his determination to wield said gemstones, familiar voices intrude. Kate and her boyfriend exchange heated words as they walk through the rose garden.

"She saw you in the hedge maze together," Kate says.

"She's lying," Harrison replies.

"Why would Lainey lie to me?"

Their voices fade as they walk away.

A few songs later, I run into Lainey exiting the powder room, her hand on the ruby amulet, and I swear, it looks brighter. When I open the door, a girl sniffles inside. "Why would she say something like that?"

"I'm sure she didn't mean it," another replies.

Back in the ballroom, Lainey's dancing again. A group of girls stand in the shadow, shooting daggers at her and the boy. I remain on the periphery, observing. Suspicious. Lainey is pouring gasoline on emotions that are already fraught—insecurity, jealousy, desire. Everything feels heightened. Like one wrong spark and the whole night will explode.

I don't get it.

Lainey was so excited to come to the ball with Rafe, and yet they haven't danced together since the opening number. Neither have Jude and I, for that matter. Ever since Rafe made his comment, a frost settled around Jude that has yet to thaw.

I spot him near the stairs with his mask in place. He stands tall, his posture refined, effortlessly dignified as he converses with Cosette Everly of the Preservation Society, Mayor Ridley, Isabel, and Rafe.

I weave between the dancers and slip into the conversation, my arm but a whisper from Jude's. The urge to touch him, to anchor myself to his presence, throbs beneath my skin. The air between us throbs, too. And yet, he's drawn himself tight, like a line I'm not allowed to cross.

"I must admit, this is a smashing success, Isabel," Mayor Ridley says. "People were a little hesitant with the change of venue. Of course, there will always be the naysayers, but I don't see how anyone here tonight could argue with this atmosphere."

"It really does feel like we've stepped back in time." Cosette casts her gaze upward, from the ornate chandeliers dripping with crystals to the carved cherubs on the cornices while the stringed quartet plays and the costumed guests glide across the floor. "I'm delighted you petitioned to move the event. Town hall pales in comparison."

"I must give credit where credit is due," Isabel replies. "I never would have thought of the idea if not for Rafe's insistence. In fact, it's thanks to Rafe that Jude and I are here at all."

The words come like a scratch to vinyl.

I can feel Jude react beside me.

Thanks to Rafe?

"He was very adamant that we join him here in Foggy Hollow for the festivities, and even more so when it came to hosting the ball in our manor."

Rafe smiles. "Yes, well, what's the point of being part of such a prominent legacy if we don't open it up to the masses?"

"If only everyone felt the same," Cosette says, her lip curling in the direction of the Bogaards, making me wonder what they could have done to offend her. "It's a very generous position to take."

"Says a very generous lady," Rafe replies. "You and your husband both." His attention connects with Henry Everly in his burgundy cravat, conversing with Loraine Pritchard, a pretty woman in her forties who sings in the choir at St. Oswald's. "It's touching to me, that he and his cousin are so close." He claps Jude on the shoulder. "It gives me hope that Jude and I might be the same someday."

Cosette blinks. "His cousin?"

"The woman he's speaking with. Loraine, I believe?"

Mayor Ridley laughs. "Henry and Loraine aren't cousins, are they?"

"Loraine is Henry's secretary." Cosette stands a little taller. "What made you think they were cousins?"

"I could have sworn that's how he introduced her when I ran into them in Elkins the other day, enjoying lunch. I must have misheard."

Cosette blanches.

Mayor Ridley gives his throat an awkward clear.

The air has been drawn out of the conversation.

All thanks to Rafe and his carefully placed comment.

The acting was faultless—innocent, oblivious.

But I'm not fooled.

Rafe is neither of those things.

"You know, Jude," he says, "it's very ungentlemanly of you to let such a beautiful date go to waste. I haven't seen you dance with Selah once since the opening number."

"I could say the same about you and Lainey," Jude replies.

"Yes, well, Lainey isn't short on suitors, is she? Meanwhile, poor Selah here is wilting on the sidelines."

Heat rises up my neck.

Mayor Ridley chuckles, like this is good fun.

"What do you say, Selah?" Rafe extends his hand to me. "Would you do me the honors?"

My skin crawls.

I don't want to touch him.

I don't want to be anywhere near him.

But I do want answers.

If dancing with him is the only way to get them, then so be it.

45
SOBBING IN THE
MUSIC ROOM

I can feel Jude's eyes on me as I take Rafe's hand and follow him out onto the dance floor. I dare one glance over my shoulder. He watches in taut stillness, the kind that crackles with tension.

The music begins, soft and slow.

Rafe sets his hand on the small of my back and draws me close. "Do you want to make him jealous?" he whispers in my ear. "It would be so easy. A well placed kiss ... "

I lean away, trying to maintain space as the melody draws us into its rhythm. Rafe sweeps me across the floor with ease. His steps are deliberate, perfectly timed, his dancing skills every bit as honed as his acting.

"It's so cute, watching you trail Lainey around like a little hall monitor. Tell me, Selah. What do you think of her performance so far?"

"She's stirring up a lot of drama."

"She's good at it, isn't she? An event like this, with so many people packed into one space. It's already ripe with emotion. Then you add Lainey and she just has a way of making it all sing."

I narrow my eyes, looking from him to Cossette Everly, who's having an animated conversation with her befuddled husband in an alcove nearby. I don't like the Everlys. They've always looked down their noses at Maggie and Walt. But I'd never go so far as to mess with their marriage for sport. "Why do I have the feeling you never saw Henry in Elkins with Loraine?"

His smile widens.

"What are you up to?"

"I thought you knew."

"I mean tonight. What's the point in having Lainey perform at all? What are you trying to accomplish by stirring up drama? How does this fit into your master plan?"

He laughs low like I've said something amusing. "You ask a lot of questions, Selah."

"And you tell a lot of lies."

He spins me in a circle, then brings me close. "You want a truth?"

"If you're capable of giving one."

"Lainey reminds me of Molly."

A shiver runs down my spine.

He wants me to feel afraid, and I do. But unlike this morning, I refuse to show it. This time, I'm not caught off guard. I know what I'm facing. I lift my chin and stare straight at him. "Are you going to dispose of her, too?"

"I didn't dispose of Molly," he says, giving me another twirl. "She did that on her own. I will admit, I did have a hold over her. The same hold I have over Lainey. The same hold I have over any of them I want. Except you. It's fascinating, the way you resist my charm."

"Your charm is poison."

"Ah, but most of your kind don't know this. And even when they do, they still can't resist. It's quite tedious, to be honest. A lion does like to hunt, you know."

He's admitting it, then.

Whatever power of seduction Seraphina possessed, she passed on to him when she brought him back to life. Molly didn't stand a chance, and neither does Lainey.

"Two hundred sixty-eight years is a long time to be bored. Imagine my intrigue, running into you that day in the graveyard. A girl not only immune to my allure, but the very one from my brother's painting." He chuckles wistfully, as though recalling a fond memory. "You were such a source of torment to him in his final days."

His words set my teeth on edge.

"What do we think? Were you a symbol of hope? He painted a girl who could not be so easily swayed as his beloved Molly. And yet, in the end, he had to know it wouldn't matter. I might not be able to have you, sweet Selah, but neither can Jude. If he tries, the curse will win."

His words cut like a poisoned blade as the music rises and we circle the floor. A small, wild piece of me wants to grab onto his lapels and beg. Plead with him to break this curse. At least tell us how. Instead, I take a steadying breath and pivot the conversation. "Why send Lainey after us about the onyx and the pearl. Do you really think we'd tell her anything?"

"Of course not. But that doesn't mean you didn't give away your hand. Your tells are louder than Lainey's flirting. I didn't think it possible, but Twig's are even worse." He glides backward, drawing me with him. "Now, I know what I only suspected before."

"Which is what?" I ask warily.

"You have them, and they're somewhere close. Which means ..." He pulls me against him, removing all the space, and trails a finger down my arm. "You shouldn't have a problem handing them over to me tomorrow by midnight."

"I think that's enough." Jude cuts between us.

"Took you long enough." Rafe leans close to my ear. "Tick tock, Selah."

Then he's gone.

And I begin to tremble, a shiver deep down in my bones.

Jude's hand finds the small of my back, the warmth of his touch dizzying and steadying all at once. "Are you all right?"

I nod, but it isn't true.

I was just dancing with a monster. A murderer. A wicked shadow that has darkened the doorstep of Jude's family for centuries.

A new song begins, soft and aching.

He doesn't ask. But he doesn't let go, either. With his eyes locked on mine, he steps closer and lifts my arms around his neck. Then he slides his hands down my ribcage, setting off a trail of sparks.

With Rafe, I wanted distance.

With Jude, I want none.

Closing my eyes, I savor his nearness. The feel of his body against mine. The intoxicating scent of his cologne. The warmth of his breath against my ear.

"I think he's going to kill Lainey," I whisper.

For a moment, he goes still—a hiccup in the middle of our dance.

"He knows we have the gemstones. He wants them tomorrow by midnight."

Or else.

The threat may have been unspoken, but it was crystal clear nonetheless.

My mind grapples for a solution.

"We can give him what he wants," Jude says. "He still can't open the tomb."

I lean back to look him in the eye.

"He needs mortal blood, willingly spilled. Whatever he is, it's not mortal."

"You think we should give him the stones?"

"If it buys us time."

The clinking of silver against glass cuts through the moment.

The music halts.

Conversations die.

Jude steps away.

And I feel bereft.

Rafe stands at the microphone with a champagne flute in his hand. "At this time, I'd like to invite all guests to return to the ballroom for a special performance by our very own Blackwillow Ballet Ensemble.

"And if I may, I'd also like to offer a quick toast." He lifts his glass. "To Foggy Hollow, for being so welcoming. I've only been here a short time, but somehow, it feels as though this town has been my home for ages." His sparkling eyes find mine. He shoots me a devilish wink. "To Isabel, our lovely hostess, who has gone above and beyond to make this event one for the ages. And to my cousin."

Rafe tips his glass in our direction. "I've cherished our time together these past two months. I was hoping we'd have longer, but I suppose I understand why you want to get back to your life in the UK. Let's make the most of the time we still have, shall we?"

Glasses rise in unison.

Polite applause ripples through the room.

Meanwhile, my heart thuds—a dull, heavy beat in my ears.

"And now," Rafe continues, "let's clear the floor for the Blackwillow Ballet Ensemble, proudly presenting 'Ashes to Light', an original piece choreographed for Foggy Hollow's Bicentennial celebration."

The dance floor begins to clear.

But I remain in place, hardly breathing.

I look up at Jude. "You're leaving?"

His expression says it all.

Finally, Rafe has given me a truth.

With my heart in my throat, I make a beeline for the nearest exit. I spot Twig and Naomi entering from the terrace and change course. Mr. and Mrs. Calloway laugh as they come in from the antechamber, and I pivot again. I head toward the far doors leading into the east wing like a salmon swimming up stream.

By the time I reach the corridor, it's empty. I tear off my mask and stride toward the conservatory. From there, I can slip into the night. I can catch a proper breath.

Jude takes my arm. "Selah, wait."

I turn on him.

He's removed his mask, too, and for a moment, his tortured beauty undoes me.

"You're just going to leave?" I ask. "Disappear?"

The same as my mother.

But I can't say those words.

They're too painful.

"I'm trying to keep you safe," he says.

"How will that possibly keep me safe?"

"If I stay, you die!"

The lights flicker.

Jude shoves his hand into his hair, then grabs at his chest like he's trying to tear out his own heart. Like doing so might show me the truth of it.

He opens his mouth.

I wait with baited breath, but no words come. We stare at each other across the impasse, a chasm too immense to cross.

He drags his hand down his face. "We just need to get through this week. If we can keep him from the tomb—"

"You think this will be over in a week? He's been waiting for two hundred and sixty-eight years, Jude. If he doesn't get what he wants, there will be hell to pay."

"Then let me pay it," he says, his voice ragged. "He needs *my* blood. If I keep it from him, he'll come after me. *In Europe.* If he wants to torment Ezra's descendants, then let him torment me there."

While I'm in torment here.

Tears sting my eyes. A knot of emotion rises in my throat. Jude looks at me like I am spun from glass and he is nothing but a hammer. But he's not the hammer. Doesn't he see? It's the curse, not him. Maybe together, we can figure out how to break it.

The sound of weeping intrudes upon my pain.

Someone is crying.

It's coming from the music room.

Together, we move toward the sound.

Jude pushes the doors open.

My blood runs cold.

Because there, in the middle of the room, stands Lainey Sikes. On top of a chair with a rope fastened around her neck.

Rafe steps out of the shadow, a serpent on legs, and sighs a theatrical sigh. "My, my. Cosette was right. We really have stepped back in time."

46
THE RIFT

At the sight of Rafe, Lainey's expression twists strangely. She cries his name on a choked exhale, like he is her knight in shining armor. And yet, her eyes tell a different story. They are wild with terror. "Please, Rafe. I don't remember how I got up here."

"Lainey, Lainey, Lainey." He tuts as he strolls closer. "I'm afraid we need to have a little chat."

"Can you help me get down first?"

"You might want to stay. See what I have to say before you make a decision."

Her body trembles.

Jude stands beside me like a lion about to pounce—frozen, alert, every muscle coiled.

"We just aren't working, you and I," Rafe continues. "I think it's time to take a break."

"A break?"

"I need space, Lain. This relationship of ours is starting to feel claustrophobic, you know?"

"But I thought—"

"I know, I know." He heaves a sigh. "You thought I loved

you. And I may have alluded to that, but Lainey, the truth is, I don't. I never have."

Mascara streaks down her face. Her chest rises and falls like at any moment it might collapse and she better get in some good breaths first. I want to go to her, climb up on that chair, and remove the rope. But it all feels so fraught. Like one wrong move could snap Lainey's neck.

"I tried. I really did," Rafe says, his silky voice cutting like the edge of a razor. "But at the end of the day, you're just ... not enough."

"Not enough?"

He shakes his head in mock sorrow.

Lainey buries her face in her hands and sobs.

The ruby brightens.

It wasn't my imagination.

It's like the gemstone is feeding off her emotion.

Rafe stops behind the chair. "I could have plucked any girl from the crowd. Bent her to my will. But this way is more fruitful. So much more emotion to work with once they've fallen in love."

Lainey wails.

The lights flicker.

My mind races.

We need to get her down. We need to get her to safety. But how, with Rafe so close? One good kick, and he could send the chair flying. I see Molly Ludwig in my dream. Her feet dangling.

"Poor Lainey," Rafe tuts. "You've never been quite good enough, have you? Not for your dad. Not for your mom. Not for me. I don't know, maybe it's better to just ..." He wobbles the chair.

With a shriek, she totters precariously.

Jude takes an aggressive step forward. "Knock it off."

"Oh yeah? And what will you do if I don't?" He gives the chair another nudge.

Lainey shrieks again.

She's terrified.

It's written all over her face.

Despite what Rafe has suggested, she doesn't want to be up there with that rope around her neck.

The ruby is practically glowing.

"Jude," I say like a warning. His eyes meet mine. If he notices the amulet, he doesn't let on. He's too fixated on helping Lainey. But in order to do that, we need to get Rafe out of the way.

"Careful, Cousin," Rafe says. "You look like you're about to do something heroic."

Jude steps toward him, his jaw clenched.

Rafe takes a slow step in return. "Playing the hero has never ended well for your bloodline. Ezra. Amos. Gabriel. Elijah. Each one tried so hard to deny themselves happiness, as if the sacrifice might shield the ones they loved. Same story, different guy. Watching it unfold has grown so redundant."

I inch behind him, closer to Lainey as Rafe begins circling Jude like a wolf. "I watched them all claw their way through grief. Endure decades of loneliness, wearing their misery like a martyr. As if they had any concept of what true misery felt like."

Lainey chokes on a sob.

The ruby pulses.

And I recall another dream.

John Vandenberg, shouting.

His son, yelling.

His wife, crying.

His daughter, seething.

So much emotion, it was almost like the rift couldn't help

itself. Couldn't resist. It needed to feed. Rafe is drumming up that same emotion now, only a hundred times stronger.

And suddenly, I understand.

Ezra's map.

The red X.

The decrepit mausoleum.

Until the flash of lightning.

For a fraction of second it was there—Dante's tomb, just out of reach. Because it exists in a different dimension, layered over ours. To get to it, Rafe must go through the rift, and he can't get through the rift unless he opens it first. To do that, he needs emotion.

Raw, unfiltered emotion.

Rafe continues his taunting as I reach the chair. Very carefully, I step onto it. I join Lainey, who is hysterical and heartbroken and making that ruby glow brighter by the second. With urgent, fumbling hands, I manage to remove the rope from around her neck and take her gently by her shoulders. "Lainey, please calm down."

But she only shakes her head and cries harder, her entire body wracked with sobs.

"Please, it's going to be okay."

"No it's not!" she wails.

The chandelier trembles.

Jude and Rafe prowl in a circle, drawing closer.

Settle down, I want to shout. *Everyone needs to settle down.*

But the words are trapped.

And Rafe is relentless. "You killed your mother the day you were born," he says.

Jude's hands curl into fists.

Fury burns in his eyes.

"How long until Selah ends up in a body bag, too?"

Jude lunges.

He tackles Rafe into the piano.

Lainey screams as the keys ring out a discordant tone.

I grab her by the arm and pull her to the ground as Rafe recovers. He rams his shoulder into Jude's chest. They crash into Lainey's chair. Jude throws a punch and connects with Rafe's jaw.

He staggers, a trickle of blood running down the corner of his mouth. He wipes at it with a sinister smile, then he picks up a nearby music stand and swings it at Jude's head.

Terror grabs me by the throat as Jude blocks it with his forearm and tackles Rafe to the ground. Fists fly. Lainey screams. And I'm shouting, too—for somebody to come, for somebody to help.

The doors burst open.

People rush inside.

Isabel.

Mayor Ridley.

Twig.

Mr. Calloway.

He wrenches Rafe and Jude apart as Isabel shrieks, and the ground begins to shake. The crystals in the chandelier chatter like tiny glass teeth.

Shouts erupt in the ballroom.

An earthquake!

Pandemonium ensues as guests run for cover.

But I can't move.

I stand by the fireplace, watching the spot where Lainey once stood. The air starts to shimmer—a thin ribbon of ghostly light that crackles and sparks. The tremble turns into a violent quake. The chandelier sways. A candelabra crashes to my feet. Slowly, the ribbon grows, longer and wider, until it splits into a gaping, swirling wound.

The shaking stops.

The world goes still.

Mr. Calloway and Mayor Ridley and Isabel and Twig look

around wildly, as though waiting for something to come, not realizing something already has.

The rift is open.

Across the room, Rafe yanks the ruby from Lainey's neck. She twists free from his grip and runs past the undulating hole like she doesn't see it at all.

Rafe's eyes lock with mine, then Jude's.

He grins a bloody grin and steps inside.

47
MARKED

We follow him. Jude and I step through the tear, and the hair on the back of my neck stands on end.

We're still in the music room.

But it's not the music room.

Whispers float in the air, disembodied and indecipherable. Joined by the confused, panicked voices of Mayor Ridley, Mr. Calloway, Isabel, and Twig. They talk over one another, their words muffled as though spoken through thick glass.

It's exactly as Simon's journal described.

We're here, but we're also not here.

There's no time to make sense of it. No time to stop and figure out why Jude and I could travel through the rift, but Lainey couldn't even see it.

We go after Rafe, through the corridor, into the foyer, out into the night, where the disembodied whispers grow louder, and the sky churns overhead—a swirling, black void that makes the ground feel tenuous. Like at any moment, gravity will let go and we will plunge into the abyss.

Jude takes my hand.

Together, we chase Rafe's shadow across the lawn, flashes of light illuminating familiar landmarks—the marble fountain, the twisted tree in the Midnight Garden. But in this world, they are distorted. Warped. Reflections in a funhouse mirror.

Fog rolls thick, billowing like waves as Rafe slips through the front gate.

We hurry after him. But when we emerge from the estate, he's gone.

Jude lets go of my hand and turns in a circle. I do the same. But I've lost all my bearings. I can't tell which way is north and which way is south. We spot a familiar tree in the near distance, but when we reach it, it's not familiar at all.

Jude scans for something—*anything*.

But the fog is too dense, and shadows swirl like sentient things.

A shiver crawls down my spine.

"We have to go back," I say. "He can't open the tomb. He doesn't have the gemstones."

Or mortal blood. Dante's comet isn't burning brightest in the sky, either. That won't happen until Halloween.

Still, Jude hesitates.

Panic squeezes my throat.

If we don't turn back now, we could get lost forever. And I swear, something is closing in, lurking nearby. We're being watched.

"Please, Jude."

His eyes find mine.

He sees my terror.

And it's enough.

Taking my hand, we retrace our steps as the fog presses in and our feet fumble over unfamiliar ground. I try to breathe. I try to stay calm. I try to focus on my hand in Jude's. Most of all, I try not to look over my shoulder, convinced if I do, I will see something terrible.

The Night Beast.

The *Nachtdier*.

The fountain materializes through the fog.

We race to the portico, my heart hammering as the sky rumbles and the dark grows darker. We need to get inside. I need a ceiling above my head, something to block out that terrifying hellmouth overhead. We're halfway up the stairs when a slurping, sucking squelch slaps the cobbled stone behind us.

A tentacle wraps around my ankle.

I'm yanked backward.

With a scream, my legs fly out from under me. I hit the ground hard, elbows scraping stone. I scramble for something, anything to hold onto, my fingers scrabbling as I'm dragged away by a writhing creature that's unfurled from the fountain.

"Selah!" Jude dives.

He catches my wrist.

The inky black tentacle coils tighter.

Pain shoots up my leg.

Jude's grip tightens.

I'm being torn in two.

But I beg him to hold on, don't let go, as the wind howls, rain lashes, and thunder cracks.

Our hands are wet.

I'm slipping ...

Slipping ...

I've slipped.

But in the very next split of a second, Jude snatches my other arm. He latches on like a vice and hauls me closer. He has a rusted trowel in his free hand. And with a primal roar, he plunges the pointed end into the tentacle wrapped around my leg.

Black, viscous fluid spurts into the air.

The creature wails, an ear-splitting shriek of a sound, and

releases me. We tumble backward as it folds in on itself and vanishes into the fountain.

I collapse on top of Jude.

His arms wrap around my waist as our hearts pound and our chests heave and the rain falls.

For a second—or maybe an eternity—he looks at me like I'm his entire universe. Like he lost me and lived a whole life without me and he's traveled back in time just to be with me.

And now here I am.

Alive.

Here.

In his arms.

His hand finds the back of my neck. In one graceful maneuver, he flips me over, and with a ragged inhale, his mouth claims mine in a storm of desire and relief, agony and urgency.

My hands grab at his shirt.

His fingers tangle in my hair.

Wave crashes into wave.

I hold on tight, riding each crest until the storm softens into something so achingly tender, so piercingly sweet, I think I might die. His lips are perfection. The taste of him, divine. I want to live in this moment forever—stay right here, forever— when something intrudes upon my ecstasy.

An icy sting.

A cruel interruption.

Like a frozen sickle carving into my skin. Right where my mother's mark had been. Even as I go on kissing Jude, I know what this is.

The curse has come for me.

48

FAULT LINES

I move aside dead leaves and twigs as birds chirp and the crisp morning air nips my skin. I cast a look over my shoulder, toward the trail.

He's late.

He probably stopped for gas and got caught in conversation with the clerk. Everybody's talking about the earthquake that wasn't an earthquake. At least, not one that registered on any richter scales. So then, what was it? The town is abuzz over one more unexplainable event in Foggy Hollow's long list of them.

The Flash of 1757.

The Fire of 1822.

The Disappearance of 1995.

And now, the Tremble of 2025.

Only this time, I know the cause.

Our town exists on a supernatural fault line. Not a fracture in the Earth's crust, but a schism between worlds. Because of that schism, we have a rift.

And a curse.

My hand moves to my collarbone. The touch burns, only the burn isn't hot but cold. I told Dad I wasn't feeling well and stayed home from church. It wasn't a lie, exactly. There's a pit in my stomach that no amount of sleep or Maggie's chamomile tea can soothe. But I never intended to stay home and rest.

A branch snaps behind me.

I turn fast, extra jumpy given the circumstances.

Twig emerges from the trees, one arm tucked tight in a sling, the other clutching a crowbar and a car jack.

"Hey," he says, his voice low and careful, like someone might hear. "I triple checked to make sure nobody was following me."

By *nobody* he means Rafe.

The two of us get to work, at first in silence. Twig wedges the crowbar beneath the slab. It takes both of our strength to lift it enough to fit the car jack underneath. Not until we descend the stone stairs with our flashlights on do I start talking. The words pour out in a gush. I tell him all about Rafe's plan. The way he used Lainey to execute it. The rift opening and what it was like on the other side.

Twig listens, his head on a swivel as he takes in our surroundings. When I use the key to get inside the crypt, he turns into a kid in a candy shop. I don't blame him. If I weren't in such distress myself, I'd probably join him. But the burn beneath my collar smarts—so sharp, I grimace.

"Hey," Twig says. "Are you okay?"

I consider lying.

But this is Twig.

He's going to find out sooner or later.

So, I pull down the collar of my shirt and show him what I have yet to show Jude.

His face turns gray.

I tug the collar back into place. "Please don't say anything to him."

"But that's—"

"I know what it is."

His Adam's apple bobs in his throat.

"Please, Twig? He's going to freak out."

"Shouldn't you be freaking out?"

"What's the point?" The mark is there. That's a fact. But maybe it doesn't have to mean what we think it means. "There's a reason Ezra painted me. Those words he wrote? Beacon. Balm. Blessing. Maybe that's what I can be."

"Do you know how to break a curse?"

"No, but that doesn't mean it isn't possible." I turn away from my friend and his very visible concern. I didn't come here to talk about the curse. I came here to protect the people I love.

"Selah? I really think you should tell him."

I pick up the pearl and the onyx. I grab the locket, too. Because why not have all the pieces to the puzzle? Rafe wants the gemstones by midnight. I'm not convinced handing them over is a good idea, but given his ultimatum, what other choice do we have?

<hr>

A haunting sonata envelops me as soon as Tulane invites me inside.

Jude sent a text.

We need to talk.

He's right. We do.

We need to devise a plan, figure out exactly how to hand over the gemstones while keeping Rafe from his ultimate goal. But right now, that goal feels small and far away. All that exists is this soul-stirring music, so filled with longing, it makes my chest ache. I follow Tulane to the music room as if in a trance. Then we reach the open doors, and whatever's left of my breath whooshes away.

The rift hangs in the air like a freshly stitched wound. A jagged seam of darkness, the edges frayed and flickering with veins of obsidian light. I turn to Tulane, but he simply bows and leaves like nothing is amiss. Like that wound is as invisible to him as it was to Twig and Lainey the night before.

I step closer, remembering the way it tore open in my dream. A violent explosion that sucked Simon and his family straight in. The police found no evidence of anything amiss other than a fallen candelabra. But what if it was there all along in the dining room? A fresh wound, just like this one. Only they couldn't see it.

A niggling thought wiggles into my brain.

Ezekiel Cotton's first claim.

Last night, I found it underwhelming and obvious. Of course mortal descendants of angels would have a strong connection to the spiritual realm. But now, stepping around the rift as it hangs there like an omen, warping the music ever so slightly, I find myself reconsidering it.

Dante wasn't the only angel to create a mortal line.

I stare, as transfixed by the sight as I am by the music. If I reached out and touched it, would my hand slip through? Is that creature from the fountain waiting for me on the other side?

I take a step away, closer to Jude.

He sits at the piano, unaware of my presence. The soft cotton of his oxford shirt pulls gently across his back, tracing the shape of lean muscle as his hands move like liquid across the keys.

I recall those same fingers in my hair.

His lips on mine.

Our bodies pressed together.

Heat blooms low in my abdomen.

The spot under my collar burns like ice.

And I wonder. Is this what masochists feel?

Pleasure in pain.

A hunger for more.

Jude stops playing in the middle of a refrain.

The room goes jarringly silent.

He sits impossibly still. Achingly forlorn. Then—*bang*—he slams the lid shut. The sound cracks through the room like a gunshot.

My heart leaps.

The rift crackles.

He pushes to his feet and kicks the stool out from under him.

It clatters across the floor and slides to a stop.

With his hands curled into fists, he turns. And for one raw, unguarded moment, before he sees me, his expression is ravaged.

I step toward him.

But he lifts his hand in a gesture to stop. To stay away. "When were you going to tell me?"

"T-tell you what?"

"Really, Selah?"

I swallow, unsure. For all I know, he went to the crypt and found the empty jewelry box. He's upset I didn't invite him to join. "I went to St. Fortuna's this morning and got the gemstones."

"I'm not talking about the gemstones."

I bite my lip.

His eyes burn as he crosses the room, as he stands in front of me. Ever so gently, he brushes my hair over my shoulder. My heart pounds like a caged bird. I wish I'd zipped up my coat. Opted for a turtleneck instead of this shirt with a scooped neck.

With his attention fixed on my clavicle, he hooks his thumb beneath the fabric and draws it aside.

His chest rises, sharp and uneven.

"Twig told you," I whisper, frustration seeping into every syllable.

"He's scared."

I roll my eyes.

"I'm scared," he says, his voice simmering.

"It's going to be okay."

With a shake of his head, he lets go of my shirt and turns away.

Tentatively, I touch his shoulder.

He turns so fast I startle. "Explain it to me, then."

"E-explain what?"

"How is it going to be okay?"

"My mom didn't die."

A bitter laugh breaks from his throat.

"No, listen," I say. "She had this same mark. But she kept living." I step closer, needing him to believe me. Needing to believe myself. "The curse didn't kill her."

Sure, Simon and his family got sucked through the rift. But no need to call that out. At least, not at this very moment.

He shakes his head again, like I'm talking nonsense. Like I don't understand. "She was put into a psych ward. She turned into an addict. A mother who walked out on her daughter."

The truth cuts.

"Maybe she's alive out there somewhere, but that doesn't make her any less tragic. All because Simon dared to love her." His voice is bitter, cracked through with pain. "I don't accept that fate for you."

"It's a tricky thing to avoid, though, isn't it?"

We both turn.

Rafe steps into the room with a shiny red apple. "I heard the two of you arguing. Thought I'd pay a little visit. Remind you of the deadline. Only to discover this fun little turn of events." He twiddles his fingers in my direction. "You can't fight fate, Jude. Unless, of course ..."

He lets the words dangle as he polishes the apple on his suit coat.

I glare, my blood boiling.

Ezra should have let him die.

Let him rot in the grave where he belongs.

"The only one who can undo the curse is the one who cast it, and Seraphina's still trapped in a tomb." He leans against the doorframe, crossing one ankle over the other.

"Help me free her and your sweet Selah won't have to—" He drags a finger across his neck with the sharp click of his tongue. Then, with a taunting lift of his brow, he casts a glance at the rift and tosses Jude the apple. "Looks like we're on the same team now, *Cousin*."

49
A SEMI PLAN

I t started with the portrait.

That's what brought us together. Jude and I were looking for answers because it was an irresistible mystery. But Jude isn't just curious anymore. He's compelled. Possessed. Unable to sleep. Scrambling for answers in a desperate race against time.

On Sunday, he studies blueprints for secret rooms and takes apart desks in search of hidden compartments like the curse's antidote might be hidden somewhere in the manor. He returns to the crypt and scours every inch of it, examining the walls, the floors, even pulling up loose stones.

That night, we give Rafe the gemstones.

Jude skips school on Monday, and somehow convinces Twig, who's never played hooky a day in his life, to do the same. They pore over ancient texts in the library—theological and philosophical. They sink deep into angelology and the Apocrypha. Anything that might provide some insight.

About angels.

Seraphina.

The curse.

And maybe, just maybe, a loophole.

Meanwhile, I take to Google.

How do you break a curse?

The answer is surprisingly thorough, and very unhelpful. Still, I try a few suggestions. Like renouncing the curse and declaring my freedom. I say it out loud, word for word, in the shower on Monday morning.

"I renounce this curse and declare my freedom!"

The mark remains.

I study the portrait for clues.

I fixate on the locket, which I can't pry open. Not with my fingers. Not with a tiny screwdriver. I try a hammer only to wake up on the floor a full two minutes later with a goose egg on the back of my head.

By Monday afternoon, Twig has utilized two years' worth of connections forged doing research for *Accounts of the Uncanny*. He and Jude visit every fringe group, every niche chatroom, follow every wild conspiracy to its bitter end. Until finally, they find a lead on a message board buried three layers deep where ghost hunters and theologians argue about the spiritual realm. A user named PaleScript mentioned a monk who was cast out for translating forbidden texts—a Benedictine archivist with several published articles about the Watchers and their influence over human bloodlines.

Twig finds his last known location. And by Monday evening, Jude is airborne. Off on a private jet, making his way to the French Alps.

On Tuesday, Twig and I carve pumpkins with his family and my dad. The annual tradition cannot be skipped, and surprisingly, it serves as a welcome distraction.

Now it's Wednesday. Just after lunch. I'm home from school trying and failing to get warm. No matter how many layers of blankets I burrow beneath, the cold will not relent. It has settled in my bones, and a feeling of heaviness sits on my chest. I can't tell if it's the curse ... or if it's just me, missing Jude.

The ache of his absence feels urgent.

Like he is water in the desert.

Warmth in the winter.

A match in the dark.

Halloween creeps closer.

Time is slipping away.

And Jude is gone.

We're spending what could be our final days apart.

My teeth chatter as I flip through the no-longer-locked tome. I study the stained glass illustrations, looking for patterns and symbols. There are several repetitive themes, but blood is predominate. A force of life, power, and sacrifice.

My phone rings.

Jude's number appears on the screen.

I answer it eagerly.

"Hey," he says. His voice, even travel-worn and tired, brings the first real warmth I've felt all day. "Just checking in. Wanted to make sure you were—"

"Still alive?"

"That isn't funny."

"It's a little bit funny," I reply, my jaw tense to keep the shivering at bay. "Are you on your way back?"

"Already on U.S. soil."

A thrill of delight zips through my body.

"Are you home?" he asks.

I consider lying. I don't want him to worry more than he already is. Me at home in the middle of a school day will definitely make him worry.

"Because if you aren't," he says, "you're not paying much attention to your carbon footprint."

I sit upright.

"Several lights are on, and your dad's working in the front garden. I'm a little concerned he might think I'm a stalker."

I smile. "You're here."

"On your front porch. Looking at a very strange jack-o-lantern. I think it might be a cowboy hat attached to a jellybean with legs?"

"It's a UFO beaming up a cow."

A low chuckle rumbles in my ear.

Ten seconds later, he's rapping on my bedroom door. He pokes his head inside—his hair tousled, his eyes shadowed—and my intuition was right. Clearly, the sight of me in bed under all these covers in the middle of the day worries him immensely.

He crosses the room in two easy strides and sits beside me, the mattress dipping beneath his weight. "You're sick?"

"I feel fine." The words aren't even a lie, because right now, with him here, I do feel fine. More than fine, actually. I cross my legs beneath the covers. It takes significant restraint not to grab his hand and pull it into my lap. Instead, I tuck my hair behind my ears and tug at my sleeves. "So, did he tell you anything helpful—the monk guy? Was it worth the trip?"

"I'm going to tell Rafe we're on his side."

I blink several times, positive I misheard.

"We'll open the tomb in exchange for Seraphina undoing the curse."

"Jude, Seraphina isn't going to—"

"I know she isn't. But we don't need her to undo anything." He reaches inside his coat pocket and removes a small notepad. "Father Odo might be the strangest person I've ever met. He wouldn't let me take photographs or make copies of anything. But he knew his stuff, and he had a lot to say. I planned to write everything down once I left. But really, it all boils down to this."

He hands me the notepad. Two lines have been written on the page in his familiar, controlled handwriting:

A curse of a fallen one may linger upon the mortal soul, but its roots die when the caster falls. From the Thirteenth Epistle.

"What's the Thirteenth Epistle?"

"A letter. Part of a collection he called *Scriptura Obscura*. Its origins trace back to a secret order in Rome from the seventh century."

I read it again, slower this time. "So if Seraphina dies ... the curse dies with her?"

Jude nods.

"Your plan is to kill her?"

The fact that he doesn't laugh or scoff at the absurdity unnerves me.

I shift in bed. "Ezra made it sound like that can only be done through supernatural means."

"Father Odo confirmed as much."

"We don't have supernatural means. Unless Father Odo gave you some sort of weapon I don't know about."

His gaze dips to my clavicle, where the mark hides beneath my oversized flannel. "I re-listened to some podcast episodes on my way home."

It takes me a second to realize he means *my* podcast. And he used the word *re-listened*. Which means he's already listened once before. I picture him in class with his AirPods in. Was it my voice in his ear all along?

The idea makes me flush.

The warmth of it feels nice.

"Which ones?" I ask, picking at a loose thread on my comforter.

"Your mini-series on religion."

Through the ages.

Episodes three and four of season two. We covered everything from Greek Mythology to Scientology and their unique beliefs in the supernatural.

"I ended up watching *Clash of the Titans*," he says.

My jaw drops with delighted surprise.

"It was a long flight," he adds ruefully.

"Did you watch the 1981 version or the pathetic attempt at a remake in 2010?"

"You made it very clear the 1981 version was the only version worth watching."

I smile. *Clash of the Titans* is one of my all-time favorites, which is probably why I spent so much of episode three raving about it. "What did you think?"

"The eyeless witches were terrifying."

"And Medusa?"

"Equally terrifying."

"Here's a fun fact. In the movie, her blood is only good for destroying things, but in actual Greek Mythology, it has the power to poison or heal. Depending on which side of the body it comes from."

"Selah."

I look at him.

"I didn't come here to analyze *Clash of the Titans*. Or discuss Greek Mythology." He's fighting a grin though, his dimple coming out to play, his hand sliding closer to my knee. "I want to talk about episode four, and the Watchers."

I nod, eager to hear what he has to say. Episode four focused on Christianity and Judaism, particularly their beliefs surrounding angels, demons, and spiritual warfare. The Watchers were angels tasked with protecting humanity. They broke their vows by loving mortal women and fathered the Nephilim—powerful, unnatural hybrids.

"Father Odo has studied them extensively," Jude says. "He's spent years digging through the *Book of Enoch*, the Dead Sea

Scrolls, the sixth chapter of Genesis. He believes descendants of Nephilim carry traces of supernatural power."

I think about Ezekiel Cotton and his first claim—*descendants of angels have a strong connection to the supernatural realm.* Father Odo has taken that concept and upped the ante.

I look at Jude, whose eyes are aglow with hope, like he thinks *he* can destroy Seraphina. And the cold in my bones seeps into my heart.

"Jude," I say with caution, "if Ezra couldn't destroy Seraphina back then, how are you supposed to do it now?"

To this, he has no answer.

"Did Father Odo have anything to say about *that*?" I press.

He expels a frustrated breath. "No. But Twig found another lead. A retired professor who taught in Ohio University's anthropology department. She specialized in folkloric studies, and piloted a class called *Curse Lore and Ritual Structure.* She published several articles about the topic."

"A curse expert."

"She might know something. I've reached out several times, but she hasn't replied." He glances at my bedside clock. "She lives in Athens, Ohio. If I don't hear back from her by the end of tonight, I'm heading there first thing in the morning."

Thursday.

The eve of Halloween.

One day before Dante's comet will blaze brightest in the sky.

Quite possibly our last day together.

I shove the disturbing thought away. And the dread that comes with it. Jude is worried for my life, but I'm worried for his. Especially if he thinks he can take on Seraphina.

My teeth begin to chatter.

He slides his hand over my knee.

The touch makes my breath catch.

"You're freezing," he says, shadow falling across his face. It's as if my cold temperature, or maybe his words, cause him physical pain. "I'll never forgive myself for being so weak."

I shake my head adamantly, because love isn't weak. No immortal ancestors or fallen angels or terrible curses will convince me otherwise. I slip my hand beneath his, palm to palm, finger to finger.

My breath trembles.

He lifts his thumb and traces my lines like a palm reader. Then he brushes aside the collar of my flannel, and ever so gently, he lowers his mouth to the mark.

My pulse throbs.

I lean toward him, my heart drumming wildly, pleasure coiling in my abdomen. Then his lips move to my throat and my fingers curl into his hair.

He pulls back, his eyes dark with desire and determination. "I'll tell Rafe tonight."

I can't speak.

I can hardly breathe.

All I can do is nod.

"I'll do whatever it takes to protect you," he whispers against my neck.

Death has become a storm cloud hovering above us. And yet, I've never felt more alive than I do right now.

50
THE REVELATION

I am a block of ice on the move—hair frozen, breath frosted —lost in the hedge maze, dead ends at every turn as shadow closes in and panic rises. I must get to him. I have to save him. But when I finally reach the center, Jude isn't there. Instead, the portrait lies on the ground like a mirror.

Birdsong fractures the silence as the locket in the painting shimmers like a sunbeam.

Ribbons of light spider outward.

The portrait splits into a gaping maw, and a black tentacle reaches out from within.

I jerk upright in bed.

My phone is buzzing.

Jude has sent a message.

He's on the road. Headed to Athens, chasing a solution I'm not sure exists. If it did, surely Ezra would have found it. But Ezra didn't find a way to destroy Seraphina. He only found a way to lock her up.

Now Jude wants to let her out.

I shiver.

Cold has become a merciless, inescapable companion.

I draw my comforter around me and step out into the hallway. It's quiet. Dad's bedroom door is ajar. He must already be out mowing the paddock or clearing the stables. I wonder if he's found the old carriage yet, and the pair of initials carved inside a heart. One of them belonged to his wife, who was here thirty years ago.

A kid in foster care, sent to Foggy Hollow. Drawn to Simon Vandenberg with no idea that Simon's great-great-great something grandfather had painted the daughter she would one day have.

Simon fell in love.

The curse was triggered.

Tragedy struck.

My mother was sent away.

But the demons went with her.

She had me.

She left me.

And because she left, we came here.

Was it all meant to be? Was this moment, right now, written in the stars? Or could she have stayed? And if she had stayed, would we still be in Ohio? What about Jude? What about Rafe? What about the gemstones and the portrait and the curse?

I kneel on the floor, pull the portrait out from under my bed, and stare at the locket in the painting. It drew him to his wife and led to the birth of his son. He hid the locket inside a jewelry box, inside a coffin, inside a crypt. Marked by coordinates inside a compass, inside a Bible.

Clues inside of clues, like Russian nesting dolls.

Maybe this is why I'm so convinced there must be something inside the locket, too.

Ezra dreamt about it. In his dreams, Seraphina wore the locket as she murdered Molly. So why did he paint it around *my* neck? Because he dreamt of me, too? And what of the words scrawled on a fragment of parchment in Maggie's office? Surely, if there was a revelation and he thought I might be its fulfill-ment, he would have kept careful track of that revelation.

I narrow my eyes.

Clues within clues.

I run my hands along the frame, feeling for a hidden latch. A secret compartment. There's nothing. I pick the portrait up, turn it over, and set it on my bed. On the backside, muslin has been nailed in place. I smooth my hand over the aged cotton, much softer than the flaxen weave of the canvas. They are two different things, with a small space between them.

Clues within clues.

With a jump of adrenaline, I search for an opening. There's not even a loose thread to pick. My eye catches on the tome set upon my bedside table, with its busted lock.

Five minutes later, I'm back with a razor blade.

As carefully as possible, I cut near the frame's edge. I work the blade along the stretcher, and the fabric starts to give—slowly, painstakingly, until finally, the muslin is gone. And there, hidden against the raw back of the canvas, are words.

With my heart in my throat, I begin to read.

This revelation was set down by my own hand in the year of our Lord 1777, though I remember it not.

What she could not claim in Heaven, she sought through blood.

A mortal line, forged to swell her might, so long as it endured.

Silver was shaped, a fragment of her divine essence sealed within.

Protection for those she named her kin, given not from love, but greed.

Yet in her reach for dominion, the seed of her undoing was sown.

By the cruelty she wrought, her end shall be fashioned.

Power unlocked by the blood of her progeny.

Fates entwined through the touching of blood.

The curse shall return to its maker.

A reckoning bound to sacrifice.

For no mortal may touch the divine and live.

- E.V.

Ezra's revelation has been here all along, recorded on the back of the portrait. I reread every line, trying to make sense of the words.

What she could not claim in heaven, she sought through blood. A mortal line to swell her might.

The subject is clearly Seraphina. It matches the information from the scroll we found in Ezra's crypt, translated by Ezra himself. Unwilling to be bested by Dante, she forged a mortal line to increase her power.

Silver was shaped, a fragment of her divine essence sealed within.

My attention darts to the middle drawer of my writing desk. I haven't touched the locket since the hammer incident. But now, I open the drawer and weigh the locket in my palm, unsure if the faint pulse is a figment of my imagination, or a fragment of Seraphina's divine essence.

Power unlocked by the blood of her progeny ...

The words jump off the page. They reverberate through my mind like a plucked bowstring.

Unlocked.

Blood.

Progeny.

My heart thuds—a heavy *glug-glug-glug* in my ears.

Seraphina created a bloodline.

Silver was forged, her essence preserved inside. And that power can only be unlocked by the blood of her descendants.

According to Ezekiel Cotton, those descendants would have a strong connection to the spiritual realm. So strong, perhaps, they'd be able to see doorways others couldn't.

I pick up the razor blade and prick my finger. A droplet of crimson pools on the tip. I touch it to the locket's clasp, and like ink blooming on paper, my blood spreads through the silver.

Slowly, it fades.

For a moment, nothing happens.

The locket sits in my palm, my blood consumed.

Then it begins to glow.

My heart beats harder as the locket shudders ... and opens.

A drop of shadow laced with thin veins of pulsing red floats inside.

A tiny black beating heart.

Ancient.

Hungry.

Waiting.

I feel its pull.

To lean closer.

To touch.

As if I were always meant to do so.

But just as my fingertip hovers over it, I stop. The final words of the revelation echo through my mind.

For no mortal may touch the divine and live.

The curse is coming to a head. It's coming for me. I can feel it in the coldness of my bones. It's as inevitable as me, here in Foggy Hollow.

My fate written in the stars.

So, too, is the task before me.

Rafe will open the tomb, and Seraphina will come out. But that is where it will end.

She will not rise more terrible than before. I won't let her. With the touch of my blood, our lives will be tethered. Our fates, entwined. And the curse that is coming for me will come for her, too.

By the cruelty she wrought, her end shall be fashioned.

Her essence pulses in my palm.

I cannot touch it yet.

But I will soon enough.

Jude is looking for a solution.

And I have found it.

A supernatural weapon.

A way to stop the curse.

To rewrite the ending of this tragic tale once and for all.

51
DEAD EITHER WAY

I've spent the better part of my life chasing ghosts, contemplating the impossible, enchanted by the uncanny, eager to prove the supernatural. Believing that life is a grand mystery nobody will ever solve. Least of all, me. But man, is it fun to try.

And sure, maybe Dr. Penny had a point. Maybe my obsession was nothing more than an outlet—a way to process my mother's abandonment, to turn it into something fantastical instead of painful.

Or maybe, it's always been more.

Not just curiosity. Not just a coping mechanism. Not just a subconscious attempt to connect with my absentee mother, who was drawn to the fantastical herself. But preparation. What if every stake out with Twig, every episode on our podcast, every fascinating mystery and wild possibility was training for this?

An uncanny fate.

An impossible destiny.

A supernatural ending.

I hand Jude my phone and pace the Midnight Garden as dusk gives way to darkness. He sits on the bench like a statue, reading the revelation on my screen. Meanwhile, I'm a bundle of nervous energy, unable to sit at all, let alone sit still.

I place my hand over the locket clasped around my neck. The tiny heartbeat within knocks against my palm. I imagine touching it. My fate and Seraphina's entwined. The curse returning to its maker. Will it happen right away, I wonder. Or will it take awhile? The revelation didn't go into that particular detail.

My phone buzzes in Jude's hand. A message from Twig, probably. Or my dad. I've been avoiding both, unsure what to say or how to act given the circumstances.

Seraphina's end will be my end, too.

But it's also a way.

To stop the cycle of suffering.

To end the tragedy that has haunted generation after generation.

Jude finishes reading. He looks up, his face pale as a ghost, and shakes his head. "We'll find another way."

I give him a helpless shrug. "There is no other way."

And we're out of time.

Dante's comet will blaze brightest in the sky tomorrow, on Halloween.

He stands abruptly.

We switch roles—I am still, and he is pacing.

He white-knuckles my phone in one hand, fists his hair in the other. "I don't agree to this."

"You don't have to agree to this."

"He needs *my* blood." He clutches his chest like he might tear out his heart. "I was willing to give it to *save* you, Selah. Not so you could—" But he doesn't finish the sentiment. He can't say the word.

I yank the collar of my shirt to the side. "I'm dead either way."

Jude winces.

I shiver.

And ache.

For him.

For us.

For everything I want but can't have. Because long ago, evil twisted something good. Poisoned something beautiful. By turning love into a curse.

"The curse will be broken," I whisper. "You'll be free to love."

"I don't care about love if I can't love you." He closes the gap between us and takes my face in his hands. "You're who I want, Selah. You."

Tears well in my eyes. Because I want him, too. So badly, I feel like I might suffocate beneath the weight of it. But what choice do I have? The end has come for me, just like it comes for all of us eventually.

"If death is my fate," I say, "it's not without choice. Either I die by the curse, or I die by destroying it." I cover his hands with mine. A tear catches on his thumb. "I choose to destroy it."

He lets go.

He turns away.

With a guttural shout of rage, he kicks the bench so hard, it splinters. "You're not the only one who learned something today," he says. "She called it a *consuming* curse. It needs to feed on someone bound to it through love. And that someone doesn't have to be you."

Before I can process his words, he's gone—storming toward the manor like a man on a mission. And I'm left dumbstruck, blinking through the confusion. Because surely, it can't be him. I'm the one with the mark. But then I think of my mother, who outlived Simon Vandenberg by decades.

My thoughts lurch to the scorch mark.

The curse needs to feed, and Jude just looked like a man determined to offer himself up as a meal.

Panic surges.

I sprint after him, but he's already on the portico, disappearing through the doors. I stumble in the dark, reach the stone steps, and bang the brass knocker.

The doors fly open.

Rafe stands on the other side.

I don't wait for a smirk or a snide innuendo. "Please," I gasp. "I need to talk to him."

He leans against the doorframe and folds his arms. "I don't think he wants to talk to you."

My panic spikes.

A *consuming* curse.

It needs to feed.

Isn't that what it's been doing—feeding on my warmth, on my life? What if Jude finds a way to turn its appetite to him? What if he's upstairs feeding it now?

I grab onto Rafe's arm. "In order to get Seraphina back, you need Jude's blood."

His expression glints with something dark and inscrutable.

"Surely he needs to be *alive* when he gives it."

Rafe narrows his eyes. "Are you telling me his plans have changed?"

"He thinks there's another way to save me. One that doesn't involve opening the tomb. A way that would—" My voice catches. I swallow a shaky breath. "Do you understand what I'm saying?"

I want him to reassure me.

Yes, he understands.

No, he won't let it happen.

I want him to give me his word.

I want his word to mean something.

He could, at the very least, look concerned.

Instead, he flips me a sardonic salute, then steps inside the foyer and closes the doors in my face.

52
ONE LAST HURRAH

Frost crunches underfoot. Fog hovers between headstones. Dawn is slow to rise, the sky a muted bruise behind the trees. My fingers ache as I plant the camcorder behind a crooked headstone, angled toward the mausoleum. When I straighten from my crouched position, I'm overcome with a bout of dizziness. The curse is hungry this morning, closer to the surface.

I can feel it beneath my skin.

Feeding on my warmth.

Feeding on my strength, too.

It's not an optimal way to go into battle. Nor is it a pleasant sensation. But I'm comforted nonetheless. So far, its appetite remains fixed on me.

"Most people spend Halloween morning worrying about costumes, not wiring up graveyards."

Twig's voice comes so unexpectedly, I nearly drop the audio recorder. He emerges from behind the mausoleum, scanning my set up.

"How did you know I was here?" I ask.

He holds up his phone, showing me the tracking app on his

screen. We synced up ages ago, mostly in the name of food—an easy way to score a biscuit any time one of us caught the other at Tudor's.

"You're avoiding me," he says, sliding his phone into his back pocket. "So I figured I'd have to come to you."

My guts squirm with guilt.

"What are you doing?" he asks.

"Helping you achieve your life's ambition." I wag the audio recorder. "If ever there was a time to unequivocally prove in some really weird stuff, tonight will be the night. It should make for some great podcast fodder, anyway."

"You think I care about the podcast if I don't have my cohost?"

My shoulders wilt. "You talked to Jude."

"He's not doing so great."

I move to a stone angel and tuck our audio recorder behind its wing—out of sight from party-goers, but close enough to catch sound if any should slip through.

Twig sits on a headstone. "So ... what's your plan, Selah?"

With a resigned sigh, I tell him.

When the time comes, I will go with Rafe through the rift. Jude will follow. Rafe will threaten. Jude will spill his blood to protect me. Seraphina will rise. I'll open the locket, touch her essence, and she and the curse will be destroyed once and for all.

When I finish, he remains as silent as the stone he sits on.

My teeth start to chatter.

I shove my hands deep into my coat pockets. "Think you can keep people away from this part of the cemetery tonight?"

He scoffs. "You're putting your life on the line, and you want me to babysit drunk teenagers?"

"I don't want anyone to get hurt."

"Just you, huh?"

He's angry.

Twig doesn't get angry.

But he is now.

My chest tightens. "Please, Twig. I need you to not be upset with me right now."

He takes off his glasses and rubs his eyes, muttering something too quiet to catch. Then he groans a loud, frustrated groan. "I wish I could go through the rift with you. We could fight Seraphina together."

"Fight her how—with our proton pack?"

"Why not?"

"Twig ..."

"No, seriously, Selah. Why not?"

"Our proton pack is filled with granola bars and bug spray. Not to mention, your arm is broken."

"But what if we made a real one? An actual scientific weapon?"

The set of his mouth, the eager tilt of his chin brings me back in time, to the summer before sixth grade, after we watched Ghostbusters 1 and 2 and built our very first ghost trap. A shoebox wrapped in tinfoil with a magnetized coil of copper curled around a pack of D batteries and a candy bar for bait. We planted it right here, in this very cemetery, convinced we were going to catch the Woman of the Woods. The next morning, the lid was off and the candy bar gone. A raccoon, probably. But Twig's conviction that it had very nearly worked was so unshakable, it made me believe too.

And now, here he is again, that same conviction locked into place as he stands from the headstone. "Something that only requires one arm to wield."

He begins to pace. I can practically see the gears turning behind his eyes—calculating, sketching mental blueprints. This has become a problem to solve. And Twig Calloway doesn't fail when it comes to solving problems.

Honestly, it makes me want to cry.

"I can't go through the rift because I can't see the rift, but I can be here. The question is—how will I know when you're here, too?" He stops suddenly, as if asking the question out loud has unlocked an answer. "The tracking app. What if it works through dimensions?"

He's not asking me.

He's asking himself.

I've seen Twig like this before, muttering his way through a plan. It's best not to interrupt.

He resumes pacing. "The EMF meter went wild at the Vandenberg estate, which means this dimension must have a magnetic field. And magnetic fields can be destabilized."

He bites his thumbnail. "I'd need some sort of disruptor coil. A pulse generator. A high-voltage power cell—like a car battery, but way stronger. There'll be a bunch of people here, just like the masquerade ball, and a fallen angel will literally be rising from the grave. With that much energy, we could tear it down completely. Forget the rift. We could collapse the barrier between dimensions."

He turns to me with bright eyes. "I could fight with you. We could try to take her out in a way that doesn't involve the locket."

"Twig, she's—"

"An angel, I know. But she's fallen, Selah. Which means she's bound to earth. Bound things have limits. They can break. Iron weakens fae. Silver burns werewolves."

"Sunlight torches vampires," I say softly.

"Exactly. So she has to have a weakness, too. Some kind of Achilles' heel."

She does.

Me.

I'm her weakness.

But I don't say it.

Doing so would be cruel.

This is his outlet.

His coping mechanism.

Twig needs a mission. He needs to believe he can tip the odds. I get it. If the roles were reversed, I'd need the same thing.

Twelve hours stretch between now and nightfall.

Jude won't take my calls or answer his door.

So I'll spend the time I have left with my best and oldest friend, building something wildly implausible and entirely useless.

And I'll savor every minute.

Our last supernatural hurrah.

53
THE SPILLING OF BLOOD

Beyond the estate gates, Foggy Hollow celebrates Halloween. Porch lights glow. Witches, pirates, superheroes, and princesses dart through yards, their bags fat with candy. Teens laugh and scream their way through the Wraith Walk before gathering in the cemetery for a costume party. It's my favorite holiday of the year, and tonight, it feels like a different world, something completely removed as I enter the music room where the rift floats like a scorch mark in midair.

Rafe waits in the dark, a rigid silhouette cut from shadow.

I take a step toward him. "Is Jude—?"

"Alive? Why, yes." He sets his hands on the armrests of the chair, pushes himself upright, and steps into the halo of light from the corridor. For once, he doesn't look flippant or casual. There are deep shadows beneath his eyes, and an unmistakable tightness in his jaw. "Are you really willing to do this?"

By this, he means helping him open the tomb. He has no idea what I'm willing to do afterward. All day, I've been gathering my resolve, summoning my courage. Despite all the planning and conniving I've done with Twig, I know there's only one way to break this curse. "We can't get her to undo anything if she's trapped in the tomb."

He looks me up and down as though measuring my commitment. Finally, with an unimpressed lift of his brow, he reaches inside his coat and removes his phone. He taps out a message and hits send, then returns the device to his pocket and draws out the ruby. It glows softly. I swear, I can hear the faint, familiar sound of Lainey's weeping—a distraught melody seeping from the amulet. Rafe lifts it into the air, then draws it downward along the rift's seam.

The room hums. Deep and low, vibrating through my chest like a tuning fork pressed to bone. Lainey's weeping grows louder. And like a fresh wound all-too easily opened, a sliver of spectral light cuts through the scorch mark.

It splits open and stretches wide.

Rafe peers at me over his shoulder, then holds out his hand. With a shaky breath, I take it. And together, we step through. Into the cold. Into the dark. Into the swirling void of two worlds twisted together, coiling in and out of sync.

Removing my hand from his, I pull my coat tight and press my palm over the locket hidden beneath my shirt. I match Rafe's long stride. Determined to keep up, to stay close, like he is safety—a testament to my terror, and the awful memory of that sucking, tentacled beast that crawled out of the fountain.

"How do you know Jude will come?" I ask.

"He won't ignore the message I sent him."

I look at the black abyss overhead. The blaze of Dante's comet is the only familiar thing. Somehow, it is fully present in both realms, its white fire painting everything in sharp silver and deep shadow. I stumble, then quickly recover. "The last time we tried finding our way in this place, we got lost."

"Last time, he didn't have the compass."

"And the tomb?"

"What about it?"

"He's supposed to *willingly* spill his blood."

Rafe presses onward.

"Is it willing if he's doing it under threat?"

"There will be no threat to *his* life."

"Just mine."

"So long as I don't take his blood without his permission, or physically force his hand, the choice remains his."

Thick, viscous fog sucks at my feet.

All around, shadows press in.

I try to swallow my fear. But it is a persistent thing, crawling right back up my throat again. Talking seems to keep it down the longest. And just maybe, if I say the right thing, I won't have to fight two demons tonight. "How do you know Seraphina wants out?"

He scoffs at the question.

"You said it yourself. Two hundred sixty-eight years is a long time. And for every second of it, she's been with Dante. Forgive me, Rafe, but they read a bit like soul mates."

Toxic ones, certainly.

But soul mates nonetheless.

He doesn't take the bait.

I keep pressing. "Do you really think she'll come out and the two of you will ride off into the sunset?"

He chuckles dryly, like my question is silly.

"She seduced you so she could reclaim her powers. Took advantage of your love to get the upper hand. From everything I've read, she never loved you back."

He whirls on me, his eyes glinting. "You make a lot of assumptions, young Selah."

I lift my chin. My assumptions are logical.

"What makes you think I want to ride into the sunset with her?"

His question throws me off balance.

"You assume because I loved her once, I love her still?"

"But ... " I blink a few times. "Don't you?"

He huffs, a quick exhalation through his nose, then continues onward.

"Then why go to all this trouble?" I ask, following him once again.

"Did my dear brother happen to mention, in all his precious journaling, how Seraphina brought me back to life?"

My brow furrows.

No. He didn't.

"My existence is tethered to hers. And for the past two hundred sixty-eight years, she has been sealed inside a cold, dark tomb. Not dead. But not exactly alive either. It's a long time to exist in such a way."

He's not talking about her.

He's talking about him.

"An immortal life in a dark and broken world is a cruel thing in any circumstance. But especially mine."

"Your lives are connected," I say.

His jaw clenches.

His fists, too.

He's not freeing her out of love.

He's freeing her so he can be free, too.

"Does that mean, if she dies ...?"

"Are you getting fanciful ideas? You think if you kill her you can get rid of me? She is an angel. You wouldn't stand the slightest chance."

But he doesn't know.

About the locket.

About the power within.

Power *I* can wield.

The ground softens beneath my foot like mossy sponge. My boot sinks. And I swear, something breathes on my neck. I twist around to look behind me, where shadows coil and crawl.

Rafe grabs my wrist and yanks me forward, this young-looking man who speaks of immortality like a punishment. All day I've been drumming up bravery, fighting back despair. Somehow, Rafe's words, of all words, have bolstered my morale. We all wish for more days in the end. More time. But perhaps, in some paradoxical twist, the very fact that our days are numbered is what makes them so special.

The wrought iron gate of the cemetery rises before us. The Halloween party is in full swing—muffled laughter, distorted music, warped voices. Costumed teenagers flicker in and out of focus, smudges of motion weaving between gravestones, unaware that I am here, too. But a ghost.

We wind up the hill. Past the oldest graves. Toward the mausoleum at the top.

The tomb.

The arch.

The three symbols etched in stone.

They're here in front of me, just like they were when the lightning flashed.

So is Twig, hiding exactly where he said he would be, crouched beside the twisted silhouette of a cracked obelisk. Inside my pocket, my thumb hovers over my phone screen, a message typed before I set foot inside the Vandenberg manor.

We're here.

As Rafe carefully slots the pearl into place, I hit send and hold my breath, counting the seconds, wondering if the message will make it through. Rafe is slotting the ruby into place when it happens—a flicker of light blinks once. Just once.

Twig's signal.

He got the message.

He knows I'm here.

And while his presence can do nothing to save me, it does everything to give me courage.

Somewhere behind the obelisk comes a faint mechanical click, followed by a soft whir. One of Twig's devices kicking on.

He's planted them all over this part of the graveyard. Not just one weapon, but a supernatural minefield. A patchwork of sensors, coils, and pulse rigs wired with hope and just enough recklessness to make them dangerous.

Then another sound comes.

Someone is calling my name.

Rafe fits the onyx into place.

Something ancient stirs beneath our feet as Jude breaks through the fog, the compass clutched in his hand, his chest heaving.

His eyes lock onto mine.

But he's too late.

Rafe grabs me around the waist and cold, sharp steel presses against my throat.

"Move any closer," Rafe says, as casual as a Sunday stroll, "and she dies."

Jude freezes.

"Please," I whisper, grasping Rafe's forearm in an attempt to create more space between my neck and his blade. But I'm not sure who I'm begging, or what I'm begging for.

For Jude to cooperate?

For Rafe to let me go?

For the curse to relent?

For fate to reconsider?

I want a different ending. But time has reached its end. Above us, the comet burns brighter. A flare across the heavens. Party-goers let out shouts of awe. They light sparklers and snap selfies and lift lanterns, oblivious to the nightmare unfolding.

All of them except Twig.

Jude picks up a rock. He brings the jagged end across his palm in one decisive swipe. Blood pools in his hand. I hold my breath as he takes a step forward, tips his palm to the stone, and lets the crimson spill.

<h1 style="text-align:center">54
WRITTEN IN THE STARS</h1>

Disembodied whispers carry on the wind, snatching hats and whipping cloaks. Spiraling gusts kick up dirt and dead leaves, sending debris in violent swirls. Contraptions tick and blink and hum, like the cemetery itself has come alive.

A ghost hunter's last stand.

Twig's minefield.

The epitaphs on tombstones glow.

Lantern flame erupts in pale blue.

Party-goers cry out, their bodies flickering and glitching as the ground rumbles underfoot.

A bolt of lightning forks upward.

A speaker explodes.

Teens scream.

Tree roots tear through soil and grass, rising like skeletal fingers from the grave.

Twig shouts my name as the tomb splits open.

Wind shrieks from within.

A black ring of fire ignites around its mouth.

A white flame shoots up from the abyss. Like a firework, it erupts in concentric circles. They widen, pushing apart the mist and the fog, until—for one heart-stopping moment—the supernatural realm is laid bare. Winged creatures. Chained souls. Ruined altars. A terrifying vision that twists into a single beam of pale light that strikes the pearl.

The ruby ignites beside it like a domino. The comet burns red, bathing the cemetery in a bloody glow. My heart burns in my chest. Rafe clutches his own. His knife clatters to the ground as corporeal veins pulse across the sky, emitting a euphoric song and a devastating wail that coalesce, then implode into a single beating ember that slowly sinks into the ruby.

The onyx begins to glow. Every other light goes dim. Lanterns and sparklers snuffed in the wind. Even the comet slips behind clouds as shadows pull free and writhe like snakes across the ground. With a bone-chilling screech, they slither up the archway and crawl into the black stone.

Seraphina's powers—to see what is hidden, to control human hearts, to manipulate darkness and shadow—have been reunited with their amulets.

Jude clambers to my side. He takes my hand and tries to shield me as the curse swells. I can feel it building like the crest of an icy wave.

The locket beats beneath my shirt—wildly, euphorically— as another rift tears open. A jagged, vertical split through the air, and through its warped shimmer, I glimpse the other side.

A mob of stampeding partygoers scramble for safety, only they don't know where to run. I spot Twig, working furiously against the wind, adjusting a rigged-up array of copper rods wired to a humming battery. Sparks spit from the panel as wind tears at his clothes.

Shadowed wings unfurl from the tomb. And Seraphina emerges, her eyes aglow. Her skin, pale and luminous. Her long, raven hair whipping in the wind, framing a face that is terrifying in its beauty.

Rafe drops to his knee.

The black ring of flame shrinks.

The wind goes quiet.

So does the chaos on the other side of the veil.

Slowly, she turns to Rafe in a gown woven from shadow and starlight. The hem tattered as though dragged through a battlefield.

"Raphael," she says in a voice that is both honey and venom, melodic and inhuman. "I thought you wouldn't come."

"Of course I came."

She traces her pale finger down his cheek.

He looks up at her, his eyes reflecting her glow. "You left me buried in a half-life, waiting for the stars to align."

"*I* left you? Oh no no, my sweet." She brings the tip of her finger beneath his chin. "You have your brother to thank for that. Please tell me you made him pay."

"Him and every generation after."

She smiles a slow, bone-chilling smile, then turns in our direction. "And who do we have here?"

"The last of Ezra's line," Rafe says. "And the girl he bleeds for."

Fear coils in my gut.

Jude shifts, like doing so might hide me.

Seraphina's glowing eyes glitter. "Is this love I see? Oh, how delightful."

She turns to the archway and lifts the onyx between her fingers—obsidian dark, glowing with power. She sighs a contented, blissful sigh as darkness spills from the stone like undulating liquid suspended in the air.

"Do you have any idea how wonderful it is to be reunited with my beloveds after so long without them?" For a moment, the darkness swirls hypnotically. Then, with a flick of her wrist, it streaks toward me with impossible speed. I stumble backward and fall. Jude tries to intervene, tries to stop what is happening, but how do you fight shadow?

It passes through him like mist.

He shouts my name as darkness curls around my neck, squeezing, tightening, lifting me off my toes.

The world dims.

My eyes bulge.

I choke—unable to breathe.

"Let her go!" Jude shouts.

The darkness releases its hold.

I collapse to the ground, coughing and spluttering as Jude crouches beside me.

Seraphina watches with idle amusement. Then she smiles venomously. "I think it's time for your friends to meet one of my darlings."

She lifts the onyx again, high above her head.

From the chasm behind her, something stirs.

A wet, slithering sound slurps across stone.

I watch in frozen horror as a tentacle emerges, slick and glistening, as thick as a man's torso. A second tentacle follows. Then a third. The creature unfurls from the mouth of the tomb like a snake uncoiling from hell itself. Seraphina raises her hand in a graceful arc, as if commanding a symphony. And the beast responds. With another flick of her wrist, it strikes.

A tentacle lashes through the veil.

It grabs a girl in a fairy costume.

The tentacle wraps around her waist and with a yank, she's pulled through the rift.

For one horrifying second, her eyes lock with mine.

I recognize her.

She's in my AP Lit class.

Her body distorts. Her scream warbles. And with a violent convulsion, she erupts in fire, then bursts into ash.

My mouth opens in a silent scream as Seraphina lifts her hand again, and the second tentacle strikes.

Another girl is snatched.

Lainey Sikes.

Twig lunges for her. With his good arm, he grabs her by the wrist. With his broken arm, he fires one of the rods. It sails through the rift as he loses his grip on Lainey. She's yanked through, her costume a horrible irony. Dressed like a fallen angel, her mouth twists in a horrifying cry as she, too, combusts in a burst of ghostly flame. And just as my body catches up with the horror, Twig is grabbed by the ankle.

A scream tears up my throat. I snatch Rafe's knife from the ground and charge as Twig claws at the dirt, kicking wildly. But he has nothing to grab. His foot is dragged through the opening. With a war cry, I drive the blade into the creature's slimy tentacle. At the same time, Jude seizes the copper rod and plunges it deep into the tentacle's base.

With a horrific and high-pitched shriek, it flings Twig across the ground and withdraws, slithering back into the shadows from which it came.

My heart pounds as Twig scrambles to safety and Seraphina plucks the ruby from the archway, like she's ready for a new toy to play with.

The ember rises. It lifts from the stone and pulses in the air.

She gives her head a sadistic tilt.

Jude gasps.

He sinks to his knees, clutching his chest, his face bone-white. I drop beside him and beg her to stop. "Stop! Please, stop!"

The ember returns to the stone.

Jude sucks in a breath.

"See how weak love makes them?" Seraphina purrs, turning her attention to Rafe, who has remained on one knee, watching the events unfold. She glides to Jude, stops in front of him, and gazes deep into his eyes as though searching for devotion or desire.

They only glow with defiance and disgust.

She pouts. "Same as Ezra, I see. Immune to my charm. A trick of Dante's I did not foresee. I believe every firstborn of his line carries the immunity. To keep them safe, I suppose. Retain the upper hand."

Seraphina rolls her eyes. "Better had he made them immune to love altogether. Then perhaps all of this could have been avoided. Ezra certainly wouldn't have begged me so pathetically to spare his brother." She sighs. "I did warn him there would be repercussions."

I feel them—the repercussions.

The curse spreads like ice through my veins.

"And now this dear girl." She tuts. "One more tragedy in a long line of tragedies."

The cold is unbearable.

Inescapable.

"I'll kill your sweet Selah while you watch," she tells Jude, her voice soft and cruel. "But you can go on in misery. That I will allow. Mind you, it will be nothing compared to two hundred sixty-eight years trapped in there, left to rot."

Seraphina reaches for the final gemstone as I pull off the locket, my hand tightening around it.

Jude meets my gaze.

His love burns like a flame, the only warm thing within me.

Seraphina lifts the pearl.

The air around it ripples, and I know what's coming. The locket may be tucked inside my fist, but once she wields the power of the pearl, I won't be able to hide it any longer.

She narrows her eyes. "What is that you have in there?"

I open my hand.

The silver chain dangles between my fingers.

Behind Seraphina, Rafe shifts, as though to get a look for himself.

"Oh, how splendid," she says with a smile. "Are you one of my own? And is that your protection? Unfortunately for you, your life matters not to me. My bloodline has become quite vast. Ridding the world of you will do nothing to diminish my power, silly girl."

"It's not for my protection."

She frowns, as though she can't imagine why it would be for anything else.

I pick up Rafe's knife and cut my finger.

Blood drips onto the silver.

The locket begins to glow.

Then it opens, and the wind returns and alarm ignites in Seraphina's eyes.

Evil may have corrupted what is good, but it doesn't get the final say. Seraphina turned love into a weapon of destruction. But all my life, love has given me strength. Maybe not from my mother, but certainly from my father, who has been there always, waiting up on his recliner. And Twig, my co-adventurer, who not only believed in the wild things but explored them with me. And the Calloways, who made sure a warm supper would be waiting for us after every expedition. And Jude, the steadfast skeptic, who in the end, would battle all the things he doubted to keep me safe.

With the strength of that love, I lower my finger to the tiny beating heart—*fates entwined by the touching of blood.*

But something happens then that I do not expect. That I did not anticipate.

Jude grabs my arm, his eyes blazing, steady and fierce. Before I can object, before I even have time to react, he takes the opened locket with the very same hand he cut with a rock.

"No," I gasp, like a sucker punch to the gut. The kind that doubles a person over.

But it's too late.

A bolt of white-hot power bursts from his chest. It lashes through the air and wraps around Seraphina's wrist like the creature she drew forth, only this one is made of light. A luminous strand of supernatural energy stretched taut and crackling with heat.

With a scream, Seraphina tries to escape.

But she can't break the tether.

Rafe shouts and lunges forward only to be lashed back. He hits the ground hard and rolls into shadow.

Jude draws me close and brings his mouth to mine.

The curse ignites.

It surges inside me like ice-fire.

Ready to feed.

Ready to consume.

But not me.

As his fingers tangle in my hair, the icy cold begins to drain, as though being drawn out. Siphoned from me into him. There's a spark of icy blue where the tether meets Jude's chest, and like frost racing across glass, it moves down the length of the lasso. Until the entire thing pulses with an eerie, electric cold.

The curse is moving.

Passing through Jude.

Coming straight for her.

With an ear-splitting cry, Seraphina tries to flee. But there's no escape. She is trapped, entwined, her fate written in the stars—not with mine, but Jude's.

Light fractures through her skin like broken glass. She is fissuring from the inside out, pressure building like steam in a kettle. And then, with a sonic boom, she bursts into pieces. Completely obliterated as the curse that has plagued generation upon generation, at last, turns upon its maker.

The world around me buckles.

Light and shadow ripple and split, then tear completely. With a thunderous snap, the veil between dimensions disintegrates.

The tether fades to nothing.

The air is cold.

The sky, full of stars.

For a moment, there is silence. So deep, it feels like the earth itself is holding its breath. I turn to where Rafe lay, and watch him disappear in fading pixels. Like a dream. Like my mother. Until he's gone. And it's just me and Jude.

For one whole, impossible second, he stares at me—triumphant, glorious. "Ezra never said it had to be you," he whispers, his voice weak.

So very weak.

Then his gaze softens.

"Jude?"

He sways.

Then he falls.

I drop to my knees beside him and cradle his head in my arms. "Please, Jude. Please stay with me."

But the light leaves his eyes and he's with me no more.

The price has been paid.

No mortal can touch the divine and live.

55
GONE

Somewhere far away, a siren wails. I grab Jude by the shoulders and shake him.

His head lolls.

There's a hole in his shirt where the tether erupted. I slide my fingers inside and tear the fabric away. Tiny black spider veins curl over his heart.

I press my ear against his chest.

But there is no sound.

And I don't know CPR.

Why don't I know CPR?

"Please," I cry, coming to my knees. Turning. Searching. My mind scrambling for something, anything, to fix this.

A figure stumbles through the dark.

Twig.

He limps toward me, dragging his left leg, blood soaked through the torn knee of his jeans. His face is ashen, scratched, and bruised. His glasses are gone. But he sees me and I see him.

He's here.

Fully here.

So am I.

Someone cries.

Someone else moans.

The sound of frightened, injured party-goers pockmarks the night.

Distant, but no longer distorted.

Somehow, we are in the same realm.

Twig stumbles. Falls. Scoops something up from the grass, then gets to his feet again.

"Is he alive?" he asks through gritted teeth.

"I don't know," I cry, searching for a pulse. A flicker of life. A shred of hope. "I don't know," I say again, wilder this time, my fingers fumbling from Jude's neck to his wrist. My own heart beats everywhere—in my ears, in my throat, in my skull. If only I could rip it from my body and share it with him.

I reach for his other wrist.

The locket is still in his hand, open and empty.

With a hoarse cry, I snatch it up and hurl it at the tomb. It cracks against stone and falls as a sob tears up my throat and memories claw their way in.

Jude on his first day of school, reading *Macbeth* in the cafeteria, debating with me in class about witches and evil. Listening to Stevie Knicks in his storage room. Watching *Tales from the Crypt* until midnight. Skipping rocks at the quarry. A glitter fight at the fairgrounds. Dancing in the ballroom. His crooked grin, a rare sight to see. But oh, when it came. He didn't believe in monsters, but he saved me from one anyway, and then we kissed.

"Selah." Twig drops beside me, his breathing ragged.

He opens his fist.

Something flickers on his palm.

A faint red pulse.

The ruby amulet.

It's glowing.

Still alive.

With power over human hearts.
And I am Seraphina's descendant.
With the ability to wield the supernatural.
My breath catches.
I pick up the ruby and place it on Jude's chest. With tears tumbling down my cheeks, I take his hand between mine and cradle it against my heart.
"Please, Jude."
I grapple for the right words.
Magic words.
True words.
"I love you," I whisper.
And I will never believe that love is a bad thing. No matter how Seraphina tried to twist it, love is not a curse.
It's a gift.
A good, life-giving gift.
My heart swells with it as tears tumble down my cheeks and I press my lips to his.
The amulet flares to life.
A red ember lifts from the stone, glowing like a tiny star. It floats in the air. Then slowly, delicately, it lands on Jude's wound. It sinks into his skin. The ruby pulses once, and the spidery black veins fade away.
Time stops.
So does my breath.
But my mind churns.
Begs.
Please, please, please ...
His finger twitches in my hand.
And his eyes flutter open. The color of changing leaves in the fall. A sob escapes—a joy-filled, euphoric sob. Half laughter, half disbelief as his cloudy gaze finds mine.
Twig slumps against a headstone.
Red and blue lights flicker in the distance.

Jude pulls my hand to his chest, where his heart beats once again. "Did it work?"

I laugh and cry and nod.

"But I'm alive?"

"Yes," I say, showing him the ruby, which pulses no more. A special power Seraphina used to hurt hearts and break hearts and stop hearts.

Its final act was life.

"And the curse?" he asks.

"That's gone, too."

He closes his eyes for a moment, an exhausted smile painting his lips. Then, as though needing proof, he gently moves the collar of my shirt aside.

The mark is gone.

He exhales softly.

"Then allow me to say the words I've been dying to say ..." His fingers curl around the back of my neck. He draws me close, his voice warm in my ear. "I love you, Selah Whitlock."

56

UNACCOUNTED FOR

Outside, red and blue lights spin in the dark. Reporters speak into microphones, gesturing toward the front entrance of Foggy Hollow General, camera lights casting long shadows across the glass. Inside, shell-shocked teens sit in the waiting room as a trickle of panicked parents arrive and a police officer moves from group to group, quietly gathering statements.

I sit beside Jude, my hand in his as we wait for news about Twig. Jude's shirt is torn open, a peculiarity on a typical night, perhaps. But tonight is not typical, evidenced by Wednesday Addams and Chucky's Bride sitting shoulder to shoulder across from us.

Wednesday weeps.

The Bride sniffles into her phone. "The police said to come here, but we just found out they're transferring Callie to Morgantown," she says. "It's really bad, Mom. Her sister had to do CPR and ..."

Her face crumples.

She can't finish.

Callie Reese is a sophomore who was flung against a stone

statue and knocked unconscious. Callie's sister, a senior named Milly, administered CPR until the ambulance arrived.

"Can you come get us?" the girl asks, wiping at the black streaks of mascara running down her cheeks. "We want to go to Morgantown."

On the television, the news unfolds. Muted footage of police tape at the cemetery and teenagers wrapped in blankets. A headline scrolls across the bottom of the screen.

Breaking: Several teens hospitalized after Halloween incident in Foggy Hollow cemetery.

The doors leading to triage hiss open and out comes Kate in a long black dress, her face still painted witch-green.

Harrison comes to his feet.

She falls into his arms.

"They're putting him under sedation now," she says. "I don't understand how he burned his foot so badly. They said it went all the way though his shoe."

Kate pulls away and looks at me like I might have an explanation. Before I can feign confusion, commotion breaks out on the other side of the waiting room.

"She's his sister." Griffin Tate gestures toward Kate, his bloody forearm wrapped in the tattered remnants of a superman cape. "Maybe he told her something. He was right there with us. He might have seen what happened to her."

The officer tries to calm him down, but Griffin will not be calmed.

"She just—she disappeared. And none of my calls will go through. They keep dropping, see?" He dials a number and thrusts his screen forward.

The call doesn't go to voicemail.

It doesn't go through at all.

My heart twists.

He's trying to call Lainey.

"I understand, son. This is all very upsetting," the officer says. "But you're not the only one having trouble. Whatever happened at the party disrupted signals. Phones are still acting up."

"I have to go back there. I need to find her."

The officer steps into Griffin's path and nods at his wrapped forearm. "You need to get that checked out first."

"But what if she's still there? What if she's hurt?"

"The scene's been evacuated. And a lot of people ran. I'm sure she'll turn up just fine. Now, why don't you tell me everything that happened while we wait for those stitches?"

Kate sinks into the chair beside me.

"Did you see Lainey?" she whispers.

I shake my head, my insides squirming.

Yes, in fact. I did see Lainey.

No, in fact, she isn't *just fine*.

I lean into Jude, thankful for his warmth, his strength, his presence—the miraculous, steady beating of his heart.

The front doors slide open.

Mr. and Mrs. Calloway hurry inside with my dad close behind, all three so focused on the front desk they don't see us sitting in their periphery.

Kate and I rise in unison and call their names.

When they spot us, they melt with visible relief.

Mr. and Mrs. Calloway wrap Kate in a hug while I throw my arms around Dad's neck. When I pull back, he takes my face in his hands, his dark brown eyes swimming with worry. "Are you okay, kiddo?"

I nod, but I can't hold back the tears any longer.

Jude comes to my side as Kate assures her parents that Twig is okay. He's injured, but it's not life threatening. Together, they head to the front desk for more information.

Dad takes in the state of Jude—his torn shirt, his well-defined upper half, his lacerated palm—as the Calloways join us.

"He has a contusion on his head that needed some stitches," Mr. Calloway says, wiping his palms down the front of his jeans, which are perpetually grease-stained thanks to his job. He takes a seat. "And a burn on his ankle and foot that required attention. They'll come for us when he's out of the procedure."

Mrs. Calloway sinks into the chair beside him, white as a sheet. "What happened?"

Kate exchanges a bewildered look with Harrison, then another with me and Jude. "I don't know. It was like ... there was this massive gust of wind and the ground started to shake, like it did at the ball. All the lights went weird, and something exploded?"

"Everyone panicked," Harrison says.

I nod along, avoiding Dad's stare, and the Calloways' too.

A throat clears.

The officer has reached us. He stands a few feet away with his hat in his hands, his expression soft. Before he can ask for a statement, however, the front doors slide open again.

A woman rushes inside with the same frantic energy as my dad and the Calloways. Only there's nobody waiting to intercept her. When she reaches the front desk, she sets both hands flat on the laminate counter. "Please, can you tell me if my daughter is here? Her name is Ivy Winslow."

The name hits me like a punch to the gut.

Ivy Winslow.

I couldn't remember it earlier, but I recognize it now. The quiet girl in AP Lit. Always drawing in a notebook. Except when we read *The Scarlett Letter*. She had strong opinions about that book.

"I keep trying to call her, but none of my calls will go through. She was at the party. Do you know if she was brought in by ambulance? Do you know if she's okay?"

I squeeze my eyes shut, trying to block out the memory of

her face—terrified, frozen in that final moment—before she …
combusted. Disintegrated. Evaporated.

Her life gone in an instant.

Just like Lainey's.

"Please check again," the woman says.

The staff member behind the desk gives her screen a quick
glance. "I'm sorry, ma'am, but she's not here."

The woman shakes her head, her hands curling into fists.

The officer steps in.

"Ma'am," he says gently. "Just because Ivy is unaccounted
for doesn't mean she's not safe."

"What happened at that cemetery?" Miss Winslow asks, her
voice edged with hysteria.

"We're still trying to sort that out," the officer replies. "At the
moment, we believe someone may have been trying to cause a
scare, being Halloween and all."

Miss Winslow's cheeks turn pink. "You think this was a
prank?"

"It's a working theory, ma'am. Equipment blew, the ground
was unstable, and many of the teens on site were under the
influence. Not a good combination, I'm afraid."

"I can assure you, my daughter doesn't—"

He holds up his hands. "I'm not accusing anyone. I'm just
letting you know what we've established so far. I promise you
we're doing everything we can to sort it out. Why don't we step
over here, and you can give me Ivy's full name and description.
I'll make sure it's passed along to everyone at the scene."

I watch them walk away with my heart in my throat.

Because it won't matter.

They aren't going to find Ivy Winslow.

Or Lainey Sikes.

I reach into Jude's lap and take his hand, thankful, so very
thankful, that Twig escaped with nothing more than stitches
and a burned foot.

57
NOT EVEN A TRACE

Fire crackles in the grate. Rivulets of rain streak the windowpanes, smudging the dreary afternoon outside. I sit in the center of Jude's four-poster bed surrounded by familiar items while he strips his wall, removing photographs, journal entries, and news articles.

I pick up the gemstones, emptied of their power, and shake them in my palm like dice, my gaze wandering from the carved-out Bible to the gold-plated compass to the charred silver husk that was once the locket.

It's Saturday afternoon.

Twig's at home, resting.

And the town is in an uproar.

Officials scramble to make sense of what happened, navigating confusion, community pressure, and outright condemnation. How was a party of such magnitude allowed to unfold under their noses on public property? And what is going on with these non-earthquakes? First, the tremble at the ball. Now teens have reported another at the cemetery. If nothing is turning up on the richter scale, then what is going on?

With a sigh, I let the gemstones spill from my hand and

reach for the family tree, curled in on itself like a scroll. I stretch it flat and eye Raphael's line, which is no line at all. Raphael II. Raphael III. Lucian. Rueben. Frank. Thomas. I brush my finger over each name. All of them were one and the same.

Where is he now?

The rift vanished in the music room. No trace of it remains, not even the faintest of scars. The destruction of Seraphina, along with the curse, seemed to have caused a supernatural glitch. Jude and I were booted from its realm. But what about Rafe? Is he stuck on the other side? According to him, his life was connected to Seraphina's. When she met her end, did he meet his, too?

I look at Jude, taking in his broad back, his slim waist as he removes Lydia Mabel's autopsy report from the wall.

"You should frame this," I say.

He glances over his shoulder.

I lift the family tree. "Hang it somewhere in the estate."

"I'd rather throw it in the fire."

"Maggie would die."

"Maybe I should give it to her, then."

I trace the branches of his lineage—one after another, marked by the curse. From Ezra all the way down to Jude's father. Heartache and tragedy passed from father to son, and I wonder, how many of them knew what was going on?

My finger pauses over the scorch mark.

Elijah Vandenberg.

I think of his suicide note. His mother's pain. His father's shame. Elijah's final request—to tell his son everything. But they refused, as if acknowledging the curse gave it power. Isaiah remained oblivious, and the train flew off the tracks anyway, an attack not only on Vandenberg blood, but on every innocent passenger aboard.

Ignoring it hadn't protected anyone.

It only kept them stuck in the same tragic loop.

Generation after generation.

Until we faced the monster head on, and broke ourselves free.

"What *should* we do with all this stuff?" I ask.

"We could put it in the crypt." Jude sets the stack of evidence on his desk. "Lock it up," he continues, his eyes on mine as he comes closer. "Throw away the key."

I set the parchment aside and lean forward. "Maybe in fifty years, some girl will find it and dive head first into a supernatural mystery."

"With her nose in every shadow." He traces the ridge of my jaw with his thumb, sending a trail of sparks along my skin.

I lift my chin.

His lips find mine.

And my insides catch fire.

The kiss is soft.

Achingly so.

Until my hands slide around his neck.

He pulls me to him so that I'm drawn to my knees, his arm wrapped around my waist, our bodies pressed together as he lowers us onto the bed, and I'm so euphorically grateful for this freedom. This gift. This tantalizing distraction. Kissing Jude Vandenberg pushes the investigation, the missing girls, and Callie Reese far, far away.

I don't want to stop.

Not ever.

But in one smooth maneuver, Jude flips us over so I'm on top of him, his arm bent casually behind his head as he rests back against the pillow, looking in complete control, and ever-so-slightly amused. Like he knows exactly what he's doing.

I narrow my eyes playfully.

He tucks a strand of hair behind my ear.

I rest my head against his chest, relishing the sound of his heartbeat when a knock sounds at the door.

Jude groans, but he gets up and answers it anyway. Isabel stands on the other side. She never came to the hospital. Not like the Calloways. Not like my dad.

I try to make out their voices, but they're low and muffled in the hallway. When he returns, he shuts the door with a soft click and drags a hand down his face.

"The police called," he says. "They want us to come to the station to give a statement."

My stomach churns.

I picture Ms. Winslow, racing to the front desk. I picture Griffin Tate, thrusting his phone in the officer's face. What is more cruel? Telling the truth? Or letting them hold on to hope?

I worry my bottom lip. "Are we going to tell them what happened?"

"They'd never believe us if we did."

He's right, of course.

Despite all the evidence, even the craziness that occurred at the ball, they'd think we were joking. Or maybe insane. Just like the Abners thought of my mother. She wanted, more than anything, to help Simon Vandenberg and his family. But the adults in her life wouldn't listen to a truth so preposterous. She doubled down and ended up in a psych ward where she was probably forced onto antipsychotics.

Was that what led to her addiction? If she'd just stayed quiet, would she have been okay? Or was it the silence that killed her?

Jude pulls me up from his bed.

"So what are we going to tell them, then?" I ask.

"A palatable version of the truth," he suggests. "We were near the mausoleum when something shifted beneath the ground. We don't know exactly what happened. We're just glad we made it out."

"So glad," I whisper.

He wraps me in a hug.

"The officer at the hospital made it sound like they think it could've been a prank." Knots twist in my stomach. My fingerprints and Twig's fingerprints are all over that part of the cemetery. "Do you think there's a chance Twig and I could be implicated?"

"No," he says.

I lean back and study his face. "That's a confident answer."

He flashes a crooked grin. "What's the benefit of money and connections if you can't use them in your favor?"

"Does this mean you'll be around to use them?"

"Why wouldn't I be?"

"Last I heard, you were headed back to your boarding school."

He kisses my neck. "Boarding schools aren't all they're cracked up to be."

"Your rock-skipping will suffer."

"My fencing, too."

"Risky business," I say breathlessly. "You never know when you'll find yourself in a sword fight."

"Yes, well." His lips travel to the spot where my mark once was, but is no longer. Like the rift, not even a trace remains. "Who needs swords when you're part angel?"

Foggy Hollow Police Department Press Briefing
Saturday, November 1, 2025 – 6:42 p.m. EST

CHIEF DOUGLAS PERRY: We can confirm that two students from Foggy Hollow High School—Lainey Sikes and Ivy Winslow—were reported missing early this morning, following an unsanctioned Halloween gathering at the town cemetery on

Friday night. We take these reports very seriously and are doing everything in our power to locate both girls and bring them home safely.

At this time, there is no confirmed evidence of foul play. However, we are treating this as an active investigation. Search and rescue operations began this afternoon and will continue through the coming days with assistance from county authorities and local volunteers.

We are also monitoring the condition of Callie Reese, who sustained serious injuries at the same gathering. Our thoughts are with her and her family during this difficult time. We urge anyone who was present at the cemetery on Halloween night to come forward, even if you think what you saw wasn't important. We are also reviewing security footage from local businesses and traffic cameras.

If you have any information that could aid our investigation, please call the Foggy Hollow tip line.

We ask the community for patience and cooperation. We know this is a frightening time, especially for the families involved. I assure you, we are doing everything we can.

58
STILL MISSING

Sunday morning, Dad and I go to St. Oswald's with the Calloways, including a very sore but very alive Twig. It's a somber service, with many prayers said for Callie Reese, in critical condition at Ruby Memorial in Morgantown. Along with Ivy Winslow and Lainey Sikes, who are still missing.

I take Twig's hand.

He holds on tight, his palm clammy.

Search parties are being organized.

Congregants are encouraged to help.

The Calloways join the effort.

Dad does, too.

Twig can't, given the state of his foot, which gives me an excuse to stay back and keep him company. I can't stomach the idea of canvasing the woods for two girls I know aren't there. We decide to watch a movie. We bypass our typical 1980s paranormal fare and settle on *The Princess Bride* instead. We watch it on repeat with the lights low, the popcorn Mrs. Calloway made untouched between us.

Mrs. Calloway and Kate return from the search around five.

Harrison picks up Kate shortly after.

Mrs. Calloway cooks in the kitchen, the smell of onion and thyme drifting down the hall. A couple hours later, Mr. Calloway and Dad return. They tuck into heaping bowls of homemade stew. Twig and I eavesdrop from his bedroom, our ears perked as spoons clatter. They speak in dulcet tones.

"They brought in bloodhounds," Dad says. "They caught a scent, then lost it completely in the back part of the cemetery."

Twig and I exchange a look.

"I spoke with Benny McCoy," Mr. Calloway says. "His sister, Elena, is on the force. She said they found some interesting gear in the area."

"Like?" Mrs. Calloway inquires.

"Some homemade pyrotechnics. A small camera. A voice recorder. And a motion-triggered flash device that was rigged up to emit a high-pitched tone."

"You don't think ... ?"

Mrs. Calloway doesn't finish her question.

It trails off into oblivion.

"Think what?" Dad finally asks.

I picture Mrs. Calloway fidgeting with a napkin, squirming in her seat. When she answers, her voice is even lower. I really have to strain to hear. "It's just ... after school on Friday, Spencer and Selah were in his room for quite some time. And, well, they asked Carl for help with several ... gadgets."

The silence that follows is deafening.

Twig and I stare at one another.

A throat clears—Mr. Calloway's, I think. "Listen, even if it was their equipment, I don't believe for one second they would manufacture a hoax. They're too smart for something like that, and too obsessed with the real thing."

A pause stretches long enough for Twig to shift beside me, the air between us taut.

Then Mr. Calloway adds, "Elena said the camera still works."

"Do you think it could have captured something?" Mrs. Calloway asks.

"I'm sure that's what they're hoping."

I gape at Twig.

He gapes back.

If the camera is still working, what in the world did it capture?

Foggy Hollow Police Department Press Briefing
Wednesday, November 5, 2025 – 3:46 p.m. EST

CHIEF DOUGLAS PERRY: After four full days of coordinated searches, including extensive ground sweeps of the cemetery, the woods, and surrounding rural areas, we have not yet located Lainey Sikes or Ivy Winslow.

We continue to follow every lead, and our team is in regular contact with the families. This remains an open and active investigation.

Based on witness interviews and available evidence, we believe the event on Halloween night was most likely a prank that escalated in unexpected and tragic ways. There is currently no evidence of abduction, and no individuals are being pursued as suspects at this time.

We know there is a great deal of speculation circulating online, much of it unverified or sensationalized. We ask the public to refrain from spreading misinformation and allow our investigators to do their jobs without interference.

Again, if you were at the cemetery party or have since heard or seen anything that might help, we urge you to come forward. No detail is too small.

This community has always come together in hard times, and we are confident that with continued effort and cooperation, we will find answers."

REPORTER (FOGGY HOLLOW GAZETTE): Chief Perry, can you comment on the status of Rafe Vandenberg? Given his connection to Lainey Sikes, is he considered a suspect or a third missing person?

CHIEF DOUGLAS PERRY: At this time, Mr. Vandenberg is not considered a missing person. He is 22 years old, and according to family and acquaintances, he expressed plans to leave Foggy Hollow following the weekend festivities. While he did attend the public ball with Ms. Sikes, we have no verified reports placing him at the cemetery party or confirming involvement in the events currently under investigation.

That said, we would like to speak with Mr. Vandenberg. If anyone has heard from him, we urge them to contact our department.

59
FROM BEGINNING TO END

The wheels of the cart squeak as I trail Maggie to the front of the store, her shawl fluttering over an unreasonable number of layers. Walt reads the paper behind the counter, muttering under his breath while Poe surveys the scene from a crooked shelf above. Walt often mutters like this when he reads the *Foggy Hollow Gazette*, bemoaning the slow, pitiful death of real journalism.

It's Saturday morning, and while I'm not technically on the clock, I don't mind making myself useful while I wait for Twig.

Maggie comes to an abrupt halt and peers down her nose, through her reading glasses, at the book in her hand. The spine reads: *Lacework for the Recently Bereaved*, and I can't help but marvel at the vast and peculiar universe of books. Somewhere out there, someone grieved a loved one and thought, "You know what would help? Needlework."

The newspaper crinkles as Walt turns a page.

I glimpse the headline.

Echoes of the Past? Halloween Disappearances Stir Memories of Vandenberg Tragedy.

Maggie must glimpse it, too, because she harrumphs. A full

week has passed since Halloween night, and like most others, she's none too pleased with the lack of progress made by the police department. According to Maggie, the last thing this town needs is another mystery.

"Looks like Callie Reese has been moved out of ICU," Walt says, turning another page.

The news hit yesterday at school.

She'd been transferred to the neuro step-down unit.

Maggie shelves the book. "I heard something rather interesting from Birdie the other night."

"Who's Birdie?" Walt asks.

She sets her fists on her hips looking truly affronted. "Birdie Temple."

Walt blinks.

"She's the one who's always bragging about having met Maya Angelou at a Cracker Barrel."

Walt stares back at her, completely stumped.

Maggie shoos her hand at him. "She's Callie Reese's great aunt. Apparently, the kids whipped up one of those online fundraiser doodads—"

"GoFundMe," I say.

"—Set the goal at fifty *thousand* dollars, if you can believe it. Birdie nearly choked on her peppermint. Said they'd be lucky to raise fifty. But lo and behold, some anonymous do-gooder swooped in like a knight with a shining debit card." Maggie lowers her sparse brows in my direction. "I wonder who has that kind of money."

Jude.

He has that kind of money.

But I'm saved by the bell.

It chimes as the front door swings open.

Twig hobbles inside with a gust of cold wind, his injured foot in a boot and his arm in a sling. Still, he manages to carry a cardboard drink carrier with three coffees, a bag from

Tudors, and a crossbody backpack strapped over one shoulder.

I rush to help him, although I suspect he's growing weary of the baby treatment. Between Mrs. Calloway and Kate, he can hardly walk two steps without one of them trying to assist in some manner.

I hand Walt his coffee and nod at the headline. "Any updates?"

He covered the Vandenberg cold case back in the day. And although he's made a few enemies between now and then, he still has connections. Which means he's been our informant when it comes to these more recent disappearances.

"Nothing new, I'm afraid," he says. "Sometimes I think they're more focused on shutting down the rumor mill than finding the actual truth."

"They're failing on both counts," Twig says, tossing me a biscuit.

The rumors are running rampant.

Conspiracy TikToks have sprouted like mold—teens speculating about rituals, cults, coverups. Most of it's satire and clickbait. But there is a growing number of earnest believers.

Some of them have discovered our podcast.

Walt unwraps a biscuit. Ribbons of steam curl in perfect spirals and fog up his glasses. "I warned them. Releasing that last statement was a serious fumble. A prank gone awry appeases nobody, especially not the parents of those girls."

"Or Birdie Temple," Maggie adds.

"If this was just some kids trying to cause a scare, two teens wouldn't be missing." Walt uses the hem of his cardigan to clean his lenses. "Or perhaps, just one."

Maggie frowns. "They messed up the count?"

"More than a few town officials seem to think Lainey Sikes ran off with Rafe Vandenberg."

So does most of the student body.

I take a delicate sip of my coffee, thankful for the weekend. I can hardly stand being in school these days. The anxious whispers. The locker shrines. The tears from kids who never once spoke to Lainey, or Ivy, or Callie. The tactless jokes. The empty seat in AP Lit where Ivy used to sit. Knowing the truth while everyone else speculates is unbearable. If not for Jude and Twig, I'd feel completely alone.

Twig shifts. "Any word on the camera they confiscated?"

Maggie and Walt pause just long enough to make me uneasy. They know about our cemetery stakeouts. I'm pretty sure they suspect the equipment was ours. But like Mrs. Calloway, neither have confronted us about it.

"If there was anything on it," Walt says, sliding his glasses back onto his nose, "no one is saying."

Twig takes a bite of his biscuit, doing a great impression of a bad actor playing the part of casual.

In truth, we're both wound tight, waiting for that knock on the door. For the other shoe to drop. For someone to show up and accuse us of murder. Twig's been especially on edge. He nearly turned himself in twice, ready to confess the gear was his, that it was all part of a paranormal investigation. Jude and I talked him off the ledge both times.

"Do they have any suspects?" I ask.

"Not a one. Don't think they will either." Walt folds his hands over the newspaper. "So, what's the scuttlebutt with the pair of you? Headed downstairs for the next episode of your podcast? I imagine season three will practically write itself after last weekend."

Twig and I exchange a glance.

We're a full week into November. Normally we'd be excited —diving headfirst into research, pinning down topics, crafting quippy titles. By now, we should have the first episode of our new season recorded. But we've been dragging our feet. It's one thing to discuss supernatural phenomena to which we have no connection, or a vague one at most. It's quite another to dig into something so close we can still feel it breathing down our necks.

"We're going to start recording today," I say to Walt, trying to inject some enthusiasm into my reply.

Twig gathers his coffee and another biscuit, I take my own, and together we make our way into Maggie's basement. We don't have much time to waste. Twig promised his mom he wouldn't be gone long, and I'm meeting Jude at noon. We've decided to return the gemstones and the locket to the crypt. The portrait, too. We'll lock them up, and put the whole thing to bed.

Twig pulls the crossbody bag over his head and sets it on the wooden table next to our sound equipment. He sinks into the nearest chair and stares forlornly at the crates in the corner.

"You okay?" I ask.

"Everyone thinks she's off somewhere with Rafe."

In a way, she sort of is. I swallow the tactless words and sit in the chair across from him.

He sets his elbow on the table and covers his eyes with his hand. "Kate was crying this morning in the bathroom."

"She and Lainey were friends."

He nods, and when he pulls his hand away, his eyes are red and teary. "I shouldn't have let go."

"Twig..."

"I had her by the wrists, Selah. But I just ... I wasn't strong enough."

I reach across the table and set my hand on his arm. "There's nothing you could have done."

"I could have held on."

"How? You with one good arm versus a demon octopus straight out of the *Mines of Moria*? Even Gandalf barely made it out of that one."

"She was so scared. And now she's gone because I—"

"There's no *I* in that statement, Twig. She's not gone because of you. She's gone because of Seraphina. And Rafe. And evil."

"We can't even talk about it."

His words come like a punch to the gut—an iron fist of truth. Here lies the heart of it: We know what happened. And we're sitting on our hands like cowards. Afraid we won't be believed. Afraid we might be blamed.

Don't Lainey and Ivy deserve better?

Callie, too?

I imagine if things had gone differently. If Twig hadn't found the ruby. If there'd been no way to bring Jude back to life. The thought takes my breath away. But I don't run from it. I force myself to consider the scenario. Jude, gone. The paramedics taking him away, not on a stretcher, but in a body bag.

Would I really stay quiet?

He broke a curse that burned Foggy Hollow to the ground, threw a whole train off the tracks, and snatched four Vandenbergs from their dinner table. He stopped Seraphina from rising, more terrible and mighty than ever before. Would I really let the public believe he died because of a prank gone awry, when in truth, he died to save me, to save our whole town?

The thought is so vile, so despicable, it makes my bones hot.

We've been dragging our feet, unsure how to return to this thing we've always loved. Telling spooky stories. Chasing mysteries. Spinning theories. Embracing the unknown.

But maybe a shift is in order.

Maybe this season, we try something new.

"What if we *do* talk about it?" I say.

Twig looks at me.

"What if we tell the truth on our podcast?" I set my elbows on the table. "The whole thing, from beginning to end."

His brow furrows. "Our listeners will think we're crazy."

"And the police might knock on our door," I concede.

"Mom will freak out."

"And I'm sure she'll tell my dad." I shrug. "But the truth will be out there, for those willing to hear it."

Evil came to Foggy Hollow.

Evil took some of our own.

But evil didn't win.

Twig's gaze meets mine, and for the first time since that monster almost dragged him through the rift, his eyes twinkle with life.

He gets out his laptop, and we begin.

60

NOT ALL WHO
VANISH STAY GONE

Cold nips at my nose as I jog through the woods. Jude and I locked the crypt and covered the door. I told him about the plans Twig and I made, knowing they would go nowhere without his consent. We won't tell a story that features his family, that features him, if he doesn't want us to. But Jude agreed. He might even be a guest.

I come to a stop in the clearing. I remove the chain from around my neck and let the key sit in my palm—a memento from a shoebox, a necklace my mother once wore. Did she think of Simon whenever she put it on? Did the mark beneath her collar burn like ice when she remembered him? If she's alive right now, is the mark still there or did it disappear like my own? When Jude broke the curse, did her brokenness break, too? Will she come for me now, healed and whole?

With my eyes closed, I picture her.

Kneeling in the garden.

Praying over her rosary beads.

Reading me a book.

I used to think my mother was Max, sailing back and forth between home and the place where the wild things are. But now I know she was never Max. She was always a wild thing. Or maybe she was made into one because of the story she was dealt.

Simon was stolen from her. She knew what happened. She tried telling the truth, but she didn't have a best friend to help, or a podcast for an outlet, or a dad to keep her safe. Instead, she was locked up in a psych ward, which is maybe where her addiction began. She stopped telling the truth. Maybe she stopped believing it herself.

Perhaps the mark faded when the curse broke, but she has other scars, the kind that aren't so visible. I have one myself, left by her because she, herself, was scarred. Trauma passed down from mother to daughter like a curse through the generations. But it's not inevitable. It isn't written in the stars. We aren't helpless.

We have the power to face it.

To fight it.

To do everything we can to stop it.

In the end, my mother wasn't stolen by some otherworldly force. She was broken by grief and circumstance.

I set my elbows on the stone lip of the well, and with a deep inhale, I turn my palm over and drop the key.

A breeze stirs the branches overhead.

They creak and sway.

And on the wind, I hear a whisper.

The soft call of my name.

I turn around.

But there's nothing.

Nobody.

Just a scuffling in the bushes.

A strange chirping sound.

Curiosity draws me closer.

Slowly and quietly, I pick up a stick, move aside the overgrowth, and gasp.

A small creature looks up at me from eyes that are glossy and luminous, with no pupils at all. Just a pair of full moons set in a pointed face covered in lavender fur. It coughs up a glowing seed, then scuttles away.

Mesmerized, I follow it.

Off the path, into the trees.

I pick up my pace as it hops into thicker foliage, darting through a curtain of ferns without so much as rustling a leaf. I hurry after it, my heart pounding as the woods grow darker around me. Quieter, too. The kind of quiet a person notices.

Like the forest is holding its breath.

For a moment, I lose sight of the creature. But then, there it is, poised on the edge of a shallow gully, nose twitching as it looks at a ripple in the air. Not a wound that is healing, but a small flickering doorway no larger than a windowpane. The creature hops through it without a sound.

I stay where I am, rooted in place, staring at this new rift, open and pulsing, when my phone begins to buzz.

I pull it from the pocket of my leggings.

The screen is alight with messages.

From Twig.

From Dad.

From Harper and Naomi.

One after another after another.

Lainey Sikes—a girl I watched combust into flame and vaporize into ash—has been found alive.

HUNGRY
IS THE
HOLLOW
K.E. GANSHERT

HUNGRY IS THE HOLLOW
TALES FROM THE HOLLOW BOOK TWO

On Halloween night, two girls vanished and the town of Foggy Hollow has been holding its breath ever since, praying for their safe return. So when one of them comes home unharmed, fear gives way to hope.

Selah Whitlock and Jude Vandenberg aren't so relieved. They know the truth. The girl shouldn't be alive. They watched her die.

Whatever happened in the cemetery on Halloween didn't stay buried.

Darkness has its claws in Jude. Selah's classmates are disappearing. Something sinister is stalking the local teens. And it has an appetite.

With panic spreading and the Appalachian winter deepening, Selah and her friends must stop whatever is feeding on Foggy Hollow before the entire town is swallowed whole.

ABOUT THE AUTHOR

K.E. Ganshert is an award-winning author of clean fiction filled with mystery, adventure, romance, and the fantastical. Her stories are perfect for readers who crave unexpected twists, strange happenings, high stakes, and romance that runs deep but never explicit. She lives in eastern Iowa with her husband and their two children.

TURN THE PAGE FOR MORE

THE RETRIBUTION OF EDEN PRUITT
GANSHERT
THE REVELATION OF EDEN PRUITT
GANSHERT
THE ABERRATION OF EDEN PRUITT
GANSHERT
THE FABRICATION OF EDEN PRUITT
GANSHERT
"A thrill ride of twists and turns."
award winning author
Becky Wade
THE FABRICATION
OF EDEN PRUITT
K.E. GANSHERT

THE EDEN PRUITT SERIES
A ROMANTIC DYSTOPIAN THRILLER

After a strange day at her new school, Eden Pruitt comes home to a jarring scene. The house has been ransacked. Her parents are gone. She rushes to the police for help, but when they return, nothing is how she left it.

Alarm turns to panic. Confusion spirals into chaos.

Suddenly, Eden is on the run, trapped in a nightmare with nowhere to turn and nobody to believe her. Except for a mysterious stranger who is as dangerous as he is enticing. Someone who knows more than he should... and might be just as perilous as the truth she's desperate to uncover.

THE CONTEST

a novel

K.E. GANSHERT

THE CONTEST
A ROMANTIC FANTASY ADVENTURE

In a world of haves and have nots, where petty crime is punishable by death and magic is forbidden, a deadly contest unfolds in secret. Twelve competitors are mysteriously invited. The winner gets one wish.

For 17-year-old Briar Bishop, this means saving her brother from execution by guillotine, and she's not going to let anything or anyone get in her way. Especially not Leo Davenbrook, the handsome High Prince, who has grown up with everything she never had and whose very presence threatens her chance at survival.

She has no idea a darker battle wages, one that could lead to a fate far worse than the death of her brother.